"For those cravi[...]
ture, Koch is an [...]
[...] op pick)

"Koch still pulls the neat trick of quietly weaving in plot threads that go unrecognized until they start tying together—or snapping. This is a hyperspeed-paced addition to a series that shows no signs of slowing down." —*Publishers Weekly*

"Aliens, danger, and romance make this a fast-paced, wittily-written sf romantic comedy." —*Library Journal*

"Gini Koch's Kitty Katt series is a great example of the lighter side of science fiction. Told with clever wit and non-stop pacing . . . it blends diplomacy, action and sense of humor into a memorable reading experience." —*Kirkus*

"The action is nonstop, the snark flies fast and furious. . . . Another fantastic addition to an imaginative series!"
—Night Owl Sci-Fi (top pick)

"Ms. Koch has carved a unique niche for herself in the sci-fi-romance category with this series. My only hope is that it lasts for a very long time." —Fresh Fiction

"This delightful romp has many interesting twists and turns as it glances at racism, politics, and religion en route . . . will have fanciers of cinematic sf parodies referencing *Men in Black*, *Ghost Busters*, and *X-Men*."
—*Booklist* (starred review)

"Gini Koch mixes up the sometimes staid niche of science fiction romance by adding nonstop humor, blockbuster action, and moments worthy of a soap opera."
—Dirty Sexy Books

DAW Books Presents GINI KOCH's
Alien Novels:

TOUCHED BY AN ALIEN
ALIEN TANGO
ALIEN IN THE FAMILY
ALIEN PROLIFERATION
ALIEN DIPLOMACY
ALIEN VS. ALIEN
ALIEN IN THE HOUSE
ALIEN RESEARCH
ALIEN COLLECTIVE
UNIVERSAL ALIEN
(Coming in December 2014)

ALIEN
COLLECTIVE

GINI KOCH

DAW BOOKS, INC.
DONALD A. WOLLHEIM, FOUNDER
375 Hudson Street, New York, NY 10014

ELIZABETH R. WOLLHEIM
SHEILA E. GILBERT
PUBLISHERS
www.dawbooks.com

First Printing, May 2014
1   2   3   4   5   6   7   8   9

DAW TRADEMARK REGISTERED
U.S. PAT. AND TM. OFF. AND FOREIGN COUNTRIES
—MARCA REGISTRADA
HECHO EN U.S.A.

PRINTED IN THE U.S.A.

For Colette Chmiel and Joseph Gaxiola,
whose help and support has been and remains
invaluable to my career and my sanity.

ACKNOWLEDGMENTS

As always, I must thank, first and foremost, my awesome, supportive, and incredibly patient editor, Sheila Gilbert; my wonderful agent, Cherry Weiner; my fantastic crit partner, Lisa Dovichi; and my main beta reader, Mary Fiore. Not only for all their help, but also for putting up with me and a host of neuroses throughout the writing of this book. Special thanks to my daughter, Veronica, who spent an inordinate amount of time reassuring me that the book was indeed good, and doing other things that I'm sure she'll make me pay for later in life.

Love and thanks always to all the good folks at DAW Books and Penguin for support and patience (yes, lots of patience was given to me for this book, for which I'm incredibly grateful). Even more love and thanks to all my fans around the globe, my Hook Me Up! Gang, members of Team Gini, all Alien Collective Members in Very Good Standing, Twitter followers, Facebook fans and friends, Pinterest followers, and all the wonderful fans who come to my various book signings and conference panels—you're all the best and I wouldn't want to do this without each and every one of you along for the ride.

Special shout outs to: my distance assistant, Colette Chmiel, who continues to ensure that I know what I'm doing when while also keeping the pirates at bay; my personal assistant, Joseph Gaxiola, who continues to ensure that I show up when and where I'm supposed to, who keeps me calm and laughing on the road, and who frequently allows me to be two places at once; Edward Pulley, for letting me steal Joseph away so much and for always helping out whenever I need it, which is often; Adrian and Lisa Payne, Hal and Dee Astell, and Duncan and Andrea Rittschof, who continue to bring their smiling faces to every event I attend, ensuring that

I always feel loved and supported; Jan Robinson for continuing to make adorable pieces of "soft artwork" related to all my books and then bestowing them on me time and time again; Robert Palsma, for continuing to like everything I do; Kay Johnson, for constant cheerleading; Lee Greenberg and Rachel Warner for all the fantastic foodie experiences and even better company at WorldCon San Antonio; authors Leo King and Thomas Olde Heuvelt for a great time talking the night away at WorldCon San Antonio; Tom and Libby for the best fudge in the world; Oliver and Blanca Bernal for always having a welcoming home; Missy "Whoosh" Katano, Colette "Sunny" Chmiel, Paul "Catman" Sparks, and my Montana Girls, Terry Lopez and Betty Russell for coming from far away to spend time with me at DarkCon; special thanks to Missy Katano for all the lovely prezzies and Betty Russell for giving me the greatest compliment anyone can—love you both; Brad "My Man" Jensen for great help at DarkCon; my Paranormal Romance Dream Team pals, authors Caris Roane, Erin Kellison, and Erin Quinn for laughs, advice, and solidarity; my Wyked Women Who Write friends, authors Jordan Summers, T.M. Williams, Sharon Skinner, T.L. Smith, and Marsheila Rockwell for fun times at cons and while eating cupcakes; Mysterious Galaxy San Diego, Mysterious Galaxy Redondo Beach, and The Poisoned Pen Scottsdale for support at cons, events, and book signings; and awesome author L.E. Modisett, Jr., who tells the best stories, for invaluable advice and encouragement.

And, as always, all my love and thanks to my husband, Steve, and daughter, Veronica. No writer could have a better family than I do and I love you both more than words can say.

THERE WAS A TIME, about four and a half years ago, when I thought the world was basically simple.

I was a single, carefree girl with a sorta-promising career in marketing, great parents, good friends, and a place of my own.

Then a superbeing formed in front of me and genetics I didn't know I had took over. I killed the fugly monster, saved the day, and won the heart of the handsome prince. Literally.

Of course, my prince didn't know he was a prince, though he did know he was an alien, even though he was born on Earth. His family was exiled from Alpha Four in the Alpha Centauri system. His very large, extended, and connected-back-through-the-ages family. All of whom are pretty much the most gorgeous people on Earth. Since they also have two hearts, hyperspeed, the ability to regenerate and heal quickly, and special talents, the fact that they're also great looking sort of seems unfair.

It *is* unfair, really. But I manage to find the will to go on.

I also discovered a much more promising career in the realm of Superbeing Extermination, and moved quickly up the ranks to become the Head of Airborne for Centaurion Division. And, just as quickly, got moved over to become first the co- and then the only Ambassador for American Centaurion. Though I've protested a lot about the Peter Principle, everyone insists I'm at least as good at this job as I was at any other. They're being complimentary. I think.

Jeff's in the same spaceship, of course, because he got shoved into being the Representative for New Mexico's 2nd District in Congress. Meaning he has to work with politicians every day. And to set the rumors straight, not all politicians are evil monsters, but most of them make us nostalgic for the superbeings we used to fight regularly.

There are plenty of nights where we argue about which one of us has the worse job. But at least we have each other.

And we have our daughter, Jamie, who's very special with a heaping side of extra. In addition to her being a human-alien hybrid, some extenuating circumstances have led to her sharing head space with a collective superconsciousness. At two and a half, that's probably a lot to handle, but she's our daughter and she's doing great with it. Overachieving is apparently our "thing."

So, you know, fantastic husband, amazing daughter, important jobs we feel challenged in, great friends, wonderful family. What could go wrong with all of that?

Wow. You really haven't been paying attention all this time, have you?

CHAPTER 1

"YOU HAVE THE RIGHT to remain silent. Anything you say can and will be used against you in a court of law."

"I'd like to say two words—Diplomatic Immunity. Then I'd like to say other words like, I want to call my lawyer, the President, my mom, and a few other people like Officer Melville." The cop helped me up into the paddy wagon.

"That's nice." Of course, he was now actually helping my lawyer into the big metal van. Amy Gaultier-White patted my hand. "You and all the rest get to go to headquarters first, ma'am. Then you can make all those calls you want to make."

"Diplomatic Immunity. We do remember what that means?"

The cop smiled as he helped several other women into the paddy wagon with me. "Yes, ma'am, Ambassador Katt-Martini. We do know."

"I'm the Ambassador for the American Centaurion Diplomatic Mission. My husband is a congressman. And you're risking pissing off a lot of important people."

"Comes with the job, ma'am."

"Why are we being arrested? Since when is arresting diplomats your job? Every woman with me is part of my diplomatic mission." In some way, at any rate. Wasn't sure if I could count the female members of Alpha Team as being part of the Embassy staff. Then again, I was the Ambassador, so

I could decide I'd officially instated them as Disturbance Attachés before we left. Minor moral dilemma solved. Major dilemma still not solved.

"You're at the scene of a disturbance, ma'am. Ambassador or not."

"I'll say it again, officer—Diplomatic Immunity."

"Yes, ma'am." The cop gave me the Concerned Officer of the Law look. "You're being moved off the streets for your own protection, ladies."

"Peaceful protest is part of our democracy," Abigail said.

"My husband's going to hear about this," Serene added. "He's an astronaut."

"I'll watch out for falling moon rocks, ma'am," the cop said to her. Wasn't positive, but I was pretty sure he was trying really hard not to laugh. "However, your own protection currently supersedes your immunity."

"Since when?" Amy asked.

"Since now." The cop closed the back doors. Nicely. But still.

"Well," Lorraine said, "at least we're not chained up or handcuffed."

"Speak for yourself," Claudia muttered.

"You tried to hit one of the officers in the face," Lorraine pointed out.

"He was being rude." Claudia looked around. "Can I get out of these now?"

"Sure. You want to break them or have me or Amy pick the lock?"

Lorraine Billings, Claudia Muir, Serene Dwyer, and Abigail Gower were all female A-Cs, or, as I called them to myself, Dazzlers. Dazzlers were, to a one, gorgeous, which was par for the A-C's course. They were also all brilliant by human standards, usually focused on medicine, math, and/or science. My girls were also focused on butt kicking.

They all looked awed and impressed. "You and Amy have finally learned to pick locks?" Serene asked.

Amy and I both sighed. "Yes, Malcolm's been working on it with us," I shared.

"A lot," Amy added, going for the Full Disclosure option.

Malcolm Buchanan was assigned to be my personal shadow. He was also pretty much the most comprehensively competent dude in covert and clandestine ops imaginable. During Operation Infiltration he'd taught the four Dazzlers with us in the paddy wagon how to pick locks. Amy and I hadn't done so well with that. So Buchanan had made it a point to ensure that we knew how. Sadly, it hadn't come that easily to either one of us, which was something of an embarrassment, but both Amy and I were proficient lock pickers now.

Amy pulled a metal nail file out of her purse. "Too slow, Kitty." She went to work.

"At least some of us made it," Claudia said as Amy got the cuffs off her and she rubbed her wrists.

The doors opened again and two more women were put in—Doreen Weisman, our last Dazzler on Embassy Duty, and Denise Lewis, who was human but frankly gorgeous enough to pass for alien.

"Diplomatic Immunity!" Doreen shouted. "Do you all understand what that term means?"

The cops smiled, nodded, and shut the doors again. "So much for Claudia's optimism," I said. "I thought you two had gotten away."

"We did, too," Doreen said.

"Someone in the crowd pointed us out," Denise added with more than a trace of bitterness.

The doors opened again and Nurse Magdalena Carter and my sorority roommate and bestie, Carolyn Chase, were both helped inside. "This is supposed to be the land of freedom and opportunity," Nurse Carter said darkly. "Not the land of oppression." She was originally from Paraguay and had joined us during Operation Assassination.

"Senator McMillan is going to hear about this!" Carolyn was the Senator's Girl Friday.

"I'm sure he will, miss," the officer said. "From more than just you."

Counted noses. We were missing one person. Sure enough, the doors opened again. Though who was being helped in wasn't on my list of Girls Gone Washington Wild.

"Lucinda? What are you and my daughter doing here?"

Yes indeed, my mother-in-law was there, carrying my daughter, Jamie. Two officers helped them in, with a third standing behind to catch them if Lucinda lost her balance.

"Thank you so much," she said to the officers. "You're all too kind, and I just want you to know how much we appreciate all the good work you do and long hours you put in."

She got very friendly smiles from the cops. "You're very welcome, ma'am. You and the little lady be sure to sit down so you don't lose your balance." The doors shut again.

"Mommy, this is so much fun! Gran'ma Luci said we could come watch you work!" Jamie bounced over to me for hugs and kisses.

Happily gave out the necessary snuggles, then handed Jamie to Amy for more of the same. "Lucinda, what part of 'you and Jamie stay at the Embassy' didn't come through clearly?"

"No part of it, Kitty," she said as she settled herself in between Doreen and Serene, opposite Amy. "I just thought it would be fun for Jamie to see what you girls were up to."

Lorraine and Amy both nudged me. "I think Kitty just wanted to be sure you and Jamie didn't get hurt," Amy said as she finished loving on Jamie and handed her to Abigail. "And I have to agree. Are you alright?"

"Oh, yes, Amy dear, we're both fine. It was quite exciting, all the chanting and jumping up and down."

Managed to keep my mouth shut but only by grinding my teeth. Abigail hugged Jamie then passed her on to Carolyn.

"You do realize it's a political protest?" Serene asked, radiating innocence. While my first impression of Serene, during Operation Drug Addict, was that she was a crazy loon, my second, third, fourth, and fifth impressions of her were Innocence on the Hoof.

However, I'd learned there was a lot more to Serene than most of us ever saw. Right now, for example, I had a feeling she was asking because she knew I couldn't do so without snarling, and she was doing it in such a way as to not upset Lucinda.

And it worked, of course. Lucinda patted Serene's knee.

"Oh, yes, dear, I know. It's part of how our great host country works, and it's important for Jamie to see that, to see how her father is a part of something so much bigger than himself."

"Jeff's always been a part of something bigger than himself," I pointed out.

"Yes, Kitty, but Jamie couldn't go into active situations with her father, now could she?"

Regardless of Amy and Lorraine's nudging, Doreen and Serene's wide-eyed "shut up, shut up" stares, and what I could feel radiating from the rest of the girls—that I needed to keep my mouth shut—I couldn't stop myself. "Um, have you been paying attention to anything that's gone on since Jamie was born?"

Fortunately, before Lucinda could reply and I could earn more Bad Daughter-In-Law Points, the doors opened again. And, once again, our new arrival wasn't anyone I was expecting.

CHAPTER 2

LILLIAN CULVER was helped inside. "Thank you, officers, that will be all."

"Yes, ma'am. Do you need anything else?" the officer who'd been doing most of the talking asked. Unlike with Lucinda, where he'd clearly been happy to help, or with me and the others, where he'd been trying not to laugh, right now he seemed very controlled and official. Presumed he knew exactly who Culver was.

"No, no, we're all good here now." Lillian turned to me and smiled widely. She was a top lobbyist, *the* top for most of the big defense contractors, meaning she was incredibly powerful and influential in this town—the epitome of a Washington insider. And, as seemed to be the "thing" here, she had "her color," which happened to be red.

Culver was an attractive enough woman, until you looked at her just long enough. Then you realized she was all bones and angles, with a very wide mouth her bright red lipstick really emphasized. I called her Joker Jaws to myself for a reason.

Right now, I was getting the Joker's smug "I've trapped Batman and all his cronies" look from Culver. Couldn't wait to hear what she wanted.

But before Culver spoke, the doors opened yet again. "Good grief, it's like a Marx Brothers film in here. We're about to be at standing room only."

Culver laughed and reached her hand down. "Nathalie, you're here, too?"

Representative Nathalie Gagnon-Brewer was helped in by the officers and Culver. "Thanks, Lillian. Kitty, I'm glad I caught up with all of you." She was a French expatriate, a former international fashion model, and a widow. Her husband, Edmund, had been a Representative from California, and he'd been murdered during Operation Sherlock. As with Jeff, the President had asked Nathalie to take over her husband's seat in Congress. And as with Jeff, considering the state of the union and the world after Operation Destruction—when everyone on Earth had learned, in a really big way, that we weren't alone in the cosmos—Nathalie had said yes.

"Wait for me, wait for me," a man called before the cops could close our now very full paddy wagon up again. Vance Beaumont climbed inside. "Thanks, guys, appreciate you holding the car for me," he said to the officers.

They nodded and closed the doors behind him. "Vance, what are you doing here?" I asked.

Vance was married to Guy Gadoire, who was to the tobacco industry what Culver was to defense. Vance spent his days thumbing through *GQ* and dressing accordingly, throwing lavish parties, and hanging around.

Despite all of this, I'd come to realize he had a functioning brain he liked to keep hidden, and he was actually a better friend to me now than I'd have ever thought possible when we first met. Same with Nathalie, of course. And while Culver and I couldn't be called friends, thanks to my "uncles" the top assassins, she and I had a good working relationship where she didn't try to push me into making bad decisions for American Centaurion too often and I returned the favor by not threatening to "call home" too often.

"I thought this was a woman's rally against the anti-alien presidential candidate," Lucinda added as Vance jumped the line and took Jamie from Nathalie—who'd just barely gotten her from Carolyn—to give her a quick "airplane flight" she loved, if her squealing with joy was any indication.

Vance gave Jamie a kiss, handed her off to Culver, and

shrugged. "I have the wife role in my relationship, in case you missed that key point, and, also in case you didn't notice, the Cleary-Maurer ticket is also anti-gay."

"And anti-woman," Nathalie added. "They aren't pro-minorities, either. Or immigrants, legal or otherwise."

Shocking me to my core, Culver both cuddled Jamie—who didn't scream in horror but instead cuddled back—and nodded. "They need to be stopped."

"Wait, what? Lillian, are you saying you were here as part of the protest?"

Culver shrugged, gave Jamie a kiss, and handed her over to Doreen. "Yes. I'm a woman, in case you didn't notice, and I'm not excited about what Cleary and Maurer both stand for."

"They stand for hate," Lucinda said calmly as Jamie clambered from Doreen and over Lucinda to get to Serene, giving Lucinda a kiss along the way. "And, as such, they need to be opposed." She looked right at me. "And our young women need to see that their role models are so opposing."

"Fine, fine, yes, I noticed everything and yes, I'll stop complaining about Jamie being here." Stood up and hugged my mother-in-law. "I just don't want either one of you getting hurt, that's all."

She hugged me back. "I know. I may have been a housewife more than a career woman, but trust me—no one will touch a hair on one of my grandchildren's heads and live to talk about it."

"So," Claudia said as she took Jamie from Serene, "do we think Adriana made it without getting nabbed, or do you think she's in a different arrest vehicle?"

"And, since we have two who were out of the Embassy against orders," I gave Lucinda the hairy eyeball, "where's Mahin?"

Before anyone could reply, the back doors opened once again. Two more men joined us—Len and Kyle, my official driver and bodyguard. They'd both played football for USC, but they weren't causing the cops any problems. "Thanks," Kyle said as the cops once again closed our doors. He stayed by the doors, blocking both entrance and exit.

Len nodded to everyone as he worked his way forward. As he reached the front of the holding area, car doors slammed—they were clearly the doors to our particular car. "Everyone, please keep your seats," Len said. He took Jamie from Lorraine and handed her to me.

"Hey, I just got her," Lorraine said.

"Sorry." He didn't sound sorry. Len pounded twice on the metal separating the cab from the rest of us, and the paddy wagon lurched off. We drove for about thirty seconds and came to a screeching halt.

The doors opened yet again, and two more people joined us. Tito Hernandez, our Embassy doctor, and Mahin Sherazi, who'd joined up with us a year ago during Operation Infiltration. Tito was literally dragging Mahin aboard.

"A little help?" he asked Kyle, who reached down, grabbed the back of Mahin's shirt, and lifted her into the back.

She was shouting in Farsi. I didn't speak her native tongue, but it was pretty clear that she wasn't saying nice things.

Kyle and Tito got the doors closed, Len did his hand-slam-on-metal thing, and we took off, this time at a much faster rate of speed. Sirens were going off around us—clearly we had at least one police car as an escort, maybe two. Maybe more.

"So, what's going on?" I asked Len. "And I'd really like an answer. Starting with what you, Kyle, and Tito are doing here in the first place. And why you all happily leaped into the paddy wagon with us instead of, oh, I'm just spitballing here, getting us *out*."

He sighed. "You weren't supposed to go to this thing without me and Kyle."

"It was, despite us having four men in here, supposed to be a women only thing. Hence why we left the men at home. Or thought we did. Mahin, you were supposed to stay home, too."

She tossed her hair out of her face. "I went with Lucinda and Jamie."

"Shocker."

"Mahin is part of our family, too," Lucinda said calmly. "And I brought Doctor Hernandez, Len, and Kyle along with us to protect Jamie."

"Wow, check and mate. Good one. Look, I appreciate the arrest solidarity, but didn't it occur to anyone that some of you staying out of jail might be helpful?"

Culver cleared her throat. "Ah, Kitty? I don't think we're actually being arrested."

"No? Then why are we in a police riot van?"

"For our safety," Lucinda said. "That's what the nice officers said."

Got a bad feeling. "Look, you all realize that we've been herded into a metal van and are being taken God knows where by God knows who, right? And that the local police have been infiltrated and impersonated before, usually by people wanting to perpetrate a great deal of malice aforethought on us? Remember? Anyone?"

The car came to a stop, the doors to the cab opened and closed, then the doors to our section opened yet again.

Had to admit—I really wasn't expecting to be where we were or see who was standing there, though it shouldn't have surprised me all that much.

CHAPTER 3

"MISSUS CHIEF, nice to see you and the rest of the gang."

"Malcolm, what the hell?"

Buchanan was tall, good looking, built, and buff, with brown hair and blue eyes. Not as handsome as my husband, but he wasn't hard on the eyes at all. Of course, A-Cs were the most gorgeous people on Earth, but most of the human guys working with us were pretty nice to look at, too—it was one of the many perks of being part of Centaurion Division and American Centaurion.

Buchanan didn't answer me. Instead he looked to Len and Kyle. "Let's get them all out and in, as fast as possible."

The boys nodded, and Len worked his way to the back, with Kyle keeping everyone in until Len was out. Then the boys started helping everyone down.

Adriana Dalca appeared as everyone other than Amy and me were out. "Convoy is all inside, gates are locked." She was the granddaughter of the Romanian Ambassador. Romania's embassy was across the street from ours, and we'd become good friends with them, particularly Adriana and her grandmother, Olga.

Olga was former KGB and could pass as the Oracle on any given day of the week. She was training Adriana in the old spy ways, as well as the new spy ways, which was good, because Adriana had saved my life almost as many times as Buchanan had.

"Nice to know we didn't lose you in the crowd," I said as I handed Jamie to Adriana and Buchanan lifted me out of the truck.

"Mister Buchanan found me as things started to get out of control and suggested we get all of you to safety."

"Nice. I guess." Something registered. "Things were out of control?"

"Oh yes. Grandmother was very concerned." Before I could ask what things had concerned Olga, Adriana turned, still holding Jamie in a protective manner, and trotted off.

"Malcolm? I'd like to know what was out of control."

"*I'd* like to know why we're at the Bahraini Embassy," Amy said, as Kyle helped her down. He and Len nodded to Buchanan, then trotted off, but in a different direction from Adriana.

Sure enough, I could recognize the architecture, if you could really call it that. In our part of town, aka Embassy Row, all the buildings were lovely, some really showing off, some making do with quiet dignity. But all attractive.

However, there was another embassy section of D.C. that I'd nicknamed The Bunker. In this part of town, every embassy was gated and secured, the buildings were set well back from the street, and no doorway was close to the gates. The buildings also weren't nearly as pretty as the ones in our area—they'd been built for stolid usefulness and defensibility, not architectural beauty.

We could have been at any embassy in The Bunker, but we had good friends in the Bahraini and Israeli embassies, and it was pretty much a fifty-fifty guess that we were within one of their heavily guarded gates. The Bahraini flag flying overhead was undoubtedly the clue that had tipped Amy off to where we were.

Buchanan grinned. "Because you have friends all over."

Looked around and finally managed to spot the six police cars that were with us. All of the cars' flashing lights were on, and they all had dogs inside. "Oh, the K-9 squad is here? Well, that saves me a call to Officer Melville." Chose not to mention that I hadn't noticed that they were here until now. Hey, they'd turned off their sirens. Somewhere along the way.

The policemen were opening their doors and helping people out, among them Mona Nejem, who was the Bahraini Ambassadress, and her Royal Bahraini Army bodyguard, Khalid.

Unsurprisingly, Jakob, Oren, and Leah from the Israeli Diplomatic Mission were getting out of another squad car. They were all Mossad, but, as Mona had explained to me during Operation Destruction, if I thought politics made strange bedfellows, it was nothing compared to the beds diplomats tended to lie in. Only she'd said it with far more class.

By now, I wasn't the least bit surprised to see my favorite reporter, Mr. Joel Oliver, also getting out of a car. He pulled a snazzy sports wheelchair out and then, sure enough, helped Olga into it, with Len assisting.

"It's a party. Malcolm, you want to tell me what the hell's going on?" One of the K-9 dogs ran over to me, whuffing happily. "Hey Prince, how's my favorite officer of the law?" I knelt down and gave Prince tons of pets and he licked my face in return.

"You'll be briefed inside, Missus Chief." He helped me up and moved us so we were standing near the embassy with the police van blocking us from the street. Prince came with us.

Looked around. Richard White was getting out of another squad car. He was Amy's father-in-law, Lucinda's older brother, and the former Supreme Pontifex of all the A-Cs of Earth. He was also my partner whenever we got to kick butt.

White was accompanied by Jeremy and Jennifer Barone, the brother-sister Field team assigned to our Embassy during Operation Destruction. Jeremy was an empath, and Jennifer was an imageer. She was also engaged to Ravi Gaekwad, a member of the team I called Hacker International, who'd also joined up with us during the gigantic alien invasion.

Rajnish Singh, our Embassy Public Relations Minister, and Pierre Duchamps, our Embassy Concierge Majordomo got out of squad cars number five and six respectively. They were ushering the kids from Embassy Daycare. Did a fast headcount—yes, all the kids. This was boding. Or else we were having a giant kegger no one had told me about. I went with precedent and figured on the former. They, like the rest of those in the cars, were hurried inside the embassy by Len, Kyle, and the police officers.

Amazingly, I didn't see any evidence of Hacker International or anyone else I wouldn't have expected to be here anyway. I was shocked that not every, single solitary person I knew was here. Maybe they were coming in their own police vans and were delayed by traffic.

"Malcolm, seriously, it's like we're at a surprise party or something."

He sighed. "In a way, you're right."

"Wow. Cryptic. Not a help, mind you, but cryptic nonetheless."

"Let's get inside, Missus Chief. All will be explained shortly."

"I guess I should be glad we're at Mona's embassy instead of at police headquarters."

"No," Buchanan said darkly. "You should be glad you're in a safe location as opposed to being dead."

Let that sit on the air for a bit. "You mind explaining that?"

"No, but not here." And with that Buchanan took my arm and, accompanied by Prince, we headed into the Bahraini embassy.

CHAPTER 4

FROM THE OUTSIDE, the Bahraini embassy was nothing much to look at. The inside, however, was very different.

Romania's entryway was very Old World Austere, but it's upper levels were Old World Homey. Our entryway was basically plain, if you ignored the marble floors, because our first floor was where we did all the "human" things. That's where the kitchen, dining room, and a lot of offices were, so our entryway led into a long hallway. Once inside, our Embassy was basically Upscale Model Home.

The Bahraini embassy's entryway was opulent and beautiful. It looked almost like you were entering a very expensive luxury hotel lobby—the kind regular people can't afford to enter, let alone stay at. There were chandeliers, comfortable looking settees, chairs, and loveseats, cherrywood coffee and end tables, lots of Turkish rugs, and a very full bookcase along one wall. The visitor's reception desk resembled a high-end concierge setup. Basically, this embassy's décor was Old Money.

Embassy staff were always in nicely tailored, expensive suits, so in that way they resembled American Centaurion. Unlike the A-Cs, who were love slaves to black and white and Armani, the Bahrainis got to wear other designers. All of them high end.

We didn't linger in the lobby, but were ushered into a larger sitting room off to one side. It was almost a duplicate of the lobby, only three times as big, with three walls of bookcases and some couches and fancy tea services on even fancier rolling trays added in.

Large or not, we had a lot of people, and the room, while not packed, seemed full. Looked around. The Bahraini ambassador wasn't present. Neither were many of the men I'd sort of expected to see, such as my husband. However, Hacker International *were* here, along with the rest of our Embassy personnel. Including Walter Ward, who was our Embassy Head of Security and who was the last guy in the world ever willing to leave his post. This, combined with the presence of all the Embassy Daycare kids, was beyond worrisome.

"Malcolm, seriously, what's going on? Why are we here instead of police headquarters or, better, the protest we were actually attending? And what the hell is Walter doing here?"

Buchanan looked around. Either my question had caught most of the room's attention, or everyone knew that Buchanan was going to be the one who shared what the hell was going on. "Everyone's accounted for?" Len and Kyle both nodded. "Including the congressman and your boss?"

This was starting to bode more than it already had. The congressman was my husband, and Len and Kyle's boss was Charles Reynolds, aka the head of the C.I.A.'s Extra-Terrestrial Division and my best guy friend since ninth grade. Of course, Chuckie worked with Jeff all the time. Maybe I was worried for nothing.

"Yes," Len replied. "They're with the rest of Alpha Team, the head of the P.T.C.U., the head of Special Immigration Services for Homeland Security, and the head of the FBI's Alien Affairs Division."

So much for that worried for nothing idea. Things were definitely serious if my mother was involved. Because, as I'd learned only about four and a half years ago, my mother wasn't just a consultant, she was *the* anti-terrorism consultant and the head of the very kick-butt and also very clandestine Presidential Terrorism Control Unit. Meaning if the P.T.C.U. was involved, things were likely to be looking grim. That combined with Clifford Goodman and Evander Horn, from Homeland Security and the F.B.I. respectively, being with Jeff and Chuckie boded. A lot. The fact that Buchanan and Len were using official titles versus everyone's names boded more. Tried not to worry. Failed.

"Fine. Okay, Missus Chief, we got a tip that the anti-Cleary-Maurer rally was going to be a target of attack from our favorite homegrown terrorists."

"You mean Club Fifty-One and the Church of Intolerance were going to share their version of righteous wrath while at the same time coming out in total favor of the Hate Party Ticket?"

"Yes. And, unsurprisingly, American Centaurion personnel were presumed to be the targets."

I was good with catching words that shouldn't belong. "Presumed. So, *were* we targets, or were we hustled off by the police to get us out of the way so we didn't become targets?"

"In part, yes. To both questions. However—"

Took the leap. "However, the rally was a great time to presume that most of our staff would be elsewhere and therefore they tried to attack our Embassy. Which has really nifty invisible shielding, I'm forced to mention."

"It also has tunnels leading into it," Buchanan said. "Evacuation was deemed necessary—evacuation of everyone, Walter included—and our good friend the Ambassadress," he nodded toward Mona, "offered the safety of her embassy."

"So, was the rest of our area evacuated or just us? And where are my dad and our Embassy Animals?" We had my parent's four dogs and three cats, two dozen Alpha Four Royal Peregrines, and more Royal Poofs than you could count in a day. That was a lot of fur and feathers I wanted to remain intact and safe. Not to mention my father, who was both a history professor on sabbatical from Arizona State University and, naturally for my life, a secret cryptologist for NASA. What Dad wasn't, though, was a kick-butt type.

My phone rang before anyone could answer. In part because I was in the Female Standard Issue Clothing—white Armani oxford shirt, black Armani slim skirt, and black Aerosole pumps—and in part because of all the "fun" at the

protest, my purse was hooked over my neck, which was why
I hadn't lost it during all the brouhaha. Considered taking it
off while I dug around for my phone and decided to stick
with the likely idea that I'd need its contents sooner as opposed to later.

Pulled my phone out on the third ring and took a look.
Blocked number. This usually indicated I was getting a
chatty call from someone trying to kill me or other people I
cared about.

"Answer it, on speaker," Buchanan said quietly.

Did as requested. "Hello?"

"Ambassador?" Wasn't a voice I recognized. It was high-
pitched.

"Maybe. Who's this?"

"Ambassador Katt-Martini of American Centaurion?"

"Could be, could be. Who are you?"

"A friend." Still high-pitched. Faked, for certain. Sounded
like someone trying to imitate Julia Child. Meaning it was
probably a man trying to sound like a woman. Or else Julia
was calling from beyond the grave. The way my luck ran, I
didn't rule this possibility out.

Buchanan made the "keep them talking" motion. Rarely
an issue for me. I was great with keeping the baddies mono-
loguing. He pulled something out of his pocket and plugged
it into my phone's audio jack. The small, blinking device
didn't affect the call.

"My friends identify who they are or I'm able to recognize their voices. So far, you're not really falling into my
Friend Zone."

"I will shortly. You need to leave the protest."

Shared a "what the hell?" look with Buchanan and several
other people around me. "Um, why?"

"It's not safe. For anyone, but for you especially."

There were a lot of people, and dogs, in here, so it wasn't
silent. But the room didn't sound like an outdoor protest,
either. And from experience, you could tell when someone
had you on speakerphone. So either the caller wasn't paying
attention or he was playing stupid for a reason.

"Where are you? At the protest, too?" They couldn't be,

because we hadn't exactly been quiet about being dragged off into the police van. Someone had to have seen us, probably a lot of someones. And I heard no background noise at all—they weren't on speaker, and they weren't with a noisy crowd.

"No. I'm at . . . headquarters." My caller cleared his throat. Probably hard to keep up the Julia Child impersonation for this long. "You need to get to safety."

"Why?"

"Because they want to hurt you."

"Who are 'they' and why are you warning me?"

"You need to stop taking an interest in the elections. They'll leave you alone if you stay out of it."

"Blah, blah, blah. I doubt it."

"Why aren't you taking this seriously?"

"Dude, I get weird phone calls like this all the time. Sometimes they're from crazed psychopaths, sometimes they're from friends in trouble, sometimes they're just from crazy people who have time to kill and have chosen me in their version of Phone Russian Roulette."

"I'm not a 'dude.' "

Interesting where you got them. "Uh, you're faking your voice. Or else you're Julia Child, and if you are, then I'd like to request an easy-to-make recipe that the whole family will enjoy that will not cause me to burn down my kitchen."

"This isn't a funny situation! And I'm not faking my voice. This *is* my voice."

"Suuuuuure it is. I believe you. Truly."

Mona and Olga were talking quietly to each other and Oliver. Decided they'd let me know if their conversation was relevant or not later.

"You need to believe me! I'm taking a terrible risk contacting you. If he finds out . . ." Julia Child dropped her voice. "He'll kill me."

"So the drama. Okay, you tell me who the hell you are, so I know why I should believe you. And, if you're really telling the truth, we'll protect you. How about that?"

Buchanan gave me another "what the hell" look. I ignored him.

There was noise on the other end of the phone. Reminiscent of when Karl Smith had been on the line with me right before he'd been murdered during Operation Drug Addict. Got another bad feeling in my stomach because I was pretty sure my mysterious caller was no longer alone.

"I'll speak with you later, dear," my caller said cheerfully. "Thank you for supporting the Cleary-Maurer presidential campaign. We look forward to your generous donation." The line went dead.

Buchanan pulled his device out of my phone and plugged it into his.

"You think that was really a woman and really her voice?" Lorraine asked me.

"No guess. You think he/she/it was really associated with the Cleary-Maurer campaign?"

"Yes," Mona said. "We recognize the voice."

Olga nodded. "It is a woman, about my age."

"Really? A woman? You're sure?" They nodded. "Okay, I'll bite. Who?"

Oliver opened his mouth to answer, but Buchanan spoke first. "That call originated from the Cleary-Maurer campaign headquarters."

Oliver nodded. "Not a surprise. I believe what *is* a surprise, and the question that needs to be answered, is—why is Cameron Maurer's mother calling to warn Kitty away from this campaign?"

"I've got another question. Was she calling to warn us, to trap us, or to ask for help?" Another thought occurred. "Or was she, in fact, using the same equipment as Malcolm in order to determine our position?"

CHAPTER 5

WAITED FOR THE SOUND of incoming bombs. None. Figured this just meant they'd launched the slow missiles. "Should we evacuate again?"

Buchanan shook his head. "Your embassy isn't safe to reenter right now."

"We could go to Dulce," Lorraine pointed out.

"No." The way Buchanan said it, I assumed this meant that the Powers That Were My Mother, My Husband, and My Best Guy Friend had said they wanted us to remain right here.

Took a deep breath. "Okay, in this order, I want these answers. Where is my father? Where are all the Embassy pets? Why is my embassy unsafe? Where are the other people who I'd expect to be here who are not in this room? And what the hell is going on?"

Oren cleared his throat. "Your father and your pets are in our embassy, Ambassador."

Leah grinned. "We're a little more pet friendly."

"There are half a dozen K-9 dogs in here. Mona appears to be quite pet friendly."

Mona laughed. "Your father has an old friend in town who is staying at the Israeli embassy, Kitty. He wanted the animals with him because he feels they would feel safer."

"My dad actually said that? And with a straight face?"

"Honestly?" Jakob asked. I nodded. "Yes, he did. I think

he misses his dogs and cats and just wanted to show the Poofs and Peregrines off. It's not everyone who has not one but two alien animal races as part of their menagerie, after all. They're quite a hit, so don't worry about them, or him. Your father is under very capable guard."

Meaning other Mossad agents were there. Which was good and also made sense—Mom was the only non-Israeli, non-Jew to ever be in Mossad. A long story I still didn't have all of, but I figured it was Old Home Week for Mossad and Dad was starting the party early.

"Rahmi and Rhee are with him as well," Raj said. "We felt that they would enjoy the company of Mossad, and they're also guarding your father."

Rahmi and Rhee were princesses from Beta Twelve in the Alpha Centauri system, aka the Planet of the Getting Less Pissed Off Amazons. They'd been sent to us by the Planetary Council during Operation Sherlock, under the guise of attending Jamie's first birthday party.

Due to some issues going on both here and there, we hadn't found a way to send them back. So, they'd become a part of our diplomatic mission, and were getting much better with the idea that all men were not enemies to be instantly smashed. They'd really bonded with my dad, which wasn't a shocker, since they worshipped Mom and he was married to her.

I'd been smart enough to not allow them anywhere near the protest, and unlike every single, solitary other person in my circle, they actually followed my orders. They lived to kick butt—which was why I'd kept them far away from the protest, lest they turn it into a riot—and sending them to the Mossad Kegger seemed like their version of heaven, so Raj was right on as always.

So, Dad and the animals were safer than safe, and I could table concerns about all of them for later, including wondering why none of the animals had shown up to protect any of us. Since the Poofs and Peregrines were both bred for protection, it seemed odd that none of them had tried to at least warn us we were going into danger. But I had other, more pressing, questions.

"That's two down, three to go. Where are my husband and the rest of those who I'd expect to see here, or, rather, expect to be in my embassy at some time?"

"Safe," Len said. "They're in Langley. All of them."

"So, there is not one living soul in our embassy?" Many heads shook. "Because my embassy isn't safe, right?" Many heads nodded. "So, how is one of the most secure buildings on Earth compromised?"

Officer Melville took this one. "We—and by 'we' I mean the K-9 team, all of us—received a tip that a dangerous package had been delivered to your embassy, Ambassador."

"That old ruse again? We have equipment that can safely check for bombs, don't we? And by 'we' I mean Centaurion Division, along with the Washington P.D. Bomb Squad."

Melville nodded. "Yes, but the tip was from a rather, ah, unconventional source. Sent to all of our cell phones at the same time. From an untraceable number." He shot me a meaningful look. At least I assumed he was waggling his eyebrows to be meaningful. Either that or he had bad gas he was holding in. Hoped I was right to go with the former.

"What did this message actually say?" And who would know to send a message about American Centaurion being in danger to the K-9 squad? And why to the police at all? Why not to Alpha Team?

Melville handed me his phone. *Officer Moe, my niece's home has been compromised with deadly gas. Please remove every living thing instantly or we will be forced to take steps. Then please ensure that her home is safe for all living things as soon as possible or we will again be forced to take steps.*

Ah. That's who. My "uncles," the two best assassins in the business. Nice to know they were keeping a very watchful eye on me. Nice, creepy, and worrisome at the same time. Awesome, I got the trifecta on this. "Wow. They are *that* good."

"How so?" Buchanan asked.

"I don't think I ever called Officer Melville 'Moe' in front of my 'uncles,' and yet they know what I called him during the first time we all met, so to speak. I'm hella impressed. And, yeah, okay, this would make me grab everyone and run, too."

Melville nodded. "We knew this had to be legit because either they'd heard you call me that or you'd told them. Either way—"

"They were right," Buchanan said.

"Why did they contact the police?" Amy asked. "I mean, for bombs, yes. But why not tell Kitty? Why not call James, or Malcolm?"

"I got a message," Buchanan said. "Mine was brief. 'Your job is in deadly danger and should visit the Middle East immediately.' So when Melville called me, it seemed obvious."

"Ah, that's why."

Everyone looked at me. "Mind explaining that?" Claudia asked.

"My 'uncles' knew Officer Melville would call Malcolm. So they could get him moving on getting all of us out of public and to somewhere other than home, with the full cooperation of the police department." Had to hand it to Peter the Dingo Dog and Surly Vic—they were hella efficient and totally in the know.

Speaking of which, Lillian Culver was in the room and I only had her where I wanted her politically because of said "uncles." Wasn't sure if this was a good conversation to be having within her hearing. Then again, it was probably confirming that they could kill her at this very moment if they wanted to. Which brought up another point.

"Um, that means they're in town, doesn't it? And they didn't call or anything to let me know they were coming."

"I'd count this as them letting you know," Buchanan said dryly. "However the package didn't come into the Embassy via conventional means. It was put into the tunnels and sent up through the basement. Which is the only reason we were able to evacuate in time."

Looked at Lucinda. "I take back any and every complaint about you taking Jamie and the others with you to the rally. You're the best mother-in-law on the planet."

She shook her head and hugged Jamie, who she'd claimed from Adriana during my phone call with Cameron Maurer's dear old mum. "I didn't know about this when we left."

"Take credit for the brilliant ideas as they come and never

apologize for them, especially when they're shown to be brilliant after the fact." Hey, that had been my motto since day one with the gang from Alpha Four, after all.

Pierre cleared his throat. "I'm sorry, Ambassador, but should the children and the, ah, non-essential personnel be involved in this meeting? Or, to put the question another way, where would our lovely Host Ambassadress like me and some of the others to take our darling little pitchers?"

Embassy personnel only called me Ambassador when people we didn't like or trust were nearby, or if I was missing something really important and they wanted me to focus on their words carefully.

Leave it to Pierre, versus me, to point out that "little pitchers have big ears" and that the kids hearing about scary things happening where they lived or spent most of their days might not be in the Happy Child Rearing Handbook. Wished he'd done it sooner, but there hadn't been time for him to do that politely, and even when he was delivering a cutting insult, Pierre was always polite. He was an excellent example for the children of how to behave in all social settings.

Mona called in some of her embassy personnel, including their embassy physician, and they took the kids, Lucinda, Pierre, and Denise off to whatever tastefully decorated room was now declared the impromptu Bahraini Daycare Center. Walter sent Jeremy and Jennifer with them as well to provide protection, and since Jennifer was going, Ravi was going, and if Ravi was going, all of Hacker International felt they were going, too. Buchanan seemed fine with this, so I didn't argue.

Tito and Mahin joined the Daycare Team, Tito because he was having a conversation with Dr. Zainal and Mahin because she was having a conversation with two of Mona's embassy staff. Fine with me—someone should be turning this into a fun time, and that meant more people protecting the kids.

Mona also took the opportunity to ask for tea service to be delivered, both to us and to the kids and their retainers. Either her staff kept the tea stuff ready 24/7 or else she had a couple of A-Cs doing kitchen duty, because tea, finger sandwiches, tea cakes, and the like appeared quickly.

"So," I said after I'd had a few sandwiches, two cups of tea, and some cakes, to keep my strength up and stress level down, "I still point out that we have the best shielding around encircling our embassy, and it covers the lower portions, too. Nasty things bounce off the shield. So, was it off or damaged?"

"No, Chief," Walter said. "However, the shields aren't made to stop gas. If they were, we'd die when shielded because oxygen wouldn't get through."

Chose not to ask why I didn't know this already and also chose not to ask myself why I'd never wondered about this, either. I'd taken chemistry and other sciences in school. Since Jeff and Chuckie weren't here, gave myself a "duh" on their behalf.

"How in the world did they get gas into our Embassy, though? Through what means? And in such a way that we were actually able to evacuate without anyone becoming contaminated or dying. And if we weren't so able, I want names and risk levels right now. I'm asking for specifics, not generalities, by the way. And I'm asking very officially."

"We don't know how they got the gas in," Buchanan said. "Which is part of the problem."

"Only part?"

"We got everyone out before the gas could reach the first floor," Walter said before I could get even more sarcasm going.

"Only just," Melville added. "If the warning hadn't come when it did, there would have been casualties." His phone rang and he answered it. His eyes narrowed and I decided I wanted to table the rest of this conversation until he was done. To be polite. And so I could eavesdrop. And have another little cake and cup of tea. Hey, the morning had, so far, been quite energetic.

Melville grunted. "Where? How many target areas? Really? Interesting. How many casualties? Oh? Good. Yes, that times out correctly. Yes. Yes, I agree. No idea, honestly, but I'll keep you apprised. Thanks, Chief." He hung up and heaved an angry sigh. "Bombs were activated at the protest. We got these folks out just in time—they detonated no more than a minute after we'd cleared the area."

"How close to where we were did they go boom?"

Melville grimaced. "The targets were around the perimeter. No casualties, just a few minor injuries. The Chief thinks in part because we were taking you all away and that created interest in where we were. The bombs weren't near you or our exit route."

"So they were set off to drive us home," Serene said. Everyone turned to her, which was wise. In my opinion, when the Resident Explosives Expert Supreme was speaking about things going boom, we should all listen.

"I don't disagree, but why do you think so?"

"Because an explosive of any decent magnitude should have hurt someone there, Kitty. But if they were done more for show, like fireworks, then the likelihood is that they were set up with a limited blast radius. Meaning they didn't really want to hurt anyone there, they just wanted them to panic."

"And frightened animals run to the safety of their nests, and we're all animals at our cores. That makes sense. So, they blow things up, and we all run into the Embassy which, if that had worked out, would have been filled with deadly gas, and we all die before we can figure out that the people inside are already dead. Officially, I hate whoever's doing this. Not that this could possibly come as a surprise to anyone."

Culver looked pissed. "You'd have taken anyone near you with you, too."

"Beg pardon?"

She rolled her eyes. Not her best look, but whatever, we were currently on the Bestest Buds side of the embassy, and I was willing to try to keep us there. "Kitty, I know you, and so do your enemies. You're a protector. So, you'd grab anyone who was terrified and try to get them to safety. And where would be safer to you than your Embassy? Meaning they'd have killed me, Vance, Nathalie, and anyone else who knew you and was nearby. Your Embassy was much closer to the protest than this one."

"Our enemies so rarely care who else they hurt while they try to hurt us, Lillian's theory both makes sense and comes as no surprise. Okay, so, if someone's loosed a deadly gas in our embassy, how is that not spreading throughout all of Embassy Row?" Looked at Olga. "Oh, God, is that why you're here?"

"No, no," she said reassuringly. "I am here because the game is afoot and Mister Buchanan felt that if your embassy was compromised, Adriana and I could be targeted as well."

Somehow she thought this statement was reassuring? Or that it indicated that deadly gas wasn't wafting through all of Embassy Row? Had to wonder about my friends sometimes. "Ah, what about the rest of the Embassies around us? And everyone else in the Romanian Embassy? And so on?"

"The area around you has been evacuated," Buchanan said. "Natural gas leak is the official cause."

"Okay, so who's risking their lives to verify that the area is secure?" Had to figure Centaurion agents would be assigned to this—hyperspeed meant they had the best chance of getting away if things were dire.

"Airborne."

CHAPTER 6

CHECKED LORRAINE AND CLAUDIA'S expressions, in case I'd heard wrong. They looked as freaked out as I felt. "Excuse me, did I just hear you correctly?"

Buchanan nodded. "Yes. Airborne is in charge of Embassy contamination cleanup and safety verification."

Tried not to let my voice hit the dog-only register. Failed. "So, the team that has only humans on it, that's the team everyone decided should go in with the deadly gas?"

Way back not so long ago I'd been the Head of Airborne. Shoved a longing for the Good Old Days away—as Olga had said, the game was afoot and I needed to focus on the here and now. Airborne consisted of Tim Crawford, who'd moved up to my old position, and my five Navy Top Gun flyboys, two of whom were Lorraine and Claudia's husbands, Joe Billings and Randy Muir. So, as I was understanding it, my guys and their husbands were tramping around Potentially Poisoned Gas Ground Zero.

"No," White said calmly. "The team with the closest U.S. military ties is using their influence and skills to ensure that those who are helping to decontaminate our buildings and those surrounding us aren't, at the same time, planting bombs or listening devices, and so forth."

"They're all in protective gear," Buchanan added.

"I wanted to go with them, Chief," Walter said. "But I was overruled."

"By whom?"

"By the Head of Security."

A year ago, that would have been Gladys Gower, who had been pretty much the most formidable woman ever, right after my mother and Olga, at any rate.

But Gladys had died a year ago. The lump in my throat that thinking about anyone we'd lost from our side always gave me was even larger when I thought about who we'd lost during Operation Infiltration.

But we'd had to go on, and I had to go on now, too. William Ward, Walter's older brother, had been moved into the Head of Security role. Meaning that he'd ordered his little brother to get to safety with everyone else. However, since Security always stayed, even when everyone else had to evacuate, that meant that the danger had been extreme. Which made sending Airborne in seem, in some ways, even more foolhardy.

Tried to think about this like Buchanan would have, since it was clear that he was in charge of Mission: Evacuation. Wanted to ask why we weren't sending the people with the hyperspeed, but reminded myself that we were doing our best to keep as many A-C powers secret as possible. As it was, Jeff being the top empath in, most likely, the galaxy was far too common knowledge.

So, this was a very public thing, and in fact the police had been called and were involved. Meaning Buchanan wanted to ensure that the police, and human military, remained obviously in charge. After all, he hadn't said that Airborne had no A-C Field Teams assisting, just that Airborne was in charge.

"Okay, Malcolm, I'll assume that you, Tim, and the rest of the team have things under control."

"I'm so flattered," he said in a tone that indicated he actually wasn't. "Really, Missus Chief, what do you take all of us for, amateurs?"

"Someone's an amateur," Vance said. "Because they let Cameron Maurer's mother call Kitty."

Chose not to mention that this was actually an impressively smooth conversational shift Vance had just advanced, and instead thank him silently and go with it. "Did they let her? Or was she trying to drive us into the Embassy to be sure we all died today?"

Vance shook his head. "She sounded frightened for you, and for herself."

"Yeah, well, good old Leslie Manning sounded all worried for her safety, too. In order to get me into a position to try to kill me. So, you know, call me Miss Suspicious, but I'm not buying into the coinkydink."

"Leslie was an android, though," Vance said. "And before you say it, why in the world would anyone spend the time and money to make an android of a little old lady?"

"I'm more interested in who the 'he' was who she feared would kill her," Mona said. "Did she mean her son?"

"There are so many options for Suspect of the Moment that we probably don't have enough to go on to guess. But I'd really like to hear Olga's opinion on my not-so-mystery caller."

Olga shrugged. "I agree with the young man—Nancy Maurer sounded sincere and frightened for more people than just you, Kitty. I would suggest that this bears investigation."

"Would that investigation be related to the deadly gas contamination, the bomb explosions, or its own special thing?"

"Why assume they aren't connected?" Amy asked. "It seems like everything's always connected."

"Sometimes." Considered who wasn't doing a lot of talking and, under the circumstances, that seemed odd. "I'd like to hear what Mister Joel Oliver has to say on all that's been going on today."

He shook his head. "I was visiting Madame Olga when all the excitement happened."

"Wait, what? You weren't at the protest? You, the investigative journalist supreme, passed up that opportunity? Pull the other one."

Mr. Joel Oliver had first come onto my radar during the festivities leading up to my wedding. That Chuckie—who I called the Conspiracy King because he'd always been into all the stuff everyone thinks is crazy to believe in, and was proven to be right every day of my life these last few years— felt Oliver was the most in-the-know reporter out there had been frightening at first.

But Oliver had proven to be a friend, and a trustworthy one at that. And when American Centaurion had been outed as being the aliens living on Earth he'd always said they were, Oliver's cachet had risen dramatically. He was no longer that lunatic paparazzo; instead he was now the man with the insider information. However, while he'd stopped being journalism's laughingstock, he'd not stopped being Mr. Well-Informed. Chuckie got at least half of his accurate tips from Oliver and his network. That'd he'd missed a big deal protest being bombed in his backyard seemed far-fetched.

"It's true," Oliver said with a shrug. "And before you ask, no, I wasn't given any tips in regard to the explosions at the protest or the attack on your embassy, let alone whatever Missus Maurer was calling about."

"Are you feeling okay?" Vance asked solicitously. He was Oliver's self-admitted biggest fan, and pretty much thought Oliver walked on water. Figured Vance was ready to demand that Tito do a full physical on Oliver. Not that I could blame him. Oliver almost always knew what was going on.

"Yes, I'm well." Oliver sighed. "I was working on . . . something else of extreme . . . delicacy." He shot me a meaningful look.

Decided to both take the leap and not say aloud where I was leaping to, which was that Chuckie had asked Oliver to do a special assignment. Clearly one that had involved Olga and her Font of Knowledge. In part because she was wheelchair-bound, Olga liked to really make you work for the answers. Oliver had the best track record with her, and also the most patience for the game.

"Okay, so you two weren't there. I'm still wondering how it is that Missus Maurer, if that was really her, thought we were still at the protest. Did we somehow not make the news for once?" Since Operation Destruction, we'd made the news with alarming frequency.

"Let's see," Mona said. She nodded to Khalid, who pushed a button on the wall, making a whole panel of books slide to the side, revealing a ginormous flatscreen TV. He had a remote and started flipping through the channels.

Khalid settled on CNN, where reporters were breathlessly

discussing explosions and asking if homegrown or foreign terrorists were responsible. What they weren't saying was anything about our being taken away by the police. Because the reporters weren't talking about explosions at the protest.

They were talking about explosions at C.I.A. Headquarters.

CHAPTER 7

I N TIMES OF GREAT STRESS, there is always the choice to freak out or to stay calm. I amazed myself and went with calm. "Malcolm, am I correct in believing that my husband, my mother, my best guy friends, the Supreme Pontifex, and several other key men attached to my diplomatic mission are all at Langley right now?"

"They were," he replied tersely, as he made a call. He stepped to a part of the room that no one was in and started speaking in a low voice.

Buchanan was busy. I could trot over to eavesdrop, but he clearly didn't want to be sharing. Fine. I turned to Serene. "Did your team happen to take care of hiding the bombs at the protest, or our removal from it?"

She was texting on her phone. "No, Kitty. I just checked. Imageering didn't have anything to try to alter. There was no footage of us being dragged away. They have nothing of use from Langley, by the way."

The word "try" wouldn't have been used in relation to our imageers a year ago. But a year ago we were hit by the best hacker in existence, Chernobog the Ultimate. She'd not only wiped all our data, but she'd put some kind of anti-imageer bug into the digital systems worldwide. We still hadn't isolated what it was that was affecting the digital feeds, but whatever it was, the imageers were blocked from all digital images.

Considering imageering talent meant that said imageer could touch an image and know everything about the person in the picture, that they were blocked was beyond frightening. Film was still "seeable" for most imageers, but right now they could read digital just like a regular human could—with their eyes only.

Christopher White, who was Amy's husband and the most powerful imageer we knew of, said that pictures took copies of people's minds and souls as well as their bodies. So whatever had been put into the digital airwaves was somehow blocking said minds and souls.

Christopher would be with Jeff and the others at Langley, as would Kevin Lewis, who was Mom's right hand man in the P.T.C.U. and also our Defense Attaché. We probably had other guys there I wasn't thinking of, too, because that's just how our luck ran. So everyone's husband was in some kind of mortal peril right now, how nice. Except for maybe Serene's and Lucinda's. Got a nervous feeling in my stomach. "Can we see if there are more attack sites than the protest and Langley?"

"Funny you ask," Abigail said with no humor in her tone. "I've been checking our bases worldwide with William and Uncle Alfred. The Kennedy Space Center was just attacked." NASA Base, where Jeff's father, Alfred, worked, was part of Kennedy. "William had already put all bases on full alert due to the Embassy being attacked, so no one was hurt."

"Why is this happening?" Mona asked quietly, while the reporters chattered on about terrorist bombings going off all over. "I mean this kind of effort, right now?"

"That is the correct question," Olga said. And whenever Olga tossed off a really obvious hint, I paid attention.

Unfortunately for those around me, I did my best thinking while running my mouth. I could give in and freak out about how half the people I loved could be blown up or I could continue to give calm and in charge a go. Really wanted to start freaking out, but instead went with thinking.

So many weird and scary things had happened this afternoon, but the weirdest had to be the call from Nancy Maurer. Start there.

"Missus Maurer called to warn me to leave the protest. But she called after the bombs had gone off there, and after our Embassy had been gassed. So why did she bother?"

"Maybe she didn't know what was going on, or where," Culver suggested. "Just that something bad was going to happen."

Lorraine nodded. "She didn't sound like she was what I'd call in the know."

"More like she'd heard something by accident and was trying to stop bad things from happening," Claudia said.

"That would make sense," Raj said, looking at his phone. "I've been researching the Cleary-Maurer campaign while we've been here, and there's a lot of press about how Missus Maurer is supporting her boy. It's clear that they're using her in a public relations capacity, but that also means they're bringing her out to a wide variety of events, including a few 'closed door' meetings where they've had her around for photo ops."

"They're going for the full-on flag, Mom, and apple pie approach," Oliver said. "Emphasis on mom, since they're using her to show that 'decent women' support them."

"But how would she have known about bombs? Would the Cleary-Maurer campaign really be willing to try to blow up their competition?"

"You'd be surprised what politicians will do to win office," Culver said dryly. Figured that, out of everyone in the room, she'd know best.

Vance cocked his head. "You know, Kitty, she said that you needed to stop taking an interest in the election and, if you did, 'they' would leave you alone."

"You think this is all related to the election?" Serene asked. "Even the bombs at NASA Base?"

"If Kitty, as the Ambassador, is making the statement that she is against the Cleary-Maurer ticket, then the assumption would be that all the A-Cs are also against the Cleary-Maurer ticket," Mona said.

"I don't tell them how to vote."

Abigail snorted. "Yes, you do. You're the Ambassador, and the Pontifex and Alpha Team agree with you. That's all it takes—we tend to vote as a bloc."

"Really?"

Every A-C in the room nodded. It so figured.

Yet something else I was getting to learn on the fly. This I knew for a fact hadn't been in the gut-busting Briefing Books of Boredom I'd finally managed to get through. They were a blur of points of parliamentary procedure, maps that merely looked like eye charts combined with mazes, and an unreal amount of if-then statements, but a statement pointing out that every A-C voted the party line would have caught my eye.

Buchanan got off his phone and rejoined us. "Miraculously, no one was hurt. Anywhere. Best we can tell is that these were all warnings, a sort of 'see what we can do?' kind of effort. Designed to frighten and intimidate without the bad side effects of killing people."

"Our enemies are starting to attempt to be humane in some way? What's this world coming to?"

"Why kill a registered voter?" Culver said. Like everyone else in my circle, she had a sarcasm knob. The horrifying fact that I was likely to become friendlier with this woman than I'd ever planned or wanted waved merrily at me. Chose to ignore this horror due to all the other crap going on. I'd save it for later, when I was feeling good about things, just to bring me back down to reality. "They want Cleary-Maurer to win, and you can't win if the swing voters are all dead."

"I wouldn't count on the 'no harm' mindset to last," Buchanan said. "The assumption is that they're trying to show that they mean business to get what they want without killing . . . but that they did this to show that they can and will kill if needed."

"Ah, so business as usual, gotcha."

He managed a small grin. "Probably. Proud of you, all of you, for not losing it, by the way."

"We're good under fire," Amy said. "But Kitty was trying to figure out what's going on and I think Vance and the others have it right—it's related to the elections."

"Okay, so we oppose Cleary-Maurer. So what? We haven't endorsed whoever's running against them, so what does it matter?"

Everyone in the room gave me the "really?" look. Was glad Jamie and the other kids weren't here—wouldn't have wanted them to join in on this look and I had a feeling they would have.

"Oh, fine, fine. Yes, okay, Senator Armstrong is running and likely to get his party's nomination. Senator McMillan's already endorsed him. And we're close to both of them and while we haven't said anything outright yet it's only a matter of time before we start waving Armstrong for President flags."

Culver, Vance, and Nathalie exchanged a look. "Ah . . ." Nathalie said. "Kitty?"

"Oh goody, something else I don't know but am going to find out. Thank God I live to learn and all that. What am I forgetting or not aware of? Other than the fact that both presidential candidates are going to be from Florida, I mean. Which is weird, when you think about it."

"I've got some news you're going to find weirder," Vance said. "Like who's being discussed, seriously discussed, as Vincent's running mate."

Took a deep breath. "Lay it on me."

Heard some steps behind me and turned to see everyone we'd been told were at Langley enter the room, my husband amongst them. As relief washed over me, I examined everyone to make sure Buchanan was right and no one was hurt. Oh, sure, I looked at Jeff the most, but he was my husband, so that was only right.

Jeff was tall, broad, and built, with dark brown wavy hair and light brown eyes. He was, point of fact, the most gorgeous thing I'd ever seen, which was the biggest reason I was looking at him the most. So I was a normal girl.

His expression matched the rest of those entering the room—stress, combined with worry, relief, and anger. So pretty much how everyone already in the room probably looked, too. However, Jeff was also looking a little uncomfortable.

Vance came up next to me and put his hand on my shoulder. "Meet the most likely vice presidential candidate on the Armstrong ticket, Kitty. You might know him as your husband."

CHAPTER 8

LET VANCE'S STATEMENT sit on the air for a bit. Because it wasn't computing. At all. While I stood there in shocked silence I got to observe.

I observed that I had nothing I could say that wouldn't sound extremely undiplomatic. I also observed that everyone was passing little signals to others in the room—Mom and Kevin to Buchanan; Chuckie to Len and Kyle; Mom again to Jakob, Oren and Leah, and then again to Khalid; Chuckie to Amy and Caroline; Kevin to Raj and White; Cliff and Horn to Culver and Nathalie; Reader to Lorraine, Claudia and Serene, and then to Nathalie; Kevin to Len and Kyle; Chuckie to Olga, Adriana, and Oliver; Gower to Doreen, Abigail, White, and Raj. It was a regular Secret Sign Fest in here.

The only ones not joining in on the fun were Jeff—who was cringing and trying not to show it, meaning that, regardless of whether or not my face was hiding my inner thoughts, my emotions were incredibly clear—and Christopher.

Christopher was the only person of our new arrivals acting normally. Well, normally for him. He was glaring. Patented Glare #1, to be exact. It was such a relief that I wanted to hug him. However, that would mean I'd have to move and speak, and right now, I didn't trust myself to do either.

"Nice way to tell her," he snapped at Vance.

"When were you planning on it?" Vance asked, sarcasm knob heading toward ten. "At the national convention?"

Managed to find my voice. "April Fools?" Hey, a girl could dream.

"It's the end of July," Christopher said. "So, no. Nice try."

"Why are Christopher and Vance the only ones talking?"

Mom sighed. "Everyone's waiting for your expected reaction." She shook her head. "So, let's get it out of the way so we can get down to business."

"Can you get out of it?" This I directed to Jeff.

He grimaced. "Not really. It's . . . political."

Managed not to offer a snide reply. Jeff couldn't be any more thrilled about this than I was. Went for the only thing I could think of—what I'd been thinking since Vance had shared the exciting news. "Has anyone considered the, ah, ramifications of the kind of . . . scrutiny a presidential or vice presidential candidate goes through? I mean *really* considered?"

Reader nodded. "It's why we were all at Langley today. Discussing. Everyone feels that things can be . . . contained."

Considered whose sanity to appeal to. Decided the guy who'd spent a lot of years sniffing around was the best choice. "MJO, can you perhaps share your extremely educated perspective on why this is likely to be the worst idea ever in the history of the world?"

"I believe that the situation could be less threatening than you believe it to be, Ambassador," Oliver replied.

"I think it's wonderful, Kitty," Mona said. She appeared to be the only other person in the room who wasn't clued in or getting secret signs passed to her. She looked quite pleased for us. I normally credited her with a hell of a lot more insight.

"It is?"

"Yes." She beamed. "Why don't you and Jeff go into one of the smaller salons and you two can discuss it as husband and wife."

Ah. Mona was possibly more clued in than everyone else. And my good friend. Because I needed to talk to Jeff and I couldn't risk saying anything in front of Culver, Cliff, or Horn, and presumably Mona realized this. Oliver probably had, too—he'd called me Ambassador and I was fairly sure he'd been lying about things being less threatening than I was imagining.

Khalid took my elbow and ushered me and Jeff out of this room, down a hall, and into a much smaller room that looked like a waiting room. "This is the antechamber to the Ambassador's offices," he said with a smile. So it was a waiting room, go me. "He's not here at the moment, so you should have privacy." Khalid nodded to us and closed the door.

Jeff opened the door leading to the Bahraini Ambassador's office. "No one there." He closed it, came over to me, pulled me into his arms, and hugged me tightly. His hearts were pounding. I hugged him back and felt his body relax a bit. "Are you, Jamie, and my mother alright? I wanted to call but Chuck and your mother wouldn't let me."

"Yeah, we're fine. Because my 'uncles' are in town and gave Officer Melville and Malcolm the scary heads-ups." Took a deep breath and moved out of our clinch. "Who in God's name thinks you becoming Senator Armstrong's running mate is a good idea?"

"Everyone, apparently." Jeff ran his hand through his hair. "It wasn't my idea."

"I guessed. Whose idea was it?"

He sighed. "Don's."

"Senator McMillan suggested you? Is he high?"

"No. He thinks it will give voters something positive to choose."

A-Cs were deadly allergic to alcohol, so I didn't drink any more because I didn't want to risk killing Jeff, or have him unable to kiss me. However, right now, I wanted the stiffest drink imaginable. "It's going to give the press a really good time."

"You don't think I'm a good choice, do you?" Jeff asked in a low voice.

"Huh?" Looked at his expression—he looked disappointed and unconfident. This wasn't an expression I was used to seeing on my husband's face. Which meant he was reading my emotions incorrectly. Then again, my main emotion had been shocked horror. Maybe he was reading me right but interpreting me wrong.

I hugged him again. "Frankly, I think you're a great choice. Jeff, you're a natural leader and you always have been. It's not you moving into a bigger position of power that worries me. It's the fact that we have some scary skeletons in our closets."

"Everyone knows I'm an alien."

Wow. Due to our enemies giving Jeff a huge amount of Surcenthumain, what I thought of as the Superpowers Drug, he was amazingly enhanced. This meant a lot of things, but one of those things was that Jeff could practically read my mind. Backed up again and looked up at him. "Did you get hurt and no one wants to tell me about it?"

"No, why?"

"Because I'm not worried about you being 'outed' as an alien any more than I'm worried that our Supreme Pontifex is going to be 'outed' for being gay—both are very common knowledge by now and why both Club Fifty-One and the Church of Intolerance are so very fond of us. I'm worried as hell, though, about the fact that you and I used to do some really dangerous work, and that work included killing a variety of very bad people."

"Oh." He sounded relieved. "*That's* what you're so upset about."

"That you're *not* upset about it worries me. A lot. But not nearly as much as Mom, Chuckie and James not being completely worried about it."

"We were discussing how to keep our former jobs under wraps, or how to discuss them, when the bombs went off."

"Cannot wait to hear the plan so I can laugh a really bitter laugh while Mister Joel Oliver pokes ever so many holes into said plan. However, are you really okay? You all look fine, but you're not really, um, reading me very well right now."

Jeff grinned. "I'm stressed out of my mind, baby, and before you point out that I've had a stressful job since I was twenty, this is a very different kind of stress. This is stress based on doing another thing I really don't want to do that I'm also not sure that I *can* do well. It's affecting my ability to read anyone clearly, even you. I can get the dominant emotions, but not the nuance. It'll pass."

"Good. And to reassure you again since you're not picking up nuance, you'll be awesome as vice president, should you get the nomination, and we all survive the campaign, and you get elected, which I in no way think is a given. The survival. I'm fairly sure that if Senator McMillan thinks you're the right choice for VP then you're the right choice."

Jeff smiled, pulled me to him, and kissed me. He was the best kisser in, I figured, the entire galaxy, and as always when he kissed me, I stopped thinking about anything else other than his mouth. Well, I thought about his body, too.

He ended our kiss and chuckled. "Thanks, baby. As long as you believe in me, I can do anything."

"Glad to be of service. I'd love to suggest that we continue this part of our discussion and go rip each other's clothes off, but we currently can't go home."

Jeff laughed. "I love that, no matter what the situation, your laser focus on the priorities remains intact."

"It's a gift."

CHAPTER 9

KHALID WAS WAITING for us down the hall and we rejoined the others. Everyone was eating, and I made sure Jeff got a snack, too.

While he was eating I sidled over to Reader, who was standing a little apart from everyone else. He hung up his phone as I came over. "Tim was checking in, girlfriend."

"I wasn't trying to see if you were calling another girl, James. But are they okay?" Looked around. "Where did Malcolm go?"

He grinned. "You're the only girl for me, and you know it. And yes, everyone is still alive and unpoisoned. Cleanup's going to take longer than we'd like, and Buchanan went to oversee that and to ensure all tunnels near our bases are devoid of other evil stuff. And yes, before you ask the question I see your mouth opening to ask, he's wearing protective gear and has Field team escorts."

"Good, good. I just like to be sure."

"Yeah, I know. You okay?"

"Physically, yes. We were very efficiently herded here. But emotionally? Hell no. I can't believe anyone thinks that we can have Jeff in a major campaign without a lot of nasty things we don't want revealed to be waved at us on the six o'clock news."

"I know. And as hard as this is to believe, everyone who's pushing Jeff to go for the nomination knows the risks."

"Awesome. Can't wait for our lives to be ruined in, what, less than a month?"

He rolled his eyes "We think we can mitigate the risks, Kitty. How stupid do you think we are?"

"Not stupid at all, which is why I'm having trouble with the notion that all of you somehow don't think that the very first thing that the paparazzi are going to uncover is that we killed Leventhal Reid."

I could manage to say the name without shuddering, but it took effort. Reid had been, hands down, the most frightening person I'd ever dealt with in my life, and that included a lot of fugly monsters, politicians with scary delusions of grandeur, and the most cutthroat corporate raiders out there.

The last year had been nightmare filled for me because we'd discovered that the Bad Guy of Bad Guys, aka the Mastermind, had figured out how to clone people and had made a new, improved version of Reid. I'd met his sorta fourteen-year-old, rapidly-aging-to-maturity self as we were bringing down the secret research and cloning facility. And unfortunately, that clone had escaped.

As had the clone of Amy's wicked stepmother and the Brains Behind Many Master Plans, LaRue Demorte Gaultier. She'd looked around twelve a year ago. How "old" they both were now was anyone's guess, but my money was on mid-twenties.

Thinking about those two being out and about always made me sick to my stomach. However, thinking about their ages gave me one last straw to grasp at.

"You know, Jeff's not thirty-five yet. So legally he can't run."

Reader shook his head as Chuckie joined us. "*Nice* try," Chuckie said. "However, he's thirty-four and a half, and he'll be thirty-five before they would take office. So, that issue can and will be avoided."

"I can't believe you, of all people, are okay with this, Secret Agent Man."

He shrugged. "Might be nice to have a truly decent person in office."

"This wouldn't be the first time."

"No, but your husband is one of the few people whose motivations I actually trust."

Considering Chuckie's massively suspicious nature, this was high praise indeed. Under other circumstances I'd have been happy. Under this one I just wanted to find what Kool-Aid they'd all been drinking and either have some myself or, better, find the antidote and administer it to everyone before it was too late.

"Kitty," Culver called, "you need to see this." She was standing near the TV, Nathalie and most of the others clustered around her.

We trotted over. We watched. It was quite a show.

All of us who'd been at the protest were on screen—being shoved into the police van. The police had managed to shield Jamie from the cameras, so one small favor there. They'd gotten a great shot of Claudia trying to hit a policeman and the rest of us yelling and fighting being shoved into the police van, though. We looked like the best-dressed, most passionate hippies in the world. Go us.

"Well," Horn said finally, "looks like you've made the news, ladies."

"At least you're not wearing linen suits anymore," Mom said. "So there's one small favor."

"Serene, I thought you said that there were no feeds of us?"

"That we'd found. Checking what's going on now." She didn't sound happy and was texting at hyperspeed. She stepped away.

Khalid turned the sound up. ". . . were our local aliens and their supporters only protesting the Clearly-Maurer campaign?" the voice-over asked. "Or are they laying the groundwork for Representative Jeff Martini's bid to become Senator Vincent Armstrong's vice presidential candidate?"

"How do the female members of our diplomatic mission being at this protest lay the groundwork for anything?" Jeff asked. "Let alone my so-called bid for vice president?"

"They'll spin it however they want to," Kevin said. "That's what the news does. No offense," he said to Oliver.

"None taken," Oliver said with a small smile. "Particularly because you're correct."

"We'll handle it," Raj added, as the voiceover continued to question our motivations and desires. "We always do."

"Could this get worse?" I asked everyone and no one. Right on cue, my phone rang. I was just lucky like that. Pulled it out. Not a number I knew. The fun never stopped here. "Hello?" Followed Serene's lead and stepped away from the group and the TV.

"Is this Ambassador Katt-Martini?" A man's voice, but I didn't recognize it.

"Could be. Who's this?"

Chuckie jerked, reached into his pocket, pulled out a doo-hickey that was a lot like the one Buchanan had used only a little while ago, and plugged it into my phone. Chose not to complain, nor to ask if I should just keep one of these plugged in 24/7.

"I'd like to get your reactions to a few developments. Are you alone?"

"This isn't a sex line, so I don't feel any need to answer that. And I'd like to get your name, rank, and serial number. Or I get to get your reactions to my hanging up."

Chuckie made the "put it on speakerphone" gesture. Shook my head. Didn't want to give my mystery caller any intel and hearing the background noises would confirm I wasn't alone. He rolled his eyes, but made the "keep him talking" sign. Managed not to snort—I was a pro at this well before today's Surprise Test Callers.

My latest mystery phone buddy chuckled. It didn't sound evil, and since I'd heard a lot of evil chuckles in the last few years, felt I'd recognize one. However, while it wasn't evil, it was something else I didn't care for—patronizing. "I'm a friend."

"Bullpookey. As I say every time someone tries this su-persecret way of pissing me off, my friends identify themselves and I can also recognize their voices. You and I have never spoken, therefore I'm having a challenge believing the whole 'friend' line you're trying to pass."

Another chuckle. "I'm not trying to be mysterious, I just wanted to be sure it was the real Ambassador Katt-Martini I was speaking to, not a subordinate or stand-in."

"And dialing my cell phone wasn't enough proof?"

"No. I needed to, ah, hear your speech patterns to be sure you're the real deal."

"Don't I feel all special? And yet, there you are, being your own kind of special by still not telling me who the hell you are. You have two seconds to spill your secret identity before I decide I'm bored and stop playing this game."

Yet another chuckle. Got the impression he really thought he was charming. Chose to practice diplomacy and not tell him that he was actually insufferably annoying. "Let me stop being rude and mysterious. I'm Bruce Jenkins, Ambassador. I'm with the Washington Post."

"Um, hi Bruce. We get the Post already." And every other paper coughed up in or around our nation's capital. I never read the papers, but everyone else in the Embassy seemed fond of them. "No need for the special renewal deals."

Oliver's turn to jerk, spin, and race over. "Bruce Jenkins?" he asked in a low voice. I nodded.

Jenkins chuckled. "I've heard about your sense of humor. You *are* the woman who told the British Consul that Aerosmith would take the Rolling Stones in either a battle of the bands or a battle of, I think your term was, 'lifelong, total hotties'?"

"Um, yeah. Ages ago." Well, a year ago. Maybe two. Or so. I tried not to keep track of the things that made me ask why I'd been given this particular job. Oliver was whispering urgently to Jeff, Chuckie and Reader, while also giving me the kill gesture. Frantically. "Bruce, what's the point of your call? I have a life to get back to."

"I'd like to interview you. Human interest piece."

This was a new one. "Human interest interview?"

"Yes."

"You want to interview me?" Oliver shook his head so hard I thought he'd break his own neck. "I don't think that's such a good idea."

"Why not? Your constituents aren't embarrassed by you, are they?"

I'd spent the start of my career in marketing and the last couple of years in D.C. and I knew a leading, trick question when I heard it. "Oh dear, the water's boiling over! Have to call you back, Bruce, bye!" I hung up.

"This isn't good," Oliver said. The rest of the room had joined us.

"Did I catch this correctly? Your caller was Bruce Jenkins?" Culver asked.

"Yeah. Supposedly from the Washington Post."

Jeff ran his hand though his hair. "Washington Post?"

"Yes," Oliver said. "There is no 'supposedly' about it."

Reader groaned. "I was really hoping you were making that up or Mister Joel Oliver was wrong."

"MJO's never wrong, right, Chuckie?"

Chuckie rubbed the back of his neck. "We need to call in everyone. This is going to be bad."

"I didn't tell him anything."

"It won't matter," Oliver said. "He'll make it up." He shook his head. "Bruce Jenkins is the worst kind of reporter you could have interested in you."

"He's a bad guy?"

"Depends on your point of view," Oliver said in a voice of doom.

"Figure you know what my point of view will be, MJO."

"Bad? No. He's smart, tenacious, trusted, and, worst of all, popular."

"Um, we could play the Guess The Reason To Freak Out Game, but I'd prefer if someone would tell me why this particular popular reporter is freaking everyone out so much. No one freaked out when you, MJO, were hot on our trail, so to speak."

"Because no one believed me," Oliver said patiently. "However, everyone believes Bruce Jenkins."

"I've never heard of him. Ever."

"You have," Culver said. "Only probably not by his real name." She looked worried—The Joker Fears Batman Has Had Commissioner Gordon Call In The Marines worried. This boded.

"And that name is?"

Oliver swallowed. "The Tastemaker."

CHAPTER 10

"**OH. THAT GUY.** He's a gossip columnist. Isn't he?"

"Yes, in a way," Oliver said. "He's quite in the know—his gossip is accurate."

"So what? So was yours and no one ever believed you."

Oliver sighed. "Yes, but my 'gossip,' so to speak, was about conspiracy theories and aliens—things most people don't want to believe. His information is of a more salacious nature, affairs and so forth, which everyone's interested in."

"Stop pussyfooting," Culver snapped. "She's not a child." Managed to keep my jaw from dropping, but it took effort. "The Tastemaker is the reason your husband is up as Vincent's running mate. Because he destroyed the reputations of the last two who Vincent was considering."

Awesome. I could officially hate this guy. "Oh. So, he's the guy who finds the skeletons in people's closets and then exposes them?" Everyone nodded. "So Jeff declines the nomination and everything goes back to how it was."

This seemed like a really good solution to me. Maybe instead of hating him I should thank Jenkins for calling.

"He can't," Cliff said. "These things aren't just tossed around casually, Kitty. This is a very strategic move, and Jeff needs to accept the nomination. It's important for everyone, your people in particular. This means, however, that Jenkins needs to be handled correctly." He gave me an encouraging smile. "It's not going to be a problem. We'll just all ensure that everyone knows what part they're to play, and we'll keep Jenkins at bay."

"I agree," Horn said. "When you talk to Jenkins again, tell him that he has to run any meetings with you through my office."

"Why yours, Vander? Chuckie's would seem more . . . appropriate."

Horn nodded. "Yes, which is why it would be a bad idea. Of all those in government who you're close to, you've known me the least amount of time. There's much less history for Jenkins to use against you, therefore."

"I agree," Cliff said. "Our three agencies deal with Centaurion Division the most, but your relationship with Chuck is well known. Anything he does to protect you is going to be taken as him watching out for his old girlfriend."

"We didn't date."

Jeff rolled his eyes. "No, but trust me, everyone on the Hill is shocked that we've managed to keep your 'affair' under wraps."

"Excuse me? Chuckie and I have never had an affair!" Well, one week in Vegas when we were much younger and both single, but that was a fling, not an affair.

"I know," Jeff said patiently. "But the two of you are so close that it's the natural assumption made in this town."

Nathalie nodded. "Those who know the two of you know the truth. But The Tastemaker isn't necessarily interested in that kind of truth."

"He didn't expose you, when you were involved with Eugene."

"No, he didn't. I wasn't interesting enough."

"And he's only come to prominence in the past couple of years," Oliver added.

"Should we have the Senator come over?" Mona asked. "This seems like a good reason to have a meeting."

Everyone started talking. Everyone other than Mom and Olga. They were both still watching the TV, as if they weren't paying any attention. I knew my mother and I knew Olga— they'd both heard everything. Therefore, if they were off pretending they weren't here, something else was going on.

Sidled over. "What's so fascinating on the news?" I asked softly. Looked like more footage of the bombings at the protest.

"Timing," Mom said.

Great. Mom was now playing Olga's game. Hoped Mona had migraine meds around somewhere. "Timing of what?"

"Of everything," Olga replied.

"You mean my phone calls, the bombings, the warnings from my 'uncles,' Jeff's potential appointment, our Embassy being gassed, or something else?"

"Yes," Mom said. Fantastic. She wanted me to figure out what was wrong. As if this day wasn't going badly enough.

As my mother was well aware, I thought better by running my mouth. Olga knew this, too. Ergo, they expected me to so run. Never an issue.

"Well, Bruce Jenkins calling right now seems related to the news stating that Jeff's going to be Senator Armstrong's VP candidate. The bombings seem related to the desire to kill us all, especially since there were bombings at Centaurion bases as well as the protest. Missus Maurer might have been cluelessly warning me, or she might have been trying to drive me into the poison gas."

"It's been a busy day so far," Olga said. Ah, so she was going to try to toss me some breadcrumbs.

"Yes, it has, and I'm clear, you two want me to pay attention and think." Turned and watched the TV with them. The others were still discussing strategy—how to circumvent Jenkins mostly.

The newscaster was saying that the police had no leads for who'd placed the bombs. Mad bombers had to be more important than a gossip columnist.

"So no one's figured out that Club Fifty-One set the bombs, probably with the help of the Church of Intolerance?"

"You know, for a fact, that they're the ones responsible?" Mom asked.

"Well . . . no." Footage of the bombing was rolling again. It was really miraculous that no one had been injured. The newscaster was saying the same. Considered. "Club Fifty-

One is funded and supported and given very bad things to use against us, but they're not really . . . good at it."

Mom's lips quirked. "No. For which I'm personally thankful."

"Glad to know you're not all for them offing your only child."

"No, I'm very attached to you." Mom looked at me. "But then, you know that."

My mind chose to give me a nudge. "Oh. You think my 'uncles' contacted everyone because they were, in fact, setting up and detonating the bombs?"

"I think the idea has merit," Olga said as Mom turned back to the TV. "However, as always, there are other options that must be considered."

"Mossad is in town and Dad's at the Israeli embassy. And Mossad would probably like to get their hands on my 'uncles,' right?"

"Among others," Mom said. "How's William working out?"

Mom had clearly been comparing notes with Olga about the best way to give someone mental whiplash. However, I was used to it from both of them by now, so only needed a couple of seconds to make the mental switch. "What would this have to do with Gladys?"

Mom's lips quirked again. I wondered if I'd done something to piss her off recently. Maybe not enough Grandma Time with Jamie. "Try thinking. Without talking. Just for a change of pace."

"Harsh." Fine, Mom didn't want me sharing my mental processes with the room. This would be harder, but not impossible.

Back to the problem at hand, then. There had to be a reason Mom was bringing up the Head of Security now, right now. And I knew she wasn't worried about William's performance— he'd added in a ton of new security, most of it based on Mom's recommendations. And per Buchanan, no one at any of our bases had been hurt, meaning that William's security measures were working just fine.

So Mom wasn't concerned about that. Ergo, Mom indeed

wanted me thinking about Gladys. Considered if I was supposed to be thinking about the fact that Gladys was dead. Or maybe take the leap from there and think about Michael Gower, who was also dead, or Naomi Gower-Reynolds, considered dead by everyone other than me, but she was on another plane of existence, at least as far as I knew, so dead to us for all intents and purposes.

Maybe it *was* Naomi they wanted me thinking about. Chuckie and Naomi had been married for six months when she died. He'd been a widower for a year now, and most of the time we just didn't talk about it, because he couldn't take talking about it. So Mom and Olga wouldn't want to bring Naomi up unless it was vital, or Chuckie wasn't here.

Risked a look at him. He seemed okay. Well, as okay as he'd been since Operation Infiltration. Bad things going on helped give him something to focus on, so that was one for the win column. A pathetic one, but still, one. Looked back to Mom.

She gave a small shake of her head. "No. Right time, wrong person."

Okay, so this wasn't about Naomi. And it probably wasn't about Michael either. Back to Gladys. Why Gladys? Why now? What about what was going on was making Mom and Olga think of her, and making them want me to think about her? And why was that the question right after I'd suggested Club 51, the Church of Intolerance, or my Uncles the International Top Assassins as the potential bombing culprits?

Because they weren't who Mom and Olga thought were actually responsible.

Okay, so there was another person or group I was forgetting. Back to Gladys. Right time, wrong person. So, Mom definitely wanted me thinking about Operation Infiltration. What about Gladys then could have any impact on what was going on now?

The people we'd captured when Gladys had sacrificed herself to ensure that Ronaldo Al Dejahl was dead and gone were still in a severe form of custody. No one had gotten anything much out of them, though because we had Chernobog's son, the hacking attacks had stopped.

Other than Annette Dier, who was a top assassin who

wanted me dead, regardless of whether she was paid or not, the rest of the prisoners were, like Mahin, all technically Gladys' half-siblings, just as she was a half-sib to White and Lucinda.

White, Lucinda, and Gladys were the only legitimate children of Ronald Yates, born when they were all still on Alpha Four and he'd been a different person. Two wives being murdered due to assassination attempts on his life had changed him, apparently. Shocker. Said different personage had included being the Supreme Pontifex of our A-Cs, which was the reason for said assassination attempts.

He'd been banished to Earth, changed his name, built a huge media empire, YatesCorp, that still existed, expanded into a variety of other businesses including robotics and any corporation we in Centaurion considered enemies such as Gaultier Enterprises and Titan Security and probably more we didn't know about yet, and had created the Al Dejahl terrorist organization. He'd also joined with an alien parasite and become an in-control superbeing, codenamed Mephistopheles, aka the Devil Incarnate. And, just to show his range, he'd become what we now called the First Mastermind. He had a lot of titles in my world.

He was a doer, you had to give him credit for that.

He'd also been a ladies' man of the highest order. And at whatever age he'd been, he favored women in their late teens and early twenties. Women in the prime childbearing years. Women he never married or kept up with. Serene was the product of one of his pairings, with an A-C girl. The now-happily-late Ronaldo Al Dejahl had been Serene's older brother, though she'd never known him, or her father.

However, while he might not have kept in touch with his many romantic liaisons, we were pretty sure that Yates had kept a record of them, and that someone, likely the first Apprentice, otherwise known as Leventhal Reid, Man of My Nightmares, had used it to track them down, which is how Ronaldo Al Dejahl had gotten pulled into the family business. Reid had become the Mastermind and found a new Apprentice, and that man was now the Current Mastermind. And we had less than no idea of who he was.

Gladys had been working on something, though, in the week before she'd died. In fact, it was a task I'd assigned to her. She was trying to find the rest of the illegitimate offspring of Ronald Yates. Other than White and Lucinda, every one of Yates' offspring we'd found were all hugely talented. That had passed on to Jeff and Christopher, and to Jeff's sisters' children. Mahin was also a Yates offspring, and her talent was strong, and different. We knew our enemies were trying to find all these people and win them over to their side. We needed to do the same.

Because she'd known she was going to die, Gladys had left details of her work behind. She'd only had a week, and she'd been more focused on finding Ronaldo Al Dejahl than anything else, but her husband had felt sure she'd made progress on determining how to find the other offspring. But we hadn't found anything anyone could decipher that would indicate if she had or hadn't found any of her half-siblings around the world.

Looked at my mother. Gladys had respected Mom, and she'd trusted her, as much as Gladys had trusted anyone. So maybe we never found anything because Gladys hadn't found anyone. Or maybe she didn't want us to find her notes.

Or maybe she'd found a lot, but had given that information to the person she thought would best handle the hunt.

Cleared my throat. "You think this was done by what I'd call our oldest set of enemies—Ronnie's Kids."

CHAPTER 11

MOM SMILED and turned to me. "Yes."

"So, have you found more of them, or are you still deciphering whatever Gladys gave you before she and I went on her suicide mission to Guantanamo?"

"You've raised such a good daughter," Olga said. "I'm sure you're very proud."

"Wow. Compliments. I'll preen later, when I'm sure that wasn't sarcasm."

"It wasn't," Olga said reassuringly.

Mom rolled her eyes. "True, but it took you long enough." She squeezed my hand. "Yes, I'm proud of you. Always. Now, continuously necessary reassurances that you're still your mother's favorite taken care of, you need to consider why everything is happening today."

"Wait, what do you mean I'm still my mother's favorite? I'm your only child. Who else would you favor? I mean, aside from Amy, Chuckie, Sheila, and Caro? Well, and James and Christopher. And probably Jeff. And, of course, Jamie. Anyway, moving on before you actually answer those questions, I want to know what you got from Gladys before I do any more mental calisthenics."

Mom shot Olga a long-suffering look. "See what I mean?" Olga chuckled. I managed to refrain from comment. Mom turned back to me. "Fine. Gladys didn't find much in the short time she was working on Project Kindred Spirit."

"*Love* that code name."

"*So* glad you approve. I was losing sleep over the thought that you might not like it." My mother's sarcasm knob went well past eleven. "Anyway, because of Mahin, we knew we couldn't just use heartbeats as an indication of potential."

A-Cs all had two hearts. Hybrids—those with an A-C and a human parent—had human genetics dominant for the outside and A-C genetics dominant for the inside. This meant that every hybrid had two hearts. At least, that had been the conventional thinking.

Only Mahin, whose mother had been a regular human woman but whose father had indeed been Ronald Yates, only had one heart. But she could move at hyperspeed, though she hadn't known she could until she'd been recruited by Al Dejahl.

She also had impressive talent which she had known about since she was young—she could move dirt around. This sounds like a big "so what" until you're saying so what when Mahin's moving twenty tons of sand at you and then the reaction is a lot more like "Oh God, oh God, we're all gonna die."

Shortly after Operation Infiltration had ended Tito had shared that Mahin wasn't technically correct for a standard hybrid. Chuckie and Mom had allowed him to test the three other Yates Offspring they had in custody and, sure enough, they all had single hearts, too.

All we'd come up with was the fact that Yates was, in genetics terms, a sport. There was nothing predictable about how his genetics would transfer to someone else, meaning that each mother's genetics had a potential to create very different children, much more so than a normal horndog man's spreading it around would account for.

"Weird abilities and the potential for hyperspeed would seem to be likely options."

"Oh, thank God you've come," Mom said, sarcasm knob heading toward at least twenty on a scale of one to ten. "It's amazing how easy it is to ask every single person within a forty year range if they've ever run at supersonic speeds or can do something odd. We should be done with our initial questioning in about three hundred years, give or take a decade."

"Wow, too much caffeine, Mom, or just wishing you were already at the Mossad Homecoming Party?"

"Both. At any rate, we've made very little progress. Charles suggested that it's high time you got involved."

"Me? Really?" Wow. At least Chuckie respected the skills.

"Yes. He feels that your, and I quote, 'random abilities and exceptional capacity to find trouble' will be invaluable."

"I'm touched. Why have you waited a year to get me involved?"

Mom sighed. "Because Charles has been very . . . focused . . . on this. It's taken him time to adjust to the idea that he can't do this all himself."

"Oh. Why did you let him?"

Mom shrugged. "He needed the outlet, and finding these people isn't as vital as everyone thinks. At least not as vital as keeping Charles focused on something other than despair. We could afford to wait for him to come around to the idea that it was time to ask for help."

"Why didn't he just come to me about it?"

"Because I needed to do it alone," Chuckie said from behind me. "For a while at least. Yes, Angela, I was eavesdropping."

Mom laughed. "That's your job."

"Yeah." Chuckie rubbed the back of his neck as he looked at me. "Mad at me?"

I hugged him. "No. You know I'm here if you need me."

He hugged me back. "Yeah, I know." He let go of me and cleared his throat. "Cliff and Vander don't want the two of us to go anywhere alone together until we have the Bruce Jenkins situation under control."

"Well, you're living at our Embassy, so that can only work so well, but whatever." Due to a variety of factors, Chuckie's apartments in D.C. somehow always getting ransacked by our enemies and Naomi's death being the two biggest, Jeff had put his foot down and insisted that Chuckie take a permanent guest room at the Embassy, at least for a while. I'd taken this to mean that Jeff was worried that Chuckie was on the edge of suicide or murder, though Jeff had refused to confirm such. Or deny it. "Though, frankly, I don't know where we're really living right now."

"No one's going into the American Centaurion Embassy for, most likely, at least another twenty-four to forty-eight hours." Chuckie grimaced. "Buchanan and William have Field teams searching the tunnel systems around every Centaurion base or stronghold worldwide, and that's going to take some time, hyperspeed or no hyperspeed. Crawford and the rest of Airborne are overseeing the cleanup and everyone's triple-checking everything, so again, taking a while."

"No argument from me. I don't want anyone dying from this, any of us especially. But where are we all going to go? Dulce? The Pontifex's Residence? Or was that attacked as well?"

Chuckie and Mom stared at each other. "No," Chuckie said slowly, "there was no activity at all around the Pontifex's Residence."

"Are we sure it's safe? Or, let me put this another way. Are we sure there's not some horrible thing—bomb, assassins, intolerant religious assholes—lying in wait for Paul and James to go home?"

CHAPTER 12

CHUCKIE AND MOM both pulled out their phones and started making calls. Olga smiled at me. "We are going to be staying with the Czech diplomatic mission. Andrei and the rest of our mission are there already. I'm sure you could house with Bahrain and Israel."

"I'm sure we could. I'm just worried about us bringing down trouble onto our friends. More trouble, I mean, since all of our neighborhood's been evacuated. Because of us."

"No," Olga said sternly. "Because of a variety of evil people. Not because of you."

Examined her expression, because that had sounded like an Olga Clue and I didn't want to miss it if it was. She looked just slightly expectant. Always the way.

"You think it's the usual two, three, or four plans going at once, don't you?"

She shrugged. "If you examine the events from a distance, they don't seem overly . . . coherent." She looked at the TV, then back at me.

Decided to take the leap. "Gotcha. They're being triggered by the same thing, though, aren't they? Jeff's sort of announcement as Armstrong's VP."

She nodded. "Your husband would be my choice out of all the options."

"You've mastered the art of making every sentence have

at least a double meaning, haven't you? I'm, as always, impressed."

Olga laughed. "It is, as you say, a skill I'm proud of."

Mom got off her phone. "I'm going to send Kevin and a team over to the Pontifex's Residence." She strode off, Chuckie following her, though he was still on his call.

Adriana rejoined us. "Grandfather wants to know when we will be joining him."

"Not just yet," Olga said. "I would like to be sure that things are . . . quiet."

Adriana nodded. "I believe it would be helpful if you could reassure Representative Martini that his accepting the nomination would be in everyone's best interests." It was clear she was talking to Olga, not me.

"Are you coming with us?" Olga asked as Adriana took hold of her wheelchair.

Had an overwhelming urge to talk to someone who wasn't going to make it hard on me or stress me out. "Ahhh . . ." Now I just had to figure out how to say that I wanted alone time more than I wanted to reassure my husband, somehow without earning major Bad Wife Points.

Prince had been snoozing with the other K-9 dogs. However, as I tried to come up with a smooth exit strategy, he got up, trotted over, and wuffed quietly.

Prince loved me and Jeff as much as he loved Officer Melville. I knew this because since those drugs had altered Jeff, they'd also altered Jamie, and, due to my giving birth to her, altered me. I'd gotten some of the nifty A-C abilities, like hyperspeed and faster healing. And I'd also gotten my own special talent. I could talk to animals. Sort of. If they wanted to communicate with me, that was.

Prince usually wanted to share the wonder that was Our Special Bond, so I was quite clear that, as far as Prince was concerned, if I wanted some alone time, then he was going to be with me and we would be alone together. He was like a canine Buchanan, but I didn't share that with either one of them, because I wasn't sure if they'd be flattered or insulted.

I was also quite clear that Prince didn't actually need to go but was enthusiastically willing to work as my distraction. He was great that way, and much easier to convince to go along with my plans than any of the men, particularly Buchanan.

"Oh, you want to go for a walk, boy? Sure thing. I think I'd better let Prince relieve himself," I said to Olga and Adriana. "I'll take him out back."

"Enjoy yourselves. We will tell everyone where you are should they be searching." With that, Adriana wheeled Olga off and, thusly covered, Prince and I headed for the doorway. No one seemed to notice. Good to see how Vital to the Cause I was.

I'd been here before and knew my way to the back. As with most of the embassies around town, there wasn't a huge backyard. However, there was an outside patio with some grass along the enclosure's walls and that was good enough for what I wanted.

"Can I help you, Ambassador?" One of Mona's many retainers had spotted us.

"Oh, I'm just heading out back to walk the dog. So to speak."

"I can do that for you," he offered. I didn't know him, but this meant absolutely nothing. I didn't know half of the Field agents I'd met over the years or the many politicians in town I'd been introduced to, sometimes more than once. My not knowing someone on Mona's staff was low on the Surprise-O-Meter.

Like all the others on staff he was dressed impeccably. He was reasonably attractive, though he didn't really look like Mona or Khalid, and he certainly didn't look like Oren, Jakob, or Leah. But all that meant was that he wasn't Israeli and wasn't from the same regions Mona and Khalid were.

Upon closer inspection he looked sort of European, with dark hair and eyes and olive skin. Then again, this meant nothing, really. With this so-not-rare coloring he could be Middle Eastern or Italian or American or half a dozen other nationalities, all things considered. He was vaguely familiar, so I assumed I'd seen him here before.

However, regardless of where he originally hailed from, I didn't want company for this little trip, company I didn't know in particular. "Oh, Prince is picky. Aren't you, boy?"

Prince knew a cue when it was offered. He bared his teeth and gave a low growl.

"Ah. Well then, would you like me to accompany you?" He was dedicated, I'd give him that. Whoever he was. Wondered for a moment if he was a spy or an enemy, but how would he have gotten in? The Bunker District embassies all had massive amounts of security, and the Bahrainis were no slackers in this regard. Especially today, I'd have to figure no one was getting in without a lot of Proof of Citizenship and so forth.

"Nope, I'm good, thanks." Headed off, Prince still growling. Suggested he calm it down, in my mind. Yeah, I could talk to the animals both verbally and mentally. Dr. Doolittle had nothing on me. Jeff's excitement about this particular skill knew no bounds.

Got to the back door and went outside, making sure the door was unlocked so we could get back inside without issue. Prince finally stopped growling, so that was good. Checked behind me. It was a glass door—bulletproof, of course, but still, glass—which made it easy to see that the Helpful Servant was still there, watching me. Maybe he didn't trust me.

Couldn't argue about this concern—after all, I had people all around me who trusted pretty close to no one. Wouldn't be a surprise that Mona had more than Khalid hanging about to cover the watching for suspicious activities.

Prince and I trotted around for the sake of faking out the guy watching us and maneuvered ourselves to a spot where we couldn't be easily seen by anyone inside, Mr. Helpful Servant specifically. The ten-foot block walls protected us from random lookieloos to the sides and back.

However, if someone was up high enough, they could see us. A-Cs had improved eyesight over humans, and I'd backward-inherited some of that. Scrutinized the area. Didn't see anyone looking out of any windows, and the only person acting suspicious I could spot was me.

"Okay, I think we're alone and unobserved, unless you spot something."

Prince wuffed that as far as he could smell, the coast was clear. Then he pointedly looked around. I knew what he was suggesting. And asking. Go me.

"Yeah, yeah, I'm on it, I'm on it. Poofs and Peregrines, please assemble."

CHAPTER 13

THE POOFS WERE ADORABLE BALLS of alien animal cuteness, with no visible ears, black button eyes, tiny paws, and the fluffiest fur ever. We'd gotten our Starter Set of Poofs during the fun Invasion Lite that was the pre-show entertainment for my wedding to Jeff.

The Peregrines had come home to roost, pun totally intended, later, after Jamie was born, right before Invasion Full Flavor, or what I called Operation Destruction. They looked like peacocks and peahens on steroids, the males multi-colored, the females all white.

The Poofs were androgynous and rumor had it that they only mated when an Alpha Four royal wedding was imminent. They were also only supposed to belong to the Alpha Four Royal Family, of which Jeff, Christopher, and Gower were all a part.

However, by now, we'd had a Poof Explosion of such epic proportions that pretty much anyone of any significance within American Centaurion and Centaurion Division had a Poof to call their own. Heck, Oliver had his own Poof, and I was pretty sure our Middle Eastern Contingent had some, too. Olga and Adriana had gained Poofs right after Operation Infiltration.

By contrast, while we had twelve mated pairs of Peregrines, they had yet to start their own flock. They were "assigned" to Embassy staff and those who worked closely with said Embassy.

Operation Infiltration was the reason the Peregrines hadn't gotten their flock expansion going. They felt they'd failed us. Because we'd lost three A-Cs and a Poof during that time. And not just any A-Cs—Gladys, Michael and Naomi had been hugely important to everyone in Centaurion Division and they'd been just as important to the Alpha Four animals. When they'd first arrived, one set of Peregrines had been assigned to Naomi and Abigail, and one set to Chuckie, too. So we had four Peregrines mourning as much as Chuckie, the remaining Gowers, and Caroline, who'd been engaged to Michael.

I was working with them on getting over the guilt, but it was slow going. Though I was doing better with the animals than the humans, this was a classic example of damning with faint praise. When your entire species has been bred for thousands of years to protect, and you aren't able to, you feel like a failure, whether you're a human, alien, or avian. Especially if you loved those you were protecting.

The Poofs had also been upset to lose the three people we did, but they'd been more upset to lose Fuzzball. Poofs weren't used to early deaths. Because, as I'd found out, they weren't really from Alpha Four. They were from the Black Hole Universe. And, according to the only authority on Black Hole People I could ask, even though Black Hole beings were immortal, they could be killed.

So in addition to my parents' cats and dogs, we had alien avians and bundles of fluffy adorableness. And I could talk to all of them. Figured it was only a matter of time until I could talk to random animals I didn't know. Maybe that would be helpful. Maybe.

I'd spent a lot of time practicing talking to all the animals in my mind, but it took more effort than speaking aloud and, besides, no one was around to hear me. Well, no person.

But I'd made the call and was instantly surrounded by Poofs and Peregrines. The Peregrines had hyperspeed and the Poofs had . . . whatever the Poofs had that was like hyperspeed only probably better.

The entire furred and feathered clan weren't here—there were always Poofs and Peregrines guarding Jamie and the other Embassy and Alpha Team kids, most of whom were hybrids, all of whom could be used as the most effective hostages ever. And many Poofs were with whoever they felt they belonged to, especially if that person was doing something dangerous.

That no Poofs or Peregrines had been in evidence during the protest, our "arrest," and here at the Bahraini embassy before now didn't indicate slacking on their part. The Peregrines could chameleon it up and essentially go invisible, and the Poofs had whatever their special powers were that allowed them to not be seen unless they wanted to be seen. So these days, I went with the working assumption that I had the Head Peregrine, Bruno, and a variety of Poofs, most likely the Head Poof, Harlie, and my Poof, Poofikins, with me at all times.

Only, this time, Bruno, Harlie, and Poofikins were not in attendance.

However, I still had a blanket of concentrated cuteness interspersed with feathered beauty in front of me. It was enough to make a girl pause. Which I did, mostly so I wouldn't step on any paws or claws.

"Hi all, Kitty would like a word." Had the Sea of Animal Love's full attention. Hard to concentrate with this much adorableness in front of me, but I'd slipped out for a reason, so Onward for the Cause. "We've had a lot of bad things happening today. First off, are all my Poofs, Peregrines, cats, and dogs safe and accounted for?"

Received quiet purrs and squawks confirming that all animal personnel were alive, well, and where they should be, wherever that was.

"Super. Now, in regard to those bad things, can any of you tell Kitty what's going on and, more importantly, how to stop it?"

The Sea of Animal Love stared politely at me. This was not the outcome I was hoping for.

"Ah, Prince, can you give it a go?"

Prince obliged and wuffed. The Poofs mewed back, the Peregrines squawked and bobbed their heads. I tried to follow the conversation. Failed. The thing about my talent was that while the animals could always understand me, I could only understand them when they wanted me to.

Prince growled. The other animals growled back. I didn't think they were actually growling at each other, though.

Prince barked, and the Poofs and Peregrines disappeared, while Prince spun around and took off at a trot. Decided questioning what the hell my supposed guardians were up to was going to be a waste of time, and took off after the police dog.

He didn't go far. Prince was at the door we'd just come out of, barking his head off. He wanted in, and he wanted in now.

Tried to open the door. The operative word was "tried." The door was locked tight. Since I'd made certain it had been unlocked only a few minutes ago, this indicated someone had gone out of their way to lock the door, and lock me and Prince out.

Prince was barking louder and more hysterically. There were other K-9 dogs inside, as well as lots of people, and no one, on two legs or four, was coming to the door. This boded in a typical and familiar way. Prince and I had been locked out for a reason, and that reason point-blank couldn't be good.

There was really only one Likely Suspect. Maybe Prince hadn't been growling to help me with my excuse for why we were going outside. Maybe Prince had been growling because he hadn't liked the way the Helpful Servant had smelled.

Contemplated my options. If the door had locked by accident, or automatically, my ripping it off its hinges would be a poor way to repay Mona's hospitality.

On the other hand, if everyone inside was in danger, there was a strong likelihood that Mr. Helpful Servant had some deadly gas he was dying to share with everyone. And that included my mother, my husband, and my daughter.

American Centaurion was a wealthy principality-territory-reservation-whatever. And we could fix whatever I messed up using hyperspeed. And no one was coming toward us, calling to us to shut the dog up, or anything else.

Dilemma over, I grabbed the door handle, channeled my Inner She-Hulk, and pulled with all my strength.

CHAPTER 14

BULLETPROOF GLASS is usually encased in steel. So are most buildings, especially those built to withstand attack. Needless to say, the Bahraini embassy had plenty of steel.

While my enhancement made me stronger than the average human, I normally wasn't up to a normal A-C's strength level, let alone Jeff's. If I was completely enraged, all bets were off. But rage wasn't always easily available, and right now, I had panic going much more strongly. Which was a pity—I needed rage or Jeff's muscles right now, because the door wasn't budging.

Tried harder. Was rewarded with the handle coming off in my hand. The less said about my falling onto my butt the better, but now I had a metal bar and no entry into the embassy. Was willing to define this as "not good."

Of course, bulletproof and shatterproof are not the same things. Decided that, as always, necessity was the mother of invention and panic was the father of ability. Started slamming the handle against the door. It did nothing other than bounce off in an impressive and, for the person holding the metal, painful manner.

Prince barked. Well, he'd been barking already and non-stop, but he changed how. He wasn't barking the All Dog Alert anymore. He was barking instructions.

Fortunately, I was a confident enough person to listen to

what a dog was telling me to do. Hey, he was a trained police professional after all. "Oh, really? Well, that's a big 'duh' for me then." Dropped the door handle and dug around in my purse for my Glock, while congratulating myself on my prescience, based on years of experience, in keeping my purse firmly attached to my person at all times.

I never left home without my Glock. Frankly, I rarely left our apartment in the Embassy without my purse and all its contents, which always included my Glock and several clips. So I was ready, willing, and able to do what Prince was telling me, which was to fire repeatedly at one area of the glass until it broke.

Stepped back, flicked off the safety and, per Prince's instructions, started firing at the high middle of the door, basically head-height for Christopher.

Sure enough, as Prince had shared, bulletproof really meant bullet-resistant. And I happily discovered, as my sixth shot caused the glass to break apart, shatterproof just meant the glass went into "safe" pieces, versus deadly shards. It was always nice when something, anything, worked in my favor.

Stopped shooting—figured I'd need the ammo shortly for a much more fleshy target. Used the door handle to break the rest of the glass away so Prince and I could get in. Proof that something was terribly wrong was easy to find—no one had so much as stuck a white flag around a corner, let alone come to see who was trying to shoot their way into the embassy. We were officially at DEFCON Bad.

"Remember that they're using poisoned gas," I reminded Prince as we both stepped through carefully so as not to get glass on our shoes or paws. "And they're certainly big into bombs and shooting people, too."

He snorted. He was a trained professional, thank you very much, and I could just stay behind him and let him lead. Typical. Every male I knew tried to shove me behind them any time danger loomed. Under the circumstances, decided not to argue and let Prince do his thing.

Which he did. He slunk along, hugging the wall, sniffing like mad, but no longer barking, or even growling. I knew he was angry and intent—but he wanted to also be silent so as to have a hope of surprising our enemy in whatever meager way we might manage after all the barking, shooting, breaking and entering.

We checked the rooms along the hallway as we slunk by them. No one was in evidence. Prince prepped himself, then rounded the corner with a low bound, me right behind him.

And then Prince and I both skidded to a stop, because there was no one in the room.

Ran out and started searching the embassy at hyperspeed. No one, not one living soul, was in evidence anywhere. Fought down the total panic and was back with Prince in the main room where everyone had been before in a matter of about a minute. To find it still devoid of anyone other than Prince, and him in an attack stance, fur up all over, growling at absolutely nothing.

I'd have told him to stop being dramatic, but we were missing a tonnage of people, all of whom were important to me in some way, particularly my daughter, husband, and mother, and there was no sign of a fight. So drama was probably the way to go.

The A-Cs could have grabbed everyone and run off somewhere, only there was no way in the world my husband wouldn't have noticed that I wasn't around to be grabbed. And neither he nor Officer Melville would have left me and Prince locked outside. Frankly, no one who'd been here less than fifteen minutes ago would have left us to whatever fate without at least trying to get to us. So the good guys running for safety was out as an option.

Meaning, what? Every living person in this embassy had disappeared without a trace. Only Prince wasn't acting like we were alone. He was acting like he had someone, or something, cornered.

"A little help?" I asked softly.

Prince wuffed, barked, and snarled, sharing that the someone was the guy he'd growled at earlier.

Okay, I could tell the dog he was talking crazy, or I could accept that he could smell someone I couldn't see. Considering that I could talk to the dog, invisibility didn't seem all that farfetched. The Peregrines had that ability, after all, though it was more like chameleon camouflage. And the A-C system had cloaking technology—we were using it here on Earth to protect the Crash Site Dome and other key facilities.

Decided to trust my gut and my dog—hey, until we found Melville, Prince was mine—and take a page from the NFL. Pointed my Glock at what I was guessing was chest height for the person I was by now praying Prince really had cornered. "The best defense is a good offense. You have a simple choice—you can decloak yourself or I can start shooting. I'm a really good shot, I can hit someone going at hyperspeed, and I have a lot of clips on me. I suggest you choose wisely."

Nothing.

However, I examined the area Prince was threatening. It was a corner with bookcases on either wall. However, if I looked just right, there was a faint outline, as if the books and wall were . . . thicker than normal. Like in the movies, when Harry Potter has on the invisibility cloak, or Sherlock Holmes was using his special hide-in-plain-sight clothes.

"Okay, you asked for it." I aimed for where I thought the thigh might be and fired.

CHAPTER 15

A MAN SCREAMED, and then, all of a sudden, Prince and I weren't so alone. I'd shot the Helpful Servant, in the thigh, too. Right on target. Why was it that when the skills were especially impressive and I was functioning like the top secret agent ever there was absolutely no one around who I wanted to impress? "Stop it, you insane woman!"

Aimed for his chest. "No. Tell me where everyone is and what you've done with them or I'm going to put more bullets into you. Not killing shots, mind you, because I want information. Oh, and in case you weren't clear, I want it now."

"I have no idea where they are," he snapped.

"Right. Because while you were waylaying me in the hallway, everyone disappeared."

"No. Because after I locked you out, prepped what I needed to, and went back everyone was gone." Nice. Even shot this guy had a sarcasm knob.

Chose to not say that this was the same thing as I'd said. In part because of the phrase he'd said that I hadn't. "Prepped what?"

He shot me a dirty look. "What do you think?"

"Honestly? Bio-weapons."

Got a mildly impressed look. "You're smarter than you look."

"And you must like getting shot."

He shrugged. "Threaten me all you want. They're going to go off shortly."

They're. Meaning more than one. Oh, goody. "You'll die, too."

"I don't care about that."

Something clicked. That More Martyr Than Thou attitude. "Oh, you're definitely one of Ronnie's Kids, aren't you? How long have you been part of the Al Dejahl terrorist network?"

His jaw dropped. "What? How—?"

"Dude, come on, spare me the pretense. Your father, your biological father, regardless of who raised you, has been shown to you to be the late Ronald Yates, founder of Yates-Corp. Also known as Ronaldo Al Dejahl, founder of the Al Dejahl terrorist organization. A group of people claiming to be your half-siblings have come to tell you about the glorious cause your father was a part of, and they've waved a potential seat on the YatesCorp Board, martyred glory, or whatever else twiddles your knobs in front of you and you've bought in."

His jaw dropped lower.

"But, of course, there's more to it than that. You have some sort of weird talent—I'm just spitballing here, but I'm betting you can go invisible in some way—and you've always known you were different. You've been taught how to go really superfast, but only by your newfound bestest buddies."

"How—?"

"Oh, come on! This is all new and exciting or whatever for you, but I've been a part of this goat rodeo for the past few years now. I know a whole lot of your other half-siblings, including one who realized she'd joined up with the wrong side and traded teams before she became a murdering monster. You might still have that option open to you, but I'm not prepared to bet on it."

"Traitors will burn," he said through clenched teeth. Apparently getting shot and bleeding profusely wasn't comfy. Good.

"Blah, blah, blah. Heard that before. Frequently. What I

don't understand is why they'd be willing to let someone with your talents blow himself up, because invisibility has got to be a superskill they're madly in love with." Heck, who wouldn't be in love with it? Had to be as good as hyperspeed in some ways.

How he'd snuck in wasn't that hard to guess now that I thought about it. Wished I'd thought a littler harder earlier, but better late than never, right? There had been a lot of people arriving, so fooling the K-9 dogs couldn't have been hard—they wouldn't have known who smelled wrong. Presumably Prince had picked up some smell—anticipation, evil intent, poisoned gas, something—as we'd been going outside.

Fooling embassy staff would have been easier than fooling the dogs—one more guy in a suit just meant he was one of our guys to the Bahrainis, and one of the Bahrainis to us.

Fooling Jeremy Barone, on the other hand, that had to have taken something. Like Jeff, Jeremy was an empath. He wasn't as strong in his talent as Jeff was—no one was, after all—but he was damned good.

"You've got an emotional blocker or overlay disc on you, don't you?"

His brow wrinkled. "No . . ." He sounded confused.

"They gave you a small disk to carry, then. Told you it was a tracker or similar?"

This earned a grimace. "Yes. Are you a mind reader?"

"I wish." So, as with Mahin, he hadn't been given all the facts. He's been primed, aimed, and fired, but cluelessly.

How he'd known we were coming here was the question, but process of elimination might have been easy to do—all of our area was quarantined, every base was attacked, and Langley was attacked, meaning that other government locations could be next. It was here or the Israeli embassy. Worried about Dad for a moment, but he had Mossad there and I had Prince and a guy about to set off bio-weapons. Dad could fend for himself for a couple more minutes.

"How long can you hold your invisibility?"

"It's not invisibility," he snarled. "I blend in with my surroundings."

So it was just like the Peregrines. Proof, as if I'd needed it, that this guy was a Yates Offspring of some kind. Wondered where all those Poofs and Peregrines I'd called in for help had gone. Hoped it was to save the day, versus being dead or captured or whatever everyone else was.

"Nice. So, how long can you hold a blend?" He glared. Decent enough under the circumstances, though nowhere close to Christopher's level. I shrugged. "If we're going to die anyway, and you seem set on that course, why not share the wonder that is you for the few minutes you have left to be you?"

Amazingly enough, this logic seemed to make him talkative. It was nice to see that my ability to mind-meld with the psychos, lunatics, and megalomaniacs remained a hundred percent consistent. "It . . . depends on how tired I am. The longest I've done is five minutes."

"Not a long time. How did you manage to infiltrate the tunnel system? It's big and had a lot of cameras in it."

"I'm bleeding."

"Thanks for the update, Captain Obvious. You're going to die shortly anyway, per you. Answer the question and maybe I'll stop pointing my gun at you. Well, no, I won't. But I might toss you something to tie your leg up with."

Prince increased his growling, to indicate that he was ready, willing, and able to go for the groin.

"Fine. I blend near the cameras and when I'm past them, I stop. Like turning a light switch on and off."

"Wow. Impressive. I say again that I'm having just the teensy-weensiest problem believing that our enemies want to lose your special set of skills, especially over an empty building."

"My killing you would bring honor to my family," he said.

"Really? You have a wife and kids and all that?"

He looked just slightly embarrassed. "No. Not yet."

"Not ever if, you know, we blow up or die from some horrible poison. Just saying. So, your mother and the man who raised you as his son, they're all for you murdering people?"

His eyes flashed with anger and hatred. "My parents are dead."

Interesting. No Yates Offspring we'd found so far had a living parental unit left. Wasn't sure if this was merely coincidence or if they'd been killed off to prep Ronnie's Kids to join the family business. But if I was a betting girl, which I was, my money was on the latter.

"So, what family are you honoring? The one that just found you somewhere in the last year?"

"How did you know that? That they made contact within the last year?"

Couldn't help it, I sighed. "Dude, seriously. Your fantastic relatives tried this with us last year. And the year before that, really. You weren't in either group. Meaning they found you between the last action and now. As in, we captured or turned the ones they found last year, and you and whoever else they've recruited are this year's models."

A flicker of concern flashed across his face. "What else do you know?"

"That you're going to bleed out soon. Beyond that, don't know your name, don't know your country of origin but assume it's somewhere in the Middle East, assume your mother was a human because you don't look drop dead gorgeous and if you had imageering ability you'd have used it already."

"Imageering?"

"Wow. They didn't tell you much at all, did they?"

He shrugged and looked down.

They hadn't told Mahin anything, either, during Operation Infiltration; just enough for her to try to kill us, but not enough to know what was really going on. Which, based on that experience, meant they thought this guy might be open to changing sides, just like Mahin had. But that wasn't a guarantee. If he'd only been recruited recently, they might not have spent the time.

Went right back to the relevant conundrum—who would want a guy who could basically go chameleon to take a suicide mission?

The answer was simple: no one. Meaning one of two things—either he wasn't really on a suicide mission, or they didn't know what he could actually do.

Examined him again. He wasn't looking at me, right after

I'd made the comment about him not being told much. This was textbook "A-C trying to lie." Only he wasn't a full A-C. But that didn't mean the human side was in charge—the hybrids I knew didn't lie well either.

Decided to go for it. "And you didn't tell them much, either, did you? As in, they have no idea that you can blend. They just figured you'd use hyperspeed to sneak the poison bombs into my Embassy. So, why didn't you share that with your new brothers in arms?"

He looked up and looked surprised. "How did you know?"

"I'm a good guesser. So, how long before your bombs go off?"

Heard a step behind me. "Never."

CHAPTER 16

"MALCOLM, WHAT KEPT YOU?"

"He was busy making us listen to see what you could get out of this guy," Jeff said, sounding annoyed, as he stepped up next to me.

"Bombs are found and neutralized," Buchanan said as he went near to Prince and the Helpful Servant. "Both the ones here and the ones at the Israeli embassy." He shot me a glance over his shoulder. "Your father 'had a bad feeling' and made Mossad do a search."

"My dad rocks." No wonder Mom thought he was the greatest. "Our prisoner here is wearing either an empathic blocker or overlay, by the way, but I don't know where on his person he has it stashed."

"Oh, I'm happy to look for that," Buchanan said, in a very calm tone that did nothing to hide the threat.

The Helpful Servant might have been suicidal, but he wasn't stupid. He reached into his pocket and handed something to Buchanan. "I thought it was a tracking device."

"Sure you did," Buchanan replied in the same calm yet totally threatening tone. "Thanks. Of course, I'm going to search you now. Struggle, try to get away, do anything I don't like, and not only will the dog bite you and Missus Chief get to shoot you some more, but I'll cause you pain like you've never experienced before."

The Helpful Servant didn't argue, or try to do anything,

while Buchanan searched him with extreme prejudice. Waited for him to demand our prisoner strip so he could do a cavity search, but I guess Buchanan wanted to protect Prince's delicate sensibilities, didn't have surgical gloves with him, or was saving that for whenever the Helpful Servant got uppity again, because he finished up and our prisoner was still clothed.

"Nothing other than the so-called tracker," Buchanan declared. "Not that I actually believe he thought this was anything other than what it actually is"

"He might have thought that was a tracker, or I might have given him the idea and he ran with it, but we'll get to that later. First, I want to know—where did you all go? Where are Jamie and the other kids? And Malcolm, how did you get back?"

Jeff sighed. "We were taken to the Israeli Embassy and Pontifex's Residence, all children included. I might say all children especially. They and all the adults with them were at the Pontifex's Residence before the rest of us. Those who are in jobs of a more, ah, protective nature went to the Israelis— probably because the Pontifex's Residence is maxed out. Not that I'm complaining about this, mind you. And no one went on their own power."

"Oh! My Poofies and Peregrines rescued all of you?"

"Seemed like it," Jeff said. "It happened faster than we could really see, but there was a lot of fur and feathers."

"Your favorites came and got me," Buchanan said. "They seemed urgently upset, so I didn't argue about going." He shot an amused look at Jeff. "Unlike some people."

"I didn't want to leave my wife alone and unprotected. Just call me a caveman."

"Later, when we're alone." Buchanan laughed, Jeff grinned, and the Helpful Servant glared. Truly, not up to Christopher's standards by any stretch. Speaking of whom. "So, is it just the two of you here?"

"No," Christopher said, as he joined us. "As the fastest, I got to do bomb return duty. Everything's with the F.B.I.'s Bomb Squad."

"Vander took control of this?"

"Yes, and he and Goodman are back in their offices. Your

mother kept Reynolds with her, though, and she's still with Jamie and the others."

"It was a little bit of a fight between him, Chuck, and Cliff," Jeff admitted. "Angela felt it was better for the overall situation, though, if the F.B.I. took point."

"Take this back to Serene," Buchanan said, handing the disc to Christopher. "She'll want to try to get something from it before it blows up."

"Oh, yes *sir*," Christopher snarled. But he took the disc and disappeared.

"Blows up?" the Helpful Servant asked. He sounded surprised. And like he was ready to pass out.

"Your new friends are just the best, aren't they? I'll bet you can't *wait* to find out what else they didn't tell you."

"Are we letting him bleed out?" Buchanan asked. It was clear he wasn't going to care if I said yes.

"Unsure. He can go chameleon, so he's useful. But he'll need the entire four-footed portion of the K-Nine squad watching him, because he's sneaky and Prince will need a break."

"You can probably stop pointing your gun at him," Christopher said as he reappeared. Hyperspeed, it was the best.

"Nope, I like our new friend right where I can see him."

"I'm not up to blending," he told me. "I don't think I can stand up any more, either." So saying he slumped down against the wall and onto the floor.

"Medical's on the way," Christopher said, as there were more steps behind me and Tito appeared, medical bag in hand, escorted by the Barones. Presumably they'd used the normal A-C hyperspeed to get here. Christopher's Flash Level was hard on even Jeff, let alone any A-C who wasn't enhanced.

Tito took in the scene, shaking his head. "We can't leave you alone for a minute, can we, Kitty?"

"This wasn't my fault! I'm not the Mad Blending Bomber."

"Blending?" Christopher asked. "Seriously? I thought I'd heard wrong before. You two were making smoothies or something?"

The Helpful Servant shot Christopher a dirty look. Maybe I could like this guy somewhere down the line. "No," I said, as Tito got to work on his latest patient, with Buchanan and the Barones standing guard and looking very threatening. "Blending is what he calls turning chameleon."

"I have a name," the Helpful Servant snarled.

"Not that he's shared it with me or anything. I'm calling him the Helpful Servant."

This earned me WTF looks from everyone in the room, other than Tito, who was busy.

"Why?" Christopher asked finally.

Said Helpful Servant managed a bitter chuckle. "Because she thought I was part of this embassy's staff when we met and I was trying to help her walk her dog."

"Got it in one!"

"Oh, fantastic," Christopher said. "This guy speaks Kitty."

"Why are you here instead of James? James doesn't complain about how I talk. Ever."

"That you know of. James is doing his job, which currently consists of verifying that our bases are secure and determining where we're all going to sleep tonight. There are multiple diplomatic missions that need to be housed and protected. And before you ask, Tim's still with Airborne verifying our embassy's status, Serene is with Horn at the F.B.I. doing things with bombs, and Claudia and Lorraine are remaining to guard the kids and Paul."

"Ah, so that's why James let you two do a flashback and cover Malcolm." This earned me a nice shot of Patented Glare #2. Chose to ignore it. "So, do we think everyone's still in danger? And by everyone I guess, based on all that's gone on, I literally mean everyone."

"Can't tell yet," Buchanan said. "The gas didn't release into this embassy, or the Israeli's, so both could be fine for habitation. We just don't know if there are more bio-weapons coming." He nudged the Helpful Servant with his foot. "Save yourself a lot of pain, and tell us what you know."

"Well they're not coming from me," he said through gritted teeth.

"He's telling the truth," Jeff said.

"You're sure?" Buchanan asked.

"Positive. I can read him now that you got that crap out of here."

"And?" I asked, clearly speaking for everyone else in the room, the Helpful Servant included.

"And he's not our friend, but he's not necessarily our enemy either."

"Oh, the enemy of my enemy is my friend? First time for everything. Usually our enemies gang up on us and become best friends forever."

Tito tossed the Helpful Servant's wallet to Buchanan, who took a look. "Interesting. Don't count on the 'friend' part, Missus Chief." He examined Tito's patient more closely. "Well, I see why they trusted you. Not Missus Chief here—I mean the people who gave you the bio-weapons to use on us. I want to know what else is going on, and I want to know now."

"Give him a second," Tito said. "I'm working without anesthetic and, trust me, this hurts."

"So, while we're being nice, who is our potentially friendly bomber, here?"

Buchanan tossed the wallet to Jeff. I would have complained but I still had my Glock out and trained on the Helpful Servant's head. Just because he appeared to be controlled and out of it didn't mean he actually was.

Jeff examined the wallet and grunted. "Yeah, interesting. According to his ID, he's not from the Middle East—he's from France. If this isn't doctored, his name is Benjamin Siler."

I was amazed. Neither Jeff nor Christopher reacted. Then again, they hadn't spent the same time with her as I had during Operation Assassination, and they certainly hadn't had to play the Anagram Game while falling down a hella tall garbage shaft.

But before I freaked out totally, had to be sure. "Siler? As in your mother was Cybele Siler, who married Antony Marling?"

"No," Helpful Servant Siler said. "Cybele was my aunt. My mother was her sister, Madeleine."

Wanted to shut up, but couldn't. Something about the total shock of it all. "Oh, my God. Your parents were Ronald Yates and Madeleine Cartwright."

Both of whom we'd killed.

CHAPTER 17

MADELEINE CARTWRIGHT had been the brains behind a lot of the Legacy Bad Guy Plans. She'd also infiltrated herself right into the heart of the Pentagon, and had been part of what I'd called the Cabal of Evil. And she'd tried to kill me during Operation Assassination.

Adriana had killed her first, but it had been a very close call.

While she and I had discussed her niece and nephew, and what her brother-in-law had ultimately done with them, with her blessing, Cartwright had never indicated that she had children of her own.

Of course, I hadn't asked. I'd been too busy learning that Marling's children were actually Leslie Manning and Bryce Taylor. Marling did great work—he'd taken his dead children's DNA and turned them into androids so real that they gave off emotional signals Jeff could pick up. If we hadn't had to break them down to their metal and wires in order to stop them from killing most of the politicians in Washington, D.C., we wouldn't have believed they were anything more or less than human.

I knew Cartwright been one of Yates' lovers. But it had never occurred to me that she might have had a child by him. Possibly because she was older than my mother.

Something didn't compute, though. Because this guy didn't look like he was in his forties. "You're too young."

Hey, it was better than saying that Jeff, Christopher, and I had combined to kill this guy's father and that Adriana and I had basically killed his mother. And it was also true.

"I know." Siler, as I supposed I should think of him now, said. "And before you confess to the fact that you killed my parents, I'm not here to avenge them. They did . . . something to me. I don't age like other people do."

"Tito, can you wave your wand and see if he's an android?"

Tito shot me a "really?" look, but he pulled out the Organic Validation Sensor, or OVS, that he carried with him. Tito and some of our people at the Dulce Science Center had created it as a way to non-intrusively determine if someone was a human or an android.

I'd been told that, other than newborns, who show as a hundred percent organic, no one is fully organic. Fillings, body art, a pin in your leg, and so on, all create an inorganic signature. There was a tipping point, of course—barring an artificial limb, you wanted to be 85% organic or more to be considered a non-android.

That we'd had to create such an item was a testament to both Marling's skills and his range—during Operation Destruction we'd managed to find and activate hundreds of androids to fight for us. But Chuckie still felt there were hundreds, maybe thousands, more that we hadn't found.

The OVS looked like the wands the TSA people used at airports to do the less unpleasant body frisks, only with a lot more blinking lights. The lights on Tito's OVS weren't blinking in a bad manner.

"He's human," Tito said. "But the OVS won't show something done at a genetic or molecular level if it's something organic, versus man-made."

"I don't know that I'm more or less human, or alien, than any of you," Siler said. He looked very pale and sounded weaker than he had yet.

"Tito, if you're done, move away from him," Jeff said. "Just in case."

Tito did as requested and came over next to me. "He's lost a lot of blood. We need to get him to an infirmary or hospital, sooner as opposed to later."

"Thanks for caring, Doc." Siler managed a chuckle. "Not going to hurt the guy who just patched me up. Your man's right, though," he jerked his head at Buchanan. "I'm not here to be your friend."

"No, you came to kill us," Christopher snarled.

Siler shrugged. "Sort of." He seemed relaxed; far more relaxed than the situation warranted, considering he had four men, a woman who'd already shot him, and a dog all ready to attack if he moved wrong.

Thinking about Adriana meant Olga was top of mind for me. What would Olga say, right now? What is the right question? I had a feeling I hadn't asked Siler the right questions yet. What would Mom say? To trust my gut. And my gut said that something was wrong with this picture. Which was typical for us.

Buchanan had been assigned to me during Operation Assassination, but Adriana had shot Cartwright and been the one to save me, because she'd been able to be where Buchanan couldn't. They hadn't been coordinated at that time, it had just worked out. But she and Buchanan had coordinated today to get us all away from the protest safely. Because alliances were made, or broken, all the time.

"Wait a second. Who the hell are you actually working for? Or with?"

Siler looked right at me. "Who do you think?" He asked this nicely, but it was a challenge. And he wasn't acting like he had when he and I had been alone. He'd been acting before, that was clear. He'd reacted in the way I'd expected him to earlier, given me canned answers in that sense, probably to test me out for whatever I knew or to see what I'd guess or how I'd reason. I mean, why should only Mom and Olga be on that bandwagon?

But this was him right now. Barring him having troubadour talent, it was unlikely that he was good enough to fake both being a hapless lackey and Mr. Smooth all within the same few minutes. Pain had a tendency to wipe out the ability to pretend to be someone else, and blood loss undoubtedly had added to it all, but more than pain and such, we were finally asking the right questions.

"Answer her," Jeff growled.

"No." I lowered my Glock. "How is it that we were infiltrated by a guy who can, for all intents and purposes, go invisible, and yet the Poofs and Peregrines didn't do squat until I called for them and Prince basically told them to get their butts in gear?"

"Because he didn't register as a threat," Buchanan replied. "But the bombs were real, and the gas deadly. And it was released in your Embassy."

"And yet we were warned and able to evacuate the Embassy, everyone was gathered up and taken to safety, we didn't lose anyone . . ." Examined Siler a little more closely. He still seemed far too calm for this situation.

Mahin hadn't been calm when she'd been in a similar situation. Because she was still new to the whole Terrorist In Training Game when we'd met her, and she was also a good person. In fact, I'd been around a lot of long-term bad people who hadn't seemed calm when they were shot and/or held captive. And I'd been around some, good or bad, who had been calm, cool and collected in the same situation.

"Three plans."

"What?" This was from all the men, in unison, other than Siler.

"There's always more going on, and Olga point blank told me she thought that we had the usual two, three, or four actions going on at the same time. Triggered by your climb up the political ladder, Jeff."

"I'm so proud." He didn't sound proud. He sounded suspicious. "What's going on?"

"Well, while I realize that Siler here would be a great addition to the Ronnie's Kids Team, if he's as old as I think he'd have to be to actually be Madeleine Cartwright's illegitimate and hidden son, he's been around longer than the first Apprentice. And that means there's a good chance he's been doing something to fill the time. And I can think of a great job for someone who can 'blend.' It's pretty much what he did today, only really ineffectively. But I think that was on purpose."

"Want to share for the rest of us," Christopher snarked, "or are we just going to have to try to decipher the Kittyisms?"

"No, I'll make it easy for you. I think Mister Siler here has been making a nice living as an assassin."

"Only sometimes," Siler said with a small smile. "Just like all of you assassinate or kill people sometimes, the dangerous ones who need to be put down for the safety of the world. Like my parents."

"Your parents weren't assassinated," Buchanan said.

"Oh, call it whatever term makes you happy. There are stories, but I'm sure most of the people all of you have killed were in self-defense in some way. I know for a fact that my mother was going to kill you, so if you're here and she's not, it's not because she had a change of heart."

"True enough. You seem very, oh, casual about all this. Are you like a living bomb or something and you're just waiting to detonate?"

He grinned. "No. And I know you," he looked at Buchanan, "are the real killer in the group. They need you. My people need me."

"How do you know all you think you know?" Buchanan asked. He, like Siler, seemed amazingly relaxed and calm. In fact, if I wanted to make comparisons, they were a lot alike, at least in terms of how they handled intense pressure situations.

"Oh, crap. France. Meaning Europe. You're with Interpol, or MI-Six or something like that, aren't you? In their James Bond Division? Or are you part of the Assassination League and you're just helping out in some really ineffective way? Or both?"

Siler jerked, just a little. He tried to hide it, but I knew it had been real and I wasn't the only one who'd caught it.

"That's it, baby," Jeff said. "Good job."

"Always glad to toss out random crap and have it work. So, which job is our new pal here doing?"

"It's not one or the other . . . it's both. He's working with your 'uncles,' but he's also infiltrating the terrorist networks targeting us and . . . more besides."

"How are you getting that?" Siler growled.

"Why do you think they gave you an emotional blocker, scrambler, overlay or whatever the hell it was?" I asked him. "I mean, surely you've done your research on us."

Siler nodded. "They didn't exaggerate about you, any of you, did they?"

"Oh, they tend to like to sell us really short, but we don't take it badly, usually because that way we get to stay alive."

"Let's have some proof that we should leave you alive," Buchanan said to Siler. "Because right now, Missus Chief, I'm on the side of kill him and let God and the governments sort it out."

CHAPTER 18

"I CAN'T GIVE YOU ANY PROOF you'd believe," Siler said, sounding unperturbed. "At least not here."

"Tell us what you were doing," Christopher said. "Because I'm with Buchanan—regardless of what Jeff got from you, I think you're our enemy and we should get rid of you before the next attack hits."

Something Cartwright and I had talked about before we'd killed her nudged. "I don't think we can kill him. His cousins were essentially killed by their father, as was their mother, in early experiments with the supersoldier drug. Their all dying is probably why Marling focused more on androids and left the superdrugs to Gaultier. My bet, though, is that the reason Siler here isn't out to avenge his parents' deaths is that he knows he was an even earlier experiment. Clearly successful."

Siler gave me a closed-mouth smile. "Despite the fact that since you've joined up you've foiled almost every major offensive sent against your people, most of your enemies still want to consider you merely stupid and lucky."

"Your mother actually didn't. We kind of . . . got along. In a sense, anyway."

"That's nice. Would that have stopped her from murdering you if she'd been able?"

"No. Not at all, honestly. If I'd promised to go away and not try to save people she might have. But I couldn't do that."

He nodded. "Because you're not like her. She was driven," he spat out. "They were all driven. No one really matters to them, not as a person, an individual. Everyone and everything's a means to an end."

"Mostly. Your uncle loved his wife, I do know that. And he loved his parrot."

"Lucky parrot. Maybe if my cousins had had feathers they'd still be alive." Siler's sarcasm knob, like everyone else's around me, went to eleven. He looked at Christopher. "I'm not telling you who I'm affiliated with. You're just going to have to trust me."

"Kitty might," Christopher said. "Jeff might, too. I won't."

"Up to you. And not my problem." The color was coming back to his cheeks. "I was a successful experiment, yes. But I think it's because of who my father was, and I'm certain that the reason Gaultier went on to create Surcenthumain was because I didn't die and my aunt and cousins did. Gaultier made the connection to my father."

"Oh. Wow. You're our Patient Zero, aren't you?"

"Patient what?" Jeff asked.

"Patient Zero is a genetics term for the first person identified with a communicable disease, or for the first genetic anomaly in a family. It's also used for computer viruses and even ideas." Everyone stared at me. "What?"

"As always," Christopher replied, "it's just strange hearing anything rationally scientific coming out of your mouth."

"See?" I said to Siler. "My friends think I'm an idiot, too."

He chuckled and stood up, slowly. "Not all of them, I'm sure." He looked at Buchanan. "So, what's your next move?"

"Funny," Buchanan said, with no humor in his tone, "I was going to ask you the same thing."

"He looks better," Tito said. "But I'd still like to get him to an infirmary, if not a hospital."

"Captain America rarely needs medical attention. Though we've already assigned that name to someone else." And I wasn't willing to give up Reader's superhero name to Siler any time soon. "Besides, I'd say what with all that disappearing, he's more like Nightcrawler."

"So glad you've assigned him a bizarre nickname," Christopher said. Opened my mouth to explain. He put up his hand. "I don't care which comic-book character it is or why you assigned it to this guy. Because I truly don't care and I'm with Buchanan—we need to figure out what to do with him. Now."

"I think we need to figure out what else is coming," Jeff said.

"I can't tell you," Siler replied.

Jeff nudged me. Took the hint. "So, are more places being set up to have poisoned gas released? And if so, why? Who's going to be assassinated? Were you going to reveal yourself to us or did we just get lucky? Where are the other Ronnie's Kids?"

Jeff grunted. "Keep going," he said quietly.

"Fine by me. So, Nightcrawler, you seemed really well prepped to act like you're part of the New Terrorist Mutant Network. So, *are* you a part of it? And, if you are, are you trying to bring it down, join and take over, or just along for the family reunion portions?"

"I'd like to know how he's been hidden from all of us for all this time," Christopher said. "Because we understand how the others were hidden—they only knew that they were different from other people before they were approached. They didn't know why. But he's too aware of what he is to have stayed in hiding all this time."

"I want to know why you faked me out earlier, too, by the way. That seemed like a lot of work for basically nothing and no reason. Unless you really wanted to off yourself and take me and Prince, and only me and Prince, with you."

"I could just kill him and we call it good," Buchanan offered.

"I really like that plan," Christopher said. "Right now, that's my favorite plan."

"Why did you have me patch him up if we're just going to kill him?" Tito asked. "I do have things to do, you know."

"I want to know if he's working with the Dingo, if he's working with the League of Assassins, if he's working with Interpol or similar, if he's working with the Mastermind and the Apprentice, if he's made a real or fake love connection with Ronnie's Kids, and if, by chance, he can point us in the direction of said siblings."

Siler sighed. "I get it. You're all just going to talk at, around, and about me until I give in or die from boredom."

"No," Jeff said. "They're going to talk at, around, and about you while you have emotional reactions to what they say that I'm interpreting. And I know you know this, because I can feel you trying to control *what* you're feeling so you can fool me. Here's a tip—you can't possibly fool me. You're good, but nowhere near good enough."

"You've been fooled before," Siler pointed out.

"True enough."

"How do you know that?" Christopher asked.

Siler rolled his eyes. "I have sources. Lots of them."

"Fine," Jeff said amiably. "But your sources should have told you that I was fooled by people who'd spent their lifetimes learning how to lie to empaths."

"Or by those using the various devices," I added.

"Thanks for the support, baby. The only empaths are within my community. And you're not a part of that community, which was one of Christopher's points. So it's pretty hard to practice lying to an empath when you've never spent any time with one. You're good, I'm sure you'll learn how. But not today."

"So, what my awesome husband is saying is that we can continue to talk at, about, and around you—and speaking for myself I can do this all day, nonstop—or you can start sharing information we want to know, and need to know."

"She can talk nonstop for days," Christopher said. "Trust me. Do yourself, and the rest of us, a favor."

"I heard that."

"Fine," Siler said, sounding exasperated. "We're on a schedule, so I'll give you some help."

"What 'we,' Kemosabe? The we that is all of us in this room, the we that is you and your many employers, the we that is you and your many illegitimate siblings, or the we that is some other kind of we?"

"More governments than just the United States' have been aware that aliens were on Earth for decades," Siler said, ignoring my questions yet again. "I wasn't hidden *by* my parents and their friends—I was hidden *from* them."

"By whom?" Tito asked.

Siler sighed. "By my uncle."

"Antony Marling hid you from his cronies? Pull the other one, it has bells on."

This earned me a dirty look. "No, not him. My mother's brother, Hubert Siler."

CHAPTER 19

"TRUTH," JEFF SAID. "Who is Hubert Siler?"

"Who is Keyser Soze?" This earned me the "you so crazy" looks from Jeff and Christopher, chuckles from Buchanan and Tito, and a still-not-up-to-our-high-standards glare from Siler. Prince shared that he thought I was hilarious, though, so there was that.

"My uncle was real. Quite real. He's the only reason I escaped to have an even halfway normal life."

"Where is he now?" Buchanan asked.

"Dead," Siler snapped. "For years. He found me, rescued me from his sisters' insanity, and we hid out until they lost interest in us."

"Sounds like a great movie. Only issue is, I'd never lose interest in someone who can go invisible, and I'm just going to spitball here and say that your parents and their buddies didn't, either."

"They didn't," Jeff said. "He's desperately trying to hide this, God alone knows why, but he and his uncle spent his childhood on the run. He's lived all over Eurasia."

"He's trying to hide it so we'll know less about him," Buchanan said. "Assume he can speak several languages fluently, possibly all of the languages of Europe, since he's been around for decades and had the time to learn. It takes money and connections to be able to run and hide like that. So the family, or at least the uncle, had both. Most likely answer is that the uncle was in intelligence work and took his nephew along."

"Or his uncle was an assassin, and also took his nephew along."

"Ah," Jeff said. "That's the right answer, baby."

"And so not a shocker. That's why you're working with the Dingo Dog and Surly Vic."

Siler blinked. "That's what you call them? To their faces?" He looked and sounded shocked, horrified, and just slightly impressed.

Controlled the Inner Hyena, though it took effort. "No, dude, I'm neither moronic nor suicidal. I call them Uncle Dingo and Uncle Surly to their faces. If you catch my drift."

Siler's horror remained intact on his expression. "And they're okay with that?"

"Oh, my God, no! I call them Uncle Peter and Uncle Victor. When we chat. Which is rarely. But, these days, always something I look forward to. If only because they're more forthcoming with the information than you, my mother, or most of my in-the-know friends. A girl likes to have someone tell her the damn poop and scoop once in a while, you know?"

"Ah, yeah. Okay." Siler looked at Buchanan. "I see why they all think she's just lucky."

"Never make the mistake of thinking that I'm willing to insult Missus Chief, or have anyone else insult her to me, especially someone who's not a close relative of her husband's." Buchanan's voice was icy. "We're not friends, you and I. I'm not betting we ever will be. She gets your respect or you get my boot up your ass."

"Malcolm's my favorite, in case anyone wasn't clear."

"I thought Len and Kyle were your favorites," Jeff said, sounding worried.

"They're my favorites, too. I have a lot of favorites."

"And you wonder why I'm jealous," Jeff muttered.

"You're my most favorite. Does that help?"

Jeff grinned. "A little." He kissed my cheek and nuzzled my ear. "A lot," he purred. Did my best not to rub up against him, but it took effort.

"Do you two ever stop?" Christopher asked.

"No. Whine about it to Amy later. So, Nightcrawler, what's the good, evil, and/or horrific word? We have a lot to get back to, including dealing with the Tastemaker, which I, personally, cannot wait for."

Siler jerked. "Wait, what? What's Jenkins doing sniffing around you?"

"Really? That's what gets you? Some gossip columnist?"

Siler shook his head. "He's more than that. Much more."

"He in your line of work? Whatever that line or lines actually is, I mean?"

"No." Siler took a step, and Prince took a leap. Siler was back against the wall, Prince's forepaws on his chest, Prince's growling, teeth-bared muzzle in his face. "Ah, a little help?"

"I'm with the dog," Buchanan said. "Where were you planning to go just now?"

"Honestly, I just want to sit down."

"Floor's free," Christopher offered, not at all nicely.

"He needs to check in," Jeff said. "He's late to do so, and he wants to tell those he's checking in with about Jenkins' interest in Kitty."

In addition to people and a pet we loved, and all of our historical data, what Centaurion Division had also lost during Operation Infiltration was confidence. We'd been infiltrated and taken over, our people controlled, kidnapped, and murdered. Imageering and Field, which was made up mostly of empaths, had been severely hampered because of all the empathic inhibitors our enemies had come up with and whatever the hell they'd done to the digital airwaves to block the imageers.

Considering that up until then we'd felt pretty impregnable, and Hacker International had felt they'd had the best of the best computer security in place, being taken over as easily as we were was shattering.

So it was nice to hear Jeff interpreting emotions again. He'd done it less and less because he wasn't trusting himself. Whatever else might come, Siler being here and giving Jeff a good emotions-reading workout was a good thing.

In the olden days—you know, a year ago—in the situation we were in, we'd have taken everyone to Dulce, gone into lockdown, and figured out what to do from there. Now, we were pretty much running lost and more than a little scared. It was an uncomfortable, unnatural feeling.

"Missus Chief, call your canine cohort off, please. He should stay ready, of course."

"Of course. Prince, we're going to let him sit on the floor. If he doesn't sit, take him out."

Siler shot me a dirty look, but when Prince went back to all fours, he sank back to the floor. "Thanks. Look, other . . . things . . . are going to happen if I don't make contact."

"Do we let him check in?" Christopher asked. "Or do we take him into custody?"

"I want to know exactly who he wants to check in with," Buchanan said.

"I want to know what the other things are," Jeff mentioned. "He's stressed about them, but the what isn't clear."

"Where would we take him *to*?" Tito asked. "Someone who can go invisible can escape police custody."

Something was nagging at me. "I have a question. I don't know if anyone can actually answer it, but Nightcrawler, if you can, do me a solid and tell me the truth."

He shrugged. "If I can."

"Okay. Is what's going on, all of it, designed to get us to do what we used to do, which would be to run to Dulce and go into lockdown?"

Siler's eyes flicked to Jeff and back to me. "Yes."

"Aha, you knew Jeff had already read your emotional answer."

"Pretty much."

"Whatever works. Okay, so here's my follow up question. Why? Why are all of our enemies, and I guess some of our friends, trying to get us to grab everyone and go across the country? Is it to protect us? Or is it to herd us into one spot and conveniently get rid of all of us in one fell swoop?"

Siler opened his mouth and my phone rang. Heaved a sigh, dropped my Glock back into my purse, dug my phone out, and took a look. Recognized the number this time.

"Hello, how's it going, Squeaky?"

"Squeaky?" Yep, it was my favorite Julia Child impersonator, otherwise known as Mrs. Nancy Maurer. "What in the world?"

"Squeaky?" Jeff asked quietly.

I shrugged to indicate that I wasn't in a position to explain this to him. Tito grinned at me, then pulled Jeff and Christopher closer to Buchanan and Siler so he and Buchanan could quietly explain what the others had missed.

Buchanan tossed me his little phone-location-finder device thing. Plugged it in like a good girl as I continued on with my phone call. "It's your new code name. I think it fits you. So, whassup?"

"How is it that you're American Centaurion's top lobbyist, let alone their head diplomat?"

"You know, I ask that question all the time. No one gives me an answer I can believe, and yet, here I am anyway. So, Squeaky, are you calling to ask for a donation, to shoot the breeze, or to relay information, threats, or requests for help?"

"I'm calling to ask you why your husband is going to be running for vice president. They wanted to hurt you all before, but now? Now I don't know what they'll do, but I guarantee it will be terrible." She took a ragged breath and I realized she was crying.

"Are you alone?"

"Right now, yes. He's not my son, not any more. I didn't raise him to hate other people, let alone hurt them. His father would be devastated to see what his son is turning into, and nothing I do or say has any impact."

"We're talking about Cameron Maurer, right? Your son?"

"Y-yes."

"When did he start acting . . . unlike himself?"

"Right after the invasion. He was so pro-alien before then, telling me all about the wonderful new world we'd see once all of your people were able to fully integrate into our society. And then, he took his family to Europe for a vacation and when he came back, he was this . . . this . . . hatemonger."

"Does your son know you don't approve of his, ah, change of heart?"

"Yes, but I gave up trying to change his mind months ago."

"Yeah, I'll bet. What about his wife and kids?"

"The children and Crystal are home in Cincinnati. Why?"

"Have they been any different?"

"Ah, well . . ."

"Cough it out there, Squeaky."

"Fine," she snapped. "I don't care much for my daughter-in-law. She's much more driven by the idea of being married to a powerful man than anything else. She seems much happier since they got back from Europe and my son . . . changed. My grandchildren are wonderful, of course."

"Of course." So, if what I was suspecting was true, Crystal Maurer wouldn't know or care, or else she was in on it because she was a typical political virago. I'd ask Culver for her thoughts later, you know, whenever we got to reunite with everyone else again. Right now, my gut told me I had an old lady to save. "Where are you? Exactly, I mean."

"I went out to get some fresh air, I mean, that's what I told them, but I didn't know where else to go or what else to do, so I went to the park."

"And your son and whoever else working the campaign, they let you go there alone? No guards or anything?"

"Yes. I come here all the time. Usually alone. Again, why?"

"This city is lousy with parks, Squeaky. I need a park name, and the major cross streets wouldn't hurt, either."

"Why do you need to know where I am?" She sounded legitimately confused. It was sweet, in a scary way.

Thought about how to say this without panicking her. Decided to go for it. "Squeaky, I'd like to know how good you are at following directions."

"Fair to middling, I suppose. Why?"

"Because I think you're in danger. Or they're using you to get to us, which means we're in danger, too. But we're far more used to danger than you are, I'd wager."

"Should I call the police?"

Looked at Prince and decided I wouldn't really be lying. "No. I'm about to bring the police to you. If, you know, you ever tell me where the hell you are."

"I—"

"Squeaky?"

"Oh thank you so much for calling, dear. It was lovely catching up. I must dash now, though. I'll see you soon, I hope."

And with that, the phone went dead.

CHAPTER 20

"**MALCOLM,** figure out how to keep Nightcrawler under control. We have a situation and I think saving a little old lady is going to take precedence over our Junior Assassin."

Explained the phone call and how it had ended while Buchanan used his doohickey to figure out where Mrs. Maurer actually was, or at least had been.

"You sure you can trust this?" Christopher asked. "She could be playing you, to get you to come save her and go right into a trap."

"She could have been, and I'm not saying she wasn't. But she was crying and I think it was real. And . . . from what she said . . . I think . . ." Considered if I should say what I thought out loud, in front of Siler. Then again, out of everyone in the room, he'd be the least surprised. "I think Cameron Maurer has been turned into an android."

To their great credit, none of the men with me asked if I was high or just guessing wildly. "Why?" Jeff asked.

"He used to be pro-alien, took the family to Europe for vacation, and came back a raging xenophobe who isn't the man this woman raised anymore."

"Sounds right," Siler said.

"I have to ask—since when do assassins take this level of interest in all this political brouhaha?"

Siler laughed. "Since always. Sometimes we're killing

good guys. And sometimes we're killing bad guys to stop them from killing good guys."

"Whoever pays best and/or contracts first?"

"Something like that. And your uncles have taken a greater interest because of you. We police our own, and you have one of our own we want dead."

"Oh, Annette Dier. Yeah, that bitch is still alive, and giving us nothing. Maybe later, after we save the scared old lady, I'll ask my mom to let you have a go at her."

Siler raised his eyebrow. "Seriously? You're going to trust me with that kind of prisoner access?"

"If we let you live that long," Buchanan said. "However, if we want to save Missus Maurer or, you know, head right into a trap, we need to move." He pulled a pair of handcuffs I didn't even know he carried out of somewhere and slapped one end onto Siler's right wrist and the other onto his own left wrist. "I'll be keeping you close. And don't think that you can use hyperspeed on me to cause me issues. Our good doctor's solved that particular problem."

Hyperspeed was hard as hell on humans—it always caused vomiting, and blacking out wasn't uncommon. Tito was amazing, however, and he'd figured out how to create a Hyperspeed Dramamine. Every human agent working with American Centaurion and Centaurion Division took it daily.

Fortunately, when we'd lost all of our data, Tito's laptop had been offline and off system. Meaning we had all his research, which had included the secret formula for this medicine. We had only his research or whatever information his laptop had held, but, as I was reminded by our scientific teams and Hacker International, some data was a lot better than none.

"You think it's a trap, Malcolm?"

"No idea, Missus Chief. I think we're going to go in ready, however."

As soon as Siler was officially in Buchanan's custody, Prince trotted back over to me. He respected Buchanan as an impressive officer, but Jeff had saved Prince's life during Operation Assassination and they had a Special Bond too, as far as Prince was concerned.

Jeff knew it, too, and though he tried to pretend he didn't think Prince was better than any other animal, he thought the dog was smart and brave. Jeff hoisted Prince under his arm and took my hand with his free one. "Where are we headed?"

Buchanan sighed. "Bartholdi Park."

"Isn't that around the U.S. Botanic Garden?" Tito asked. "That's close to the Capitol."

"Which makes a lot of sense for where she could go alone," Buchanan said. "She was at Cleary-Maurer headquarters earlier, and that's not too far from the Gardens."

I grabbed Tito's hand, and Christopher took Siler's uncuffed one. Thusly connected, we headed out of the embassy. "Should we lock up behind us?"

"No," Buchanan said. "I've asked for teams to come in and verify that the building is sound." He looked at Siler out of the side of his eye. "Unless there's something else you'd like to tell us about."

Siler shook his head. "No, if you found all the bombs, it's clean."

"How many were there?" I was just curious about how badly Siler had wanted to kill me and himself.

"Seven," Siler replied.

"Eight," Buchanan countered.

Siler stopped. "No. There were seven."

"He's not lying." Jeff sounded worried.

"We found eight," Buchanan said. Christopher nodded. "One was on a shorter timer than the others."

"I only put seven in. How many did they find at the Israeli embassy? I planted seven there, too."

"Eight again," Buchanan replied. "And one there was on a shorter timer than the others. We assumed it was the trigger and the others were on separate timers in case triggering didn't work."

"No. They were set to give me plenty of time to ensure I was out of range and so was anyone who we cared about, and by 'we' I think you know who I mean, and by anyone we cared about, I mean Miss Katt here and those in her ever-widening circle."

"Wow, you're big on dropping the clues all of a sudden."

The only people who called me Miss Katt with any regularity since I'd married Jeff were my "uncles" the assassins. Meaning Siler wanted us to know that he was working with them, without confirming so out loud. Why was the Question of the Moment, which I filed as question fifty-one after the fifty other Questions of the Moment this afternoon's festivities had identified as being vital to answer.

"We need to be sure there aren't any more bombs in here, or in the Israeli embassy, especially since there are a ton of people *in* the Israeli embassy." Why I was the one having to point this out was just another one of Life's Little Mysteries today seemed determined to share with me.

"We can't do this and save Missus Maurer at the same time," Jeff pointed out.

"Malcolm, Nightcrawler, and Christopher could stay here and search. Christopher could get them to safety if needed. And the four of us are equipped to handle anything."

"We are?" Tito asked.

"Hush."

Buchanan made the exasperation sound. "I can't believe I'm saying this, but fine. By now, Missus Maurer could be long gone, either via abduction or simply a lack of patience waiting for you to show up to save her. Or their trap could be all set up. Or all of the above."

"Keep in touch," Jeff said. "Find out what Siler was going to tell Kitty before she got this call, too. Trust me," he said to Siler, "they'll use far more unpleasant methods than mine. Cooperate, you'll be happy you did." Then we took off.

I stopped us as soon as we were out of sight of the embassy, which, thanks to hyperspeed, was a second later. "Jeff, you and Prince need to go to the Israeli embassy."

"Yeah," he said as Prince shared that he didn't have Tito's Special Hyperspeed Dramamine and hacked. But, even though Jeff was still holding him, he hacked away from us. What a good dog. "I picked up what you want to do. I'm not wild about your plan, though."

"My parents and some of our closest friends are at the Israeli embassy, and while we all think everyone's found all the bombs, Siler may be the only one who can be sure. Everyone else, besides the six of us and Prince, are at the Pontifex's Residence. Siler confirmed that everyone's trying to herd us. Maybe it's our friends who want us in Dulce. Our enemies probably just want us all somewhere they can blow up conveniently. You know everyone's going to listen to you more than me on this one."

"Not necessarily." Jeff's turn to make the exasperation sound. "I don't want you going alone, and before either one of you start listing your competencies, you're not A-Cs."

Dug my phone out and made the call. He answered right away. "Missus Martini, how go things wherever you happen to be?"

"Interestingly as always, Mister White. I need you and your mad skills over at Bartholdi Park. Please don't tell anyone where you're going, if you'd be so kind. Jeff will be there shortly and share the news at that time."

"As always, I live to serve. I'll bring your catsuit with me?"

"Indeed. I should be there in, oh, five minutes. If I don't get lost."

"Ah. Won't be a moment." He hung up.

Shrugged and dropped my phone back into my purse. "Richard will meet me."

"Actually," White said from behind me, "I felt it would be wiser to find you and have us go together. I'm sure Jeffrey would prefer that as well."

"How did you know where we were?"

White held up his phone. "GPS tracking. I had our computer specialists teach me how to track anyone using my phone."

"Wow." That had never occurred to me. Decided to save being bitter that White hadn't shared until now for a later time.

"Dog with me or you?" Jeff asked, in the resigned tone of someone who's played out the argument in his head already and has accepted his crushing defeat.

"You. Officer Melville will be worried about him."

Prince was done barfing and he barked. He objected to this plan. Emphatically.

"Or, um, Richard could carry Prince."

Prince wuffed that this was far more acceptable.

"The dog is insisting on going with you?" Jeff's tone was now Man Resigned to Living in a Mental Institution.

"Yes."

"I'll go with you, Jeff," Tito said, clearly trying not to laugh. "I want to make sure everyone there is fully organic anyway. I think we're going to want the reassurance."

"How will Kitty and Richard know if Missus Maurer is a human or not?"

"We'll wing it."

"Oh," Jeff said as I leaned up and kissed him. "So, routine."

CHAPTER 21

JEFF GAVE PRINCE TO WHITE, White took my hand in his free one, and the three of us zipped off.

"Glad you're here, Mister White."

"I realized I'd be waiting for you for hours if I didn't ensure I was with you to navigate."

"I'll hurt you later, Rick honey."

"Is it time for our supersecret code names, Kathy?"

"Could be." Brought White up to speed on what had transpired since Prince and I had gone outside. "So, I don't even know where we start to figure out what the hell is going on," I said as we reached an alley near the park where we could stop running at hyperspeed and so "appear" to human eyes without any humans seeing us do so.

"I believe we're heading for the most urgent issue," White said as he put Prince down and the dog started to again barf his guts up. White handed me sunscreen.

"Wow, call you Mister Thoughtful. Thanks. How'd you know I'd need a refresher?"

"I know how fast you sunburn, we were heading to and are at an outdoor location, and what with all the excitement, it seemed likely that reapplication of protective creams hadn't occurred to you."

"Wise man always plans ahead. But," I said as I slathered the sunscreen on my face and any other exposed skin, "I think bombs all over the place, some containing poisoned gas, are more urgent than even my remaining sunburn and skin cancer-free or Missus Maurer's suspected abduction."

He shook his head. "No one, and I do mean no one, has been harmed. You yourself remarked on this earlier. The status remains the same. More bombs have gone off around the city, however. Key locations, no one injured, not too much damage. No one has claimed responsibility yet, not even the Al Dejahl group."

"Really? That seems . . . even odder than everything else."

"We all agree with you. James has kept all bases on high alert. Dulce in particular is being searched from top to bottom, drainage pipe included."

Didn't say anything about the pipe—because I couldn't. I was prevented from speaking about what was unusual about the drainage pipes in the Science Center, even when I was with White or Gower, the only other people who knew the truth about the A-C's God in the Machine. Said "God" prevented us from talking about him unless we were in his presence.

Algar wasn't really a god, though. He was one of the Black Hole People and a major criminal as far as they were concerned. In our part of this galaxy, he was the Operations Team for all of the A-Cs worldwide.

When I'd first joined up, I'd nicknamed the Operations Team the Elves, because they did all their work by what seemed like magic, even though Christopher had given me a very scientific answer, and I'd never, ever seen or met one of them.

Turned out, my magic idea was closer to the truth, not that I could crow about this to Christopher, or anyone else for that matter. Since the beings from the Black Hole Universe, which included the Poofs, were so far advanced from those of us in the Milky Way galaxy that the tricks they could pull certainly seemed like magic. Algar had an entire planetary population thinking that there were A-Cs, and lots of them, doing the Operations jobs, when in fact all of Operations was made up of just one rakishly handsome dwarf from another universe with a seriously impressive set of skills.

Algar was also something of a jerk, though a jerk who cared about us, at least in his own way. I called him the King of the Elves whenever we were talking, and I always meant it sarcastically.

For certain, Algar knew what was going on. But now wasn't the time to try to contact him to see if I could extract any kind of hint.

There was another entity I'd have liked to talk to. ACE was a superconsciousness that had been set up by the Alpha Four system to watch over Earth and keep us all, Jeff and Christopher in particular, basically on the planet. Like Algar, ACE's powers were so vast that, compared to the rest of us, it was a god, too. I'd channeled ACE into Gower and that had been great. For a while.

But ACE had done more than it was supposed to in order to protect Earth and the beings on it that ACE cared for—and our observer loved all of his "penguins," though he did have his favorites. Turned out that even gods or godlike entities have to answer to their own versions of the Supreme Court. ACE had been taken from us, and only Naomi's last minute mega-power surge and sacrifice had brought ACE back. But not as he'd been before.

ACE now resided in Jamie, which partly helped to control him, and in a larger part protected her. Due to the fact that I wasn't willing to have scary discussions about people trying to destroy the world with my little girl, I couldn't talk to ACE as I'd been able to in the past. Now, Jamie needed to be asleep—so ACE could keep the conversations from her—and it didn't hurt if I was asleep, too. My dreams were a lot funkier than they had been, but I was getting better with interpretation. However, now was a poor time for a nap.

Prince finished barfing as I finished with the sunscreen. Dropped the rest of the sunscreen into my purse and we started off.

As the three of us wandered around the park area, looking and sniffing for a little old lady who was crying, looking scared, or being dragged off, I really wanted to ask either ACE or Algar what the hell was really going on. But while ACE would want to tell me but probably couldn't, and Algar could tell me but undoubtedly wouldn't, accessing either one of them was out of the question for right now.

"You see or smell anything?" I asked finally.

"Nothing untoward," White said.

Prince wuffed that he smelled and heard a heck of a lot, but no one nearby was in distress, at least not the kind of distress we'd been expecting.

"Think it's a trap?"

"I believe that Mister Buchanan has a tendency to be correct. However, that doesn't mean Missus Maurer was lying to you. Your penchant for protecting the weak and innocent is well known."

"Yeah, Lillian Culver said the same thing earlier."

"She thinks quite highly of you."

"Oh, fantastic. She's one of the Dealers of Death, you know."

"I do. However, we need her and she needs us. And of course Monsieur Gadoire."

"Two out of three ain't bad, right?"

White stopped walking and looked at me. "There's another Dealer, correct?"

"Alcohol, since Lillian covers weapons and Gadoire tobacco. Probably others. I don't pay a lot of attention."

"I'm shocked to my core."

"Sarcasm is still such an ugly trait in a Retired Pontifex."

"And my shame still knows no bounds. Who is the person in charge of the Alcohol lobby?"

"No idea, I'm sure Lillian or Vance know. Why?"

"Why hasn't that person tried to curry favor with us?"

"Because we don't drink?"

"We don't smoke, as a rule, either. And yet, Monsieur Gadoire wants us on his side."

"The Cabal of Evil didn't include an Alcohol person, that's true. But why does it matter? Or, more importantly, why does it matter right now?"

White sighed. "Gideon Cleary's family own one of the top distilleries in the world. Per Mister Joel Oliver."

"Other than pointing out how at odds with him we are and how well funded his campaign will be, I'm still not seeing your point."

"We've been on this planet for decades. The assumption,

which no one has said anything to alleviate, is that those who approached you and Jeffrey when you became the ambassadors were those who already had relationships with the former Diplomatic Corps. And yet whoever lobbies for the quite large, powerful, and wealthy alcohol collective has never approached either one of you. I find that odd."

"I find myself again thinking you should be our Head Diplomat. I also find myself thinking that we've wandered this entire lovely park and haven't found our target. I realize you're passing the time by trying to make me think of whatever you think the bigger picture is, but honestly all I see is a lot of crap flying at us from all directions, and all I really want to do is hunker down and avoid getting hit."

"Could that be the plan?" White asked.

"It does seem like everyone wants us herded to Dulce, yeah. But why is the big question. We don't seem infiltrated, or if we are, everyone over there is acting completely naturally and doing their jobs just like always."

"I don't believe we'll be infiltrated as easily, or at least in the same way, again," White said quietly. "Gladys killed Ronaldo and sacrificed herself for a reason."

Prince pricked up his ears and listened intently before I could reply. It wasn't exactly silent around here, so I wasn't sure what he was picking up, but he was clearly hearing something. Something that, as he shared while he trotted toward the street, we needed to investigate immediately. He waited for us and we crossed the street together, going into the main Gardens.

"Think she went in here or was taken here?" I asked White as we trotted along behind Prince, who remained quite intent.

"I think it's the most secluded and likely to be unpopulated area around here, at the moment."

"Normally I'd disagree with you, because this is prime wandering the gardens time if you're a tourist. But what with all the bombs going off, I'd bet most tourists and everyone else are trying to stay inside. It's sure less crowded around here than I'd have figured, especially since there was a protest nearby not all that long ago."

White and I looked at each other. "That would seem to be

the case, wouldn't it?" he mused. "And as you frequently point out, our enemies like to have their attacks do double duty, at minimum, if at all possible."

We were pulled away from this line of reasoning by Prince's low growl. The Gardens had a pretty, sunken water fountain at the far side from where we'd started, and we were now close to it. You took a short flight of steps down from the main Garden area and there it was, looking sort of geometric and sort of *Alice in Wonderland*, at least to me. It was very shallow—so shallow that a parent wouldn't worry about letting their toddler play here, not that this was a play area.

There were a few tables with umbrellas and chairs scattered about. But what Prince was growling at wasn't the tables—it was the fountain. Or, more correctly, what was in the fountain.

A woman was facedown in the water. And while the water wasn't all that deep, it was deep enough for someone to drown in if they were unconscious.

White and I didn't hesitate, we both ran to her at hyperspeed. He picked her up and got her out of the fountain. He had her down on the ground and was doing CPR on her within a second.

To prevent myself from cursing the fact that I hadn't insisted Tito come with us, I looked around. There was no blood that I could see, either in the water or around the fountain. Did a fast check for lurkers nearby—none.

Prince did his own check and I went with him. He went to the edge of the street and stopped. The assailants had taken off, probably in a car. "Good try, boy. We'll find them later. I'm pretty damn sure they work for her son's campaign."

We trotted back to White. Our victim was sitting up. She looked soaked in front and banged up, but miraculously she both wasn't bleeding and was breathing. The tightness in my chest relaxed. "Squeaky?"

She nodded. "I said I was going to meet a friend in here. Those thugs insisted on coming with me. I went to look at the water and someone hit me on the back of my head and shoved me down. I . . . I don't know how you found me."

Patted Prince's head. "We have the best police dog in the

world on our team. Squeaky, meet Prince, the Dog Who Always Saves the Day."

Prince gave me a lick to show his appreciation for his Special Title, then trotted over to Mrs. Maurer and gave her a good sniffing. He then snorted, growled, and wuffed.

"Yeah, got it. Richard, Prince says the scent he was following is on Squeaky here, too. He'll recognize it if he smells it again. Apparently her assailant is dedicated to the entire line of Axe Apollo products and has a particularly icky sweat signature to go along with his less than stellar taste in personal fragrances."

"I'm overjoyed to not have a canine's sense of smell," White said. "How did he recognize the specific personal body care product, though?"

"Officer Melville is very thorough. Prince can identify every manufactured scent on the market today. Along with every illegal substance. He's The Super Sniffer." As he'd proved during Operation Sherlock. I had full faith that if Mrs. Maurer's assailant was in range, Prince would find him.

"Impressive. We need to get Missus Maurer to Doctor Hernandez."

"I feel fine, now that I'm conscious and can breathe. I'd like to get into some dry clothing, though."

"Not sure we want to take you home. I'd normally suggest that we just take you back to our Embassy and have our people outfit you, but that's not an option right now."

"I think I'll go wherever you suggest, Ambassador. And Mister White." She gave White a fluttering smile while he gallantly helped her up and gave her a manly, comforting smile in return. He was dating Nurse Carter, but White was absolutely a ladies' man of the highest, smoothest order. Realized that he'd probably inherited that trait from his father and filed it away for later consideration.

As White stood Mrs. Maurer up, the sky darkened. Not a lot, but as if there were cloud cover. In Arizona, where I'd grown up, or New Mexico, where I'd lived once I'd met Jeff and the rest of the gang, cloud cover in July and August indicated a potential monsoon. We hadn't lived in D.C. long enough for my natural weather instincts to alter. I looked up, to see whether we had heat, a passing overcast, or storm clouds overhead.

Only, there were no clouds in the sky at all.

There was what looked like a sort of film, like a tint you'd put on your windows to limit the amount of sunlight coming through. The film went as far as I could see.

My gut, always on duty in danger situations, mentioned that this didn't look natural. Or good.

"Ah, Richard?" Pointed up.

"What? Oh. Oh dear."

"What is that?" Mrs. Maurer asked. "It doesn't look . . . right."

"To me, either, Squeaky. And I just want to be on record that I have a very bad feeling about this."

CHAPTER 22

OF COURSE, I was correct. I'd have been proud of my ability to never be wrong about horrible crap happening, but I'd have given a lot to be able to say I was merely a Nervous Nellie.

The film or whatever it was got closer, as if it was contracting, and doing so at a very fast rate of speed. I was pretty damned sure that it *was* contracting.

In less than a minute, I felt rather than saw something go through me. Saw it go through everything else. Which was nice, since I hadn't had anything freaky happen to me for at least thirty seconds and I was feeling the withdrawal symptoms.

The film going through me felt like I'd heard people describe a ghost walking through them—like something cool and clammy had passed through my body. I was good with never feeling this again.

"What just happened?" Mrs. Maurer asked weakly. "That was rather . . . awful."

"ACE is not . . . alone in the universe, is he?" White asked, voice carefully guarded.

"No. Oh, wow, you think?" There were other superconsciousnesses out there. Some had been put in place in the same way ACE had been—by Alpha Four or another planet with some really bossy, controlling beings in charge who wanted to keep other beings firmly on their own planets.

Some were different in their reasons for being. But those other superconsciousnesses were the ones who had held ACE captive, for want of a better word, before Naomi had somehow freed him.

I had no idea what ACE's release status was—we didn't talk about it, the few times we'd talked over the past year. But if it worked even remotely like our prisoner releases did, then ACE would have some kind of superconsciousness parole officer.

My hopes that said officer had come by, taken a look, and left were quickly dashed. The fountain started bubbling oddly. We all watched as the water coalesced and formed into the figure of a humanoid. Since it was literally made of water, it was hard to guess if it was supposed to be male or female, but a lack of curves indicated male.

The Water Man turned toward us. "We wish to speak to the leader." Its voice was bubbly with a weird echo, like a lot of water going down a drain quickly. It wasn't the worst sound in the world, probably no worse than Mrs. Maurer's voice. But I wasn't a fan.

"Awesome. I can call my mom and see if she can arrange a meet and greet, but before we take you to visit the most powerful man in our country, who the hell are you, why the hell are you here, and what do you expect to gain from coming here in this way?"

The Water Man stared at me. At least, I thought he was staring. He was literally made of water, features and all, so it was hard to be sure. It was easy to see through him—it was like looking at a person-sized aquarium with really clean glass—but not to see "him," so to speak. Wondered if I put my hand into him if it would go through easily, come out wet, or something else. Was so glad my mind had added these thoughts into an already overcrowded mix.

"The leader is here."

"Yes, yes, the President's in D.C. But, impressive water show or not, he's not hanging about waiting for weirdoes from outer space to drop by to shoot the crap or make bizarre demands. He's actually, you know, running the country."

"We are here to speak to the leader."

"Yes, leader, got it. Why you chose to do your big manifestation right here, in front of the four of us only, is beyond me, but whatever makes you happy. Or watery. Or whatever."

Water Man turned to White. "We came directly to the leader."

"Richard, do they think you're still the Supreme Pontifex?"

"I don't know that they'd know me," White said slowly. "If that were the case, my thought would be that they would want to see Paul, versus the President, but I could be wrong."

Mrs. Maurer spoke before I could reply. "Excuse me, but do you feel that the leader is one of us who are right here with you?"

"Yes." Water Man sounded relieved.

"I see." She cleared her throat and pointed to Prince. "Is this who you think the leader is?"

"No." Water Man now sounded like he now thought we were all idiots.

"Good," Mrs. Maurer said. "I just wanted to be sure." She put her hand on my lower back and nudged me forward. "Our leader is very modest."

"Huh?"

Water Man stepped toward me. "You are identified as the leader."

"By whom? And is that person in their right mind? Or do you now just think that I'm the leader because Squeaky here pushed me forward?" Maybe this thing expected us to pick a leader and I'd just been volunteered. Stranger things had happened—like my entire career with Centaurion Division.

Water Man stared at me. I was starting to be able to see facial features. Meaning I was pretty sure its eyes were narrowed. "Willful stupidity will not help your case."

"It's never hurt it before."

"You will not speak to us in this way. We *will* speak to the leader."

"Excuse the hell out of me? I don't know who or what you and the rest of your collective are, or where the hell you came from, but you're not exactly being clear with what you want, and who you want to speak to, not to mention why you're here."

Water Man raised his hand up. Had a feeling it was to slam said hand right down on my head. Had to figure this wouldn't be good. Decided not to find out. Slammed through the Water Man. Felt like a lot of water—like all the water in the fountain, and then some, was all concentrated into this one figure. Again, I wasn't a fan. On the plus side, I wasn't wet when I got out the other side. Damp, but not wet.

The Water Man reformed and came at me. "Violence is not the answer."

So saying, it swung at and hit me. Felt as bad as I'd expected it to, but I shoved through the fist and it wasn't quite like a giant wave crashing on me. Close, but more like having a Gatorade bucket dumped over me as opposed to a tsunami. Had the feeling the Water Man hadn't been trying all that hard.

"So why are you using it, then?" Spun around and got into a crouch. Fighting in the Armani Fatigues wasn't all that easy, but I'd worry about that later. Right now, I had a water thing to try to take down.

The Water Man imitated my stance. We lunged at each other. Again, going through him felt odd but I wasn't hurt or wet, just a bit damper than before.

We both landed, spun, and did this a couple more times. I was about to ask if this was some bizarre meet and greet or mating ritual from the Water Man's part of the cosmos, but before I could, and before either Water Man or I did anything else, Jamie was there, standing in between us, her hands palms out toward my assailant.

"Get away from my mommy, you mean thing!"

CHAPTER 23

THE WATER MAN EXPLODED, as if he'd been a water balloon.

Picked Jamie up and gave her a big hug. Didn't ask how she'd gotten here—she'd proven at four months that she was able to time warp herself anywhere.

She'd been kept from time warping by ACE when she was a baby, and by the Poofs and Peregrines during Operation Infiltration, always for her own safety. Clearly, either she'd overcome their abilities, or ACE, the Poofs, and Peregrines approved of Jamie's coming to me right now.

As all of the Peregrines and what really looked like all of the Poofs appeared, figured I'd bet on the latter. "Jamie-Kat, thank you, but why are you here?"

"That bad thing is here to take Fairy Godfather ACE away from us." She sounded angry and distressed.

"Are you sure it's bad?" Just because it had attacked me, that didn't necessarily mean it was evil. Could just mean we hadn't hit it off properly. Certainly wouldn't be the first time.

She looked uncertain and twitched. "Kitty, ACE must clarify for Jamie." It was unsettling hearing the halting, just slightly uncertain way Jamie spoke when ACE had control of their shared consciousness. It had been weird when it had been via Gower, but he was a grown man. With Jamie it was almost frightening. "The being Jamie dissipated is not gone."

True enough. As ACE spoke Mrs. Maurer pointed to the

fountain. The water sloshed back into the fountain, coalesced again, and started to re-form.

"Lucky us. What is it and why is it here?"

"It is the one sent to check on ACE. And it wishes to speak to ACE's leader."

"Why is it yapping with us, then?" Perhaps Mrs. Maurer was wrong. Of course, the Water Man had said I was the leader, but perhaps it had been reacting to her assumption.

"ACE's leader is Kitty," ACE confirmed helpfully.

"Oh." Shot a glance at Mrs. Maurer. She had a "told you so" expression going. White didn't look surprised, but that might have been because he was busy texting at hyperspeed. "Fantastic. So, what do I need to tell your parole officer in order to get him, her, it, or they to go away and leave us alone?"

The Water Man was fully formed and sloshed over to us. "We are here to observe and report."

"Super. And attack."

"You attacked us first."

"Best defense is a good offence."

"We do not understand you."

"So very few ever do, Sloshy. So few ever do."

"We are not named Sloshy." The Water Man didn't sound amused. Whatever.

"You are until you share your real name with us. Why are you made of water?"

"You are made of water."

"No. We're mostly water, but we're all fond of things like skin and bones and fur and hair and such. If you're trying to imitate us, you're doing a terrible job."

"No, we are trying to emulate the most prevalent thing on this planet."

"Water isn't sentient," Mrs. Maurer said.

"Everything has sentience," the Water Man replied.

"Ah, metaphysics. Not my specialty and college gets farther and farther away every year, don't you find? Let's just agree that there's sentience and then there's sentience."

"Yes, all things have sentience."

"Speaking of being willfully dense. Let's put this another

way. Humans are the dominant life forms on this planet. And you know it, or you wouldn't have formed to look sort of like one of us. So stop playing whatever game it is you think you're playing or, better yet, go home."

The Water Man stepped closer. "Stay away from my mommy or I'll do it again," Jamie said, in her own voice. "Only more."

"I have a little girl and I'm not afraid to use her." Had a thought. Something had indeed been trying to herd us to Dulce. "Jamie, did Fairy Godfather ACE want us all at the Science Center because it would be safer?"

"I think so, Mommy."

"Right. Oh well, good effort, I suppose. At least there were only the few of us around to witness the arrival of Sloshy, here." Few if I didn't count the Poofs and Peregrines, that was.

"We are *not* named Sloshy." Water Man sounded offended by this nickname. Good to know my track record in this regard remained unsullied. Wondered if they knew Lilith Fair, or what was left of her, from Operation Invasion and decided that of course they did, and they were probably on her side. "We are a supreme consciousness from what you call the Eagle Nebula."

"Blah, blah, blah, Sloshy. And I'm the Head Diplomat for American Centaurion, but you don't hear me bragging about that to everyone I meet."

"We are here to ensure that the one you named ACE is not acting against our laws."

"And what if he is? ACE belongs Earth and Earth belongs to ACE. You and the rest of the interfering busybodies out there don't factor into that equation."

"So we have been told. However, the fact remains that our laws supersede yours."

"It so figures. Might likes to triumph over right all over the universe, I see."

Didn't ask who'd told them about our relationship with ACE, mostly because I could guess and that guess was Naomi. Didn't want to bring Naomi up, especially not around Jamie. She, like the rest of us, still missed her A-C godmother terribly and asked when she was coming back all the time.

Had to figure this was bad for all of us in a lot of ways. One of those ways wasn't obvious to most, but the likelihood was that this superconsciousness doing an unplanned home inspection would make Earth stand out on the greater Universal Plain. And that meant it was now more likely that the Black Hole People who were hunting Algar would notice Earth.

I wasn't sure of a lot of things, but I was certain that Earth couldn't afford to lose either ACE or Algar, let alone both of them. And I was equally certain that in any intergalactic and inter-universal fight that seemed likely to be looming, Earth was in the Biggest Loser role, aka the Battleground. Always the way.

"So, just what laws of yours has ACE supposedly broken?"

"Interference."

Interesting. Algar was on the run because he *hadn't* interfered—he'd allowed Free Will to such an extent that an entire solar system and all its billions of inhabitants had been destroyed, the effects of which had hit both the Alpha Centauri and Earth systems. It was, in reality, ultimately why our A-Cs were here on Earth.

But apparently the Superconsciousnesses Collective didn't want their kind to interfere. This was a confirmation of what ACE had felt and Algar had told me. But it was indeed bad for us and for ACE because ACE had interfered a lot. It was why we were all still alive, and by all I meant every living thing on the planet.

"So, you don't feel that the protection of all life on this planet was a correct thing to do?"

The Water Man shrugged. Not the worst sight in the world, but unsettling. Sloshy was really an apt name for him. "That is not what ACE was created for."

"You didn't create him. The people who did create him did so to make him a living alarm system—to watch and to harm. He chose to change what his purpose was to something better. Why is that wrong to you so-called supercreatures?"

"We are too powerful to interfere."

"Ah, the old 'you'll call us God' argument. Here's the thing—ACE has told those of us who know what he is that he's not God. We believe him. End of problem. Have a great trip home. Don't miss swinging by the Alpha Centauri system and telling them what to do, either. I'm sure they'll love meeting you as much as I have."

"We are not leaving at this time. We have agreed to observe ACE and how ACE interacts with all of you. If we deem that ACE is remaining within our laws, we will allow ACE to remain. If we find otherwise, we will remove ACE from Earth. Forever."

Handed Jamie to Mrs. Maurer, then stepped up to the Water Man and got right in his face. "You'll take ACE from us and against his will over my dead body, Sloshy."

"That can be arranged."

"Yeah? Then you'll be interfering. I guarantee I have someone out there who will be more than capable of pointing that out to your damned Supreme Council or whatever you call yourselves. You want to play hardball? I'm more than game and have only this to say—bring it."

Water Man stared at me for a few long seconds. Then he nodded his head. The water sloshed. It remained unsettling.

"Your challenge is accepted."

Whoops.

CHAPTER 24

THE WATER MAN backed off and dissolved, water flowing back into the fountain as if it had never left. The film-type thing came up from out of nowhere, expanding through us and out again, until it was so far away I couldn't see it.

"Ah, did you intend to challenge . . . whatever that was?" Mrs. Maurer asked, as I watched the sky to see if something nasty was going to come down out of it and attack.

"Sorta. Sorta not. Mister White, your thoughts?"

"I think we had more of an audience for this than you realized."

Turned around to see Jeff, Chuckie, Reader, Gower, Tito, Buchanan, Siler, and Christopher standing behind White and Mrs. Maurer. To a man they looked shocked and rather horrified. Oh good.

Cleared my throat. "Um, you know how I say it's not my fault when this crap happens?" They all nodded. Apparently no one trusted themselves to speak. "Well, this one was. My fault, I mean."

"We heard, girlfriend," Reader said finally. "All of it."

"How long were you there?"

"Nightcrawler can extend his blend by touch just like the rest of them can extend the hyperspeed," Buchanan answered. "So we were here for quite a lot of it."

Now that I looked more closely, Chuckie had his hand on Jeff's neck, which meant he'd been applying his Vulcan

Nerve Pinch to keep Jeff from charging. Kind of wished Chuckie had shown less restraint.

"I know. I screwed up. It's just . . . that entity thing is threatening ACE. And I promised ACE I'd always protect him."

"It's okay, Mommy," Jamie said, as Jeff took her from Mrs. Maurer and Tito started examining his latest patient. "They won't attack right away."

"Well, there's that. I guess."

"I can't express how happy I am that Jamie was involved in this," Jeff said in a tone that indicated quite the opposite.

"That *wasn't* my fault."

"That thing was trying to hurt Mommy," Jamie said reproachfully. "You'd have gone, Daddy. Why shouldn't I?"

"Because you're a little girl," Jeff said. "Mommy and Daddy are supposed to protect *you*, Jamie-Kat."

"I knew what to do," she said stubbornly.

"She did. She dissipated Sloshy."

"I don't want to know. At this moment. I'll want to know later. Right now . . ." Jeff looked around. "Why are we the only people here?"

"We were wondering that ourselves just before Sloshy showed up. No idea, but my bet is that either ACE or Sloshy kept everyone else away somehow."

"Maybe ACE should return to me," Gower said. Jeff nodded and handed Jamie to Gower. Gower was big, bald, black, and beautiful. Like Chuckie, Abigail, and Caroline, though, for the last year what he'd also been was quieter and sadder. Losing your brother, sister, and aunt in less than a week will do that to a person, religious leader of an entire race or not. "That way we can keep you out of the line of fire," he said to Jamie as he gave her a kiss on her head.

She hugged him. "No, Uncle Paul. Fairy Godfather ACE has to stay with me."

"What happened at the embassies?" I asked, before Jeff and Gower could start arguing with her, and in hope of a subject change, at least for a few minutes.

"Someone else planted the bombs Siler didn't," Chuckie said. "Not a bomb signature we recognized, but Vander and

Serene have all the bombs so that's in their court. We've evacuated the Israeli embassy as well, though, just in case."

"Where is everybody staying, then? There's already not enough room at Paul and James' place. Are we all going to Dulce? Where I think ACE was trying to get us to go, by the way."

Reader shook his head. "Paul and Jeff cannot leave D.C. right now, for political reasons. Alpha and Airborne are staying here too, because it's clear that wherever you go, so goes the action, girlfriend."

"I'm sorry I screwed up."

"We'll fix it," Chuckie said, as he rubbed the back of his neck. "Somehow."

"I hope we can get the world governments armed and ready fast," Christopher said. "And not aiming the bombs at each other."

"Maybe we can negotiate a diplomatic solution," Gower said. No one pointedly mentioned that this was actually my job, but their expressions did that for them.

All but Siler. He barked a laugh. "You all seriously think she blew it?"

Everyone looked at him. "Yes," Jeff said. He ran his hand through his hair. "Sorry, baby, but this is worse than when you declared war on the United States, and far less simple to fix."

Siler rolled his eyes. "Come on. I was watching. Nothing shows up like that thing did, ensures that everyone in the world knows something's around, and then hangs out to merely shoot the shit and idly threaten. It was here, testing her to see how she'd react to its threats."

Reader nodded slowly. "Yeah, that makes sense."

"Why am I always the one the intergalactic bullies want to test out?"

"You're a protector," Chuckie said quietly. "You always have been. And that's what it was here to determine, wasn't it? Who was going to stand up for ACE, and were they going to be afraid of something exponentially more powerful than they were, or were they going to go toe-to-toe with the aggressor?"

Siler nodded. "That's what it looked like to me. It wanted

to see if she was going to back down, try to negotiate, or just attack."

"Nightcrawler, I have a name and I'm right here. Call me Kitty, Katherine, Missus Martini, Miss Katt if you just have to fall in line with the rest of the Assassination League, or even Wolverine."

Siler grinned. "Okay, Wolvie. Anyway, I think aggression was actually the right response."

Everyone stared at him, even me. "You mind explaining how you've reached that conclusion?" Christopher asked, speaking for all of us.

"I think I understand," Mrs. Maurer said. "You don't come across a galaxy to just check in on someone, even if it's not a long trip for you. That . . . Sloshy . . . came to check us out. Why? Are more of his kind coming? He was being willfully stupid on purpose, why not be goading you for a reason? Perhaps they want to be able to declare war because you challenged them, but I'm with . . . Nightcrawler, did you say? I think the outcome was exactly what Sloshy wanted."

"Squeaky, I just want to applaud your embrace and acceptance of the nicknames. Welcome to Team Megalomaniac. Speaking of which, where're Megalomaniac Lad and the fly-boys? I'd really like some comic relief right about now."

Reader flashed the cover boy grin. "That's your job, too, girlfriend."

"You're the best at it, though, James."

"Babe, I'm the best at what I do . . . everything I do."

"Hey, that's *my* Wolverine line. You need your own line, Captain America."

"The love in the fountain's great," Jeff said, interrupting our witty repartee. "And even if Siler, Chuck, and Missus Maurer are right, we still have to have a plan of defense or, laughably, attack. Uncle Richard, any ideas?"

"I'm wondering why, if Missus Martini's bravado was taken as a challenge and accepted, the Entity Currently Known as Sloshy backed off."

"Mister White, you're my favorite."

Jeff groaned. Buchanan shook his head. "And I lose favored status just that fast."

"Oh, Malcolm, you're still my favorite, too. But I think Mister White has a point. Why not just do whatever? Why take off to fight another day?"

Chuckie cocked his head. "He who fights and runs away, lives to fight another day. Whatever it was, it wasn't winning against you."

"I honestly don't think Sloshy was trying all that hard."

"I think it might have been," Mrs. Maurer said. "You were involved. We were watching. All of us." She patted Prince's head.

"The animals . . ." Looked around. The Poofs and Peregrines all looked right at me and gave me a full blast of the Sea of Animal Innocence Look. "Oh. Wow. Really?"

"I do think so," White said. "It makes the most sense."

"Really, what?" Jeff asked in that resigned tone he'd perfected by now. "So far, nothing that's happened today makes sense to me, and I include the fact that I'm somehow a vice presidential candidate in that statement."

"I think what Richard and Squeaky are insinuating is that Sloshy didn't go for it because the Poofs and Peregrines were here." And a superconsciousness from the Eagle Nebula would be likely to know that the Peregrines were powerful. Chances were also good that it was aware that the Poofs weren't from around here.

The Water Man might have backed off because of the animals. It also might have backed off because it realized that if the Poofs were here, then Algar was here, and that could offer a unique opportunity for Sloshy to have a chat with the Black Hole People. Even odds for either option. Or both.

Needed to talk to Algar. Oh well, everyone, good or bad, wanted us there anyway. "James, I don't care about the political crap."

"This is news?" Christopher muttered.

Ignored him. "We need to get to Dulce, even if it's just for the night. We have personnel from three very full embassies to house. We can freaking take a gate back if Jeff or Paul are desperately needed, you know, like we used to do all the damn time. I'm making another unpopular decision and saying that we're all going to the Science Center, and we're going there now."

CHAPTER 25

AFTER THE USUAL ARGUMENTS, which I won, and the usual protests, which I ignored, I played the Head Diplomat card yet again, White and Buchanan backed me, and floater gates were provided, for us and everyone else we wanted or needed to house.

Gates were A-C technology that allowed you to travel from one place to another in a matter of seconds. They looked like fancier airport metal detectors that were also doors to nowhere. But they worked like the most amazing and yet nauseating travel system ever.

The gates had been the bane of my existence from day one with Centaurion and nothing—including getting some A-C talents and powers—had changed this. Normally Jeff carried me through a gate transfer. Under the circumstances, however, I decided to tough it out and show whoever and whatever was watching that I could walk through a gate with the best of them.

Fortunately I had just the right amount of food still in my stomach, so I neither tossed cookies nor dry heaved. It's the little victories you cherish.

The Dulce Science Center was the main base for all of Centaurion Division worldwide. It went fifteen stories down and I still wasn't really sure how wide it was. Rather than waste valuable time and mental space on knowing its exact size and layout, I went with the simpler idea that it was probably about the size of five Pentagons and let it go at that. My lack of ability with mazes was, by now, legendary, and I saw no reason to sully that proud reputation.

In my first couple of years with Centaurion Jeff and I had lived on the lowest level, the fifteenth floor, in what I called his Human Lair. It was the only set of rooms in any regular A-C facility that looked like humans had designed it. Not that the A-Cs lived diametrically differently from humans, but they didn't have the same adoration of TVs that humans did, for example, and they tended to go for hotel room-type functionality instead of sloppy hominess.

I still missed the Lair, but I'd gotten used to the Embassy by now. And, due to the fact that a lot of human politicians and the like came into the Embassy regularly, it was far more "human" than the Science Center felt the need to be. The one bright spot I could see so far was that we'd spend tonight in the Lair.

We arrived on what I called the Bat Cave level. It was loaded with computer terminals, screens straight out of *Minority Report*, machines and equipment that, four-plus years in, I still didn't even try to identify, and lots of human and A-C personnel, all beavering away at their assigned tasks. Other than when we'd been infiltrated or had to evacuate for some reason, the Bat Cave always hummed with efficiency.

Field and Imageering Main were also on this level, and Reader trotted off to do the Worldwide Check on the Troops thing. Saw Jeff and Christopher both shoot longing looks toward Reader's retreating backside. Not because they'd turned gay during the trip from D.C. to Dulce, but because they still missed being the Heads of those divisions. I could relate—there were many days, today being Exhibit Number One, when I missed being the Head of Airborne more than I could express.

Speaking of Airborne, Tim and the flyboys were also back with us, which was a relief in a variety of ways. Unsurprisingly, they were all for fighting Sloshy and none of them felt I was a major screwup for basically telling a visiting superconsciousness to suck it. I loved my guys.

"I'm with Kitty," Matt Hughes said, after Christopher had explained why we were, we presumed, screwed.

Chip Walker nodded. "Best defense is a good offense."

"Chip and Matt are my favorites."

Jeff groaned and Jerry Tucker shot me a betrayed look. "Hey, I thought I was your favorite. I think your plan's the right one, too, even if I don't know what it is."

"Well, that's true, you are my favorite, Jerry." This was actually true, but choosing between my favorites was like picking ice cream flavors—they were all great in their own way.

Tim pulled the flyboys and Jeff away before they could continue to discuss my brilliance and love for them. People were milling about, working, doing things, having meetings, but no one was asking for my input. Which was fine, because I'd done enough of that for right now.

In the days before what I called Operation Destruction and the rest of the world called the Terrifying Alien Invasion That Almost Destroyed Us All, we'd have had to either high-security brief, memory wipe, or memory alter everyone who we'd had to bring along.

These days, it was more like they were getting a special private tour. Mossad were certainly treating it that way. There were a ton of Mossad agents who'd been at the Israeli embassy, and, to a one, they were loving being at the Science Center. Oren, Jakob, and Leah, by benefit of being our close friends, were gaining major Envy Points from the rest of their crowd for having been here before.

My parents were here, too. Mom was, of course, discussing strategic military response options to address my latest screwup, but Dad was organizing tours. Dad had far more people clustered around him, therefore, and he was clearly enjoying himself.

Surprisingly, the entire K-9 crew was here, too. Prince was happy to be reunited with Officer Melville, and vice versa, but it was kind of weird to have the police here. However, Reader felt they were targets due to their known association with us, a fact Siler confirmed as I sidled over to where he was, since he was in a part of the Bat Cave that wasn't loaded with people.

Buchanan had uncuffed him, based on Jeff's assurances

that Siler wasn't feeling enemy-like toward any of us. There were a variety of empaths keeping tabs on him, though, Jeremy Barone included. Rahmi and Rhee were also on Siler Duty, and they were, as always, slavishly devoted to their assigned task. However, since I'd asked for a little privacy, they and Jeremy were standing about ten feet away, watching everything Siler did.

However, when a variety of D.C. bigwigs, Senators Armstrong and McMillan included, arrived, along with their spouses and close aides, I had to ask the obvious question. "Are we bringing every single person we know here, or is that just my impression based on seeing every single person I know here?"

"They need to be protected," Siler said.

"Fantastic. My grandparents aren't far away, are they?"

"All family members are with your in-laws, per what I heard. Because they, like the others, need protection. Trust me."

Made sense. Martini Manor was gigantic and could easily handle my extended family. They certainly had before. It was probably another Old Home Week for everyone over there.

"You keep on saying that, and yet I'm not so sure that I should. By the way, do we need to pull my 'uncles' in, too? And I'm asking that seriously." I'd figure out how to keep Mom, Chuckie, Kevin, and everyone else from arresting them. Somehow.

Siler gave me a long look. "You're truly serious."

"Yeah. They protect me. I think, if we're trying to cover everyone who knows and even sort of likes us, that they deserve that protection, too."

"No wonder they care about you." He sounded sincere. He looked sincere, too. And a little wistful.

"Dude, if you're actually our friend and not going to try to blow us all up now that we're all finally herded here like so many lambs to slaughter, then that care and protection extends to you, too, you know."

"No wonder they're afraid of you. Not your uncles—your enemies."

"Since when are our enemies afraid of us?"

"Not 'us.' They're afraid of you, you specifically."

"I discovered I was Evil Genius Enemy Number One when Jamie was born. But I've never noted that any of them are afraid of me."

"Oh, they are. I think the thing you're calling Sloshy is afraid of you, too."

"If you say so, but I don't see it."

"No, you wouldn't."

"Care to explain that?"

"Maybe later. I actually do want to call your uncles. Doubt they'll want to come in, though. Not with what seems like all of Mossad here, not to mention your mother."

"Ask anyway. If they need to hide with the rest of us, then they get neutrality. This is A-C land, not U.S. or Israeli." Technically. I hoped.

Siler gave me a half-smile. "I'll let you know what they want to do." He stepped off to make his call, his guardians following right behind him.

Needed to get out of the crowd and find a laundry hamper. Or at least a private room. Considered going to the second floor, but, frankly, the unused drainage pipe would be the best choice, and the easiest entrance to that was on the fifteenth floor.

"Heading down to check out the Lair," I told Jeff, who was chatting it up with his political allies.

He shot me the hairy eyeball. "Be careful, and don't leave without me."

"Wasn't planning on going anywhere but downstairs to make sure the Lair's all ready for us. Want to be sure the Operations Team have things for Jamie in there, too."

Jeff looked slightly relieved, probably due to the fact that I hadn't said I wanted to see what the Elves were up to in front of a variety of senators and representatives. I knew he couldn't tell what I was feeling—not that I thought there were emotional blockers or overlays around, but because Algar kept anything about himself blocked.

Dad had Jamie, so all was fine there. Everyone else seemed busy. Well and good. Headed to the elevators and down to the fifteenth floor. It was time to try to take a meeting with the King of the Elves.

CHAPTER 26

I COULD NEVER BE IN AN ELEVATOR without thinking of Jeff, particularly an elevator in the Science Center. As always, the damned Evil Genius League was making me try to thwart their convoluted and heinous plans instead of having fantastic sex with my husband. I really hated these people.

Boring, solitary elevator ride over, I exited and headed to the Lair. In addition to other things, this floor was the high-security prisoner holding area. Every prisoner ever held down here that I knew of had escaped somehow, usually via ACE-like means. Or by being let go because someone felt sorry for them. Wondered why the A-Cs had high-security holding cells at all sometimes.

Random thoughts about this floor taken care of, I entered the Lair. It was really one big living room/sitting room/den with a connected master bedroom with bathroom and big walk-in closet. Everything that had been here before was here now.

Went into the closet. Unsurprisingly, we had plenty of clothes in here, for me, Jeff and Jamie. Decided to get out of the Fatigues and into clothes that would allow me to work better.

Jeans, Converse, and my 4th of July Aerosmith shirt on, I felt a lot readier for action. Things were always better with my Bad Boys from Boston on my chest.

"Yo," I said as I dropped my dirty clothes into the hamper, "King of the Elves, we have a situation. I'm sure you're aware of it, but we might want to discuss what's going on, just for fun and all."

Nothing.

Sighed to myself and sat down on the floor. Dug through my purse and pulled out my iPod. Algar enjoyed his jokes, and he liked to leave me musical clues. Plus I hadn't heard any music since we'd gone to the protest, which seemed like forever ago, but was really only several hours ago. But still, that was a long time with no tunes, at least for me.

Sure enough, my iPod was on a playlist I'd never created. "Really? 'Songs in the Key of Flee.' Cute. So does that mean you've done a runner, you think we should do a runner, or someone else is doing a runner? Or are you just, as you always are, being a galaxy-class jerk? You know I'm going to go into the pipe and visit the reclamation plant where you live if you don't show up, right?"

Nothing. Really hoped this wasn't Algar's Goodbye and Good Luck message. Put in my earbuds and took a listen. First song was "Elevator" by Flo Rida and Timbaland. I normally thought of this song the same way I thought of "Love in an Elevator" by Aerosmith—a song about having sex with Jeff in one of my favorite places to have sex.

"I don't want to reaffirm life by doing the deed right now. Well, I tell a lie. I'd love nothing more than to go have lots of great sex with Jeff right now. Thing is, we have a Science Center chock full of people, a lot of scary crap going on, and I need to beg you for a clue much more than I need to remind myself why it's great to be Jeff's woman. Or do you just want to watch the Elevator Porn Channel right now?"

Scrolled down. Huh. "Elevator" was repeated over and over again. Clearly, Algar wanted a word in a specific location, and this one wasn't it.

Never let it be said I couldn't take a huge hint. Got up and trotted right back to the elevators. Got in and took a look at the buttons. "Reclamation" was a selection. This wasn't a button available normally—and unless it had been added by the A-Cs in the ten minutes between my exiting and returning to this elevator, Algar was enjoying himself.

Pushed the button, felt the gentle Time Warp feeling of a non-gate-transfer, and the doors opened to show a big room with three large water tanks in it. They were all connected with pipes and metal walkways. It looked almost legitimate, like there really was a reclamation plant inside the Science Center. Only it didn't smell, at all, of anything, and the water in all three tanks was pristine—I knew this for fact, since I'd gone swimming in one of them. From the bottom up.

Stepped out onto a metal catwalk and took a look around. The elevator doors were gone. I knew they'd never really been there. Algar used this area to do his Black Hole Operations Magic, and considering he'd made it so that no one had noticed that a pipe that started on ground level and ended up fourteen or fifteen stories lower never, ever slanted downward, among other things, his making me think I'd taken a weird elevator ride was pretty much nothing.

I'd only been here a couple of times, and both of them were surprises for Algar. So I'd seen some things I knew he hadn't really wanted me to see. Proof of this was that this time, I didn't see either the pile of glittering Z'Porrah power cubes nor his unmade bed and other personal items. The room was pristine and almost sparkling.

"Expecting an inspection?" I asked the nobody who was here.

"Same as you are," Algar said from behind me.

I jumped and spun around. Managed not to scream, but only just. "You just live to make an entrance."

He shrugged. "It keeps things from getting dull."

Algar was a dwarf by human standards. What he was by Black Hole Universe standards I didn't know. But by my standards he was indeed rakishly handsome, with tousled, dark wavy hair and eyes that were the real clue to him not being from around here—they were an unnaturally bright green.

I figured he'd liked hanging around the A-Cs, and humans even more, because he could blend in here. All it would take was a pair of colored contacts and he could walk down any city street anywhere on Earth. I often figured that he did.

"Speaking of blending, was all this to ensure that Siler couldn't use his chameleon powers to follow me and find out about you?"

Algar's lips twitched. "Do you seriously think I couldn't block him?"

"I seriously know I've surprised you by showing up here unannounced. Therefore, if I can do it, someone else can do it, too. Potentially using one of the Lost Power Cubes."

"You haven't found the one in Gaultier yet."

"No, we haven't. The one that was in the Underground Cloning Facility O' Horror is long gone, however. Unless you had the Poofs get it somehow. Oh, Harlie, Poofikins, come to Kitty."

The Poofs appeared out of nowhere, purred at me, then saw Algar, gave mews of joy, and bounded to him. He petted them and their purrs became quite loud. "No, that one is still buried. It's unlikely to be found."

"Unlikely doesn't mean impossible, does it? You should visit Tenley. I'm sure it misses you." Tenley was the Head Poof on Alpha Four. I was fairly certain Tenley and Harlie had been the original Poofs Algar had brought with him from the Black Hole Universe.

"I wasn't under the impression you wanted to talk about the Poofs," Algar said, as he sat down, cross-legged, on the catwalk we were both on, Poofs in his lap. "But to reassure you just a little, I have a blocker up against the one, and it really is only one, missing power cube. No one can enter any A-C base or facility using that particular power cube."

"Well, that's a comfort." And it explained why the Yates-Mephistopheles in-control superbeing hadn't taken over before I was born. Only not quite. "How long has that been in effect?"

Algar rolled his eyes. "Before you all discovered the cubes, I knew about them. The main bases and the Dome were all blocked from power cube entrance by me. As the Poofs found the others, there was no reason to continue to keep them from fully functioning."

"What about the one Terry gave to Jeff and Christopher?" Terry was Christopher's late mother. She'd found and programmed a cube right before she died. Well, right before Yates and/or Mephistopheles had infected her with something that killed her.

"That one also. It wasn't in my best interests for someone to be able to just show up at the Science Center using a power cube."

"Uh, I did."

He grinned. "That you did, lassie. That you did."

Any time Algar used his fake Irish accent, I knew he wanted at least a minor subject change and for me to also spend some time thinking about whatever it was we'd been talking about. "So there's really only one power cube not accounted for?"

"Yes, really only one unaccounted for. The one you've had a year to find and yet haven't. That one unaccounted for power cube."

We had a power cube in the Embassy, in the isolation bedroom that was attached to our suite, as a matter of fact. "Including the one in our Embassy that's had a bunch of strangers in it thanks to our being evacuated to escape from poisonous gas?"

"The one in the Embassy is safe. I altered it. Just a little. Differently from how I altered the one that you haven't found yet."

Thought about it. "Oh. Has to be used by me or by someone friendly to me, doesn't it?"

"It's always gratifying when you prove you're smarter than the average ape."

"Thanks ever. So, why do you care so very much about this one last cube?"

He sighed. "Because it's the one thing that truly allows your enemies their biggest advantage over you, whether you realize it or not."

CHAPTER 27

"**WELL, THANKS FOR THAT.** I know it's powerful and important, we all do. And we've looked for it."

Algar shook his head. "Not hard enough."

"We've had a lot going on, in case you didn't notice."

"I noticed. I told you you'd hurt your enemies badly. You were supposed to spend the time gaining an advantage."

"Well, we've done our best, Headmaster Elf. We can't just snap our fingers and have it all work out, however. We lost all our data, meaning we've had to focus most resources on re-creating what we can, finding what we can, and coming up with new things. While also, you know, trying to decipher the Cloning Code Books."

"That's your father's area."

"Oh my God, are you complaining that my father isn't doing this fast enough? He may still be on sabbatical, but he's got other things he has to do for NASA, you know."

"Not impugning his reputation."

"Just mine, got it. Amy's been blocked from taking over Gaultier Enterprises at every turn, meaning our access has been extremely limited. Even with that, Chuckie, Vander, and Cliff each did an official search, with a warrant, and a zillion agents each. They all found exactly nada that resembled a power cube. They didn't find much else unsavory, either."

"I didn't tell you to look only in one place."

"You didn't tell us to look at all. We did that using our

own free will and such, which should make you all kinds of happy."

"What did you find other than the power cube?"

"I know you know, but I'll humor you. We found exactly nothing untoward. Amy thinks that our commando raid on the cloning and drug-making facility alerted the Gaultier Board and they've moved all the questionable stuff elsewhere. Chuckie agrees and also feels that the power cube isn't in the Gaultier Research facility in this area and potentially never was. He thinks it's probably in Europe somewhere, most likely with all the rest of the badness Gaultier was working on."

"You should listen to him more often. He's only wrong about a couple of things."

"I listen to him all the time. And I know, he was wrong about where Hoffa was buried."

Algar nodded. "That's one thing. The other thing he's wrong on is much more important, though."

"You going to tell me what that is?"

"What do you think?"

"Yes?" Hey, you couldn't blame a girl for trying.

"No."

"Figures. You willing to tell me if the power cube in my Embassy is still there and still safe?"

"Yes."

"So, is that you saying you're willing or you saying it's safe?"

"Yes."

"I hate you."

"So you claim. I thought you were here for something other than discussing the power cubes and what you haven't done to find the one that allows your enemy to go almost anywhere in the world without issue."

Sat down next to him. "No, you're right. And I'm *so* sorry. I may have mentioned that we've been trying to recreate all our data? And also somehow protect the data we still have and are re-creating from people more tech savvy than our top computer personnel, who, until last year, were considered top in the entire world? And, while we're not doing much on those fronts, we're also working to find all the missing Yates Offspring. Oh, and trying to keep all the various protestors and alien haters off our backs. Plus, you know, do our regular jobs that everyone still expects to be done to the utmost of our abilities."

"So, you haven't been focused on the thing that really matters."

"Seriously? The missing power cube is your damage? Dude, *you* have the ability to freaking find it or tell me where the hell it is. If you can block it so that no one using it can get into an A-C base or facility, then you can certainly fetch it or have the Poofs fetch it. Utilize your free will and do me a solid."

"I can't. Not in this case."

Stifled a groan and the urge to hit him. "You mean you won't. Fine. Then let's get to what I'm currently seeing as the big problems. I want to discuss everything that's going on and everything that's coming."

He laughed. "That's a lot of things. You won't live long enough to talk about everything that's going on and coming."

"Oh, you're pulling the old Must Be Literal ploy? Fine. I'd like to know what we're going to do about ACE's parole officer, the Being Currently Known as Sloshy."

"I don't plan to do anything about the situation. It's not my bailiwick."

"Seriously? You're not planning on fleeing?" Held out my iPod.

He didn't look at it. He also didn't reply. Thought about the lyrics to the only song that was currently on this particular playlist, over and over again. "I'm not going with you, if that's what you're suggesting. Unless you're taking all of us, and by 'all' I mean all the residents of the planet."

"No, I couldn't do that." He sighed. "You'd be better off somewhere else."

"Yeah? Why is that all of a sudden?"

"Because you challenged an entity so powerful I'm not sure your brain can grasp it."

"Oh, blah, blah, blah. I can grasp how powerful you are. I know how powerful ACE is. I can make an educated guess.

And before you say it, yes, yes, we puny humans have no real concept of everyone else's incredible cosmic powers. But to continue to quote the Genie from *Aladdin* . . . you're still kind of stuck in an itty bitty living space, cosmos-wise."

Algar laughed. "True enough. But to reassure you, because that's what you really want, I'm not planning on leaving. At the moment anyway."

"I really want so many things, but yes, that was one of them. Is the issue with ACE going to attract the beings after you?"

"Potentially. But since I don't plan on being actively involved, it shouldn't create undue attention."

"We need you to be involved."

"Didn't we have the Great God Algar discussion when we first officially met?"

"Yes, we did. Didn't we have the whole With Great Power Comes Great Responsibility chat, too?"

"Yes. Free will. It's important to me."

"And to us, too. Not losing one of our two real protectors is important to everyone."

"Most don't really know what ACE does or doesn't do here, and literally only a handful know what I do here. No loss if we leave."

"Oh please, pull the other one, it has bells on. It doesn't matter if an ant understands what the sun does—but if the sun is taken away, the ant will die."

"Interesting analogy."

"I'm clear on how all you Super Special Advanced Beings think of us."

"Oh, I see you as Naked Apes."

"Yeah." Wondered if this was a clue. "Think I should contact the Planetary council and ask them for help?"

"I'll give you one for free. No. They have their own problems right now."

"Fantastic." So much for our outer-space allies. "You want me to let Sloshy take ACE away, don't you?"

"Doesn't matter to me."

"You're lying. With ACE gone you'll lose superconsciousness scrutiny of this planet. At least, so you think. But

I think they'll just send someone else, someone who won't actually care about us like ACE does."

"Immortality is a lot of dullness interspersed with extreme excitement. This is an extreme excitement moment. I'm enjoying it."

"I'm not. ACE is in my daughter. That means my daughter is in danger. And if ACE leaves my daughter, she's in more danger. And if the Superconsciousness Council tries to take my daughter with them and ACE, I'm going to find out how to destroy the entire universe to get her back. That exciting enough for you?"

Algar stared at me for a few long moments. "You're scared."

"I'm neither suicidal nor moronic, so, hell yeah, of course I'm scared."

"And yet, you're not capitulating to the superior being. Instead, you challenged it."

"Yes. As has been pointed out, not my most shining moment."

Algar gently put the Poofs into my lap, stood up, and patted my head, rather lovingly, all things considered. "No. I consider it your most shining moment to date."

Then he snapped his fingers.

CHAPTER 28

I WAS BACK IN THE LAIR, sitting on the bed, Poofs still in my lap. "Huh. As usual, not really getting the answers or help I was hoping for. Algar bats a thousand again."

The Poofs looked up at me expectantly. Then they both hopped off my lap and curled up on the pillows, still giving me expectant looks.

"You think now's a time to nap?"

Got a look from the Poofs indicating that they were concerned I'd hit my head somewhere along the way.

"Oh. Time to try to go to sleep and maybe talk to ACE. I knew that."

Received looks that clearly said they hadn't fallen for my lame excuse and I could stop pretending I hadn't been totally clueless.

"Fine, fine. It's been a hell of a stressful day so far, I see I'm forced to mention. I'm also forced to mention that, stressful or not, I'm not all that tired."

The Poofs indicated that this was too bad, and yet, they also didn't care—it was time to nap. Always the way.

Figured some music could help. Unfortunately, I didn't have a Music To Bore Myself To Sleep By playlist, or anything by Jack Johnson. I tended not to have boring music. Considered the myriad choices on my iPod. Jewel was always an option, but I just wasn't in the mood. Decided to randomly spin the dial. Ended up on Foster the People's

Torches album. As good a choice as any other. Put the iPod into the nice docking station we had in here and turned it on low.

As "Helena Beat" started, I lay down and the Poofs snuggled up into either side of my neck. My neck was my main erogenous zone, but thankfully whenever Jamie and the pets snuggled there, it was just nice, not arousing. Jeff was probably even happier about this than I was.

The Poofs started purring, which was always nice and relaxing. Took a deep breath and closed my eyes. Normally it took exhaustion or a number of great orgasms provided by Jeff for me to fall instantly asleep. However, either Algar or the Poofs, or maybe even ACE, were assisting, because I could feel myself slipping into sleep.

Half expected my "favorite" dream, where I was in front of a congressional hearing and screwing up. But someone decided to be kind. In a sense.

I was in a gray, formless mass. I'd seen this when Michael and Fuzzball had visited me in my sleep. Had no idea if this was a real place, or just what those in charge of my subconscious—which, in these cases, I never truly felt was me—wanted me to see. Why anyone would want me to see gray nothingness was beyond me, but why ask why?

Looked around. I wasn't alone. Sadly, neither Michael nor Fuzzball were in evidence. Neither was anyone else I wanted to see.

No, I was hanging out in the gray nothing with none other than Mr. Supreme Evil, Mephistopheles, as he'd been in superbeing form—big, blood-red, and seriously fugly.

Mephistopheles looked like a giant faun—sorta humanish on the top half, goat-like for the bottom parts. His arms were human-like, but his fingers ended in claws. The curling horns coming out of his forehead, his huge bat-wings, and the hair on his lower body were also blood-red. You had to give it to him—he had a theme, and he stuck to it.

"Are you kidding me? This is what I went to sleep for? Nightmares?"

Mephistopheles stared at me. "You. Why are you here?"

"Got me, Mephs. I was pretty much about to ask you the

same thing. This is my dream, though, so I think you must be here because I'm stressed out about your offspring. Or something like that."

"You were to create my offspring."

"Oh, good point." Right. There were no reproductive organs on any of the in-control superbeings I'd ever seen. "Fine, Ronald Yates' offspring, then. He's a part of you."

Mephistopheles shook his head. "No. I allowed him to die. He died separately from me. We are not bound in the . . . ," he looked around, ". . . afterlife?"

"You're asking me? Seriously? I have no idea what's going on. I took a nap in the hopes that my daughter was also napping so I could talk to ACE and see if I could get even the slightest clue about all the bad that's coming down on us. You were not in my expected equation." Thought about this question. "But, barring someone having gotten poisoned gas into the Science Center, I'm not dead."

"I am." He didn't sound angry, or sad, just matter-of-fact.

"Yeah, you are. We killed you. You were one hard parasite to kill, I might add."

He nodded. "I remember." He sat down on the gray nothing. "What can I assist you with?"

"Um . . . you're offering to help me?"

"I believe I am here to help you, yes."

"Why? We were enemies."

"No. I wanted to join with you. We were adversaries, yes, but not enemies."

"I remember it differently."

"I'm sure you do. However, I know I'm dead. And you are not. So, we are together here for a reason."

"Why you, versus Ronald Yates?"

"Perhaps because what I know is of more use to you than what he might know."

My brain decided to join the party. Algar had watched over the solar system Mephistopheles had ultimately destroyed. Ergo, Algar knew Mephistopheles, and Mephistopheles might know Algar, as well. But that relationship wasn't what I needed confirmed.

The question was, who'd "brought" Mephistopheles

here—Algar or ACE? Then again, it might not matter. If I was talking to Mephistopheles, I wasn't talking to either one of them, meaning the other Busybody Powers That Be couldn't really say they were interfering, or not interfering, depending on their particular slavish devotion.

So, what could I ask of Mephistopheles that would be relevant to what was going on? Had no clue. Decided I'd just start randomly asking things that I'd wondered about and see where it led me. Or, as I liked to think of it, routine.

"Why did you blow up your own sun? In your original solar system, I mean."

"My people were not . . . behaving as I wanted them to. I threatened them with destruction. They didn't believe I'd destroy us all if my demands were not met. But I did. I knew we would go on, and would find other worlds to conquer."

"Yeah. That didn't really work out like you'd planned."

He shrugged. "Those are the risks of power, and power plays."

"True enough. Speaking of risks, your people were used as cannon fodder by the Z'Porrah, when they attacked Earth."

His eyes narrowed. "Are they still here, the Z'Porrah?"

"No. We ran them off. With help. But still, off."

"Good. So, who opposes you now?"

"Many people and things. My husband, your sort of grandson, is somehow running for vice president of the U.S. and the people on the other ticket are nasty haters. You'd love them. I have some powerful gossip columnist after me. I'm worried that the campaign or the gossip monger are going to reveal things, like us killing you."

"None of your people would care that you killed me. You would be considered heroic. However, killing my counterpart, Yates, that will create problems. And all the other humans you've had to kill over these past years as well."

"Yeah, exactly. We also need to find all of Ronnie's Kids, as well as figure out what all our other enemies are planning. But that's business as usual for us."

"Why do you care about finding Yates' offspring?"

"They're all hella powerful in some way. Well, most of them. Depends on their mothers, really. And we're pretty sure there are a lot of them. We need to see if we can get any of them onto the side of good. We were able to flip Mahin. And for all I know, we may flip Nightcrawler, too. Or at least keep him in the neutral zone. But there are others, and if we can find them, we have a hope of showing them the right path, sort of thing."

"They are not powerful because of me."

"You're sure? You combining with him didn't alter his genetics?"

"It did. But his genes, his power, is what was passed on, not mine."

"That doesn't sound possible."

Received the "really?" look. Nice to know even the big fugly monster could shoot that one on me. "Many things that are real don't seem possible to small minds. No offence meant."

"Oh, none freaking taken. I don't get it, and you can break down and explain for my tiny mind."

"Touchy. My powers cannot be passed along in the way all of you reproduce. In order to share myself, I must become a part of you."

"So, you 'are' the parasite? All the rest is just your . . . window dressing?"

"Yes, in essence. In the same way that you are not the bag of skin and bones you present, but instead infuse the skin and bones with your essence."

The parasites were their souls. I'd pretty much always figured this, but it was sort of sad to know that we'd destroyed Mephistopheles' people completely.

He seemed to know what I was thinking and shook his head. "Death is not the end. It is also not what we are discussing. We are discussing life."

"True enough. But if you combined and altered Yates, I don't see how that doesn't alter him all the way around."

"Possibly because our genetics cannot pass along in the way yours do and his did. I could not have mated with you as you did with your husband, or as Yates did with many women. We do not reproduce in the same way. By successfully combining with him, I altered Yates, but I could not alter the genetics he would pass along. Think of me as being a separate, yet fully integrated, part. When he mated I was not with him, in that sense. I was there, in my dormant state. But I was not mingled. We only combine when we are in our natural forms."

"By natural you mean the forms like this one, what you were on your home world?"

"Yes. So the power would come from him. In these instances."

"That makes sense I guess. Richard and Lucinda have no powers, but that just means their mother was a weak link. Gladys was incredibly powerful, and she was born well before Yates was exiled to Earth. He was what we call a sport, in our form of genetics. Is that why Tito can't make more progress on the Yates Gene Research he's been doing? And why our enemies haven't, either, at least to our knowledge?"

"Yes. Yates' genes were exceptional. It was why he and I could combine and survive." He eyed me. "Yates was not the only one with exceptional genes."

"Yeah, I'm sure Jeff and Christopher are loaded with exceptional. Nightcrawler, too, or he'd be dead."

"More than them. But you should focus on the most urgent problem. Is finding these offspring the most urgent?"

"No, I guess not. At least my mom doesn't think so. I guess the biggest problem, really, is the superconsciousness from the Eagle Nebula, named Sloshy."

"Named that by you?"

"How'd you guess?"

"It rings of you. And I assume 'Nightcrawler' has another name. I doubt his mother gave him that one."

"Wow, even dead beings of my nightmares have sarcasm knobs. I'm just that kind of lucky. Nightcrawler is Benjamin, the son of Yates and Madeleine Cartwright, when she was still Siler. Why are you here, really? Just missed having someone to be sarcastic at?"

He rolled his eyes. It was icky. Shocker. "These are your questions?"

"Blah, blah, blah. It's not like I was prepared to see you, you know. We weren't prepared for any of this."

"Yes. And that is a problem. By now, vigilance should be your watchword."

"You know, it's funny, it *is*. And yet, since we don't have insights into our enemies' many plans and schemes, nor do we possess a bunch of telepaths, we're constantly surprised. Just keeps life interesting. Anyway, how do we get rid of Sloshy, without him/her/it taking ACE away? And without hurting my daughter? And the various consciousnesses ACE has joined in over the years?"

"Why does it matter if ACE leaves your world?"

"Aside from the fact that ACE protects us and he's residing inside my daughter? I promised him I'd protect him. I can't do that if I allow something to take him away against his will. I'm sure you don't need to ask me why I don't want my daughter hurt in any way. Or why I don't want to lose those who ACE joined in, either."

"No, I understand. You challenged the entity." A statement, not a question.

"Yeah, I did. Someone you know seems to think it was a great plan. No one else does."

Mephistopheles mouth moved in a way that, charitably, might be called a smile. "You are good at that. You challenge those who are far stronger and more powerful than you are." He reached out. Managed not to cringe—it was a dream, meaning he couldn't actually hurt me.

And he didn't. He, like Algar before him, patted my head. Gently. "You protect the weak and helpless, but you also protect the protectors. We have a name for that, where I come from. It isn't pronounceable in your language. And it doesn't translate well, either, beyond what I've just said. But it is a name of great honor."

"Was it a name you had, before you lost it and killed everyone?"

He nodded and stood up. "It was. Sometimes I . . . miss that name. I have to go."

"I don't get to know the name or the word or whatever?"

"No."

"And you're leaving? I don't know what to do. Or what's going on. Or anything, really, including why I bothered to nap."

He shrugged. "Perhaps it will make sense to you once you wake up. Or not. That's not my problem." He turned to go.

"Hey, do you happen to know who your Apprentice's Apprentice would be?"

Mephistopheles turned back and cocked his head. "No. That was something Yates did. I did not . . . pay attention to it."

"Now I know you're lying. You were intimately involved in all that Mastermind and Apprentice crap."

"No. I had my own plans of conquest, and he had his. At the start, they did not intersect. As he aged, and his illness spread, I was able to take more control. His plans for his children were not aligned with mine. And mine were the only plans I cared about. His plans were small. I would have conquered the world. But for you."

"Yeah, I get that a lot. So you don't know who his Apprentice was?"

"It was who you think—Leventhal Reid."

"Who was Reid grooming as his ultimate Apprentice, any idea?"

Mephistopheles nodded. "The one you are not suspecting." Then he gave me another shot of what passed for his smile and faded away.

CHAPTER 29

WOKE UP AS **"PUMPED UP KICKS"** started playing. Either I'd slept through the entire *Torches* album and it was going around again, or ACE, Algar, or, somehow, Mephistopheles had ensured that I got all the information I needed in less than one song. Based on the way things were going, bet on the latter.

Not that I felt I'd gotten much in the way of actual information. But perhaps the secret meanings would become clear to me somewhere along the line.

Sat up and looked around. Sure, it had been less than five minutes, but now, I wasn't in the room with just the two Poofs. What looked like every animal we had and then some were in here, too. Including my least favorite avian in the galaxy.

"Kitty! Kitty! Kitty!" Sure enough, Bellie, the Parrot O' Love, was also with us. Well, at least she sounded happy to see me, as opposed to ready to kill me. Put that one into the win column, in part because there was just so little *in* the win column right now.

"Seriously? You're all here? Bellie, too? Why isn't Bellie with Mister?"

"Mister says Bellie has to be safe! Bellie loves Mister! Bellie loves Jeff!"

"Yeah, I know." Jeff was, sadly, going to be overjoyed that this bird was with us. So much for all those happy thoughts of sexy times. I was never having sex with Bellie in the room, or even within hearing distance. Figured if Bellie could imitate me during sex, Jeff might seriously leave me for her.

Wondered if Oliver had sent Bellie down here to ensure that Siler didn't see her. Sure, he hadn't been privy to our conversations, but Oliver had his ways.

Of course, according to everyone else, so did the Tastemaker. Wondered when Jenkins would call me again, then knew it would be soon, and when it was just totally inconvenient. Readied myself for his call to come in at any minute.

Of course, if the animals were in here right when Algar put me here, I had to figure he'd sent or put the animals in here, too. So, maybe it was time to stop being Megalomaniac Girl or The Dream Chatter and switch back to Dr. Doolittle.

"Everyone, Kitty would like a word."

"Word! Word! Word!"

"Yes, thanks Bellie. I think we're called to order now."

"Called to order! Called to order!"

"Bellie? Shut it or become dinner. You choose."

Had to give her this, Bellie was one damned smart parrot. She shut up.

"Good job. Now, speaking of jobs, Kitty has the teensiest feeling that some of you were either not doing your jobs, or were doing jobs that someone else, mainly He Who Is Supposedly Too Awesome To Be Named, has given you. Who's going to fess up first?"

Lots of shots of the Sea of Animal Innocence look, even from the K-9 dogs. No one offered any answers, and they were all doing the thing where I couldn't figure out what they were thinking.

Gave up. "Bellie, back to you as Spokesbird. Tell me both what I want and what I need to know."

"Vance! Vance! Bellie loves Vance!"

"This is your big reveal?"

"Hey, Kitty, you in here?" Vance called from the entryway.

"Aha. Okay, Bellie, all is, sort of, forgiven. Back here!" I shouted.

Vance picked his way through all the many pets. Bellie

flew to him, squawking happily. She settled on his forearm, the better for his other hand to be able to stroke her head. "Wow, are you running a grooming business on the side?"

"Hilarious. Take the parrot with you when you go. But before you go, what's up?"

He shrugged and sat on the side of the bed. "Everyone's doing officially important things. However, since I'm not Mossad or a political bigwig, I couldn't go along on one of the guided tours. Meaning I could help babysit the kids, or find you and go over theories. Chose you. Be flattered."

"Totally am." Sort of. Though honesty forced me to admit that on at least two occasions Vance had called what was going on correctly, and in a big way. Perhaps he could do so now. "What do you think is going on?"

"You mean that I know about and can comprehend?"

"What else could I mean?"

"There are things going on I don't know about. You could catch me up to speed on them, and then I could give you theories."

"Nice try. Why don't you give me your theories for what you know about? You may know more than I do, after all."

"About the Tastemaker, yes, I obviously do. But he may not be your only problem."

"He's a problem I'm not prepared to handle. So, let's tackle him first."

"I would but he's straight. And, frankly, the pickings in and around your diplomatic mission are always of a finer quality."

"We're flattered. Sort of. Okay, so Bruce Jenkins is straight. Lots of people are. So what?"

Vance sighed. "If you want to know how to defend against someone, it helps if you know how they tick. He's straight, unmarried, not dating anyone seriously, no children, no pets. And while he could go after anyone in town, he picks his targets carefully."

"Why is he so powerful and yet Mister Joel Oliver had to have an alien invasion happen to get a modicum of respect?"

"As you were told earlier, it's because Jenkins deals with salacious gossip."

"So, when Esteban Cantu was trying to blackmail me, and Senator Armstrong, with dirty pictures of me and Chuckie and then me and the good Senator, why were those sent to MJO instead of Jenkins?"

Vance looked thoughtful. "You want my gut feeling?"

"Sure. I go with my gut all the time."

"Yeah, I know. I've climbed around on the rooftops with you, if you'd care to remember. I still have nightmares about that."

"Did you come to whine or are you going to share your gut's thoughts on my question?"

"Oh, fine. I think the pictures were sent to the *World Weekly News* because it was presumed they'd print them. In addition to everything else, it would have driven a wedge between you and Mister Joel Oliver, and even more so between him and Mister Reynolds. Plus, why get Jenkins involved if we were going to be bowing to our new alien overlords within a few days anyway?"

"Yeah, I can buy that one. So, why sic him on me now? Why not earlier? Why at all? But mostly, why now? We're clearly in the midst of another attack from one or more of our enemies, but that happens regularly. So why did Bruce Jenkins call me today?"

"When probably matters, too. He called you after the bombs had gone off."

"Meaning after our embassy had been gassed. I need to ask Nightcrawler about that."

"I'm not even going to ask who the hell that is. One weird thing going on around you at a time."

"If it was only one thing. So, back to the big question—why sic Bruce Jenkins on me at all, let alone right now?"

"It seems obvious."

"Not to me."

Vance sighed again. "Two reasons. The first is even more obvious than the second, so let me share that one. Listen, I'll speak slowly."

"I'm pretending to listen but actually ignoring you."

"Trust me, it seems that way. Frequently. But reason number one is that your husband was just announced as the most likely vice presidential candidate. Jenkins called within minutes, possibly within seconds, of that being mentioned on the news."

"Oh. Yeah. I knew that. Right. Okay, I'll give you the 'duh' on that one." Maybe I should have really tried to actually nap. I was slipping, because I'd made this assumption earlier and had, literally, forgotten. Sloshy had sort of thrown off my groove.

"Especially since Jenkins ran off Vincent's last two most promising running mates. The wrong VP candidate can destroy a ticket, but Jenkins has been getting rid of people who would have made good leaders for the country."

"He hasn't gone after Senator Armstrong?"

"He's tried, but it's easier to screw up the VP candidate. Seems less like campaign interference."

"I suppose, and before you whine, I'll trust that you know this landscape a lot better than I do. So, what's behind Door Number Two?"

"Again, this seems obvious. He called when he called because Bruce Jenkins is on your enemies' payroll, and nothing distracts a person like being hounded by the Tastemaker."

CHAPTER 30

"YOU THINK THEY WANT Jeff distracted?"

Vance rolled his eyes. "I don't play stupid with the people who actually know I'm not a moron. You can return the favor and stop playing stupid with me when we're alone. I thought you trusted me."

"I do." Somewhat. Well, all things considered, more than a lot of people. "And, dude, I'm not intentionally playing stupid. I'm just sort of overwhelmed right now."

"Yeah, and that's what I meant. They haven't sent Jenkins after your husband as much as they've sent him after *you*. You're the one they want distracted. And before you try to pooh-pooh that idea, I've seen you in action enough now that it's clear that you've got to be high up on your enemies' hit list. In fact, my guess is that you're their number one target."

This was true, but something I didn't think any of us had ever mentioned in front of Vance. Might not be remembering it—the way the day had gone and these last few minutes had proved, we might have said it in front of him an hour ago and I just didn't recall—but if we hadn't, he'd made this leap correctly by merely looking at things mostly from the out-side. Hopefully he'd made other leaps that were correct and could help.

"Okay, so I ignore Jenkins and that solves that problem, right?" I asked with probably far too much hopefulness.

Sure enough, Vance gave me a look that could only be

described as snide. "Oh, of course. Because that will solve everything *and* insure that Bruce Jenkins instantly loses interest and stops sniffing around. Totally going to happen. Let's just go shopping and not worry about anything, problem's completely solved."

"Wow. I think that, on a scale of ten, your sarcasm knob was turned to about twenty."

"Good. Means I'm getting through. No, you can't ignore Jenkins. Sorry. You have to deal with him."

"If only I knew how. You know, I didn't actually see this one coming, God alone knows why."

"I'll second that. But you didn't see it coming because you don't read the papers and you had no idea who he is. And before you try to lie and say you stay up on things, Pierre confirmed that, the few times you pick up a newspaper, you only look at the funnies and the sports sections."

"Not my fault newsprint is dead."

"Right. So, anyway, for most people in this town, the Tastemaker calling them would be cause for panic. For you, it was an opportunity for you practice your on-the-fly sarcastic comebacks."

"As if you're not making sarcasm an art form?"

"Did I sound disapproving? But that just proves you have a lot more potential for disaster than your husband would, and that's not actually meant as an insult."

"It's true, too. You know, we were both in military positions before being moved into the diplomatic mission. What are the chances that anything we did that might be considered an, ah, impropriety will be brushed aside as part of our military duty, let alone part of our time in covert and clandestine ops?"

Vance shrugged. "If they're for you? You're patriotic heroes protecting the world. If they're against you, you're psychopathic killers on the loose and no one's safe while you're around."

Mephistopheles had essentially said the same thing. Couldn't wait to tell Jeff about my dream. Maybe I'd save it for a time when he was feeling relaxed, just for maximum effect. "I can guess which way Jenkins is going to go, then."

"Yeah. It's the same way the Kramers have gone. I don't know if you ever thought of Marcia as your friend, but she and Zachary both have come out for Cleary-Maurer."

"I never could stand her, so no loss. And no surprise, either. That's got to suck for you guys and Nathalie, though. You were all close."

"Whatever. This is politics—things change all the time. They couldn't swing with the new world order, so they're going to fight it. Just know, and be sure Jeff knows, that they're not your friends."

"I'm sure Jeff knows already." Barring Kramer wearing an emotional overlay or blocker, always a possibility, Jeff would have picked up the animosity ages ago. The Kramers not becoming cronies wasn't a surprise. That we were friends with anyone from my Washington Wife class at all was the shocker. "So, I guess no help with Jenkins from that side, though. Any other political way to affect him?"

"Not really, no. He has everyone running scared. I'd normally suggest bribery, but I've got to figure that your enemies have more money than you and have offered him as much as he wants to get you, so that option's out."

"So's killing him, right?"

"Only because it's now going to be known that he's after you, and if he dies right after trying to speak to you I think it'll be suspicious."

"I was kind of joking. You'd be okay with us killing him?"

He shrugged again. "He's not my friend. He's trying to hurt people I consider my friends. However, it's not an option, so the moral quandary is over. No, what we need to have is a plan of attack to circumvent him, give him just enough right information that we can make him believe the wrong information, and figure out how to keep him more distracted by you than you are by him."

"Piece of cake. If only we had cake." Now I wanted cake. Fought back the overwhelming desire to ask the King of the Elves for a cupcake or two.

Vance shook his head. "You don't have to come up with this. You have people for that. I'll handle it, with Pierre and Raj. They both run interference for you already. I'll go over the game plan with them and we'll get you set up—before Jenkins catches you."

"Really? You'd do that for me?"

Vance gave me a funny look. "Yeah. You're my friend. Wouldn't you help your friend out?"

"Yeah, I would, and I do. I just . . ." Reached over and took his hand. "I just don't take it for granted. Thank you."

He squeezed my hand. "I know we haven't been friends as long as you have been with a lot of these other people. But you made sure that all the mess created by Lydia Montgomery didn't blow back on Guy. Even if we hadn't been friends before then, we'd have been your lifelong friends afterward."

"Good to know."

He grinned. "I know you don't like Lillian all that much, but she respects you, and she wants to stay on your good side. Not sure how much help she can be, but I'd be willing to bet she'll help as much as she's able to."

"She lobbies for some of our biggest enemies."

"There's lobbying and then there's being in someone's pocket. She knows Titan's against you guys. You've proved which side is the one more likely to win in a fight—she'll drop Titan before she drops American Centaurion."

This was news. Hopefully good news, too, but wasn't sure if I should count on it. However, it reminded me of my conversation with White from what seemed like days but was really only a couple of hours ago. "Hey, who's Guy and Lillian's Dealer of Death counterpart for alcohol?"

"Why?"

"We've never met him or her."

"Well, based on what I think you mean, if you're looking for the full group that you'd call the Dealers of Death, you need to include the people who cover the fast food, hazardous waste, oil drilling, and firearms lobbies, not just tobacco, alcohol, and weapons manufacturing. To have the full set and be able to call Death Dealer Bingo."

"Touchy much? And you forgot Big Pharma, but we already know they hate us."

"Bingo."

"Hilarious. Okay, who are they, all of them? Because none

of them have ever approached us. Guy and Lillian did, but
not these others. And it would seem like they'd all hang together."

"I'll be offended later, because it's not like it's the first
time any of you have insulted my husband and friends and
what they do for a living."

"Dude, seriously, if you can look me in the eyes and, without breaking eye contact or laughing, and also with all sin-
cerity, tell me that smoking doesn't cause every damn disease
we think it does, I'll apologize."

He snorted. "Right. Anyway, I assume you have some reason, other than idle curiosity at an inopportune time, for why
you want to know?"

"Yeah, I do. First off, it seems weird—Lillian approach-
ing us right away, with all of our potentially destructive alien
technology, makes sense. But Guy doing it doesn't. At first I
thought we'd never met whoever handles alcohol because we
don't drink. But we don't really smoke, either, and Guy
doesn't seem to care at all. So if we're somehow so influential that the head mouthpiece for Big Tobacco wants to be our
friend, why doesn't the head of Big Booze feel the same
way? Or the rest of the ones you named?"

"Okay, what's second off?"

"Why aren't you guys friends with these other Dealers of
Death? You're pals with Lillian, and other influential people.
Why are these who it would seem you'd have a lot of affinity
with not in your circle? Lillian and Guy are tight, that much
is obvious. But I've never heard Lillian mention the firearms
person, and Guy hasn't mentioned the alcohol lobbyist, not
even in passing."

"What else?"

"Gideon Cleary's family is part of Big Booze. But we
weren't enemies of his before this campaign started, at least
not that we knew of. And, regardless of their relationship or
lack thereof with Lillian and Guy, where are the firearms
people? We use guns, all the time. We must buy them from
someone. And yet whoever runs that lobby has never dropped
by to shoot the breeze, let alone try to influence us. Why
hasn't the Big Pharma lobbyist come by to see if he or she

can work the magic and make us part of their team? I can understand the fast food, oil drilling, and hazardous waste people giving us a pass . . . right up until I think about your husband, and then I'm right back to the question of either why Guy wants our favor or these others don't."

"Anything else?"

"Probably. My husband was essentially appointed by the freaking President. That alone would make him seem special, even if they didn't know he was an alien. But they do, and everyone else does, too. And even after we were exposed and Jeff was made a Representative, none of these people have approached us. And before you ask, Jeff tells me about all the lobbyists who talk to him, because it's assumed they're going to try whatever with him, then head for me as the presumed weak link, to see if they can get in that way."

"I have a simple answer for why we don't hang with Simon Hopkins, who's the head of the Alcohol lobby. It's probably the same reason he doesn't try to make inroads with all of you, either. He's a huge homophobe."

"Last time I checked, GLBT folks drank just like straight folks."

"They do, and Simon would never admit this out loud. But, you know, when you're gay, you're able to spot when someone hates you merely for *being* gay. Simon was friendly with your former Diplomatic Corps, because none of them were gay and your religious leader at the time was straight. The moment those people left and Paul took over as Pontifex, Simon was done with all of you."

"Wow, well, I wasn't asking about this to send invitations to dinner."

"Yeah, I know. Lillian had the choice to remain friendly with him, by the way—Guy and I would never ask her to compromise her work for us. She chose us and she and Abner never do anything with Simon or his wife."

I was having to radically alter my opinion of Lillian Culver, and I wasn't enjoying having to do so. However, I'd clearly sold her very short, because I'd have never expected her to choose loyalty and what was morally right over getting ahead in any way.

Vance smirked. "Yeah, she had to change how she thought about you, too. Don't worry, it's all part of the wonder that is D.C. You'll get used to it."

"In about a million years. What about the others?"

"You know, I'm kind of with you, it doesn't make any sense for why they haven't approached you. But, as for who they are, Niles Berkowitz is the head lobbyist for Big Oil, Talia Lee is who covers Firearms, oh and she's tight with Janelle Gardiner from Gaultier Enterprises."

"That so figures, and might explain why she hasn't approached us. Who else?"

"Myron Van Dyke is your Big Pharma guy, and he's tight with Quinton Cross."

"Gaultier's all set up, aren't they?"

"Yeah, they are. I'm sure that's why Amy hasn't won her fight. Thomas Kendrick from Titan is Lillian's client, of course, but he's so new, he hasn't made a lot of relationship connections like the others have. His connections are still more military in nature. Lux Carr is Hazardous Waste and Kingsley Teague is Fast Food."

"Lux? Kingsley?"

He shrugged. "I don't question other people's names. Lux seems to like her name, and Kingsley makes a lot of jokes about his that tell me he not only likes it, but he thinks he should be called King Kingsley."

"Fantastic."

"It gets better, and I know you'll appreciate this one, they're both tight with Amos Tobin."

"Well, he ran a variety of fast food franchises before he took over YatesCorp, didn't he? And God alone knows what all YatesCorp is into, but I know it's more than we even know about. So I guess those love connections make sense. That's Dealer of Death Bingo for me, then, right?"

"Right, based on what you were talking about, at any rate."

"Poor Ansom Somerall doesn't have a buddy? That seems wrong."

"He does, it's Berkowitz, sorry, forgot to mention it."

"So figures."

"All of them know each other, of course, and I wouldn't say any of them are enemies, though not all of them are friends with all the others. Speaking of Ansom, by the way, I think you also should consider—"

William's voice came over the intercom. "Excuse me, Ambassador." It was still weird hearing him instead of Gladys, especially because William was unfailingly polite and Gladys had never felt the need to bother. Shoved the pang down. Gladys would be the first one to tell me to pull up my Big Girl Panties and handle the business of protecting her people.

"What's up, William?"

"You're needed in conference. Immediately."

CHAPTER 31

RESISTED THE URGE TO CURSE or sigh. "Super, we'll be right up. Or over, depending on where we're meeting."

"Fifteenth floor conference room, Ambassador. Only you were requested."

"Gotcha. Over it is." The com went off and I looked at Vance. "Well, I guess you and I have sort of formed a plan for one of the many problems. You want to go find Pierre and Raj and get that rolling?"

"I'm going with you to this meeting. They can tell me to leave, but I'm not going to wander off just because I'm considered useless."

"You're not useless, so, yeah, come along. Besides, for all we know, Pierre and Raj are there, too."

"By the way, why have you been playing that one song over and over?"

"I have been?" Listened. Sure enough, Foster the People was still on, but instead of the album playing, only "Pumped Up Kicks" was on our personal airwaves. Figured this was some kind of a clue from Algar. Filed it away to pay attention to later.

"Yeah. Nonstop."

"Whatever. It's a good song." Grabbed my iPod out of the dock and dropped it back into my purse. Looked at the animals. "We'll continue our discussion later. For now, um, those of you who need to stay here, stay here. Everyone else, go back to your assigned person or people or come along with Kitty."

Bruno, Harlie, Poofikins, and Prince and his K-9 crew all came with us. Happily, Bellie stayed in the Lair. Wondered about my new definition of "happy." Didn't care for it all that much.

"So, you lived in those rooms?" Vance asked as we left the Lair. Noted he had an unattached Poof on his shoulder. Well, it probably had been unattached at one time. Now? Now I'd ask what Vance had named it later. But at least that meant that Vance and Guy were truly our allies. So, another one for the win column, go us. Poof Power, and all that.

"Yeah. I liked it, too."

"Right by jail cells?" We were passing the containment area. "You enjoyed living next to your people's version of County Lockup?"

"They aren't used a lot. Besides, the other housing here is kind of . . ."

"Awesome. Like a luxury hotel. I can see why that would get dull." Vance's sarcasm knob was back at eleven.

"The automatic alarms every morning suck. You literally have to have every person's feet on the floor and not be sitting down on the bed for them to turn off." And the sound-proofing was far better in the Lair, possibly because we were several floors away from the others sleeping. Not that this was any of Vance's business, Poof on his shoulder or not. "Besides, how do you know about the rooms on the transient floors?"

"We're all staying here at least overnight, per everyone, just to be safe. The Alphabet Agency Bigwigs you hang with and are related to are worried about all of your allies' safety, and I can't blame them."

Vance and I and our animal honor guard finally reached the giant conference room and joined what appeared to be pretty much everyone. We were missing the Mossad and Israeli and Bahraini embassy personnel we didn't know well, and, thankfully, the kids and those on Daycare Duty, but otherwise pretty much everyone else was in attendance, including the

Mossad, Israeli, and Bahraini folks we did know well. Heck, even Mrs. Maurer was in attendance.

"Good of you to join us, Missus Chief," Buchanan said quietly. He and Siler were both leaning against the wall just inside the door. Siler was again cuffed to Buchanan for whatever reason.

"I like to make an entrance."

They both chuckled as Vance went one way and I went the other, toward Jeff and Christopher. The room was normally set up in a round, but today we had the Corporate America Classroom setup, with U-shaped lines of long tables and chairs curved toward the far end of the room. Alpha and Airborne were in the front, with Jeff and Christopher in back for whatever reason.

"You really need to go everywhere with an entourage, don't you?" Christopher asked as I settled into the available chair between him and Jeff, animals settling in behind me.

"Blah, blah, blah. As if Toby's not in your pocket right now?" Did a fast headcount. In addition to everyone I'd expected, Gadoire was in the room. Vance sat between him and Culver.

"Whatever," Christopher muttered.

"What were you up to?" Jeff asked, somewhat suspiciously.

"Vance and I were having wild sex with all the animals. It's our new thing."

Jeff laughed. "Fine, fine, I'll stop. I wasn't actually trying to be jealous."

Patted his hand. "No, you're just good enough at it to do it on autopilot. So, what's our newest damage?" Had to figure something more was going on than just a meeting, or else they wouldn't have had William call me in.

"More bombings. Still no one taking anything more than minor damage. Still unlikely that's going to last."

There was a giant TV monitor in the room that we were set up to be looking at—similar to the ones in Field and Imageering Main in the Bat Cave—and we were being treated to a variety of screen-within-screen shots. Figured we were here instead of Main because of how many people we had with us. A whole heck of a lot about covered it.

Serene and Horn were on one screen, Cliff was on another, and other images were on the other screens, mostly of bombings and protests. The screens were set up for video conferencing, so everyone on the other sides could see all of us in the room. This looked and felt like a War Room meeting.

Said meeting was in full swing and no one seemed likely to interrupt in order catch me up. No worries, I had a decent grasp of what was going on. And most of what was going on right now was recap.

Got bored fast, since I'd personally lived most of what was being recapped, so took in the room some more. Was pretty sure that no one on the other side of the screens could see where Buchanan and Siler were standing. Wondered why Buchanan had them in this position, but filed it away to ask about later. Went back to the screens.

Cliff was clearly in his office. I'd seen it. It was typical D.C. High-Up Worker Bee Dull and Semi-Stately. However, I'd also been to Horn's office, and he wasn't in it. I hadn't seen whatever F.B.I. bomb defusing area he and Serene were at—in fact, I had no idea if they were in the D.C. area, back here at Dulce with everyone else, or in another clandestine location—so I concentrated on their screen. Which was why I caught sight of a younger Dazzler who looked familiar.

Nudged Jeff. "Who's that with Serene and Vander?" I whispered.

"Our niece," he replied in kind.

"You have a tonnage of nieces and nephews, Jeff."

"But only one old enough to be working outside of school. That's Stephanie, Sylvia's oldest. You know her." Sylvia was the eldest of Jeff's five older sisters, and she'd married and started her family first as well. Stephanie was the oldest Martini grandchild, therefore.

"Yeah, just haven't seen her since . . ." Since shortly after I'd had to kill her father, Clarence Valentino, during Operation Sherlock. He'd been a major traitor and had been trying to kill me and a lot of other people, but he was still her father, and while Sylvia had understood, we'd given their children the old Killed in Action story.

Stephanie was, like all female A-Cs, gorgeous. But she'd changed a lot in the past couple of years, leaving the awkward teenaged stage for the more mature, almost-a-real-young-adult stage. She'd be about 19 now.

Thought about the high-security cells again. Clarence had been released from them by Alfred, Jeff's father, because Sylvia had been so upset by his incarceration. He'd then been taken out of the solar system, along with Ronaldo Al Dejahl, by LaRue DeMorte Gaultier, via a ship stolen from Alpha Four. Our lives were always filled with fun complexities like that.

So Stephanie had to know her father was a traitor. Maybe her younger siblings didn't know or weren't clear, but she'd been old enough to understand everything that had been going on, and all Dazzlers were not just great looking, but also brilliant. How hard would it have been for her to put two and two together? And if how she'd been when we first met was still how she was, she wasn't afraid to speak her mind.

But I hadn't heard anything from anyone about Stephanie's reactions to what had happened to her father, or what he'd done to her people, other than the usual platitudes everyone, human or alien, says during and about bad situations.

Jeff and I had talked about how to deal with his sisters and their families, in part because most of their husbands had worked for the former Diplomatic Corps and weren't exactly confirmed to be on the side of right. Jeff had felt that my not trying to make amends with anyone and just letting him, Alfred, Lucinda, and White handle it was the right way to go. And because of his empathic talent, I'd acquiesced.

So, other than Marianne's family, who we saw fairly frequently, we only saw the rest of his sisters and their families on holidays or when jobs crossed, which was rarely, and I'd been busy enough that I hadn't thought about it a lot. Marianne was the youngest of Jeff's sisters, so I had the most in common with her, and her youngest daughter, Kimmie, had been our flower girl, so we were more closely bonded.

I was an only child, and these days I worked with most of my closest friends—I didn't miss or even think about sibling interaction when Chuckie, Amy, and Caroline were right there, let alone Reader, Lorraine, and Claudia. And Jeff and Christopher were always together, which, though they were cousins, tended to cover my sibling thoughts about either one of them.

All of the Martini grandchildren were talented—about fifty-fifty empaths to imageers—and all of them were closer to Jeff and Christopher's levels than normal A-C standards. Kimmie was empathic. But I had no idea what talent Stephanie had. Wondered if, in addition to anything else, she was, like Camilla was and Doreen was learning to be, a Liar.

Camilla was undercover in Gaultier Enterprises somewhere, and Chuckie wouldn't let me contact her. So asking for her expert opinion was, sadly, out. Doreen was across the room and it would take too long to explain to her why I was suspicious. It wouldn't take all that long, really—Doreen was high up there in smarts on the Dazzler Scale—but any time could be too much time.

Wondered why I was stressing about Stephanie right now, other than the fact that I'd seen her somewhere I wasn't expecting. Maybe because of the song, "Pumped Up Kicks". It had a cheerful, earwormy tune, but it was about a kid getting ready to go off and kill people. And Algar was a lyrics-focused clue giver.

The conversations washed over and around me—I concentrated on the screen with Serene, Horn, and Stephanie in it.

Horn and Serene were sitting—it looked like they were either waiting for their cue to talk or had already; they seemed alert and interested but not like they were going to be adding in at the moment. Stephanie was behind them, and she appeared to be taking notes.

"What's Stephanie doing with Vander and Serene?" I asked Christopher, who was on my other side, in a whisper, since Jeff seemed to actually be paying attention.

"She's working for Vander as one of his assistants," he whispered back. "Favor to us kind of thing. And it's good experience for her."

"Yeah. Who asked for her to be put into that position?"

"Why? What's wrong?" He didn't sound annoyed or snarky—he sounded worried. Good.

I hadn't taken my eyes off the screen. So I saw when Stephanie looked up and saw me. Her eyes narrowed and she shot me a look of pure venom. Her gaze shifted—the venom was being directed toward Christopher, too.

Considered this. She'd been the one who'd given Christopher and all the rest of the guys keychains as Arrival Day presents when I was pregnant with Jamie. Those keychains had had bugs in them, bugs put there by our Enemies of the Day at that time, which had included the former Diplomatic Corps, and Clarence.

Those keychains were part of how Christopher had been manipulated into becoming a Surcenthumain addict. I'd thought, we'd all thought, that Clarence had tricked her into doing it. Most had assumed Stephanie had no idea there was anything untoward inside her gifts. And no one, not even Jeff, maybe especially not Jeff, had asked her if she'd known what she was doing.

And if we asked her now, what would all the empaths feel? Nothing wrong. Because if she was working for our enemies, then she was one of the first people who they'd given an emotional overlay device to. Maybe she'd been the main tester for them—see if your Uncle Jeff can tell that you hate his wife's guts, and your Uncle Christopher's guts, too.

Algar had been warning me. That meant there probably wasn't a lot of time. We'd lost far too many people I cared about last year—I wasn't willing to lose Serene, and I had a feeling she was going to be the first in the line of fire. Her son, Patrick, was almost as talented as Jamie, and he didn't have ACE inside him. They'd tried to get Patrick, and by extension, Jamie, last year by holding his father hostage and torturing him. That was why Michael and Fuzzball were dead—they'd been killed trying to protect Brian.

Serene would be an even stronger lure for her son, and that would mean that it was Horn who was going to die first, so that we would all know the situation was serious. Okay, so Serene was second in the line of fire; made things worse, not better. Plus, the death of the guy in charge of the F.B.I.'s Alien Affairs Division, especially at the hand of an A-C, would be bad for us in more ways than I could count.

Took Christopher's hand in mine. "Do you trust me?"

To his great credit, he neither tried to drop my hand nor asked me if I was crazy. "Yeah, I do."

"Then get the two of us to wherever Vander and Serene are at the fastest speed you've ever used in your life."

CHAPTER 32

I'D EXPERIENCED CHRISTOPHER'S Flash Level of speed before. But this was faster than he'd ever used with me yet.

His Surcenthumain boost had expanded his talents to a frightening degree. But after a while, the new abilities had all faded, leaving him back to his just regular Better Than All The Other Imageers level. But his hyper-hyperspeed had stuck around.

For whatever reason, Christopher had held onto all the extra speed ability the drug had given him, and then some. He and I still worked regularly on my reverse-inherited A-C abilities and talents, but he also worked on his own. And especially after Operation Infiltration, he focused on speed and distance.

Field agents had to be able to run twenty-five miles at a go. Jeff and Christopher had always been able to do fifty. But now? Now Jeff could do several hundred before he overtaxed himself. And Christopher was up to a thousand miles without breaking a sweat.

And I was about the only one who knew it.

Part of this secrecy was simply because we wanted to keep whatever edge against our enemies that we could. Part was that we didn't really relish the idea of Jeff and Christopher having to submit to a battery of tests to figure out why they could now perform at this level in terms of hyperspeed prowess.

This meant, however, that Christopher was faster than

even regular A-Cs could see, so presumably to those in the conference room, we were there and then suddenly we were not. Was distracted from this thought because, as we sped up fifteen floors and out of the Science Center within the blink of an eye, I realized someone was holding my other hand. And I was pretty sure that someone wasn't Jeff.

I was prepared to pretty much black out, because of how hard this speed level was for anyone other than Christopher to take, so it was a shock when I didn't. It was also a shock that, once outside, we weren't heading toward the east coast. It was more of a shock to look to my left and see Buchanan and Siler there.

"How the hell?"

"He knows you well," Siler said, jerking his head toward Buchanan. "And I'm fast."

"Almost there," Christopher said. "I'll stop just before we're on top of them so you can all throw up."

Thought about it as we whizzed by things I couldn't even make out we were going so fast. "I don't need to."

"Me either," Buchanan said. "No idea why."

"It's me," Siler said, "my touch transference. I could explain it now, or we could do whatever the hell you're planning on doing."

"Where is the there we're almost at?" I asked Christopher.

"Home Base."

"Oh, a nice trip to Area Fifty-One. I guess that makes sense. But why are Vander and Serene here? You said they'd gone to Vander's Bomb Unit place or whatever."

They all stared at me, even Christopher. Hoped he wouldn't trip on something.

"There's a bombing range here," Buchanan said as we approached the Nellis Air Force Base and didn't actually go into it. "At Groom Lake."

"And they used a gate to get here, Kitty," Christopher said slowly. "And I assume they came here because Serene wanted to blow more things up than the F.B.I. felt comfortable with."

"Fine. And yes, I'll give myself the 'duh.' Let's get this rescue mission rolling!"

"There's no water," Siler said as we ran across the so-called lake.

"It's a salt flat," Christopher said as we reached a concrete bunker on the far side from Home Base. "Get ready, I have no idea what our mission actually is."

"Stopping a Second Generation Traitor from doing something very bad."

"Stephanie?" Christopher asked.

"Yep."

"Okay, I can make the logic leap." He wrenched the door open and we zoomed in.

Once inside, we stopped. Sure enough, none of us needed to toss the cookies. The benefits of having Siler around seemed good so far.

There was no one in the entry area. That this place had an entry area was kind of surprising. There was more to this bunker than one room to hide from bomb blasts within. It was a lot larger than I'd expected it to be, too. Figured the A-Cs had something to do with all of that and chose not to ask about it, lest I get another "duh" added to my ever-growing pile.

Could hear the sound of voices. ". . . have no idea where they've gone or why." Mom. Sounding tired, pissed, and suspicious.

"Is everything alright?" Horn was talking. Good, he was still in here.

"We're fine here." Chuckie's voice. "They've only been gone a minute. Let's continue. If there's something going on I'm sure they'll let us know."

"They disappeared." Cliff's voice. "I think that's significant, Chuck. Especially since they didn't tell anyone where they were going, and Kitty had just gotten to the meeting as it was."

"I think Kitty forgot something, that's all." That was Jeff. Had to figure he'd read my emotions, at least before we'd taken off. He probably couldn't read them now—had to assume Stephanie had an emotional blocker or overlay on her person. "I'm sure she and Christopher will be back shortly. Serene, why don't you tell us what you and Vander have discovered."

Serene started sharing things about explosive ranges, the differential between older and newer self-destructs on various blockers we'd found, and other bomb-related things. My ears shared that they were done listening for now.

While she happily prattled on about weapons of varying degrees of mass destruction, we crept through what looked a lot like the Bomb & Weapons Superstore. Had to figure Serene spent a lot of time here. As her current recap was illustrating, she loved explosives and considered her work with them to be like getting to do her favorite hobby full time. And she was scary good with them, too. The best we had, and that was saying a lot. She was, per Chuckie, one of the best the government had access to.

And yet, the Yates Family Players hadn't tried to recruit her. Club 51 had drugged her in an attempt to kidnap her and hold her prisoner in order to use her skills. But no one had approached her to sway her to the cause of Yates Solidarity. There was something vital about this that I had to figure out.

Only, you know, after we saved Serene and Horn from Stephanie.

"Hold on," Siler said in a low voice. "I'm going to blend us all so they can't see us. Be as quiet as possible."

Blending didn't feel like any A-C talent I'd experienced before. It was kind of gently tingly. Assumed the feeling allowed the blended to know when they were and weren't chameleoned up.

Thankfully, I could still see the three men with me. So, still holding hands, walking slowly, and stepping softly, we went to the doorway of the partitioned room our quarries were in.

The three of them were seated exactly as they had been a minute ago, when we'd been in the conference room at the Science Center watching them on our video screens. Only we were looking at their backs, so Stephanie was the closest to us.

Who, as we peered like creepy stalkers into the room, wasn't really doing anything aggressive. Wondered if this was going to turn out to just be a big misunderstanding. If so, I was going to look like the worst aunt-by-marriage in the history of the world.

Wasn't sure if we could be caught by the video feed—the doorway wasn't in a direct line with it. Sure, we were technically invisible, but Siler had said he couldn't hold it long. He might have been lying, or he might have been telling the truth, and if that was the case, we were going to appear out of nowhere soon.

Stephanie's phone beeped. I could tell it was hers because she grabbed it and looked at it. Text, not call, because she texted back, at hyperspeed. Then she stood up.

"Excuse me, I need to clear up something on Mister Horn's calendar."

Horn looked at her over his shoulder. "Don't be too long."

"I won't be a minute." Stephanie headed out of the room.

Buchanan tugged at my hand and we followed her, still slowly and quietly. She wasn't walking slowly, though. She headed for the door.

Looked back at the room. She'd left her phone on the conference table.

Well, no time like the present to either save the day or be shunned out of Jeff's entire extended family.

Dropped Buchanan's and Christopher's hands. "Her phone's a bomb!"

Then I launched myself at Stephanie.

CHAPTER 33

CLEARLY NO ONE had realized the four of us were in here, because I heard both Horn and Serene give the screams people do when they're completely startled.

Stephanie jumped and spun around. She saw me, turned, and ran for the door. But I caught her before she reached it.

"Going somewhere?" I asked as I grabbed her arm and managed to spin her around.

She hit at me, but not with any real skill. So no one had trained her in fighting. "Leave me alone!"

"You hit like a girl." I slammed a fist into her stomach. "And I note you're not at all surprised to see me here." Whoever had sent her the text had clearly told her to roll her part of the plan, and I was pretty sure said texter had also told her to assume we were here already.

She kicked at me as I managed to get behind her and wrap both of my arms around hers and her torso. "Get off me, you bitch," she hissed as I squeezed.

"Is that any way to talk to your aunt? Besides, it's hard to handle a call when you leave your phone behind. I'm just trying to make sure you do a good job."

A man's hand grabbed the back of my shirt. "Out," Buchanan said. "Now!" He tossed us both toward the door, which Siler was holding open. How and when they'd taken the cuffs off I didn't know. Decided now wasn't the time to worry about it.

"Get off me!" Stephanie screamed. "You're ruining everything!"

"Unless it was a surprise party with clowns, cake, and balloons, I'm sure we're not."

"I wish my daddy had killed you."

"Yeah, I know. We killed him instead. These things happen."

She struggled more, and because she was an A-C, she was strong. However, I was both trained and enhanced. Also however, she managed to knock us both off balance. We went to the ground. I ensured she was on the bottom.

"Let me go! We need to get out of here!"

Serene and Horn ran out, her pulling him, Christopher right behind them. Once we were all outside I realized Christopher also had Stephanie's phone. "Get away from the building!" He ran off.

Buchanan hauled me off of Stephanie and grabbed her at the same time. She tried to get away, but Serene grabbed her other arm and she wasn't going anywhere.

Siler grabbed my free hand and Serene had Horn in hers. We took off, away from both the building and the lake, meaning toward the base of the nearby mountains.

Christopher rejoined us, without Stephanie's phone. "Down!"

We all ducked and covered right as the bombs went off. Impressively. Both something in the middle of Groom Lake, which was where I assumed he'd thrown the phone, and the building we'd just been inside.

"Phone was the trigger," Christopher said. "But the entire place was rigged to blow."

"Yeah, we see that. Everyone okay?" Everyone assured me they were okay. "Great. Then someone beat the truth out of Stephanie. Or let me do it. I'm all for doing it. Start with asking who sent her the text telling her to go ahead and blow things up."

"Did you happen to look?" Buchanan asked Christopher, as he took over holding Stephanie, who was struggling a lot. She stopped as her uncle stood behind her, locked his hands around her upper arms, shoved her arms next to her torso, and shook her gently.

"Stop it, now, or I'll do something you won't like that I might feel badly about later. Yeah," Christopher said to Buchanan, "I did, actually, while running with a bomb that was ready to go off. Blocked number."

"Fantastic. So, can I hit her then?"

"Stephanie did all that?" Serene asked, sounding shocked. Everyone other than Stephanie and Horn nodded. "But why?"

Stephanie glared at us. She was pretty good. Not up to Christopher's standards, but a lot closer than most managed. I gave her a Bronze. "You deserve it."

Serene looked even more shocked. "What do you mean? What have Vander or I ever done to you? Vander gave you a job and was planning on training you to become an F.B.I. agent. I've only taught you some things about explosives. How have either of us hurt you enough to make you want to kill us?"

"She doesn't want to kill you because of that, Serene. And I can practically guarantee that she's not grateful for the opportunities, either. She was moving herself into a position to hurt us. Not just you two, all of us."

"I know Kitty's right. But why are you doing this?" Christopher snarled.

Stephanie tossed her head. "Killing traitors isn't wrong."

"Wow, I hope one of us recorded that, so when your mother tries to get you released, we can play it for her and she can understand why we're not letting you go."

She smirked. "I'm not going to stay captured long. I'm valuable."

"As an undercover agent, sure. As a captured traitor, I doubt it."

"I have a much bigger part to play than this," she replied with a heavy dose of haughty. I'd heard that before, from her father. And . . . someone else. Recently. Tried to remember who, because it was probably important.

"Ah, Kitty?" Horn said.

The current situation shared that I'd have to search my memory banks later. Right now, what was going on was requiring my full attention. Because I turned around to see Siler holding Horn.

Siler was also holding a gun, and it was up against Horn's head.

CHAPTER 34

WOULD HAVE ASKED how Siler had gotten his hands on a gun, but we'd been in a well-stocked munitions bunker, everyone had been distracted, and he had hyper-speed.

Said the only thing I could think of. "Well, this is an interesting new wrinkle. Oh, and, what the hell?"

"Let her go," Siler said calmly.

"Is this a joke?" Christopher asked.

"Are you laughing?" Siler countered. "No? Then assume it's not a joke. You let her go, give her to me, and I'll let your man here live."

No one was near enough to Siler and Horn to do anything, and Siler was an assassin with a lifetime of training who was also an A-C with probably more talents than he'd told us about. Felt stupid for trusting him. Checked Buchanan's expression. Apparently I didn't feel as stupid as Buchanan did. Go us.

"Do it," I told Christopher. Received a nice shot of Patented Glare #4 as he reluctantly let Stephanie go.

"Come here," Siler said to her. She trotted over to him, Triumphant Smirk on High. "Hold his hand." Stephanie took Horn's hand as requested. Siler looked right at me. "I need to help a kindred spirit, Miss Katt. It's nothing personal, I just have a job to do. The same as you do." With that, the three of them disappeared.

"Wait," Buchanan said to Christopher, who looked ready to run, as he grabbed his arm to keep Christopher here.

"He has Vander," Christopher snarled. "I need to catch them. I can follow their footprints."

"No. And that's an order. Take it as if it came from the P.T.C.U., because it does."

"If he hurts Vander it'll be on you," Christopher said. But he didn't try to leave.

Buchanan nodded, let go, went to where Siler had been standing, and knelt down. "Give it a moment." He picked something up off the ground and put it into his pants pocket. "He'll drop Horn shortly, I'd bet."

Sure enough, there was a tiny figure in the middle of Groom Lake. "It's Vander," Serene said, sounding relieved and confused. "I don't understand what's going on."

"Join the club." Christopher zipped off and was back momentarily with Horn, who got to add insult to injury and spend some time throwing up. We were all going to miss Siler's ability to pass along the Anti-Nausea Connection.

"I can't see Stephanie or Siler," Serene said. "They're out of my range."

"I didn't see any trail I could follow once they dropped Vander," Christopher said. "No idea why not, considering what they were standing on, but why the hell didn't you let me go after them in the first place?" he asked Buchanan.

"Because it occurred to me that Stephanie had to have had an exit strategy."

"What?" Serene asked. "Why would she?"

"Because no one blows up things in the middle of nowhere to hang out, I get it, Malcolm." Contemplated asking him what he'd picked up off the ground. Realized he wouldn't tell me. Another thing to be saved for later. "But I was thinking she'd run to Home Base crying hysterically."

"I'm sure that was her main plan. But she didn't come up with all of this on her own—and that means there was a backup plan in place for extradition. You heard her, she thinks she's valuable even though she's failed at her mission."

"So what?" Christopher asked. "She's a teenager. She thinks she's important regardless of the situation."

"Good call on the teenaged psyche, Christopher, but Malcolm thinks someone's out here, waiting for her, or, I guess them. And if they don't get them, they're going to attack us."

"No, Missus Chief, I assume they're going to attack us anyway. Which is why I didn't want the person who can get us away to safety the fastest to run off straight into an ambush, because I assume we have other A-Cs helping her as well. Were you really unable to think ahead when you were in an active position or are you just incredibly rusty?" he asked Christopher.

Buchanan was treated to Patented Glare #5, then Christopher turned to me. "Okay, Kitty, fine, I can see your point. We need to get over to Home Base, then, since someone thinks we're going to be attacked."

"You sure we shouldn't look for Stephanie's pals?" I asked Buchanan as he took my hand and Serene's.

"Yes, Missus Chief, I am," he said as Christopher grabbed me and Vander. We zipped off to Home Base, but at regular hyperspeed, for which I, personally, was grateful.

And arrived just as Jeff, Chuckie, Reader, Tim, Gower, and White walked out of the maintenance shack that hid the external gate on the base.

"Why is Paul out here, in danger?" Christopher asked, while poor Horn dry heaved. Tito clearly hadn't passed along the Hyperspeed Dramamine to him. Bummer.

"Because this is part of my job," Gower said calmly. He looked around. "I don't see any danger, though."

"It's handled for now," Buchanan said. Saw him pass a sign to Chuckie, but no one else seemed to catch it.

Wasn't sure if I'd seen it because I was expecting it, or if Buchanan had wanted me to. His Dr. Strange powers included the ability—which he, Mom, and Chuckie insisted was merely honed over time and experience, versus actual superpowers—to not have anyone notice him if he didn't want to be noticed. So far, I hadn't found that this ever failed, so if I'd seen something, chances were that he'd wanted me to. Interesting, and yet another thing to be put into the Ruminate On This Later file.

Reader nodded. "Tim and I need to check in. We'll be

right back." Those two headed off into the big building that housed most of our activities here.

"Why did you use the external gate?" Christopher asked.

"We figured we'd have to head right to you, son," White said. "And you were all outside."

"How'd you know where we were?" I asked Jeff.

"Really? I followed your emotional trail. It was clear until you reached that bunker, and then you went off my radar. So I knew where you were and that someone had an emotional blocker on them. The block stopped about a minute ago, which we're told coincides with a lot of things exploding that no one at Home Base was prepared for."

"So the blocker was in her phone? Interesting choice. Similar to putting bugs in key chains. We always thought Clarence had come up with that idea, or the people he was working for. But I think Stephanie's been willingly complicit for the past few years at least."

"You mind bringing us up to speed?" Chuckie asked. "Because, trust me, we're not all on the same page. For instance, most of us don't know why you and White took off in the first place." He looked around. "And where the hell is Siler?"

"Start at the beginning," Jeff said to me, in the tone of a man who's resigned to hearing things he doesn't want to.

"Ah . . . as to that . . . Stephanie gave me the stinkeye, and then did the same to Christopher . . ." Filled them in on all that had happened since my gut had shared that Stephanie was a traitor. No one disparaged my intuition, mostly because things had clearly gone boom, so there was that. "Siler helped us get everyone to safety, though," I shared in conclusion, "so I'm still sort of surprised by what he did."

"He's an assassin and not our friend," Christopher said. "He told us as much. So it's not actually a surprise. Though," he added to the dirty looks Buchanan and I were shooting him, "I'll give you that he was sure being helpful earlier."

"We'll deal with it," Jeff said. "We always do. It'll be fine."

"I understand why you got the feeling something was going down," Chuckie said, smoothly getting us off of the mistake in trust I and Buchanan had made. "And clearly, you were right. However, I don't understand why our various enemies wanted to blow up Vander and Serene."

"I agree," Serene said. "It's not like we had anything of importance in the bunker. Well, explosives and weapons, obviously, but I mean information-wise. Our research isn't here, or what's left of here. I mean, we did some of the research there, live testing mostly, but the results are sent back, now, to the Science Center as well as Charles and Vander's divisions."

"Not Cliff's? This seems like something Homeland Security would be extremely interested in."

"No. I mean, they *are* interested, very much so. But he gets the information after the F.B.I. and C.I.A. have done their work on it. Chain of command kind of thing. So, nothing but supplies and equipment were destroyed. It doesn't make sense."

"They were trying to kill the two of us," Vander said as if it were obvious. Which, in a way, it was. But he wasn't used to the levels of weird we got to deal with on a regular basis—in my world, nothing was ever simple or obvious.

"But *why*?" Chuckie asked patiently. "Think about whatever you two have found recently. Not today—I'm willing to bet that whatever triggered this didn't happen today because this took planning—but recently enough that it could cause our enemies worry."

"Stephanie didn't act unusual until you arrived at the big meeting, Missus Martini," White said thoughtfully. "I was watching her, actually."

"Why?" Chuckie asked. "It could be relevant."

White shook his head and sighed sadly. "It's not relevant, Charles. I was watching her because I was proud of her."

"So does that mean Kitty's arrival at the meeting was the trigger?" Jeff asked after a moment of sad, awkward silence.

"Trigger for what?" Christopher asked. "All of this, whatever this actually is?"

"Perhaps. Why was she giving you the, ah, stinkeye, son?" White asked.

"She hates me now?" Christopher replied. "Why does it matter?"

"Because she wasn't shooting that look at anyone else, other than you two," Buchanan said. "And Mister White is right—she didn't do anything untoward until Missus Chief arrived."

"But the text she got, that came after Christopher and I had left the meeting, when you all were discussing where we'd gone and Jeff was trying to cover. Someone gave her the go-ahead, and I think that someone figured we were on our way to the bunker."

"That would indicate someone who knows you well," Buchanan said. "And also indicate someone who was a part of the meeting."

"Maybe," Chuckie said. "It could also indicate exactly what you thought earlier, the reason you didn't let White go after them—that she had an accomplice, at least one, out here, hidden, who told her that she had company and it was time to put the plan into high gear."

"So, do we search for them, have our people here at Home Base search for them, or just give up and go home?" Gower asked as Reader and Tim rejoined us.

Reader shook his head. "Home Base has nothing, other than relief that no one died. Nothing showed as unusual until everything went boom."

I was about to say something when White's eyes widened and what seemed like cloud cover darkened the area. "Missus Martini . . ."

Spun around to see what he was looking at.

Sure enough, there wasn't a cloud in the sky. Instead, we were treated to the whole film encircling the Earth thing again. This time it didn't go though anyone, for which I was grateful. However, instead of water, there was a dust devil spinning. This wouldn't have been unusual for where we were, but it was forming near to us, and that meant around a whole lot of fighter jets. None of which were moving.

The dust was forming into a shape. A person shape. It so figured.

"Everyone? I have two things I want to say. First is that our timing remains consistent, meaning awful. Second is this—someone get Mahin here, faster than fast."

CHAPTER 35

MAHIN'S TALENT WAS THAT of earthbending. Well, she called it something else, in part because she'd had a sad childhood bereft of cool comics and animated pop culture and so had never seen *Avatar: The Last Airbender*. Well, before she'd met me she hadn't seen it. Now, that error had been rectified.

She could call it whatever she wanted, but basically Mahin could move sand and dirt around with her mind. And right now, I figured we needed someone who could do that, because I was fairly certain the Entity Formerly Known as Sloshy was now going to be Known as Sandy.

"It is time for the challenge," Sandy Formerly Sloshy intoned. No longer sounded watery. Now it sounded dry and crumbly. Wasn't an improvement.

The looks weren't an improvement, either. Whereas before it had been sort of see-through, now it was solid, but constantly shifting, as if it was made of a zillion sand ants bustling around in their humanoid-shaped anthill. Was so very sorry my mind had come up with this description.

Heard Reader on his phone, sounding stressed and official. He was requesting military aid.

"James, don't. That won't work. Serene, get Vander inside and out of here, and by out of here, I mean back to the Science Center, with you."

"Kitty, are you sure?" she asked. "It looks like you could use my help."

"No, both of you, get out of here. And, seriously, someone *get* Mahin here." Stepped closer to Sandy Formerly Sloshy to be between it and the rest of my team.

"Handled," Christopher said. "I took Serene and Vander back, as well. They're both safe now. Well, as safe as any of us can be at the moment."

Clearly he'd decided that everyone with us was smart enough to figure out that we hadn't used a gate to get us here in the first place, meaning they were smart enough to realize that Christopher's Flash Level was great and getting greater.

Heard the sounds of someone throwing up. More than one someone. Chose not to look behind me so I wouldn't break eye contact with Sandy Formerly Sloshy and so I also wouldn't have to see whoever tossing their cookies. I was smart like that.

"You rock."

"I brought Tito, too, because he insisted. And the princesses."

"You're a military genius, never let anyone tell you different. Tito, make sure Christopher doesn't need adrenaline—he's done a lot of long distance high speed running in a short period of time. Girls, once you have your stomachs back under control from Mister Christopher's Wild Ride, I need the mad skills. Rahmi and Rhee, make me the happiest leader on Earth and tell me you brought your battle staffs."

"Of course we did," Rahmi said, sounding just slightly offended.

"What do you take us for, amateurs?" Rhee added.

"Nope, but you know how you spell assume." Despite the situation, Chuckie started laughing. Always nice to have an appreciative audience, even if said audience only had one member.

"Excuse me?" Rahmi said.

"I don't understand you," Rhee added.

"So few ever do. We have a situation. Meet Sandy."

"Sandy?" This was chorused by everyone, the superconsciousness included.

"Well, this was Sloshy, but now, since he/she/it has changed elements, we're going with Sandy, because it's more accurate. Or the Entity Formerly Known as Sloshy. Take your pick."

"Sandy." Again, chorused by everyone, superconsciousness included. And it was definitely the loudest, too. Nice to know it had a preference.

"Okay, so, Sandy, why here, why now, and what, if any, are your rules of engagement? Marquess of Queensberry rules? MMA octagon limitations? I know you are but what am I basics?"

Sandy Formerly Sloshy stared at me. Kind of. It was hard to be sure. But it seemed to be staring. And what was pretending to be its mouth was sort of hanging open. "We don't understand you," it said finally.

"So freaking few ever do, Sandy. So freaking few ever do. It's my cross to bear but I manage to find the will to go on because I live for crap like this to happen to me. And so far, never disappointed, so thanks for keeping my record intact."

"You are . . . being funny?"

"Sure. Why not?"

"Right now? When you are about to fight for your right to exist?"

"I fight for my right to party all the time." Tim started laughing at this one. Good to know I was keeping it light for everyone. "Look, we have a ton of situations going on, so could you please just explain your supposedly neutral but actually evil plan so we can roll? I have a couple of traitors to try to catch up to and time's a wastin'."

But before Sandy Formerly Sloshy could reply my phone rang.

"Hang on, Sandy, hold whatever deep thoughts you're having, won't be a mo'." Dug my phone out and looked at the number. Vaguely familiar. Took a wild guess. "Hel-lo Bruce Jenkins." Heard everyone behind me groan. Sandy Formerly Sloshy looked discombobulated, at least as much as a sifting sand creature could.

"Missus Martini, how are you?" My ability to remember which random numbers went with which random callers remained excellent. I was on a roll.

"Busy, Bruce. And that's Ambassador Martini to you, I'm sure. But back to how I am. Busy, busy, busy. Like you, trust me, wouldn't believe. What, therefore, can I do for you in thirty seconds or less?"

"I'd like that interview now, if it's convenient."

"Wow, you're a reporter for the Post and yet you don't know the definition of the word 'busy.' Sad times out there in the fourth estate." Really wanted to hang up, but figured that since I was also hoping to defeat Sandy Formerly Sloshy in some way, that would mean we had a later and possibly even a tomorrow, meaning pissing Jenkins off totally was probably not the right plan.

"Oh, I'm sure you can dedicate a few minutes to help your husband's campaign."

"I can, Bruce, I can. Only, not right now. Seriously, I have people. Call them. Set up a meeting. Attend the meeting. Ask me all your probing, personal, inappropriate, leading questions loaded with innuendo and hidden meanings then. Stop calling me like this or other papers will start to believe that we're having an affair."

"Speaking of affairs—"

But before Jenkins could share whatever Affairs Theory he had going, Sandy Formerly Sloshy reached out and took my phone out of my hand. "She . . . is . . . BUSY!" it thundered. Impressively. Very loud and echoey with a whole Wrath of the Gods thing going, too. Figured that would hold good old Bruce Jenkins at least for a few minutes.

Then it hung the phone up and handed it back to me. Politely.

Took my phone and slid it into the back pocket of my jeans. Hopefully no sand had gotten into it. I could get a new one quickly from the Science Center, but that would leave me without a phone right now. Though, based on the quality of calls I'd been receiving today, that might not be a bad thing. "Thanks. He's a real jerk."

"He is," Sandy Formerly Sloshy agreed. "Stop thinking of me like that."

"Like what?"

"As Sandy Formerly Sloshy. Pick a name. Just one."

"Wow, you superconsciousnesses are super freaky about naming, aren't you?" There was something about this I needed to figure out, and more than anything else, I needed to figure it out right now.

"The form many times creates the thing," Chuckie said quietly from right behind me. "And observation tends to create affinity." Resisted telling him I loved him because none of us needed Jeff to have a Jealousy Attack right now. But it was always nice to have the smartest guy in any room, or on any airfield, covering your back and doing some of the heavy thinking.

"Sandy is a real name. Sloshy and Sandy Formerly Sloshy are not." Sandy sounded insulted.

"You were reading my mind? I call shenanigans. And that's also totally unfair in all the various rules."

"ACE reads your mind, all the time." Now Sandy sounded defensive.

"Yes, but ACE isn't trying to hurt us."

"I am not trying to hurt you, either. I am here to ensure that the ACE entity behaves properly, as required by our laws." Now Sandy sounded defensive, whiny, and a little bit hurt.

It could and was reading my mind. Jeff was probably far too busy blocking everyone's stress from himself to take the time to read me. Might as well just say what I was thinking and share the wonder that was my thoughts with the others, who were not able to read my mind.

"You're touchy about names, but you don't actually have any until you show up here. Why don't you name yourselves?"

"It is . . . not allowed."

"Uh huh. Is that because you'll become a real, for want of a better word, person? Because you like the name Sandy, don't you? And you want us to use it. And you used the word 'I.' In all the time ACE has been here, he's never used that word. And we call him a 'he' but we could call him a 'she,' too. 'It' is more appropriate but we humans tend to find that a rude thing to call a living being because we're admittedly gender focused. But you've manifested as male both times we've seen you, so that means you're also identifying as a particular gender."

"Sandy can be a man or a woman's name," Reader said conversationally. "It's one of those good, ambiguous names."

"You are trying to win me over to your side," Sandy said as if this was, somehow, surprising.

"Well, we'd rather be your bestest buds than fight you, yes. And since we want to buddy up and all that, duh."

"Duh?"

"It means 'obviously,' only it's ruder. We say that to each other all the time. Kind of a relaxed, joking, buddy thing."

"You want me to be your . . . buddy?"

"Better than being our enemy. We'll settle for frenemy if needed. Means an enemy who's also friendly to you, or vice versa. Depending on the being." Siler might have fallen into this territory. Yet another line of thought I'd have to follow later. If we got a later.

"I could destroy you, you know."

"Yes, we know."

"I wouldn't be so sure," Mahin said. "Right now, your entire essence is within the sand construct you've created."

"So?" Sandy now sounded belligerent. Hoped this wasn't going to get ugly.

"So, I have you bound," Mahin said calmly. "You are contained within the sand."

"You are not powerful enough to do that." Sandy sounded just a little bit doubtful however.

Mahin came and stood next to me. She shrugged. "Try to leave."

Sandy shrugged back, which was no less icky than when it had been a water man, but in a different way. The sand really looked like a bunch of ants or other tiny insects, moving over each other. Really hoped this wasn't the case.

Sandy burst apart, sand flying everywhere. Or, rather, sand trying to fly everywhere. It was captured in what seemed to be a large bubble, but one made of other sand. Looked at Mahin out of the corner of my eye—it was clear she was concentrating.

"It's still in there," she said through clenched teeth. "It can hear you."

"Sandy my friend, I don't think this outcome is what you were expecting. However, we're actually nice, pacifistic people. Well, my husband's people are. My people are bloodthirsty killers who delight in conquest. Guess who's in charge of this particular outcome?"

"I am not your enemy," Sandy said from within the bubbling sphere of sand. Sounded even weirder and even more dry and crumbly this way. I wasn't a fan.

"Wise choice. We have a saying here, though, that I like a lot: Prove it."

Sandy was quiet for a few long seconds. "How?"

"Promise me, in whatever way your kind promises, that you're going to leave ACE alone, let him stay with us on Earth if he wants to, let him leave Earth if he wants to, let him interfere as much as *he* feels is right, not as much as you all feel is right."

"And if I refuse? She cannot hold me in this form forever. The moment she tires, I will be free."

"No problem. If you refuse, we'll fight you. If we lose, I'll go with ACE, wherever you take him. And . . ." Well, no time like the present for the Big Gamble. "I'll name all of you."

The sand that was Sandy started roiling around. Mahin staggered. "It's panicked," Jeff said as he ran to us and held Mahin up. "I can feel it, blocks or no blocks."

Gower stepped closer. "She doesn't want to hurt you, Sandy," he said gently. "Or your people. We don't want to fight with you, any of you. We just promised ACE we'd protect him as he protects us, and we will honor that promise."

"It is against our laws," Sandy wailed. I'd heard ACE wail like this. And just because we could destroy something didn't mean we should.

Was about to say something to try to calm the situation when Sandy proved that it was right—Mahin couldn't contain it for long.

CHAPTER 36

THE SAND FLEW EVERYWHERE, all over us. Worried that Sandy was going to try to do something really horrible—like burrow into our skin—but thankfully all it did was form another dust devil.

A really big dust devil. Bordering on tornado. Not good.

On the other hand, every A-C was probably faster than a tornado, and the princesses were from the Alpha Centauri system and like all the beings from there, speedy. Meaning only half the men standing with me, and every human working at Home Base, was in danger. Considering this was an air base and A-C reflexes were so good that they actually couldn't drive or fly because they'd destroy the machinery, that meant a lot of humans. Back to not good.

Took a deep breath and really hoped I was doing the right thing. "Mahin . . . do your best to get Sandy under some kind of control. The rest of you, help her. Don't bring in military, they can't fight this."

"What are you planning to do?" Jeff asked suspiciously.

I'd challenged Sandy. And I'd fought him before. If I was right—and I really hoped I was—the only one who'd have to deal with Sandy, therefore, was me. "What I have to."

Took off running, so Jeff and Chuckie both just missed grabbing me—Jeff because he was still holding Mahin up, Chuckie because he wasn't an A-C. Someone else caught me grabbed my hand just before I hit into Sandy, though.

"Paul, let go—" But before I could insist Gower get back, or he could actually choose wisdom, we hit the tornado. And were instantly sucked up into it.

Unlike when he'd been Sloshy, we didn't go out the other side of the tornado. Which was disappointing in a variety of ways.

Gower's hold on my hand tightened, which was fine with me. I now knew how Dorothy and Toto had felt inside the tornado. Only I knew we weren't going to end up somewhere awesome like Oz.

Struck out with my free hand and my feet. Wasn't sure if I was having any effect, but I also wasn't being hurt. Despite being inside a violent whirlwind of sand, my face wasn't being hit and I could safely open my eyes. To see Gower not fighting at all.

He was still and calm, and as I slowed my thrashing, he pulled me to him and held me. "I don't think violence is the right answer," he said. "In this case, anyway."

There was less sand hitting me now that I was staying still. I could tell we were moving, not just randomly around, but in a direction. Hoped it was toward Groom Lake, versus through billions of dollars' worth of military equipment.

Felt something going around me. Sand was sticking to us now, but not in a hurtful manner. Realized what Gower undoubtedly already had—if we were inside Sandy, then Mahin had something solid to start to build control around.

"Close your eyes, Paul."

"Ahead of you."

"Yeah, picked that up." Gower and I remained still. Felt more pressure, which I assumed was more of Sandy's various grains being pushed against us. As this happened, the spinning slowed down proportionately.

Felt like hours but it was probably only minutes and the pressure was intense, but the spinning had stopped completely. We were on the ground, and on our sides. And then we were on Gower's back, our other sides, on my back, and so on. Realized someone was rolling us.

The rolling stopped. So figured they had us and Sandy wherever they wanted us. The issue was now that Gower and

I were trapped inside of Sandy, and I wasn't willing to bet on
how long before Sandy would decide to let us smother.

We started to vibrate, faster and faster, and then felt a
hand grab my arm and tug. Tightened my hold on Gower, but
whoever was pulling was stronger than me, because I
couldn't keep my arms locked.

I sailed out of the giant ball of sand and into Jeff's arms.
"Ooof. Couldn't you have tossed her a little less enthusiasti-
cally?" he asked Christopher, whose arm was back inside
Sand Ball Sandy.

"It's hard to do this through Mahin's control. Unless
you'd like to give it a go," Christopher snarked.

Groom Lake was fairly circular. Home Base was located
on the southern part, with low mountains opposite around the
northern portion. There were roads all around it, some paved,
some not, because this was an active airbase and people
needed to get from one side to the other, and not all of those
people were A-Cs. The bunker that had blown up had been
on the northern side of the Lake.

We were on the eastern side, happily far from both Home
Base and the still-smoldering remains of said bunker, near a
small outcropping of rocks that, because of the flatness of the
Lake, seemed quite tall. So, happily, there was nothing
nearby to hurt or damage other than all of us. Chose not to
question my current definition of "happily."

The princesses were holding the ball steady. It appeared
to be taking all their strength, which considering that those
from Beta Twelve were stronger than A-Cs, meant Sandy
was fighting back—hard. And yet, I hadn't been able to tell
when I was inside it.

Mahin was clearly still concentrating with all her mental
capacity and being held up by Buchanan. Chuckie and Tim
were touching her. Got the distinct impression she was getting energy from the three of them. Hoped it wasn't going to
hurt them—Tito was here, but he and White looked like
they'd already done the energy drain thing and were regaining their strength for the next round.

"No thanks," Jeff said to Christopher as he put me down.
"You're the fastest. You, stay," he said to me in the stern voice

he still somehow thought I obeyed. I only obeyed it in bed, or when he was telling me to do what I was going to do anyway, but apparently Jeff was Mr. Optimism. "Ready to catch Paul whenever you find him."

"I was holding onto him, I just couldn't keep hold. But he's fine," I reassured Reader, who wasn't looking any happier with me than Jeff was, and who also looked like he'd taken his turn with Mahin. "Why are you shaking? Sandy wasn't actually hurting us, I promise. Paul will be okay."

"Adrenaline shot," Reader said. "In a vein, versus heart, so it's not as bad as it could be." Looked around. Yeah, White and Tito were both shaking, too. And Tito was prepping more syringes.

Christopher grunted and Gower came flying out of the sand ball. I assumed I'd looked just like this—limbs askew, clothes disheveled, a giant fish being flung out of the sand ocean, complete with writhing. Only Gower was bald and I wasn't—figured my hair was probably terrifying to look at right now. Made the executive decision not to look in a mirror.

Jeff ran to catch Gower and thankfully White did as well, because it took both of them to catch him and not all go slamming into the ground.

"Thanks," Gower said, as they put him down. "Sandy wasn't hurting us—"

"So Kitty said," Reader interrupted. "I'll ask you what I know Jeff wants to ask her. What the hell were you thinking?"

"I was thinking that I need to go mano-a-mano with Sandy because I think that's what he's expecting."

"I was thinking that was exactly what Kitty was going to do and that she shouldn't," Gower said. "So I went with her." He shrugged. "I say again, Sandy wasn't actually hurting us. At all."

"That's true. So, is Mahin drawing energy from other people? And if so, how?"

"Yes, she is," Christopher replied. "I thought it would be a useful thing, to see if we could do it, so that in case we were in battle and no one could get adrenaline or whatever, that we could share energy. Hyperspeed works through touch, after all and Abigail and . . . Naomi used to do that all the time, essentially, and they were able to connect with me, Kitty, and Tito, as well as others. I figured, if they could do it, maybe we all could do it. So, Mahin and I have been working on that, since her talent is so externally focused."

We all stared at him.

"What?" he asked, shooting us all Patented Glare #1.

"I'm going to relish what I'm about to say. We're all just shocked to hear anything like intelligence and thoughtfulness in terms of powers and training coming out of your mouth."

"I'm not an idiot and I'm not exactly inexperienced in battle, or training." I got a shot of Patented Glare #3 all to myself.

"Yeah, I know. See how you like it when your friends and family insult the skills? Excuse me, I just want another moment to revel in this total Got You Back moment."

"Whatever," Christopher muttered.

"Kitty's right," Chuckie said. "About both the impressiveness and the fact that you're usually the head jerk insulting her at any given time. Save the wit retaliation effort, however, because we still have this situation to deal with. What do we do about Sandy here? Power from the rest of us or not, Mahin can't hold this forever and we can't all afford to be drained into unconsciousness, either."

"Paul, what do you think we should do?"

Gower stared at me for a moment. "You really want my opinion?"

"Would I have asked otherwise?"

"I suppose not. I think we should stop treating Sandy as our enemy. Differing views and rules don't mean beings are evil, just different from us. And it's powerful enough to have destroyed us all already . . . and hasn't."

"So, you'd like to try diplomacy?"

"If you're willing." Gower's lips quirked. "Interstellar diplomacy *is* your specialty, you know."

"Supposedly."

"Sandy panicked," Jeff said. "When you threatened its people. It wasn't feeling aggressive until then."

"Yeah, that 'I shall name you' thing really is their Achilles' heel, isn't it?"

"Make a decision," Tim said. "Mahin and the rest of us can't hang on with this much longer."

"I have to either contract the ball, and therefore destroy the contents, or release it," Mahin said through gritted teeth. "I have enough left to destroy, if you want me to, Kitty."

Took a deep breath and really hoped Gower was correct and I was doing the right thing. "No. Mahin . . . let Sandy go."

CHAPTER 37

THE SAND BALL DISAPPEARED. Mahin and the three men with her all visibly wilted. Tito trotted over and gave the four of them adrenaline shots. We were all going to be the most jittery people on the planet for a while. Hoped we were still going to have a while.

Sandy reformed quickly. Rahmi and Rhee moved into fighting stances, battle staffs at the ready, but Sandy did nothing aggressive toward them or anyone else.

The sand was still shifting in that totally icky manner, but he looked far more formed—definitely male, definitely humanoid. "Why did you release me?" he asked, sounding confused but not angry. "I did not ask for release."

"Not out loud, no."

"Your actions weren't harmful," Gower added. "Threatening, yes, which is why Kitty charged. But you didn't hurt us when we were inside you."

"And therefore, we didn't want to hurt you in return."

"We call it mercy," Chuckie added. "It's a concept you'll find throughout our history. Not used nearly enough, but still, one of our better qualities."

"Yes . . ." Sandy said. "And those showing mercy are not always . . . rewarded."

"No," Gower agreed. "Not always. We prefer to look on the positive side of life, however. We understand why you're here. You have a job to do. We just don't want you to harm our world. And taking ACE away will harm us."

"But our laws must be obeyed," Sandy said.

No time like the present to try what Gower wanted, which was to talk, versus fight, our way out of this. "Why?"

Sandy stared at me. "What do you mean?"

"I mean 'why?' As in, what makes your laws so wonderful that they apply to everything, everywhere? I ask because it seems to me that, sometimes, interfering is the right thing to do. You know, like Paul interfering and coming with me, Christopher interfering and pulling us out of you, and my interfering with Mahin and telling her to let you go."

"They are . . . our laws."

"Laws, yours, yes, got it. Only, here's the thing. In our world, when we realize that we have a law that is no longer relevant—like not being able to give a moose an alcoholic beverage if you're in Alaska—we either ignore it, change it, or repeal it."

"What do moose have to do with this?" Sandy asked.

"I'd like to point out that even visiting superconsciousnesses don't get the Kittyisms," Christopher said. Clearly he was still smarting from my getting him back. Good.

"Everyone's a critic and I take back that 'military genius' compliment I gave you only a few short minutes ago. Anyway, Sandy, what I'm trying to say is that laws are, many times, meant to be broken."

"Usually by you," Tim said.

"I heard that."

"Why are you all so . . . calm?" Sandy asked. "This is a dangerous situation. You have challenged, we have accepted, the time of conflict is here. Yet you all . . . joke?"

We looked at each other, then back at Sandy. "We're not calm," I explained. "We've all just become really good at panicking with style. Oh, and stop with the 'we' bit, Sandy. Once you go 'I' you never go back."

"It's not allowed."

"Really? Well you said 'I' earlier. More than once, so it wasn't a slip of the supertongue. Does that mean you've broken the laws, too? And you like your name, to the point where you demanded I think of you as Sandy, not as anything else. To me, that says you have formed a more solidified persona, an individualized identity if you will."

"You don't have to leave Earth right away," Chuckie said casually, as if it was just a thought, no big deal kind of thing. "Not if you don't want to. We've already offered ACE safe haven. You could certainly have the same arrangement."

"Why would you do that?" Sandy asked.

"Good for us, good for you," Chuckie said.

"You wouldn't have to stay here, either, you know, if you didn't want to. ACE isn't required to stay here by us. He stays because he wants to."

"But too much dependence makes lesser creatures weak."

Interesting. So they really thought they were doing the right thing. And Algar's people thought they were doing the right thing, too. What this meant I wasn't sure, but I suspected that the bottom line was that no one, not even the hugely powerful, really knew, and everyone was just doing the best they could.

"Yes," Sandy said. "That is true."

"What is?" Jeff asked. "We didn't say anything."

Sandy pointed to me. "She did. And . . . I understand what you mean, and what you are comparing."

Managed not to tell the powerful superconsciousness we were carefully negotiating with to shut up, but it took effort.

I will not tell them, Sandy said in my mind. Speaking to me in the same way ACE did. Or rather, the way ACE had, before he'd been funneled into Jamie. I understand the need for . . . discretion.

Good to know. So, this has been, at least up until now, a lot less horrible than it could have been. Why is that?

I am not here to punish anyone on Earth for anything, not even for giving ACE a name. Or . . . giving me a name. You are the one who named . . . Lilith, are you not?

Wow, that little battle made your radars? Nice to be right. I hoped.

You would be surprised. Though, possibly not. But yes, we all know of the battle. You and ACE defeated Lilith and the woman she resided in, in part because you named . . . her.

Look, I don't really 'get' the naming thing, why it, to you guys at least, makes you weaker. But to us, it makes you more tangible, more real.

That is the danger. For us, it is *the* danger.

Oh. You know, I didn't do it to hurt you. Or ACE. Though I did do it to beat Lilith.

I believe you have a saying, all is fair in love and war.

Yes, we do.

We understand that. I . . . understand that.

So, what happens now?

Now . . . does your friend, the brilliant one you are so proud of, does he speak for everyone?

He speaks for those of us who matter. I sincerely hoped.

Hope. That is a very human thing.

Right, ACE could read my deeper thoughts. Of course Sandy could, too. Is that bad?

No. It is . . . endearing.

Ah. Do you feel the passage of time as we do?

No. For us time moves more slowly and more quickly at the same time. I cannot explain it to you, your minds cannot grasp the concept, and that is not an insult. This was purposefully left out of your creation and kept out of your evolution. It is a . . . dangerous concept for younger races.

Do you see everyone, like ACE does?

Yes. It was why I entered all of you when I first arrived. I have observed you all in the time I have been here. For you, it only seems as though it has been hours. For me? It has been millions of your lifetimes, while still happening in those same hours you comprehend.

The form influenced the thing and observation created affinity. Sandy had been here, observing like ACE had. But for a much shorter time. However, I'd given it a name, a name it didn't like, but a name, nonetheless. And it had taken a form, a humanoid form. And then it had spent time, more time than I could comprehend, observing things with names and similar forms. And then I'd given it another name, a name it liked. A name it wanted to hold onto.

Why did you have a change of heart so much faster than ACE?

ACE was created. I was . . . formed.

Born? Or created out of the cosmos?

We are all made of stars. But as you would understand it, yes, I was born. ACE was, therefore, more controlled. ACE had to fight against programming. I am reacting to indoctrination, to training. But I was born with free will.

Ah, the old free will thing. It's a biggie out there in the superpowered cosmos, isn't it?

It is a, as you say, biggie right here, too.

You see ACE as a lesser being to you, don't you?

Before, yes. Now? No. Now I understand the dilemma ACE has faced all this time.

What dilemma is that?

The dilemma of loving those you want to protect. It makes the desire to interfere infinitely stronger.

Parents go through that. I want to protect Jamie from everything, and so does Jeff. But we can't.

Even ACE cannot. But I now understand why the deal was struck for ACE to return to your daughter instead of . . . Paul.

Paul is used to sharing headspace, you know. Wondered if Gower had also gone into Sandy in order to show the superconsciousness that his head was a safe haven. Probably.

Ah. And now you make the offer you know I will find hardest to resist. I understand why ACE calls you his leader.

You can't take on a real human form, can you? That's why you're utilizing the elements around you wherever you're 'landing.'

Correct. None of us can attain solid forms such as

yours. Unless we co-join. Some have done that in the past. They corrupted and were hailed as gods. Some were good. Some were not. All interfered.

ACE was careful about the interference. And neither ACE nor Paul has declared themselves a god. Jamie won't either.

You cannot say that for Jamie. Not yet. However, if ACE will do with her as he did with Paul, then you should not need to fear. And, I agree about Paul. I have looked into his heart and mind and he is a good person.

Yes, he is. And ACE will protect Jamie, and himself. So, some of that 'become a god' thing will be dependent upon what you and your people do, you know.

I know. And I . . . will consider your offer made on Paul's behalf.

He'll make it himself if you need or want him to.

No. Not just now. He sounded slightly evasive.

Ah, you and Paul were talking about this while we were inside you, weren't you?

We may have been, yes. However, I must take the time to think about the ramifications, because once that decision is made, it cannot be rescinded.

So, speaking of which, what happens now?

Now, I will allow you, and ACE, to continue on without my interference.

Wow. Thank you.

You say that as if it were not a foregone conclusion.

Sandy, dude, I take nothing for granted.

Yes. It is one of your greatest strengths. That, your almost suicidal bravery, and your ability to trust those that the evidence says you should not.

Is that a clue of some kind? Or just a backhanded compliment?

I suppose you will find out. I will . . . see you later, Kitty.

Later as in soonish in our terms, or later as in a long time from now?

Both.

Why are you leaving?

Because I have much to consider. And you have much to deal with. Soon. In your terms. Very soon, and very much.

Oh good. Or, as we call it, routine.

CHAPTER 38

YES. I understand why ACE wants to interfere. The urge is overwhelming.

Oh, give in to it and give me a little hint.

You are wasting great time, worry, and effort on a foregone conclusion.

Wow. That's your idea of a hint? Was one of your kind the Sphinx or something in a previous millennium?

Possibly so.

And with that, Sandy dissipated in front of us. The sand blew away, but this time, there was no tornado or backward dark film phenomenon. So either Sandy didn't need to do that and it had all been for show—always a real possibility— or his idea of "gone" was actually doing more Earth Walkabout.

Had the distinct impression that, in addition to other things, Sandy had discovered a sense of humor. Hoped that was a good thing, though that hint of his was a lot more like what Algar liked to pass off as help than anything else.

"What the hell?" Jeff asked. "It says it understands us and then leaves?"

Realized that Sandy had done what Algar normally did— moved me out of time to have a conversation. But it was something ACE had never done.

Whether that was good, bad, or indifferent, it didn't matter right now, though. I knew a "you're about to be attacked" hint when I heard one.

"We're about to be attacked."

"By what?" Christopher asked.

"By whom?" Chuckie added.

"By something or someone we've spent a lot of time, worry, and effort on, when whatever they or it are is a fore-gone conclusion. I think."

Chuckie cocked his head at me. "Repeat the clue exactly."

Shrugged. "Okay. 'You are wasting great time, worry, and effort on a foregone conclusion.' That was it. Oh, and that we'll have much to deal with, in our terms, very soon. Which I'm pretty damned sure means we're about to be attacked. So, um, battle stations. And all that."

"You told us not to bring in military," Reader pointed out. "So we have nothing to battle with."

"We are here," Rahmi said, sounding offended.

"And we have our battle staffs," Rhee added, sounding just as offended.

"I meant the rest of us," Reader said quickly. "We need to get some better weapons than we have on us."

"Too late," Tim said, as he pointed northwest, toward the mountains, nearish to where the exploded bunker had been. There was a road that went through the mountains, and something was coming down it. Something that was stirring up a lot of dust.

A-C eyesight was better than human, but that something was still far away and small. We all squinted. "I can't tell what that is," Jeff said. Everyone else agreed that they couldn't, either.

"Should we investigate up close?" Rahmi asked, now sounding eager. For the princesses, this probably hadn't been a very exciting mission so far.

However, I didn't like separating when we had no idea of what was going on. "No, not yet."

The princesses sighed, but moved forward and faced the oncoming whatever it was, clearly in order to be the first line of defense.

"I wish we had binoculars. I'd like to have a clear idea of

what's heading toward us, as opposed to sending someone from the team to scout."

"I could do it, but whatever, hang on," Christopher said. He zipped off.

"Seriously, baby, why not let the girls take a look?" Jeff said. "They're as fast as we are, and what could hurt them?"

"Oh, fine. Rahmi, Rhee, stay together, don't engage, just zip there, observe fast, and come back to report."

The princesses shot Jeff a look of gratitude and raced off. They returned before Christopher.

"There is a herd of animals running toward us," Rahmi said, sounding like this was, once again, not the excitement she'd been hoping for. "We don't know what kind."

"Big animals?" Gower asked.

"About the size of Duke," Rhee said. Duke was my parents' Labrador who was, like the rest of their dogs and cats, living with us in the Embassy. "They have tusks and what look like quills."

Christopher returned, binoculars for all in hand. "I have Home Base on alert, just in case whatever's coming is dangerous."

"Looks dangerous," Tim said. "Though I'm not sure if this is an attack or the filming of a show from the Discovery Channel."

Sure enough, the binoculars provided proof that there were a ton of animals all stampeding down and out of the mountains. Lots and lots of animals. As near as I could tell, all the same kind.

"Are those . . . wild pigs?" Jeff asked.

"No. They're not pigs. I'm pretty sure they're javelinas, or peccaries if you're not from Arizona."

"Distant cousins to pigs, in that sense, and hippos," Chuckie said. "They're native to the Southwest, and other parts of the country, too."

"Wasn't Natural Studies great? God, I miss college—nothing crazy ever happened there."

"You and I remember college very differently," Chuckie said.

"Everyone's a critic."

"Glad I put Home Base on alert," Christopher said. "Those hava-things look nasty."

"Javelinas. Ha-va-LEE-nas. It's not that hard a word. And there's a problem with the javelinas."

"Beyond that they're stampeding toward us and we're not getting out of the way?" Tim asked.

"We can outrun them," Christopher said. "Trust me. Tito gave me enough adrenaline that I can run us all to D.C. if I need to."

"You're back to rocking, Christopher. And yeah, Tim, the stampede is the issue—not that there is one, but that there are enough javelinas to create stampede conditions. There are an awful lot of them. I don't think anyone's running a javelina ranch nearby. So where the heck did they all come from?"

"I want to know why they're heading for us," Buchanan said. "Something has to be driving them or drawing them, and since there's no food for them here, driving is the option that wins."

"They're still a ways away," White said. "The binoculars make them seem much closer than they actually are."

"No kidding," Tim muttered.

White went on as if he hadn't spoken. "So I doubt we need to panic. As Christopher said, we can run away."

"I'd like to run away," Tim said. "Those things aren't tiny."

"Oh, as Rhee said, they're about the size of a Labrador."

"There are a ton of them and I don't want to have a *Lion King* death," Tim said.

"A what?" Christopher asked.

"Oh, Megalomaniac Lad, you complete me. It's a movie, Christopher. One of the many animated masterpieces from Disney. And Tim, relax. I just want to figure out what's causing the stampede and then we'll run away from the desert not-really-piggies, okay?"

"There," Buchanan said. "Just coming off that road."

Dust was blowing up, but not from the javelinas. They were creating dust, but this dust was behind them. It wasn't like the dust Sandy had created. It was sort of shimmering and looked vehicular in nature.

Sure enough, a dune buggy with two people in it bounced over something and so above the dust. The driver and passenger both didn't look familiar, but it was clear from how they were driving that they were herding the javelinas.

"Think it's just some kids joyriding?" Reader asked.

"Maybe," Chuckie replied. "They don't look armed."

"The way this day's been going, no," Buchanan said. "Assume they're armed in ways we can't see."

"Well, what are they armed with? Javelinas?"

"I'm going to refer to the poignant and terrifying Death of Mufasa scene from *The Lion King*," Tim said, "and say 'yes,' the big pigs that aren't really pigs but look enough like warthogs to pass are large enough to trample us. Let's get a couple of tanks and herd them elsewhere."

"I see you were traumatized as a child. Poor Megalomaniac Lad. We'll work on that."

"That seems like a reasonable plan, however, trauma or not," White said. "But we don't want the animals harmed if possible, and tanks would certainly be harmful. I wonder, Missus Martini, if you could, ah, use your talent to calm them down or send them in another direction?"

"Worth a shot, Mister White." Concentrated. I'd never tried to mind-meld with an animal I didn't know. Got nothing. Concentrated harder. Got more nothing. Decided to call in backup.

"Harlie, Poofikins, come to Kitty." The Poofs arrived on my shoulders. "Good Poofies! Can you help Kitty tell the javelinas to calm down or run back home?"

Poof reactions were not what I was expecting. Both Poofs jumped down and turned large and in charge. When the Poofs were in Protect and Attack Mode they were as big as Jeff, with a mouth full of razor sharp teeth. Still fluffy, though.

Harlie roared, and every Poof attached to every person here arrived, all large and toothy. Whether they'd been in everyone's pockets or not was a Poof Mystery I didn't have time to try to solve right now. They clustered up near the princesses, who were in front of the rest of us again in their standard Protect and Defend postures, presumably for the same reason—to form a protective barrier.

"What's going on?" Jeff asked. "Beyond the obvious."

"I have no idea." Concentrated on the Poofs. "Uh oh."

"Uh oh? That doesn't sound good, baby."

"It's not. Um, Mister White, is the Doctor Doolittle talent unheard of on Alpha Four or just really rare?"

"I'd assume there were always a few with the right affinity to communicate with at least the Royal Animals. However, it's not an officially known talent, like being an imageer."

Looked at Mahin. "But then again, neither is earthbending, and we have one right here. And an airbender in captivity."

"I'd like to go back to the 'uh oh,' " Reader said. "What's going on, Kitty?"

"I think one of the people in that dune buggy can talk to the animals. Someone's trying to tell the Poofs to attack us."

"Can we run now?" Tim asked. "I mean that seriously. I'm ready to run without an A-C to help me."

"Are the Poofs, ah, agreeing with whoever's telling them to attack us?" Gower asked.

"No, thankfully. Whoever's doing it is seriously pissing them off, though. But I can't talk to the javelinas. Or rather, I have no idea if I can or not, because Animal Man over there is occupying my animal interpreters' full attention. I'm kind of with Tim—we might want to get out of here."

As I said this, felt something weird and looked down. The salt and earth that made up Groom Lake was covering my feet up to the ankles. Tried to pull my foot out. The other sucked down a little.

"Nobody move their feet, and that's an order! Rahmi and Rhee, that order includes the two of you!"

"I'm going to hate this, aren't I?" Jeff asked.

"Not as much as Tim's going to. I think the other person in the dune buggy can move earth like Mahin can, or something. Because we're now in quicksand. And since Home Base uses this for a runway, there's no way in the world we just stumbled onto the quicksand patch."

"Could Sandy have done this?" Buchanan asked.

"No. Sandy warned us this was coming." Pulled out my phone to call Home Base for help but it rang before I could dial. "Serene, we need help."

"You have no idea. Kitty, you need to drop whatever you're doing and get back to the Science Center."

"Um, not sure we can. Tell me, fast, what's going on."

"This is on every news channel—the people being accused of setting all the bombs earlier today are . . . us, Centaurion Division."

CHAPTER 39

COULD ONLY THINK OF one thing to say. "Well, that's another fine mess we've gotten into."

"Kitty, they're calling for you, Jeff, Paul, and James. Everyone wants a statement."

"Serene, my current statement is 'help, help, we're all trapped in quicksand about to be trampled by a stampede of javelinas.' I don't think that's the statement we want going out to the world, but I'd really like you, personally, to concentrate on it."

"What are javelinas?"

"Peccaries. Wild not-really-pig-things. About the size of a Labrador. We have a lot of them heading toward us with intent to run right over us. And we're stuck. In quicksand. Don't ask how. Ask how you're going to get us out of this."

"There are a hundred if there are ten," Tim said. "Frankly, there are probably two hundred at least. I'm officially panicked. Just so you know."

"And we're living Tim's Greatest Fear because he saw *The Lion King* at an impressionable age, so, um, any help, Serene? Any at all?"

"Can't Mahin get you out?"

Looked over. Mahin was clearly concentrating. Nothing was happening. "If she can, not in time."

"I put Home Base on alert," Christopher said, looking around. "No one's coming."

"Because this doesn't look like anything dangerous to us, yet," Reader said. "However, we have another issue, because I'm calling Home Base and no one's answering."

"Oh, fantastic. Serene, either their telecommunications is down, someone's jamming them, or Home Base is once again under enemy control."

"I'll find out and call you back."

"Wait—" But she'd already hung up. Slid my phone back into the back pocket of my jeans. "I think Serene's doing something. Not sure what."

"Can the Poofs move?" Tito asked.

Took a look. "Doesn't look like it. But that may mean nothing. Harlie, can you all just get Kitty and everyone else out of here?"

A roar that ended in a mewl said that, no, they couldn't. The Poofs were as stuck as we were. Considering nothing had stopped the Poofs before, this was the definition of "not good."

"I can probably pull you out, baby," Jeff said.

"Maybe, but that just means you'll go down in the quicksand faster. We need a better plan. Or, better yet, planes. Tim! Call and scramble your team."

"Already on it, but it's going to take them a few minutes. They're at Dulce, where we have no jets, and James locked down the Dome and all the gates before we came out here, just in case. So Serene's having to reverse those orders and there's protocol involved that takes more than a second, A-Cs or not."

The men all got onto their phones, since we had no other options. No one's calls sounded like they were achieving anything other than stress.

The princesses had their battle staffs activated. "Rahmi, Rhee, see if you can use the staffs to cut yourselves out of the quicksand."

They tried, but pulled the staffs out of the sand quickly. "I could barely hold onto my staff," Rhee said, sounding shocked.

"I as well. And our staffs seemed to have no negative effect on the quicksand, either," Rahmi added.

Tried to see if any of us were near an edge. The quicksand looked slightly wetter and browner than the rest of the ground nearby. White was nearest to an edge, but the only chance he'd have to get out would be to fall over and try to grab the sand and salt and use that to pull himself out, meaning he'd get to suffocate nice and fast. Since we had no convenient trees with branches or vines hanging down just within our reach, pulling ourselves out was a non-option.

The princesses' battle staffs were just too short to reach an edge. There was no way any of this was a random happenstance.

Had to hand it to whoever had set this up—they'd rolled with the punches exceptionally well, or else this was always part of the plan. And it might have been, since Stephanie had felt confident she was still important.

How they'd created quicksand right where we were and when they wanted it, quicksand that Beta Twelve battle staffs couldn't hurt and could also hold the Poofs captive, was beyond me. However, LaRue had come back from the far reaches of space with Poof traps, most likely courtesy of the Z'porrah. So far, those traps were the only things the Poofs were helpless against, but one thing that could hurt the Poofs was one thing too many.

It was a good bet that whatever was creating the quicksand had the same element or whatever it was added into the mix. And it was an equally good bet that someone at Gaultier Enterprises, Titan Security, or even possibly YatesCorp were involved in the creation of whatever this actually was that we were all trapped in.

But what and who had created whatever was holding us wasn't important now. Getting out of this unscathed or with minimal scathing was.

"Mahin, any luck?"

"No, but I think . . . I think his talent is helped by the vibrations. If we can get the animals to stop running, I can probably free us."

"That's the thing, isn't it?"

The Poofs were clearly really stuck, because they weren't moving, but were instead roaring. That was probably increas-

ing the vibrations but I wanted the Poofs to stay large because if they went small they'd go under the quicksand in a
matter of moments. Plus I also wanted them able to eat the
javelinas if necessary.

Especially since I could see the javelinas clearly without
binoculars. They were still far away, but the dune buggy was
making sure to herd them toward us, and they wouldn't be far
away for too much longer. Time to call in reinforcements.

Concentrated. I had no idea where they were, but hoped
that our bond worked over long distances.

Jeff grabbed my hand. "Hang on, baby. I don't care if I
sink, I'm getting you out of here."

Opened my mouth to tell him no, but instead of words, a
cacophony of screeching came out. Fortunately, this stopped
Jeff. Also fortunately, it wasn't me making the noise.

The Peregrines had arrived.

CHAPTER 40

WE HAD TWELVE MATED PAIRS, and all twenty-four birds showed up, making an avian line between us and the javelinas, in front of the Poofs and princesses, Bird Shrieks on Maximum, claws forward in full-on Attack Mode, wings spread impressively.

The javelinas may have been mind controlled but they were still animals, and while they ate smaller animals as well as plants, they were prey for larger predators. And the Peregrines were doing their best to sound predatory, and twenty-four of them in one, big, screaming line looked pretty damn large. That combined with the Poofs and princesses with activated, glowing battle staffs behind them seemed to affect the javelinas more than their mind control.

The sounds of panicked squeals and gnashing tusks was combined with a lot of chaos, as the stampeding herd either went around us or tried to turn around.

"My God," Tim said. "What's that smell?"

"They're also called the skunk pig. I'm just happy the smell isn't commingling with our blood right now." Gently pulled my hand out of Jeff's—I didn't want him doing something manly and protective right now, because it would likely get him and the rest of us smothered.

"I am happy about that," Reader said as Tim gagged. "But the smell may kill us anyway."

"We're still trapped, with a lot of panicked animals around

us," Chuckie accurately pointed out. "Any ideas? We don't have enough ammunition to kill them all, and I can guarantee the dune buggy's going to stay out of the range of our guns."

True enough, the dune buggy had stopped far enough away that I was pretty sure no handgun was going to hit it.

"Bruno, my bird, someone needs to stealth it over to that dune buggy and attack with intent to seriously maim!"

Two Peregrines disappeared—Bruno and his right-wing bird, Harold. Human screams added to the mix.

"Nice," Tito said, as he tossed his medical bag to the side, so that it wasn't in, or at risk of being in, the quicksand. "I'm going on record as a bad doctor because I don't plan to patch them up."

"That actually doesn't sound like you," Chuckie said.

"I'm the shortest. I suffocate in the quicksand first. Well, me and Kitty. I say they can bleed to death."

"I'm with Tito. Mahin, any luck?"

She was concentrating, and making lifting motions with her hands. All of a sudden, her Poof shot up out of the quicksand and sailed over the javelinas.

This was great in that one Poof was free and it headed toward the dune buggy roaring like it was auditioning for Tim's *Lion King* revival. Javelinas scattered in all directions, some toward us, most away. A couple got past Peregrines, Poofs, and princesses to get themselves stuck in the quicksand. Couldn't pass judgment—we were stuck in the quicksand and we were supposedly a lot smarter.

Lifting the Poof free of the quicksand was bad, however, in that all of us sank down a little more. I was in the quicksand up to my calves.

"At this rate, Tito and Kitty will be underground, and Crawford and Reader might be too, White also, before enough of us are freed," Chuckie said quickly. "Mahin, you can't do that maneuver again."

"She could free a few more before we're in danger," Reader suggested.

"One, if you're up to it, Mahin," Chuckie said.

"Why a Poof?" Christopher asked.

"They're lighter." Mahin concentrated and Harlie flew

free. And the rest of us sank down a lot farther—Tito and I were in the quicksand at mid-thigh.

Harlie started chasing off javelinas, while the Peregrines continued to ensure most of the panicked animals went away from us and the princesses sent those who made it past the Peregrines flying with well aimed hits.

"That's it, Mahin, no more, and that's an order," Chuckie said, Voice of C.I.A. Authority on Full. "We moved down farther the second time than the first. And before anyone wants to complain or suggest we try again, I can guarantee that I've done the math and it's only going to get worse."

"Only idiots argue with the smartest guy in the quicksand, Chuckie. But, why isn't this quicksand stuff stopping? Animal Man appears to have lost control of the javelinas, so how is his companion keeping the concentration going under these circumstances?"

"Who says the driver is actually the one controlling the ground?" Jeff asked.

We all looked around as much as we could, which wasn't all that much, because movement meant sinkage. We were all facing the oncoming herd, so northwest. Looking northeast to west was fairly simple. Looking south and southeast wasn't, because the act of trying to turn and look over our shoulders sent us all a little bit lower.

Called the Peregrines over in my mind. They disengaged and flew to us. There were enough of them that, if they were strong enough, we could each grab a Peregrine's feet and have them pull us out. Was about to ask them to try this when the quicksand under each bird shot up, wrapped around their feet, and pulled them down with us. The Peregrines screamed and struggled, but they were caught, too, just like the rest of us.

The Peregrine's screams brought Bruno, Harold, and Fluffball back from their attack to try to help the other animals. This was a mistake, and before I could warn them to get away, more quicksand shot up and they were captured, too.

This left Harlie, only, out. I sent the Poof a mental message to stay back from the quicksand, which it did. So one small thing going right.

Now that their attackers were captured, the guys in the

dune buggy revved it up and started gathering the javelinas again, clearly with intent to have them run us over, or at least add in weight to the quicksand so that we'd all sink more. Sure, this wasn't acting like real quicksand should, but I was pretty damn sure it wasn't real quicksand. Not that this knowledge helped us at all.

The latter option seemed to be the one, as more javelinas ran in and were quickly trapped. Their struggles meant they sank quickly, but they also caused the rest of us to get sucked down more, bit by bit.

Harlie went after the dune buggy, but the damage was still done. The guys in the dune buggy, seeing the enraged, giant Poof after them, turned tail and left. Harlie chased them for a ways, but then stopped suddenly and headed back to us. The dune buggy had either really revved it up or disappeared, because it wasn't anywhere I could see anymore.

The javelinas were screaming for help. They weren't to blame—they were just innocent animals being used by our enemies—they didn't deserve to die, and certainly not like this.

Since having Jamie and getting all those reverse-genetic powers, the one thing I'd really learned was that, in danger situations, rage was my friend. Through all of this, all the weird and danger and worse that had gone on today, I hadn't gotten enraged. Angry, sure, upset, worried, and so on, but not enraged.

But as I looked at the javelinas struggling in the quicksand and thought about the fact that, as usual, the bad guys were harming things weaker than themselves simply because they could, I felt the rage start. But I needed it to be a rage worthy of the term "berserker."

Looked at the Poofs. They were trapped, too, and they were never trapped. That meant both that whoever was doing this had something truly extra under the hood, and also that my Poofs were probably terrified. The Peregrines were terrified for sure, based on their bird screams. And everyone else with me had to be frightened. Sure we'd all faced battle situations many times, but we were far more helpless right now than I could remember any of us being before.

All of this was probably to get Jamie, Patrick, and the other hybrid kids to time warp themselves over here to save us. Or it was just a plan to kill those of us here and then take care of everyone else who was conveniently herded into the Science Center. Or to get the Dome unlocked. Or other things I was too stressed out to come up with. The options were many. My options were few.

One of the javelinas made terrified eye contact with me and suddenly I could talk to it. Or rather, it could talk to me. And what it was saying in javelina was easy to decipher—it was terrified and asking me to save it somehow.

Tried to tell it and the other trapped javelinas to calm down, but even if they understood me, they were too close to going fully under to listen. Panic made animals stupid.

And we were animals, meaning I was probably being stupid. Rage was great. Thinking while enraged was better.

While some of us had long-range talent ability, most didn't. And even if whoever was creating the quicksand did have talent that could be used from far, far away, he or she had to be close, because otherwise said sandshifter wouldn't have been able to grab the Peregrines.

And there were rocks behind us. Rocks that were above the quicksand line.

"Jeff, Chuckie, Malcolm—I think whoever's doing this is on the rocks behind us," I said as softly as I could in order to be heard, which wasn't as softly as I'd have liked. But I had to figure the animal screams would block a lot from whoever was doing this to us.

"That'd be great if we could get out or even turn around," Jeff said in kind.

"I've managed to look behind us," Buchanan replied, also quietly. "There's no one there."

"But we know someone who can make himself and anyone else he touches go invisible." Did my best to relax and sent a message to Harlie. The Poof roared and raced behind us.

Because of how we were stuck in the quicksand, Jeff was on one side of me, Buchanan the other, and Chuckie was between me and Buchanan, a little behind us, but not so far back that he wasn't in my safe viewing range.

So I was able to see that both Buchanan and Chuckie had their guns out, and, as Harlie raced behind us, I watched both men bend over quickly, so that they were looking upside down, between their legs.

Heard shouts and screams, from more than one person, and then both men fired their guns. While half upside down, and through their legs. If we all survived, the image would be one I could use when I needed a laugh. However, survival wasn't a given at this time, so the Inner Hyena wasn't at risk of coming out.

Both men cursed while the javelinas freaked out even more.

"Not sure if we hit anyone," Chuckie said as they straightened up. "But if we did, no one's visible."

"We didn't hit the Poof," Buchanan added, before I could ask. Harlie stayed on the rock, growling.

Could have sworn I saw someone running and another shimmering off in the distance, but before I could really tell if it was Siler's chameleon look or just wishful thinking, I was distracted by the princesses urgently calling my name.

"We are about to be under new attack," Rhee called.

"We believe," Rahmi amended, sounding worried. "Something is coming."

"Now what?" I asked, undoubtedly speaking for everyone, as we all used the binoculars to see what they'd spotted.

Something new was heading down from the road in the mountains, the same road the dune buggy had come from. Only this made far less sense to be here than the dune buggy had. Spotted what might have been a shimmering behind it, but it disappeared before I could be sure.

"Is that what I think it is?" Tim asked.

"I'm not sure *what* I think that is," Gower said.

"It's something that really shouldn't be here, not in this particular area. It's a combine harvester. Used in farming. Which is not something Home Base is particularly noted for."

And, of course, said combine—blades merrily spinning—was heading right for us.

CHAPTER 41

"**O**KAY, WELL, killing us is certainly today's plan."

"Who the hell has a combine harvester out here?" Tim asked, sounding as freaked out as I was pretty sure the rest of us felt. "Is Old Macdonald living on the other side of these hills?"

"There are facilities in the mountains," Reader said, "but none of them are related to farming, storing farm equipment, or hoarding javelinas."

"Why a combine harvester, for God's sake?" Tim wasn't giving this one up. "Won't something that big sink in this stuff, too?"

"Yeah, but the blade is gigantic enough that it might not sink in. And even if it did sink, it would just make the rest of us sink faster." Mostly because it would likely be on top of us, slicing our heads off or dicing us up while shoving us under with no hope of getting out.

"This was planned out," Chuckie said, voice taut. "I'm sure the only thing not going according to plan is that Vander and Serene are still alive and not caught in this with us. So, glad you sent them back, Kitty."

"I wish I'd sent all of us back."

"I still can't get free of this stuff," Christopher said. "So if the Poof and the shooting scared off whoever's doing this, either they just moved where we can't see them, or their work here is done."

"That's it," Jeff said, as he reached over and grabbed the back of my jeans. Mahin was close enough on his other side that he could grab her with his other hand.

"Jeff, don't! It'll shove you under!"

"I don't care," he said calmly. "But I refuse to let my wife and the other non-warrior woman under my protection die, especially not in the way our enemies have planned."

With that he pulled. Hard.

Jeff was big and brawny, and while he wasn't bodybuilder muscled, he was definitely Greek God muscled. I could see his biceps bulging as he strained against the quicksand. But the quicksand didn't have that special Surcenthumain boost.

For a moment I was really sure my clothes were merely going to come off in his hands, but Levi's were made tough. And apparently, Armani was as well, because Jeff grunted and then, with a sound that was reminiscent of the biggest, sloppiest slurp in the world, Mahin and I flew out of the quicksand.

Practice meant I was able to land in a roll and jump to my feet. Mahin didn't land as smoothly, but she wasn't hurt. I pulled her to her feet and spun around, to see the rest of our team now sucked down a whole lot more.

Reader, Tim, and Christopher were in the quicksand up to their chests. The princesses, Gower, White, Buchanan and Chuckie were in quicksand to their waists. The animals were all down, most of the javelinas and Peregrines barely keeping heads above the surface, and Tito and Jeff, because he'd done the pulling effort for me and Mahin, were in the quicksand up to their armpits.

Which, in a way, was good. Because that was the last little thing required to flip me into the level of blinding rage I needed. Even with the fact that everyone had their hands in the air and were essentially waving them like they just didn't care, I wasn't able to focus on much other than the fact that my husband, friends, pets, and other helpless animals were all going to smother soon.

We couldn't risk getting near the quicksand, because if the sandshifter could grab the Peregrines, he could also grab me and Mahin again.

"Mahin, get onto that rock with Harlie. I have no idea what to tell you to do, but have the vibrations slowed down enough that you can do something?"

"Not really," she said. "Kitty, have you noticed that there's nothing on us, or on Harlie? None of that stuck to us, which is technically impossible."

Looked down. Sure enough, there was nothing on us. We weren't even damp. Come to think of it, the quicksand hadn't felt damp, or icky, or even grainy. It had felt smooth.

"Tell Chuckie about this. Keep them occupied and not moving. See if Harlie can calm down the other animals somehow."

"What are you going to be doing?"

Pulled my iPod out, put my earbuds in, and hit play. "What I always do. Improvising and going with the crazy."

As I took off for the combine "Blow Me (One Last Kiss)" from Pink came on. Great, it was a good song, good beat, angry lyrics. Just hoped it wasn't Algar being prophetic and telling me I'd never see Jeff alive again.

When I was this enraged, the skills flowed perfectly. I was as good a fighter as Rahmi and Rhee, as fast as Christopher, and almost as strong as Jeff. So I reached the combine in a matter of moments.

The two guys from the dune buggy were driving it, which figured. On the plus side, this hopefully meant there weren't a million more people with dangerous farm equipment on their way.

It was a John Deere combine, and it was gigantic, with nasty blades on a very wide track—if it reached my friends and family stuck in the quicksand, it would only need one pass to turn them all into mincemeat.

Ran around the blades and jumped onto the side. The driver and his passenger were inside a glass-enclosed cabin. Grabbed onto one of the side-view mirrors and part of the roof and swung my lower body forward and kicked the glass as hard as I could. It cracked, and I kept on. It broke soon enough.

Swung again and kicked the passenger in the head, which knocked him into the driver. This caused the combine to swerve, or really, since this wasn't the most nimble of vehicles, to slowly change course.

Now I swung into the cab. I was moving so fast that I was able to grab the passenger and slam him back against the cab a couple of times until he was obviously unconscious.

Unfortunately, the driver was still driving and he started hitting at me. I hit back. I also grabbed the wheel and cranked it hard to the left, to hopefully pull the combine off course even more.

I was winning this particular battle until someone else joined the party. Two someones. Siler and some guy I'd never seen before both jumped in. Once inside the now very crowded cabin, Siler hit the other guy with a sucker punch, grabbed me around the waist, and yanked me out. We fell onto the ground, and he rolled us away from the combine. We ended up several yards away, with me on my stomach, him on top of me.

"I'm really going to kill you, you jerk!"

Siler pulled out one of my earbuds. "Glad you're making it look good," he said quietly in my ear. "But I don't think we're being observed anymore."

"What the hell—"

I'd have asked him what he meant and what was going on, but the combine exploded.

CHAPTER 42

SILER GOT OFF OF ME, and I scrambled to my feet. He was nowhere I could see, but I couldn't take the time to look around much, since I had to run away from the explosion and flying metal.

Having run track all through high school and college, I'd learned to never look behind me when running like crazy. Sprinters who look behind them lose the race, so I went by the philosophy that what was behind me didn't matter. The few times I'd broken that rule had only proven why the rule was a good one.

So I didn't look back, I just ran like crazy away from the combine. Stopped when I reached the base of the northern mountains and turned around. Parts were still flying through the air, but none were going to have a shot of coming near me—I was far away from where I'd started.

Fortunately, the combine had been in the middle of Groom Lake when it exploded, so the others weren't at risk of being hit with debris, either.

The combine being blown up was great, in that it couldn't kill everyone. But Jeff and the animals were still close to suffocating in the weird quicksand, and I couldn't see anything clearly from all the way across the salt flat.

However, what I could see was that nothing and no one was coming out of Home Base. Considering we'd already had two big explosions, Christopher had gone to get binoculars and supposedly put them on alert only a few minutes ago, and considering there had been a stampede, a dune buggy, and a combine cruising around in a highly restricted area, by now someone at Home Base should have been taking an interest.

Figured this meant that we were indeed infiltrated in some way. Meaning no help could be expected from anyone there. As I contemplated my next move beyond running back and trying to pull everyone out at once—which I had to admit was going to be impossible—I shoved my other earbud back in and the music changed. "Firestarter" from The Prodigy hit my personal airwaves. Chose to take this as a suggestion from Algar.

Parts of the combine were burning. So there was fire. Maybe fire would destroy the weird quicksand that wasn't real quicksand. Worth a try.

However, how to get the fire over was the question. My brain nudged—the same people who'd just blown up in the combine had been driving a dune buggy earlier. So, where was it? And what else would I find if I found that vehicle?

Reader had mentioned facilities in the mountains. I actually knew where those were. Not because I'd memorized Home Base's layout and surrounding areas or anything responsible like that, but because Jeff and I had snuck off there to be alone in the early days of our relationship. There was a road that led into them, and that same road also connected to the smaller road that went over a pass between the mountains, the road the dune buggy had herded the javelinas through.

Took off running, but I didn't bother with the roads. I was going so fast that going up the small mountain was no big deal.

Crested the top and sure enough, there was the dune buggy. I was faster than it, though, so that wasn't what I wanted. Searched the area.

There were no people in evidence, and it wasn't a hard area to search, considering it consisted of four stationary satellite dishes and a couple of small bunkers. One of which was marked as Supplies. Wrenched the door open to see a nice selection of weapons including a flamethrower. Grabbed it, then wrenched the door of the other bunker open. It still held a fully functioning radio transmitter setup. Might be useful later.

Put the flamethrower on, then took off, back down the mountain and across the Lake. Took the time to run around the remains of the combine. Saw people parts within the wreckage and decided a full examination could wait for later.

Arrived as the music changed to "Let's All Go (To The Fire Dances)" by Killing Joke. Clearly fire or similar was going to do something positive. Or else Algar just wanted to watch the world burn.

Thankfully, everyone's heads—persons and animals— were still above the surface. In fact, most of them hadn't gone down too much lower than when I'd left. Other than Jeff. He was up to his neck and his arms were under as well. Good or bad, the rage left me in a whoosh, to be replaced with fear. This wasn't a good change.

"How goes the offensive, Missus Martini?" White asked calmly. Focused on the fact that he was calm and tried to relax somewhat.

"I think Animal Man and the sandshifter, along with their driver, are dead. Pretty positive Home Base is infiltrated or in some kind of other trouble we're going to hate. What's going on over here?"

"Mahin's keeping us up," Chuckie said. "Don't distract her."

"Jeff, are you okay? Why are you lower down than when I left?"

"Chuck and I figured out how to keep the animals all up. It moved me lower. I'm fine."

"Do I want to know?"

"Probably not. I'll ask you about the exploding tractor later. Why do you have a flamethrower, baby?"

"Um, I think I can burn everyone out."

"Are you serious?" Tim asked. "You're going to save us by flambéing us? That's your plan?"

Couldn't tell them why I thought this was the right thing to do. Not only could I not mention Algar, but no one was going to be excited that I was taking direction from my iPod. "Um . . ."

"It's not real quicksand," Mahin said through gritted teeth. Everyone looked surprised, so I figured Mahin hadn't mentioned it earlier. Decided I'd berate her for not following orders later. Like when we were all still alive later.

"Right! It's not. It didn't stick to me, Mahin, or Harlie, and real quicksand would. I think it's got whatever the Poof Traps were made out of in it."

"How?" White asked.

"Siler helped the sandshifter to seed the area we were standing in, that's my only guess." Wasn't sure if I should mention that Siler had been the one to blow up the combine, with the three people who'd attacked us inside. As with berating Mahin, maybe later. There was something else I needed to think about. One word. How.

"So you think burning it will work?" Gower asked. "How?"

This wasn't the "how" I was hoping to concentrate on. How did the combine get here? Felt sure that if Olga were here, she'd be confirming that this was the question.

"No," Chuckie said thoughtfully, "it could work. It might make it more liquid, both the sand and whatever the element or elements in it that make up the Poof Traps. Serene's team did a lot of research on those—extreme heat affected it. It's going to be tight, though, Kitty. The difference between warm enough and boiling is slight."

"But no pressure!"

"We are willing to be the first," Rahmi said. Rhee nodded.

"I don't think I can get to you two easily, because of the Peregrines. In fact, the only one who isn't blocked by a lot of animals and is also near the edge of the quicksand patch is Mister White."

"No way," Christopher said. "You're not using that near my dad."

White shrugged. "I'm in the best position, son. It will be fine. I'm willing, Missus Martini."

"Do you have any idea how to use that thing?" Tito asked.

"Um . . ." Before I could share that I had no actual clue,

my music switched to, of all things, "Cool, Cool Water" by The Beach Boys. At the same time, the air near me shimmered.

"Who's coming?" Christopher asked. "No one's advised any of us that they're sending help."

Realized how everything had shown up here when, by all rights, Home Base should have spotted everything—javelina herd, dune buggy, and combine—and removed them well before we'd ever known of their existence.

"The bad guys are using gates somehow. I've seen shimmering around the areas where the dune buggy and combine have shown up." And around where I thought Siler and the sandshifter had gone. But they'd come back, because the combine had blown up with the guy I assumed was the sandshifter in it well after I'd seen that particular shimmering.

"That's impossible," Reader said.

"Nothing's impossible," Buchanan said.

"Especially because the technology has been here for decades," Chuckie added.

Turned toward the shimmering floater gate. "Please let this be help. Or else I'm going to use the flamethrower for something other than getting all of you out."

CHAPTER 43

HAPPILY, it was the flyboys who stepped through, and extra happily, they were all equipped with ropes and harnesses.

Jerry shook his head. "We can't leave you all alone for a minute."

"All hell's breaking loose and here you all are, enjoying mud baths," Hughes said chidingly.

"Shocking disregard for what's important," Walker agreed.

"It's a good thing we're around to actually do the real work," Joe said as he dropped a thick lasso around White, who moved it to under his armpits.

"And you've brought the animals in on it, too," Randy said. "I'm ashamed of all of you, I really am."

"The levity's great," Jeff said dryly. "But some of us are actually up to our necks in this stuff. Speaking for myself and the animals, if you pull the others out, we all go under, so don't pull the others out."

"Don't make me flame you," I added. "Though, admittedly, I can see you as Johnny Storm, Jerry. At least based on attitude."

"I'm touched. But we can't lose a fine member of Congress," Jerry said with a grin. "Especially when it's one of the only members we like."

"Home Base is infiltrated," I shared apropos of trying to get them back onto the situation at hand.

"No, actually, it's not," Joe said.

"Yeah," Randy said. "It's actually worse. Presidential order was given to Home Base to not assist in anything going on out here."

"What?" This was shouted, or a variation, some with curse words, by everyone other than the animals and the flyboys. Even the princesses. Even Mahin. Happily, no one went any lower into the quicksand, but I didn't figured we'd be lucky twice.

"You guys! Stop distracting Mahin or everyone's going to go under!" Wasn't sure any of them would listen to me, but it was worth a shot.

"Oh, relax, it was faked," Hughes said.

"A very good fake," Randy added.

"But it took Angela a while to get that cleared up." Joe lassoed Chuckie and Buchanan who both followed White's example and put the thick leather around their chests and under their arms.

"Meanwhile, we weren't allowed over here," Walker added. "Dome was on lockdown and the presidential order kept it locked, despite Serene's screaming."

"She can really scream," Jerry added. "I may have permanent hearing loss."

"That's awesome, guys, but my husband and my pets are about to die, so consider me lacking in levity. And holding a flamethrower. Just sayin'."

More shimmering and Lorraine, Claudia, and Serene stepped through the floater gate, followed by Melanie and Emily, Lorraine and Claudia's mothers. They all had packs of equipment and such with them. "Actually, we don't think anyone's in danger now," Emily said briskly.

"Tell that to the javelinas and Peregrines," Jeff said. "And me. I'm not feeling all secure."

"I can barely keep them up," Mahin said. "And I'm all that's keeping them above the surface."

Serene shook her head. "We did some infrared and spectrum analysis from the Science Center—you should all just pull out without issue."

"Seriously, Jeff almost popped a vessel pulling me and

Mahin out and when he got us out, everyone else went down. I think this stuff has to be superheated in order to release them."

"No," Lorraine said. "It needs to be superheated to be destroyed. You can relax," she told Mahin.

"I can still feel the weight," Mahin said.

"I'd personally appreciate being really certain before Mahin stops holding me up," Jeff said. "And I'm going to share that the animals all feel the same way."

Claudia stuck something metal into the quicksand. She was near enough to be grabbed and pulled into it, but nothing happened. Presumably the dead sandshifter had to control that. So, one for the win column. She pulled out what was obviously a sample and Melanie took it and examined it under what I realized was a field microscope that was attached to goggles.

"You look like something out of a steampunk novel."

"Is now the time for the Kittyisms?" Christopher asked, voice strained.

"It's an alternative, eclectic aesthetic," Claudia said. "A reimagining of history."

"You should get out more," Lorraine added.

"I think it's quite cool, steampunk," Melanie shared. "But that's beside the point. This is now dormant."

"Doesn't feel dormant," Tim said. "I still feel amazingly trapped."

"You are, but we can get you out," Emily said. "We just need—"

"Cool water." Sent a mental message to Algar to make up his mind. Decided I was getting enough mixed messages and put my iPod back into my purse.

"Yes," Lorraine looked impressed. "Good call, Kitty."

"What were you going to do with the flamethrower, though?" Serene asked. Innocently. I knew she was faking the innocent and probably laughing at me. But she kept it all inside and had her Innocence on the Hoof look look going strong.

"I was going to superheat the quicksand to get them out. Because it sounded like a workable idea at the time."

"If it was still active it would have been," Emily said.

"Think of this element—which is not from Earth, but I'm sure we all knew that—as something similar to silicon. When it's heated it becomes malleable. Heat it enough, though, and it breaks down and literally burns away."

"Are the Z'porrah from a colder planet?"

"We think so," Serene said. "It would explain why super-heating this destroys it, versus just changes its properties. But that's not the only possible explanation."

"Based on dinosaurs and lizards, them coming from a warmer planet would make more sense," Emily said. "But we haven't spent a lot of time on the Z'porrah, and what little we had was lost last year, so they've been a low priority data rebuild."

Wondered if Algar would agree with that. He hadn't been happy with anything we'd done this past year, perhaps this was another failing on our parts. Now, of course, wasn't the time to find out.

Claudia was on her phone. "Yes, cold water. Now. Or else I'll ask the head of the P.T.C.U. to personally come see why you didn't verify that 'presidential' order. Yes, she's quite upset. I think the phrase 'ready to put a cap in yo ass' about covers it."

"I'm so proud."

"It was a lot easier to deal with Home Base when Colonel Franklin was in charge," Lorraine muttered.

"Save that thought for later. And I do mean that I want us thinking about this later. But, you know, after everyone's out and safe and all that."

"Thanks so much, since I'm still in here up to my neck," Jeff said. "But I appreciate Angela's help. I'd appreciate everyone else having the same urgency. Right now, the only person who seems intent to keep me alive is Mahin. And I'm incredibly grateful for that, Mahin. Please ignore the others until everyone's out safely."

"Relax, Jeff, the water's on its way," Emily said. "It's a good thing this was going on here. It's night on the East coast."

"Not that it's going to stop all the accusations," Serene said. "It's bad. Cliff and Vander are trying to keep things controlled, but they're not having a lot of success. And with all of you here, it looks like we're trying to hide away or avoid the questions."

"No one knows what happened?"

"Well, yes, those with the right clearances. But it's not as if we can tell the general public that all of you were kidnapped and stuck in alien quicksand, now can we?"

"I suppose not. By the way, our enemies were using floater gates to get everything here, like the combine harvester and, I'm sure, the poor javelinas, too."

"How?" Reader asked. "We monitor all gate activity worldwide."

Serene jerked. "But not when the Dome is locked down."

CHAPTER 44

"WHAT DO YOU MEAN?" I asked. "We've used the gates when we were in lockdown. We do it all the time."

"Yes, but it's monitored differently," Serene explained. "When we're in lockdown, the Dome is considered our most strategic and vulnerable location. So while we can and do use the gates when the Dome is locked down, it takes itself off the grid, if that makes any sense."

"It does," Chuckie said. "The Dome becomes self-functioning and stops monitoring other locations, is that right?"

"Yes," Reader said. "That's why all airport gates are calibrated for the Dome—in case of lockdown, or any other emergency, they'll still work to get our people to safety. However, this means that if someone's using an unauthorized gate, we wouldn't spot it."

"They could run on a different frequency, too," Tim suggested. "The Dome would spot that under normal situations, but under lockdown, it would become almost impossible to spot."

"Assume that's what they've done, because I saw shimmering, just like for floater gates, behind the dune buggy and the combine."

"Should we even ask?" Hughes asked.

"I'd rather wait for Kitty to tell us about it," Walker replied.

"Everyone's a comedian."

The water truck finally trundled up and a couple of guys in uniform got out, attached a hose, and, under Emily's direction, carefully watered down the quicksand.

"Get the animals out first," Jeff said. "And that's an order."

Reader nodded. "I agree."

Once this stuff was wet, Jerry stepped on it. It held him and neither yanked him down nor trapped him. He pulled one of the Peregrines out. It slid out easily, cawed its thanks, and went to Mahin and Harlie.

I followed Jerry onto the now-hardened quicksand surface—it was like walking on wet sand at the beach in Cabo. Was fairly sure both Jeff and I would have preferred to be in Cabo right about now. Maybe later, if we all got a later, we could go there for a little family vacation.

While Jerry handled the Peregrines, I went to the Poofs. Harlie went small and jumped onto Mahin's shoulder. The other Poofs went small as well, making it really easy for me to pull them out, especially since I did it at hyperspeed. Finished up and helped Jerry with the remaining Peregrines. Received much telepathic animal love, which was nice.

Poofs and Peregrines out, we now had to deal with the javelinas. Thankfully, whether they'd realized everyone was here to help or one of the other animals had calmed them down, they didn't squeal or struggle.

Because so many were trapped and because they weren't tiny, the javelinas required all who weren't in the quicksand to assist, two to an animal. While the others pulled out the peccaries, I slipped lassoes over everyone else. Other than Jeff, since the only option was to put the lasso around his neck. "How are we going to get you out?" I asked him quietly, as I knelt down and stroked his hair.

"We'll think of something, baby."

"I can do it," Mahin said. "Once everyone else is out."

"Really, you can stop putting out the effort," Lorraine said. "It's all dormant."

"You think so, but I can feel it," Mahin said calmly. "The surface is hardening, yes. But the water hasn't seeped in enough. Once all the animals are out, while you pull the others out, I'll be keeping Jeff up."

The other gals started to argue with her. "Stop it!" Everyone looked at me. "Look, this is Mahin's area of expertise. If she says she feels that this crap is still active, then it's still active. She's the only reason we're still alive to be having this argument. It doesn't matter who's right, especially since the likelihood is that both sides are. Focus on what you can do, and doing it quickly, and stop taking her concentration away."

Dazzlers were, to a one, smart. And not given to a lot of arguing in the face of logic. They all closed their mouths, nodded, and got back to the business at hand.

There were a lot of javelinas trapped, so it took a while, even using hyperspeed. The sun was starting to set when the last one was released back into the wild. But they didn't go anywhere, just milled around looking frightened and confused.

"Bruno, Harlie, can anyone get the javelinas home? I don't know where they came from, but it wasn't right here. There's a good chance they came from far away, and were herded through a floater gate." Bruno squawked and bobbed his head. Harlie mewled, and then, all the Poofs, and all the javelinas, disappeared.

"What are they doing?" Jeff asked.

"The Poofs will take the javelinas home and scout the area, to see if they can spot anything, like where our enemies are hanging out."

"Good initiative," White said.

"How are we getting everyone out at once?" I asked. "Or are we doing it one at a time again?"

"It'll be harder with the people, because they're bigger," Serene said. "We need to lift them straight up if we can."

The flyboys all looked at me and shook their heads. "Tim, it's a good thing you took over Airborne," Hughes said. "Kitty's losing her touch."

"Heartbreaking," Walker added. "How our mighty has fallen."

"I'll hurt you all later. Okay, fine, you're going to get a plane and pull them out?"

"Helicopters, but why get bogged down by semantics?" Jerry said with a grin.

Claudia and Lorraine grabbed their husbands, Joe grabbed Hughes, Randy grabbed Walker, and they all took off.

"Jerry, you're not going?"

"Someone has to handle things here on the ground and you're not up to it." He winked at me. "We can only have a couple birds in the air anyway, since we're dealing with a small area."

The airmen who'd brought out the water truck backed it off under Emily's direction. But she kept it nearby, just in case.

"Kitty, you'll need to be off of the area," Mahin called.

"I don't want to leave you here." Kissed Jeff's forehead.

"It'll be okay, baby. I promise. And if I go under, I'll hold my breath."

"Good. You can hold your breath a long time." He'd proven that when I'd taken an impromptu swim in the Potomac, after all.

Kissed his forehead again, then trotted over to join Mahin, Melanie, and Emily on the rocks, which timed out nicely, as the helicopters arrived.

Lines were lowered and Jerry attached them to everyone other than Jeff. Christopher, White, Rahmi, Rhee, and Tim were hooked to one chopper, while Chuckie, Buchanan, Tito, Gower, and Reader were hooked to the other.

The wind from the choppers was intense and my worry about Jeff increased. He couldn't take a deep breath before going under if he had sand and dirt flying into his face.

Jerry got off the now mostly solid quicksand and gave the all-clear sign. He stayed down there just in case.

The choppers lifted up at the same time and everyone pulled out easily, looking like we had a lot of human fish on the lines. The choppers flew off slowly, in opposite directions, so they could lower their charges and not interfere with Mahin and Jeff.

Which was good because Jeff was still stuck, and I could tell that Mahin was struggling. Sure enough, Jeff went under. Managed not to scream, but only because I was too frightened.

Leaped behind Mahin and held her. "Melanie, Emily, touch her! Mahin needs our energy or Jeff's going to die!"

They did as requested. Mahin shuddered, then tensed her whole body. Jeff shot up, with the same sucking sound Mahin and I had made. "Hold her up!" I shouted to Melanie and Emily as I took off.

Got to where Jeff was landing at the same time as Jamie's Poof, Mous-Mous, did. Considering the Poof had been, to my knowledge, in the Science Center until a second ago, this was both a relief and a shock.

Mous-Mous went large and shoved me out of the way as Jeff landed on the Poof. "Ooof!"

"Are you okay? Jeff? Mous-Mous?"

Jeff slid off and Mous-Mous went back to small. It jumped onto Jeff's shoulder and nuzzled him, then jumped to my shoulder and nuzzled me. It was fine, thanks for asking. With a purr, it disappeared, presumably heading right back to Jamie.

I grabbed Jeff and hugged him tightly, which wasn't that easy since I still had on both my purse and the flamethrower. Didn't care.

Jeff kissed me, deeply. As always, fantastic. Not long enough, but then, an hour straight of kissing him really wasn't long enough. "Thanks, baby," he said softly, as he ended our kiss. "Always nice to know that you care."

"You know I do. You can't drown in quicksand on me. Especially not when we haven't had sex since the night before."

Jeff grinned. "I can't tell you how much I appreciate your laser focus on the priorities."

CHAPTER 45

THE OTHERS WERE DOWN AND OUT of their rescue harnesses, and the choppers were on the ground. The water truck was still here, too.

Because it was summer, even though the sun had started setting a few minutes ago, we still had light, probably for at least another half an hour. Realized it was really late, because sunset in the Southwest at the end of July was usually close to eight in the evening.

Was glad Mom, Dad, and especially Lucinda were with Jamie—her grandparents would ensure she got dinner, took a bath, and went to bed on time, and Lucinda wouldn't be involved in any of the action, meetings, or planning sessions, so she could and probably would stay with Jamie in the Lair.

"Should have kept the combine in one piece," Reader said as we all congregated back at the rocks and Tito retrieved his medical bag so he could give Mahin and Jeff both some adrenaline. Jeff got to take it in a vein instead of directly into his hearts, so I counted that in the win column. "We could use it to dig this stuff up."

"We're bringing in lighting and large equipment," Jerry said. "It'll take a while to transfer, though. Requiring a floater gate as big as the one we used right before Kitty's wedding."

"Should we do that?" Contemplated if now was a good time to mention Siler's part in the combine explosion. "Dig this stuff up, I mean, not use a floater gate." My brain nudged.

"Yes," Mahin said, wincing as the needle went in. "I believe it will remain active if we don't remove it all."

The Poofs returned in their standard small sizes, and went back to their owners. Poofikins and Harlie were with Jeff, but they gave me an earful.

"What did they say?" Jeff asked while he pretended he wasn't petting them.

"The javelinas were herded from all over. The Poofs were able to get them back to their homes. No signs of any bad guy lairs near the javelina homelands."

"Why javelinas?" Tim asked. "Just to freak me out that much more?"

"No." Thought about it. "Mahin says the quicksand maker needed the vibrations to help him do his thing. Maybe he needed a certain frequency in order to get his stuff to work right, and the javelinas have the right frequency."

Chuckie nodded. "That's a good theory." Glad he'd mentioned this before Christopher could say I was an idiot. "Let's check that out," he said to Serene. "And see if their stampede frequency might have helped the creation of the floater gates our enemies used, too."

Wanted to know why my brain was nudging about the floater gates when what I really wondered was why I was holding a flamethrower. It wasn't needed, and hadn't been needed. Clearly the gals had all known what to do. Sure, Mahin had been right, but she hadn't needed fiery help, either. And though they'd said that fire could destroy this stuff, we actually wanted to save and study the special quicksand, not destroy it.

So, why had Algar given me those clues? He'd tossed out the water clue before I could flame anything, so maybe I'd just interpreted wrong. I'd gotten the fire clues after the combine had exploded but before our cavalry had arrived.

My brain nudged harder. I needed to ask something. "How would you run an illegal floater gate? What equipment would you need?"

"It would depend on the setup," Serene said. "There are a variety of ways."

"Radio would be the easiest," Reader said. "But that

would also be the least accurate, and most likely to have issues."

"Oh. Wow. Um . . . Rahmi and Rhee, stay here and guard. Anyone else who's pissed and in the mood to wreck stuff, and possibly enemies, follow me. Anyone staying here who isn't officially on Amazon Guard Duty, check all the databases for someone reporting a John Deere combine having been stolen this evening."

Took off, back toward the part of the mountains where I'd found this flamethrower in the first place.

I wasn't alone, and hadn't expected to be. "Where are we going?" Jeff asked, as he grabbed my hand.

"To the radio setup that I think our enemies are using against us," I replied, as White grabbed my other hand. He had Chuckie, Buchanan, Tim, and Reader along as well. "Mister White, I see you're doing the heavy lifting, so to speak."

"I live to serve, Missus Martini."

Reached the mountain but took the roads, rather than going up the side. At hyperspeed it would add a couple of seconds, but ensure that no one tripped on anything.

"Why here?" Christopher asked from Jeff's other side, as we wound up the mountain.

"I found the flamethrower up here."

"One day I'll understand how your mind works," Christopher said. "That day is not today."

"Whatever. The dune buggy was here. There are satellite dishes here. There's a storeroom, where I got this flamethrower. And there's also a bunker with what looked like a full radio setup."

We arrived. The dune buggy was where it had been before, but the doors to both the bunker and storeroom were closed. And I was pretty sure that I hadn't taken the time to close them.

"We're not alone," Buchanan said quietly. He and Chuckie already had their guns out. Reader and Tim followed suit. Figured I could go for my Glock, but since I had a flamethrower, might as well use it. "No chatter."

Buchanan used hand signals and indicated that he wanted

the satellites, buggy, and weapons room searched. Christopher zipped off and was back momentarily. He shook his head. So, no one was there, meaning if someone was here, they were either inside the radio bunker or invisible. Wondered where Siler was, and then figured if he was here, we'd find out.

Jeff stayed with me and tried to put himself in front of me, but I indicated the flamethrower and, after a lot of eye rolling and frowny faces, he gave up and stayed next to me instead.

Once we had that figured out, looked around to see the rest of the guys giving us the "really?" look. Shrugged and looked to Buchanan. He was clearly trying not to laugh and also clearly asking himself why, yet again, he was forced to work with others.

But he soldiered on and gave hand signals for us to fan out around the building. I decided the flamethrower and I should stay near the door. Buchanan didn't argue, and I ignored Jeff's pantomime trying to get me to go around to the back.

Buchanan took one side of the door, Chuckie took the other. The door opened out, but that wasn't an issue. I nudged Jeff. He nodded, went to the door, ripped it off the hinges, came back to me and pulled me out of the way, all in about a half a second.

Buchanan and Chuckie went into the room. "Clear!" Chuckie called.

The others rejoined us. "Nothing and no one," Reader said.

"Guess you were just jumpy," Christopher said to Buchanan. "It happens."

"Not to Malcolm. At least two of you block the door, please, so no one can get in or out." Turned around and pulled the nozzle into my hands. "I don't know a lot about how to use a flamethrower," I said in a normal tone, as I walked to the weapons storage area. "But I'm going to practice. Right now. All over this area. Starting with this weapons storage thing. And then I'm going to burn the building down. And the dune buggy. Or, you can come out now and I won't let anyone shoot you. Possibly."

"Who are you talking to?" Jeff asked.

A man stepped out of the weapons room. "Me."

CHAPTER 46

"GOOD GUESS," Siler, who was now de-cloaked, said. "Not a guess, really. I think you heard us coming and went in here, where you figured we wouldn't look too hard."

He smiled. "Yes. Oh, put the guns down, it's just us here right now."

"I don't feel warm and fuzzy about putting our guns down," Chuckie said.

Siler looked around me. "What about you?"

Checked. He was talking to Buchanan.

Who, gun still out and aimed at Siler, reached into his pocket and pulled something out. He looked at his hand. "I have no idea if this is giving me good intel or not."

"Really." Siler sounded bored. "You realize you can't shoot faster than I can run, and I say that knowing you're all trained to shoot A-Cs." He looked back at me. "You have the right idea with that flamethrower—you need to destroy this entire setup. It's been compromised since Home Base was infiltrated last year. And no one's bothered to verify its security in all that time."

Didn't have to look at the expressions on the faces of the men with me. It was clear Siler was essentially telling them, Chuckie, Reader, and Tim especially, that they were failures.

"This isn't part of our jurisdiction," Jeff said, before Reader or Tim could say anything, Commander Voice on

Full. "It's part of the U.S. government's portion of Home Base. And it's used to ensure that test planes don't bomb the wrong areas. The C.I.A. has no jurisdiction here, and neither does the F.B.I. This is Department of Defense territory."

"It is. However, it's also being used by your enemies to do a lot of really nasty things."

"Including create floater gates?" I asked.

Siler nodded. "Yes." He looked back to Buchanan. "You could raid it now, but if you do, you'll lose some of them. If you're willing to trust me, then I can send you a signal for when to show up."

"What is this 'it' you're talking about?" Tim asked.

"And why should we trust you?" Reader added. "You helped Stephanie escape."

What was going on between Siler and Buchanan dawned on me. "No, he didn't. He put a tracking device on her and then helped her to escape so she'd go back to 'it,' which is wherever the bad guys' base of operations is. That's why Malcolm picked something up out of the dirt—you'd dropped the homing device for him. Oh, and giving myself a duh—that's why you mentioned 'kindred spirit' to me, too."

Chuckie and Buchanan both jerked. "When did I tell you that name?" Chuckie asked.

"You didn't. Mom did. Yes, shocking one and all, she shared classified intel with me that matters to my job and longevity. Try not to be looking too amazed, guys, you're hashing my Figuring It Out buzz."

Siler smiled slowly. "They're going to be so proud of you."

"My 'uncles'?"

He nodded. "I'm the only one who had a shot at infiltration. I've met quite a number of my half-siblings in the last year, but I've never seen Stephanie before."

"Meaning she reports in to a different cell," Chuckie said. "She believed you were on her side?"

"In addition to helping her escape, he helped the sand-shifter capture us, and I'm sure we were being watched, so yes." The men with me started grumbling. I put my hand up. "He also blew up the combine that got rid of said sandshifter,

Animal Man, and whoever their driver was, *and* got me out of it before it blew. So, I again am willing to think that the enemy of my enemy is my friend."

"I didn't feel him," Jeff said.

Siler shrugged. "I was given another emotional blocker. Feel free to take it from me for study. I understand you haven't made much progress due to the explosive fail-safes on these."

Jeff grumbled, but Siler taking another blocker made sense. Sandy had said this was one of my strengths, that I trusted people others thought I shouldn't. Like Siler. And Mahin. And Serene.

Which begged a question. "Nightcrawler, do you think any of your half-sibs could be turned to the side of right? I mean, Serene and Mahin are with us. Maybe if we'd found Ronaldo early he'd have been on our side, too."

Siler shook his head. "You all really don't understand what you're up against, do you?"

"What do you mean?"

He sighed. "Look, one thing at a time. Are you going to destroy this area in your attempt to capture me, or are you not?"

"Oh, gotcha. You need your excuse, too. Are we getting to capture you so that you can impress everyone and escape again?"

"I'd appreciate it," Siler said with a grin, "but it's up to you."

"Is there any intel we can get out of the radio room?" Chuckie asked. "Before we let Kitty burn it up, I mean."

"Tim and I already checked while you were all chatting," Christopher said. "More thoroughly than I checked the weapons storage," he added, shooting Patented Glare #5 at everyone. In the dying sunlight it was quite impressive.

"We've got some things, but it's pretty clean." Tim shrugged. "It's not their base, just where they've been jamming us, eavesdropping on us, and the like." He sighed. "Jeff, Siler's right—we screwed up."

"No," Jeff said calmly. "We didn't. We didn't check an area none of us ever used for anything related to our jobs or our community. Mistakes happen. To all of us. Christopher and I wouldn't have checked this if we were still the Heads of Field and Imageering, and God alone knows why Kitty checked today."

"I was looking for a weapon and figured that Home Base wasn't going to be a wise place for me to go." This was true enough, really. "You and I had been here a couple times, so I knew about it. If we hadn't been attacked like we were, I'd have never come up here, or even thought about it."

"We can spend the time recriminating and absolving ourselves later," Reader said. "Right now, I'd like to capture the king here and burn this sucker down. You've been all dressed up with nothing to burn, so go to town, girlfriend."

"Goody! Bruno, my bird, you around?"

Sure enough, my Faithful Guardian was here, thrilled to still be alive and ready for action.

"Please clear out any animals in the vicinity, would you? Kitty doesn't want to hurt anything that isn't involved in all the nasty conspiracies."

Bruno squawked, we were joined by the other male Peregrines, then they all flew off. Heard some cawing and such, then Bruno returned to share that the task was accomplished and the few animals foolhardy enough to be hanging around here were relocated to somewhere a tad safer.

Buchanan showed me how to work the flamethrower, and I practiced on the satellites while the A-C men destroyed all the equipment in the radio room and the human men searched the dune buggy to verify it had nothing bad on it including bugs, took possession of all the weapons and other items in the storage shed, and transferred them into said vehicle for easy transport.

"Ready, baby," Jeff said, after I'd lit up the last satellite. "Should I worry about how much you're enjoying setting things on fire?"

"Nope." I flamed the storage room, then headed for the bunker. "Only worry if I ask to do it more than once an Operation."

"Oh, that makes me feel so much better."

"Whatever." Among the things that were in our possession

was a small propane tank. Took it from Tim and tossed it into the bunker. "Whoever's driving the dune buggy, take Mister White with you so he can kick butt if necessary and get going. Everyone else, I think we should all be ready to run. Really, really fast. And I'm specifically talking to Christopher on the fast part."

"Give us a minute or two to get out of range," Reader said, as he got into the driver's seat and turned on the dune buggy. Happily, it didn't explode. White got in and they took off.

Everyone left hooked up with Christopher and Jeff took hold of me. "Am I going to hate this?" he asked me.

"Probably. Or it may make you feel all vindicated and happy. Or maybe that's just me. Malcolm, if you'd please do the honors and help out." I flamed the bunker, paying special attention to the propane tank. After a few seconds, Buchanan shot the tank.

The explosion was impressive. And since Jeff had grabbed me around my waist and we moved so fast that he didn't bother to flip me around as we hightailed it out of there, I got to watch it the entire way down the side of the mountain.

It didn't make up for being stuck in creepy quicksand and all the other crap that had gone on today, but it sure felt like a nice start.

CHAPTER 47

A PLETHORA OF FIELD AGENTS were on the scene when we got back. Since we had Siler "in custody" and we also had a now-bigger situation to handle, we decided to do Christopher a favor and requested a floater gate.

Four out of the five flyboys were in the choppers. Per Jerry, they were taking them back to Dulce, so we'd have aerial options if necessary. Since we had no helipad I had no idea what we were going to do with two helicopters, but decided that was Tim's area and let him handle it. Gave myself some major Personal Growth Points, too. The dune buggy and its contents were hooked to one of the choppers and also taken to Dulce.

Once we were back in the Science Center, I was assured that all was reasonably well and Jamie was reportedly in bed asleep. I wasn't so sure I believed that, but I was starving and we were in the middle of so many situations I wasn't sure I could keep track, so I decided to earn some more Bad Mommy Points and believe the lie. Either she really was asleep or Jeff was in the same boat, because he didn't demand to see her, either.

Happily, Pierre had dinner waiting for us, and Mom joined us in the commissary. Everyone but Jerry, Rahmi and Rhee—who'd gone to wait for and help the other flyboys when they and the choppers arrived—was clustered together at one long table, but Mom didn't sit.

"I won't keep you from eating," Mom said, after she'd given me and Jeff her Breath Stopping Bear Hug that was her standard for whenever one of us in the family had had a close brush with death. Since meeting Jeff, I'd had a lot of those hugs from my mother. "And I'm not going to demand all the details right now, either. Just know that you're going to have press attacking you tomorrow, and please do what Raj wants."

"What does Raj want?"

Mom's lips quirked. "To handle this properly. We're in a family suite with Alfred and Lucinda, and Jamie's staying with us tonight. So are all the pets. Jamie's fast asleep, and all her grandparents are gently requesting that the two of you don't wake her up just to say goodnight."

"We wouldn't have done that," Jeff said, sounding offended.

Mom snorted so I didn't have to. "Right. Lucinda was quite clear that she expects you to think that the four of us are incapable of watching your child for one night without your supervision. However, *I* expect you to let your daughter sleep." The way she said this made it clear that if we wanted to wake our daughter up, it had better only be because Siler had dropped more bombs.

"Pardon us for wanting to see our daughter after close brushes with death," he grumbled. Under his breath. Jeff knew when he was beaten.

Mom rolled her eyes but didn't grace this with a reply. "Kitten, you and Jeff eat and get some sleep. I realize it's not that late, but it's been a busy day for everyone."

"Yeah. Speaking of everyone—where's Amy and Brian and everyone else I'd expect to be at least poking their heads in to see if their spouses, friends, and relations are unscathed?"

"They know you're unscathed. They also know you're in Centaurion Division's version of a Top Brass meeting. As such, everyone's leaving you alone."

"Right. These are the same people who have never left us alone in any meeting, ever, if given even half a chance to add in their two cents."

Christopher coughed. "Like someone else we all know."

He looked at Melanie and Emily. "More than one someone, really." They shot him the Mother's Icy Stare.

"That sort of proves my point. 'Off limits' usually means 'hurry up and get in on it' to our extended team." Looked at Mom's expression. "So what else is actually going on?"

She sighed. "*Fine*. In addition to this being considered an off-limits meeting, all military and Field personnel are on duty in some way. And all non-military personnel are in the library enjoying a party being run by your father. Everyone has already eaten and the assumption is that some of you will go to the party when you've finished eating and find your spouses, significant others, and so on, and some of you will go to your rooms." She looked right at me and Jeff for this last part. Noted that both Chuckie and Buchanan looked like they were trying not to laugh.

Chose not to rise to that particular bait. Mostly because I knew perfectly well Jeff and I weren't going to hit that party. "I thought Dad was watching Jamie. And does everything that's gone on today really scream Party Time?"

"Lucinda is on Jamie duty at the moment," Mom said with a heavy dose of Long Suffering in her tone. "And it's not a wild party like your grandparents normally throw. This one is more sedate. Pierre approves."

Jeff relaxed, though. "It's fine, baby. Your father's just trying to make the best of the situation we're in."

"You mean that my father is hosting the Dulce Kegger. I'm touched to know that he's looking at all the crap that's gone on today as the Ultimate Party Excuse." Had a feeling he was secretly thrilled all the drama was going on because, from the little I'd seen, it was impressing the Mossad folks. "And of course Pierre approves. It keeps people distracted and gives him more things to do perfectly on the first try."

"More of you could take a lesson from Pierre," Mom said, sarcasm knob at eleven. "On the other hand, you're alive, and well, and none of you are scathed. I can ask your father to run in here and have him perform the Birkhat HaGomel blessing if it'll make you happy, kitten."

"Well, a little extra thanks for surviving danger wouldn't go amiss, Mom."

"I'll be sure to let your father know." With that she kissed my cheek, passed a couple of signs to Chuckie and Buchanan, gave Siler—who was handcuffed to Buchanan again to keep the "he's our prisoner" fiction going—a long once-over, nodded to everyone else, and headed off.

Once Mom was gone we got down to the business of stuffing our faces and making general chitchat. After I'd eaten an entire steak and half of my giant baked potato, finally felt strong enough again to ask a couple relevant questions. "So, did we locate any information on a stolen combine?"

"Yes," Serene said. "However, I don't know that it's going to help us much."

"Stolen right from a John Deere dealership," Claudia said.

"Where was it located?"

"Buckeye, Arizona," Lorraine said. "No idea why they chose that location."

"It's part of Pueblo Caliente's metro area, and it's rural." Looked at Chuckie. "Think they were trying to get into Caliente Base by any chance?"

"Maybe. They might have been able to bounce or boost their signal based on proximity. But, as so often seems the case, we don't have enough information to be able to tell, and we destroyed anything we could have examined." Chuckie shot Siler a look that said he wasn't convinced burning down the radio bunker had been a good idea.

Siler picked it up, too. "Unless you wanted to airlift the entire building here, leaving that active was far more dangerous to you all than destroying it."

Before this devolved into an Alpha Male Bickering Session, I decided to pursue the question Siler had avoided earlier. "So, what did you mean that we didn't know what we were up against when I asked about your many brothers and sisters out there?"

He sighed. "I mean you're wasting your time. You've gotten the only Yates progeny you're ever going to have on your side already."

"Explain that," Jeff said. "Because our experience says otherwise." Serene and Mahin nodded. Serene was sitting next to Siler, White was across from him, and Mahin was next to White and Christopher. Had a feeling the girls were kind of hoping for a little Family Reunion Time. Couldn't blame them, really.

"Does it?" Siler chuckled bitterly.

"Yes, like I said before, based on Mahin and Serene. And also like I said before, maybe if we'd known Ronaldo existed earlier, and had found him when he was younger, things would have been different."

"Well, you'd have had to start a lot earlier than you did. As in, well before you, personally, even knew aliens were on the planet. Frankly, you'd have pretty much had to start at birth. Ronaldo was taken from his mother by Yates when he was just a baby."

"Why?" Jeff asked. "To hide that he was born out of wedlock?"

"Hardly. No, he took him because Ronaldo was his 'first' son—Mister White was a traitor in his mind and I was already hidden, so Ronaldo was the first one Yates could actually get his hands on."

"Call me Richard," White said. "You *are* my younger brother, after all, Benjamin." He patted Mahin's hand and gave Serene his fatherly smile. Yep, the girls were in Family Mode and White knew it.

Siler shot him a half-smile. "As you wish."

"Did Yates raise Ronaldo as his son?" Gower asked.

"Not really. Ronaldo didn't have Richard's leadership potential, and it was soon apparent that he wasn't very bright, at least not by A-C standards."

"Really? There are dumb A-Cs?" Tried to come up with any I'd met. Failed.

Claudia and Lorraine both coughed. "We've known a couple," Lorraine said. Knew what they were referring to—Operation Fugly might have been years ago now, but Jeff and Christopher had certainly had a very "duh" moment about how alcohol could be used as a weapon. So, okay, maybe dumb occasionally, but it was usually more that A-Cs didn't normally put thing together the way a human would.

"Hilarious," Jeff replied while Christopher graced them with Patented Glare #4. "But yes, baby, as with any population, we have those that don't hit the mental standards that the rest of us do."

"If you say so." Duh moments or not, the A-C's versions of dumb were MENSA material for the rest of us, but I'd had the pleasure of tangling with Ronaldo more than once, and I had to admit he'd never struck me as the same league as the A-Cs I spent time with. He was certainly nowhere close to Serene on the smarts scale, and she was his full-blooded younger sister. "So, he tossed Ronaldo off into an obscure part of the world and did what with him?"

"Ensured that the talents he had were at optimum and expanded."

"To my knowledge, most troubadours don't really do mind control, do they?"

The A-Cs at the tables shook their heads. "It's influence, but it's more of an emotional control than a mental one," Jeff said. "Under most circumstances, that is."

"The average troubadour is using tonal inflections, facial expressions, and body language to get someone to do or think what they want them to," Christopher added.

Managed to refrain from mentioning, yet again, that, despite the disdain given to it by the majority of A-Cs, troubadour talent was actually quite impressive.

"Troubadours use persuasion," Gower added. "Ronaldo used manipulation."

"Gladys Gower wasn't the only person whose mind Ronaldo could enter and affect to the degree he was able to," Siler went on. "It's a big reason why he was a very successful businessman. Ronaldo also had an actual flair for business, and Yates encouraged that. He had a good life, really. Probably a lot better before he was activated to start carrying on with the basic experiment, which was to create a superrace of those with the Yates genetics and a few other specially selected genetic samples."

While I didn't argue with the superrace theory, especially considering what we'd been through these past few years, I did think about the timing of when I was pretty sure Ronaldo had been activated. Didn't time out right for Yates to have activated him. At all.

However, Siler seemed to have comprehensive information. Whether we'd get all of it out of him was the question. "So, was Yates always marching under the Purity of the Race Banner? He had a lot going on for such a single-minded goal."

"So did Hitler," Siler said. "But it all ends the same way."

"Can't argue with the logic." Had a theory, but I wanted a few more answers first. "Okay, but what about all the others?"

"He kept track, but he never kept contact with any other than Ronaldo. Ronaldo was a good son, at least in the ways our father would see it, and that was, apparently, enough for him."

"Why not? It seems stupid to avoid all the kiddies if your entire plan is to make them into your own genetically enhanced army."

"Honestly? I think he found better and more loyal options outside of his genetic pool."

"You mean like Herbert Gaultier, Antony Marling, and your mother, right?"

"Among others."

"Yeah. Leventhal Reid had to have been a better 'son' to him than even Ronaldo could be."

"Definitely. Reid was far smarter, for starters."

"And he was politically connected," Chuckie said. "So that had to have been advantageous as well."

Siler nodded. "Yates also had proportionately more daughters than he did sons."

"That doesn't seem right."

"Why not?" Gower asked. "Based on the Yates offspring that are on our side—and counting Aunt Gladys and, if we can safely assume so, Siler here—we have four women and two men."

Chuckie nodded. "If those numbers are representative of his general genetic drift, it's easy to believe two thirds of his children are women."

"But, other than Serene and Mahin, we've only seen guys."

"Expect that to change," Siler said.

"I'm back to asking why you think we can't swing these women to our side, then," Jeff said. "Our track record seems good."

"And because of that, it'll never be good again," Siler said. He looked at Mahin. "You've ensured that."

CHAPTER 48

"EXCUSE ME?" Mahin sounded shocked and horrified. "I haven't had contact with any of them since they murdered . . ." she glanced at Gower guiltily.

"My brother," Gower said gently. "And we believe you, Mahin. Don't worry."

Siler shrugged. "That wasn't an accusation of evil activity. However, the reason they've spent this year finding, prepping, and brainwashing the others is exactly because of you." He looked at me. "And you, of course."

"Mind explaining that? 'Cause I don't see the 'of course' in regards to me."

"Sweetly naïve. Not your best look. But I'll explain for the apparently slow ones in the room." Siler grinned at Claudia and Lorraine, who both laughed. Jeff rolled his eyes and Christopher hit us with Patented Glare #2.

"Yeah, explain for all the slow of wit," Tim said. "Because I'm with Kitty. Why would she be the reason they *don't* flip?"

"I get it," Chuckie said. "You're the one who ensured Serene flipped to our side, Kitty. Not Brian—you."

Serene nodded. "Ultimately, that's true, Kitty."

"And you're the reason Mahin flipped," Chuckie went on. "You and White for Mahin."

"I didn't do any of it," Christopher said. "Buchanan and Kitty's father did more."

"But you were there," Chuckie said patiently. "For her and Serene. So was Jeff, but you were the one they were doing a different kind of brainwashing on. And Kitty figured that out, too."

"Ah, Operation Confusion. Good times . . . good times."

"Other than our getting Jamie, were they?" Jeff asked.

"Everyone's a critic. So, you're saying that because we'd stopped three attempts, they felt it was three strikes and they were out?"

Siler nodded. "Essentially. But I'm saying 'you' specifically, not 'all of you' generally. The assumption—which, after spending time with you, I think is completely accurate—is that there's at least a fifty percent chance that any of the Yates progeny who interact with you are going to flip to your side. Especially the women."

Considered this. "You know, I kind of bonded with your mother. Right before she tried to kill me and Adriana arrived to save the day."

"Not a surprise. Hell, you've flipped the top assassins in the world to your side. And if you could make my mother like you, then you have a lot more persuasive power than you realize."

"We . . . kind of . . . understood each other."

"Exactly. So, your enemies made the decision to spend this past year bringing in the rest of the Yates progeny and brainwashing them. They're good at this kind of persuasion, and these people aren't going to join you now, because you stand in the way of everything they want."

"Money, power, ruling everyone else?" Reader asked.

"That, and regaining their family glory, seats on the Yates-Corp board, and more. They've been promised a lot." Siler shook his head. "If I'd had all this offered to me when I was young and, more importantly, alone, I'd probably have gone for it, too. They're very persuasive, and they're offering something most of these people have never had."

Looked at Serene and Mahin and it wasn't hard to guess what was the biggest thing our enemies were offering. "Family."

Siler nodded. "Yes. You offer it, too, and you all mean it. Which is part of why you're so dangerous to them."

"You're not like them. At all. Neither are Serene and Mahin."

"I was," Mahin said quietly.

"I could have been," Serene added. "If I'd been approached differently, especially since they were drugging me."

"It was clear that kidnapping wasn't going to be effective," Siler said. "It's why they haven't tried it since."

Serene nodded. "Even crazed with the Surcenthumain they'd given me, it wasn't that hard to tell you were trying to save me."

"Well, when the drug's hold ebbed and you were able to hold onto the sanity, yeah. And you're smart." A couple of alligators chasing us with intent to snack also had to have helped Serene grasp reality. Wondered if I could find Alliflash and Gigantagator and move them into the Zoo somehow. They'd certainly keep Hacker International on their toes.

"Smart means nothing against good brainwashing techniques," Siler said.

"Oh, it does," Chuckie replied. "But I agree—even the strongest can break."

"Well, we had Serene's catnip, remember—Brian was on our side."

She laughed. "True enough. But really, it was all of you who made choosing the right side easy. Not that they ever asked me to join them. As Benjamin said, kidnapped isn't the same as being recruited."

"That's true, however, Serene was also *in* the A-C community," White said, shooting Serene another fatherly smile. "Not as tightly in as she is now, but still, within it, with family. Perhaps they would have tried brainwashing her if they'd been successful in their kidnapping attempt."

"Heck, they brainwashed Clarence, and Stephanie, and they certainly weren't kidnapped. Ever." Wondered if the tracker Siler had on Stephanie was really going to show us where the Yates Gang was hiding.

"This is true," White said. "But unless Benjamin is going to tell us that Clarence wasn't really Stephanie's father, I don't believe we have anyone else identified within the community who might be a hidden Yates child." Felt Jeff tense.

"No, Clarence is really her father," Siler said. Jeff relaxed. Took and squeezed his hand. "Your community's views on out-of-wedlock births meant that Yates couldn't just cruise through every available A-C woman."

"Because he knew what would have happened on the home world and could see how Serene's mother was shunned, meaning nothing had changed on this world, and if there were enough women being shunned with no corresponding man to shun at the same time, someone would make the connection."

"Right. However, Stephanie has Yates blood in her, and from the little she told me when I was helping her get away from all of you, that's what they're using to keep her on their side—the proof of her true blood-right."

"Fantastic," Jeff muttered. "What are we going to tell Sylvia?"

"We'll handle it," White said gently. "Somehow."

Time to get off Stephanie, at least for the moment, and back to the rest of the matter at hand. Now wasn't the time to point out that all of Jeff's sisters and all their very talented children had Yates blood in them, too. Nor to mention that, out of his remaining four brothers-in-law, only one was considered trustworthy at the moment. I'd save that stressful conversation for another time.

"Okay, I get why they didn't turn Serene. Mahin flipped to our side, though. So why not others?"

"Because the people in charge of their side of Project Kindred Spirit have found all the remaining Yates progeny," Siler said. "They have an accurate list, no searching required. The original plan was a slow recruitment process, add them in as needed. What went down between you and them last year, though, made them speed things up. They collected all the remaining siblings and they've spent this past year brainwashing them."

"They tried the brainwashing on Mahin," I pointed out. "And it didn't take."

"Not really," she said. "I mean, it was started, yes. But I

was found and activated right before the attack last year. They didn't spend a great deal of time prepping me. For anything." She looked down. "If they'd spent the time, things might be very different."

"No, I refuse to believe that. You and Serene both had the option to go to the Dark Side and you both chose doing the right thing when it mattered. And you have, too," I said to Siler. "So, based on what you're saying, either they're still flippable, or the three of you are nothing like these others at all."

"Listen, I'm *just* like them. Every scared, scarred, lonely person is, in that sense, just like them. However my uncle saved me from that life and that temptation. And yes, I consider being a top assassin to be a far more worthwhile and decent career than what these people have as their motivation."

"I'd rather spend time with hired killers than the Mastermind and Apprentice, too. You dudes definitely have more honor."

"Maybe. However, you need to remember that what all of you care about and what I care about rarely align."

Siler was really good at saying that he didn't have the same goals as us. Yet he knew what was going on with us and with his siblings. All of them. Maybe he cared about us because of White, Lucinda, Gladys, Serene, and Mahin. Thought about it—maybe only because of Serene, at least initially. She was younger and would have been in much more danger from Yates than Siler's three older half-siblings. Same with Mahin, at least once she was found and activated.

And yet Yates hadn't tried to get Serene, which was really stupid. Maybe Mahin's mother had managed to keep him off and away somehow, but Serene had been orphaned young. And her A-C family hadn't really loved her; Brian had confirmed this when he'd gone to meet them after they'd gotten engaged.

Serene got a Daddy Crush on White within days of meeting him, and I was fairly sure she'd had a Daddy Crush on Alfred, too. Serene had longed so much for parents, for a family, to really feel accepted and included, that she'd been primed to become Ronald Yates' Good Little Girl well before I'd ever met her. And she was amazingly powerful, the perfect Yates Test Subject. And yet he'd never even so much as looked her up, let alone tried to bring her "home."

"Are all the female Yates progeny more talented than the males? Proportionately, I mean. Jeff's mom has no talents and neither does Richard, unless you count charm."

White laughed. "Ah, I'm always reminded of why Jeffrey loves you so much, Missus Martini. However, while Lucinda and I might have no talents of our own, clearly the genetics were passed along. Christopher's probably came mostly from his mother, but Alfred is also un-talented, and Jeffrey is immensely powerful."

"True enough," Siler said, thankfully before anyone who might be thinking about the rest of the Martini Clan's potential to join the Yates Army shared their thoughts. "But to answer the question, yes. The women are, for the most part, stronger than the men. Not all of the offspring have talents, mind you, but those who do are all powerful. However, if I could choose who would be on my side, I'd take all the women, versus the men."

"So, while Yates knew what was going on with his kids in a very general way, he'd lost active interest in any of his children once he had his Good Son in Ronaldo."

Siler nodded. "Pretty much, yeah."

Which, aside from confirming that Yates was a misogynist— something his rampant womanizing with sweet young things had already more than illuminated—confirmed something else. Time to toss out the theory I'd put forward a year ago and see how accurate it might be.

"It was Leventhal Reid who kept the real black book. And you, of course."

CHAPTER 49

SILER STARED AT ME. "Yes to both. How'd you figure it out?"

"Are you saying he was in cahoots with Reid?" Jeff asked.

"Cahoots? Really? When did you grab the Old Person's Urban Dictionary?"

"I'm serious, baby."

Buchanan nodded. "I'd like to hear, right now, how Siler here has the same information as Reid would have."

"I want to know how you know that Leventhal Reid was the one who kept the list," Siler said.

Rolled my eyes. "Dude, seriously. Think about it. I'm sure Yates started the Little Black Book—he'd have had to since Reid was a lot younger, right?" Siler nodded. "But still, based on what you said, he didn't care much, it was more of a list of conquests, versus a list of potential allies."

"Yes. Once he had Ronaldo he seemed . . . content, I suppose."

"It's the little things you treasure. However, Reid, aka the first Apprentice was—and, sadly, is again—a sick, scary psychopath, but he also had vision and he was great with long-term planning. It doesn't take much to guess that he'd pay attention to all the women his Mastermind, also known as Yates the Horndog, had screwed and was screwing, for all the reasons that have pretty much defined my life since meeting Jeff."

"Okay," Siler said slowly. "That's accurate. But how did you realize I was . . . keeping track? Separately," he added with a snide look for the other men around the table who weren't looking overwhelmingly friendly.

"Oh, stop everyone. It's been a long day and everyone's jumpy. And, Nightcrawler, you were paying attention because you knew what your father had done to you and you wanted to at least have the option to step in, or be prepared for who you'd have to go up against. You can go invisible. That's a hell of a skill, and I'm sure you put it into use for more than contract killing."

He nodded. "It began as self-preservation. My uncle was concerned that my father would just continue his experiments and I'd have even more enemies."

"But he didn't. Because he'd realized there were better ways to achieve his purpose."

"So how did you guess that Reid was the one keeping the list, as opposed to my father, I mean?"

"The timeline for Project Kindred Spirit. The action against Serene didn't go into effect until after Yates was dead."

"Ronaldo was activated even later," Chuckie added. "Unless he was involved from the beginning and just laid low."

"No," Siler said. "He was activated right when you figure he was."

"Around the time when Jeff and I got married."

"Yes. And instantly got pregnant. That's when a variety of plans kicked into high gear."

"Is there anything you don't know about all of us?" Reader asked.

"No. Think of him as Malcolm's counterpart in the Assassination League and it'll be easier to accept. So, Reid tried to get Serene, and then we killed him. But once Reid was dead his Apprentice, who we now call the current Mastermind, took over and got things really rolling."

Siler nodded. "Yes. Short period of adjustment, bigger plans immediately after."

"Each iteration has gotten more . . . vicious," Gower said. "Yates was bad, Reid was pretty terrible, but the current Mastermind is . . ."

"A psychopath," Chuckie said.

"They're all psychos, Chuckie. Sadly, in addition, this one has a serious hard-on for hurting you. Basically, for the current Mastermind, the operating statement is: This Time It's Personal. Nightcrawler, by any chance, did you ever meet Reid's Apprentice who's now our Mastermind?"

"No. I wasn't his friend or business associate. My uncle kept me as far away from my father and his cronies as possible. Anything I did or learned was from the shadows, in that sense. And it's not as if there was an announcement in the media that Leventhal Reid had promoted So-and-So to Apprentice."

"So touchy. How about whoever's in charge of Project Kindred Spirit? It could be the Mastermind or someone else who's gotten to run with their own action. Have you met the Head Creep?"

"No. I'm not trusted enough. At all. They think they're using me, but the people in charge have stayed out of any day-to-day. They're set up in a typical bureaucratic fashion, so it's easy to keep lower-level and newer grunts in the dark."

"Do they realize you can blend?"

"Yes, but they think they're the ones who taught me to really use the ability. Same with hyperspeed. There's no record of me in the 'black book' because I'm impersonating one of my half-brothers."

"Is he still alive?" Buchanan asked dryly.

"That's need-to-know. And you don't."

"How is that possible?" Christopher asked while Siler and Buchanan side-eyed each other. "That there's no record of you, I mean. I'm clear on how easily you could kill someone."

"I'm not sure, but I've seen the record that Reid kept for my father and I'm nowhere."

"How'd you see it?" Chuckie asked. "Especially if you don't know who the current Mastermind is?"

Siler stopped side-eying Buchanan and gave Chuckie a full on snide look. "I looked at their book twice—once when my father was alive, and once right after Reid died. Blending gives me certain advantages. You're supposed to be the brilliant one, you figure it out."

"Your mother kept you out of it?" I suggested, in part to forestall the fight.

"Maybe. My name wasn't in their listing. No reference to me was there. There's a significant gap between me and the others. Ronaldo was over a decade younger than me, and he's the first born of the rest of the Yates progeny. Perhaps that's why; I was considered too old to influence."

"Maybe," Reader said. "But that's a significant gap. We know for a fact that Yates was screwing around during that time."

"But we're fairly sure Ronaldo was born before Yates combined with the Mephistopheles parasite," Melanie said.

"In fact," Emily added, "we're pretty sure that all but one of the Yates children we've found so far are older than the Yates-Mephistopheles pairing."

"So, first there's a big gap between Siler and his next kid, and then he starts screwing around with intent to create, but before he even knows the parasites are coming," Tim said. "That makes no sense."

"Maybe his plan changed," Lorraine suggested.

"I'm sure it did," Tito said. "If our estimates about the timing of Ronaldo's conception are correct, that would time out to around when Yates was diagnosed with cancer."

Looked at Siler. "Your life expectancy was increased. Maybe they didn't know for sure because your uncle took you, but they might have figured that out before you left. And even if they didn't know, there's nothing like real biological relatives for all your donor needs."

"I think that's the answer, Kitty," Tito said. "Yates was probably making as many babies as he could to have an organ and cell farm."

"That would also explain why he didn't take an active interest in them," Reader said. "Just keep track and make sure they're around. Why risk getting emotionally attached to someone whose lungs you're going to rip out, literally?"

"And once Mephistopheles joined with him, he didn't stop because he had a new lease on life," Tim said.

"Why not?" Chuckie agreed. "Get enough of your own genetics out there, available for whatever uses necessary, including experimentation to find a formula that will allow you to live forever."

"Based on what we saw last year, Reid would certainly have been enthusiastic about that idea," Buchanan added.

That would also make sense in regard to my dream with Mephistopheles. Mephistopheles would certainly see a "live forever" kind of plan to be small. Mephistopheles wanted to rule the galaxy, not just hang around on one planet making babies and cackling evilly.

"Yates was originally from Alpha Four, too, remember, and that would mean he knew about Beta Twelve."

"We remember, Kitty," Christopher said.

Ignored him and went on before anyone else could chime in about my stating the obvious. "Maybe this is where the cloning idea stemmed from, or when he and Reid decided to get it rolling."

"It wouldn't surprise me," Siler said. "At all."

"The timing would be about right for our science, too," Chuckie said. "Especially if we assume that those working on the cloning, organ harvesting, and whatever else were all brilliant, in on the schemes, and not sharing with the general public."

"Sounds like them in a nutshell," Jeff said.

"Can Surcenthumain actually extend life expectancy?" Claudia asked.

"We don't have enough samples to be able to tell," her mother replied. Emily looked at Siler. "However, whatever they gave you sure seems to be doing so."

He shrugged. "Yes. And I'd assume that whatever Gaultier created from the original serums used on me does something similar to what the first drug did to me. But there are side effects."

"That you've experienced?" Melanie asked.

"There are always side effects," Tito answered. "Even the most benign drug has a side effect."

"Yes," Siler said. "The side effect on me beyond dramatically slowed aging is the extension of my touch—that I can make others blend as I do, that I can calm the effects of hyperspeed on anyone I'm touching. There may be more, but I haven't spent time trying to find them."

"Bullshit," Chuckie said calmly. "You've spent your entire life finding out. That you don't want to tell us isn't a surprise. But stop the bald-faced lying. It's tiresome."

"Before the love in the room gets overwhelming," Reader said quickly, "and just to confirm, whoever's in charge of their version of Project Kindred Spirit has completed that project, and there's nothing we can do about it?"

"Not a thing, and that's not a lie," Siler said. "I'm sorry, but it's literally a waste of your time, and, frankly, will put you in far more danger than any of them would be worth."

"I believe him," Buchanan said. He and Chuckie passed some very hard to spot signs between them. I was just so used to people passing signs today that I was looking for it automatically now.

Chuckie nodded. "Fine. We'll write off trying to find them and if Kitty works her magic on one or more of them, we'll enjoy saying 'told you so' to you, Siler."

So, this was what all those entities were trying to tell me was a waste of our time and focus. Oh well, I hated the idea of giving up, but at least we knew.

Siler chuckled bitterly. "Oh, don't worry about finding them. They're going to find all of you. And soon."

CHAPTER 50

"IF WHAT YOU PUT** onto Stephanie actually works, we'll find them first." Buchanan gave Siler another side-eye. "*If* it really works. And isn't a trap."

"It works. And anything can be a trap if you go into it stupidly, and I know you know that. However, *they* all know where *you* are. You're incredibly easy to find. They aren't. And, as I told you earlier, Stephanie's not going to Headquarters. She's part of a cell. Until I can identify all the cell locations, or at least the ones readying to attack you, clearing out one cell only lets the others know you're on to them."

"Don't they kind of know we're on to them?" I asked. "I mean, we just took out three of them and foiled Stephanie's assassination attempt. Plus we didn't die in the bomb or poison gas attempts. Surely someone at Bad Guy Central has noticed all that by now."

"They've noticed. However, your stopping those attempts doesn't indicate that you know that their version of Project Kindred Spirit exists."

"True enough," White said. "So, we'll hope, for the moment at least, that our enemies don't know that we know about them. So, what else don't we know, Benjamin?"

"The Yates group is supported by the Al Dejahl terrorist network, and functions as that network does. Plus, they have Club Fifty-One and those lunatic church people helping them, too, even though most of those probably don't realize it."

"So, all our enemies are combined?" Jeff asked. Siler nodded. "Why now? And don't say my nomination as vice president, which isn't even official yet. No one pulls together four different groups like this in a day."

"They haven't been pulling them together in the past day," Siler said, patience clearly forced. "They've been pulling them together for the past year, at least. Probably longer."

"Definitely longer." Of this I was sure. "The Mastermind runs the long game much more than going for the short win, though he's not against getting an easy one whenever he can."

"True enough. Meanwhile, instead of doing the same, you've all been very stupid about something quite important. Two things, really." Siler was channeling Algar, how nice for us.

We were all quiet. Speaking for myself, I could guess one thing we'd been stupid about—Jeff's family's potential for turning traitor—but I was at a loss for what the second would be. Everyone else looked uncomfortable or confused. Mostly uncomfortable. Had a distinct feeling everyone had come to the same "I know this one" idea I'd had and everyone else was also at a loss for what was going to be behind Door Number Two.

Siler rubbed his forehead. "My God, you can't all be this dim." He looked around the table. "No. You're not dim. You've all figured out at least one of the things I'm going to say, I can see it in most of your expressions. But you don't want to say what you're thinking, because you're worried that you'll hurt someone's feelings, maybe everyone's. But," he shrugged, "I don't care about that. So I guess I'll be the one to say it aloud."

Decided that if this was going to come from anyone, it might be better coming from me. "He means that we're all avoiding mentioning that if Clarence already went and Stephanie's now gone to the Dark Side, who's to say that the rest of Jeff's nephews, nieces, and brothers-in-law haven't done the same thing? At least, I really hope that was one of your big reveals. And yeah, no one wants to say that, because they're pretty much all kids."

Siler nodded. "That was one, yes."

"Kids are the most susceptible to this kind of enticement," Buchanan said.

"I'd like to point out that we only found out about Stephanie today," I said. "So we weren't really being stupid about it."

"Her father was a well-known traitor," Siler said calmly. "You should have suspected every member of his family, instead of acting like he was an anomaly."

"He's right," Buchanan said. In a way that told me he'd already been considering this for far longer than just today.

"We've been watching them," Chuckie said, confirming my latest suspicion.

"The C.I.A.?" Jeff asked, sounding like he was ready to get angry.

"Yes, and the P.T.C.U. Since Jamie was born. Subtle surveillance, nothing intrusive. However, we haven't found anything, and that includes indications that Stephanie was a traitor. Otherwise, I'd have never allowed her to work with Vander."

"Time to up that surveillance to extremely intrusive," Siler said. "Incarceration wouldn't be too severe an option."

"We can't just assume they're all turning traitor," Jeff said. "I don't want my sisters and their families spied on, let alone arrested for no cause."

"I agree," I said quickly, before anyone could counter Jeff's legitimate concerns. "But you, Christopher, and Serene need to do a Superpowers Summit and check every one of the kids, and their parents, too."

"If they're part of the expanded terrorist network they'll already have emotional blockers or enhancers on them," Chuckie pointed out.

"We could take a family photo and Serene and I could try to read it," Christopher suggested.

Serene shook her head. "Whatever they've done, it's getting worse. We're having less and less success with any image, even film that isn't old. We can try it, but I don't know that we'll learn anything."

"And it could tip off any who might be traitors, too."

Chuckie shook his head. "I hate to say this, but the best option for finding out who's involved or not from the Martini family is through Stephanie. And Siler's the only one who can access her with a hope of getting the truth."

"Great," Jeff growled. "So before we send you off to pal up to my niece, what's the second thing we're all missing?"

"From knowing you, I realize that my saying that the best thing you could do was to hire me to assassinate the entire Gaultier Board, along with the heads of YatesCorp, Titan Security, and Club Fifty-One will be met with gasps of horror and a complete unwillingness to take the easy way out of this situation."

"That's correct," White said. "We don't murder. Everyone at this table has had to defend themselves and others, many times using deadly force, but we don't do it willingly, or with any form of relish or enjoyment. And we won't."

Gower nodded. "If that's your other suggestion, we're not interested, and we won't be interested."

"As I said. By the way, professional assassins don't get enjoyment from killing. It's a job, it's what we do. We get satisfaction from a job well done, but not joy."

"Annette Dier loves killing, trust me. And, honestly, if I can murder her, I'll do it with a lot of relish." The domino of events during Operation Infiltration were set into motion by Dier, and she'd enjoyed killing Fuzzball and Michael both.

"You say that, but none of you seem to live in the world of revenge, and that's what you're talking about with her," Siler said. "But she's not a professional. She thinks she is, and she's skilled enough. But you're right—she enjoys it. She's just a psychopath who fell into a career that allows her to kill people without ramifications."

"She's locked down in the bowels of the earth and she's never coming out," Reader said. "I think that's a ramification."

"Yes, and that brings me to the other thing you're all missing."

"Not killing people?" Claudia asked. "Because that's where I thought you were heading with this."

He smiled. "No. The other important thing you're missing

is that you have the best leverage in the world to utilize against the only person who can truly affect your enemies where they live, so to speak."

"If you're talking about Russell Kozlow, the son of Chernobog the Ultimate, we've been working on that for a year," Chuckie said. "And we've gotten nowhere."

"Because you're not willing to play hardball." Siler shot Chuckie a very derisive look.

"We're the C.I.A. We invented hardball." Chuckie returned the derisive lob with a bored, been there, done that volley.

"And yet you're nowhere." Siler hit back with an overhanded snide. "In part because you were focused on the waste of time project."

"Waste of time per you," Chuckie backhanded with dismissive disdain. "We still have no proof that you're not full of it. Odds are at least fifty-fifty that you're playing some kind of game with us."

"What are you suggesting?" Buchanan asked, before Chuckie and Siler could complete their Special Verbal Tennis Match. "It's easy to tell us that we need to use a prisoner to flip an asset. It's a lot harder come up with a way that will work."

Siler looked up, to the heavens, apparently. "Why me?" He heaved a sigh and looked back at the rest of us. "All this talk of flipping and getting enemies over to your side, and yet none of you have come to the obvious conclusion?"

"You're kidding," Christopher said. "You want Kitty to interrogate Kozlow?"

Siler looked like Buchanan frequently did—wondering why he was forced to lead the Scout Troop and, worse, forced to work with others.

Thought about it, and the light dawned. "You want me to make contact with Chernobog herself."

"At last," Siler said. "One of them has understood."

CHAPTER 51

THERE WAS MORE DISCUSSION about this, of course, but the logic of the idea was overwhelming, and ultimately logic won out.

The decision was made to get Hacker International and Olga onto the Hunt for Red Chernobog in the morning. In part because it had been an exhausting day and in other part because we all knew Hacker International would want to do this utilizing Science Center equipment and that would mean they'd be moved in here permanently within a week. Jeff was adamantly against this option, so we'd have to wait until we could all go home.

I had more questions, but I was tired, and just wanted to go to bed. Maybe even to sleep. But hopefully not right away.

Jeff picked this up, of course, which was one of the benefits of being married to the strongest empath in the galaxy. He adjourned our meeting and while most of the gang headed to the party my dad was running, Jeff and I headed down downstairs. Sex on the horizon—booyah!

"I can't believe you're okay with everything Siler's suggesting," Jeff said, as we cuddled but didn't have sex in the elevator. Sex booyah delayed. Disappointing.

"I think he's probably right, and there's not a lot of risk with me trying to talk to Chernobog." Jeff opened his mouth, presumably to argue, and I hurried on. "Besides, I think Siler's much more on our side than he wants us to know."

"Yeah, I get the same underlying emotion from him that I got from Mahin and Serene when they first joined us—the longing for family. It's lessened in Serene now, and somewhat in Mahin, but I can still recognize it. And he's got it, too." The elevator doors opened and we headed for the Lair. "But wanting to be a part of a family or not, I don't know that we can fully trust him yet."

"Well, that'll keep life exciting, right?"

"Only my girl."

We arrived to find that all the pets other than Bellie were gone, presumably with their owners and/or Jamie. That Bellie was with us still was very disappointing, however.

Bellie shrieked her love of Jeff to the heavens and they had their Man and Bird Reunion while I contemplated flowers lest Jeff realize how close I was to wringing Bellie's neck.

Though a thought occurred. "Bellie, where is Mister?"

The bird looked right at me. "Mister said Jeff is Daddy for now."

"That bodes. Com on!"

"Yes, Ambassador?"

"Hey, William, how's tricks? And by that I mean, where in the world is Mister Joel Oliver? Literally."

"He requested that, once you asked after him, I tell you that he's doing his job and following leads."

"What leads?"

"I asked, but he wouldn't say. He just said that when you asked this, to tell you that he was investigating the thing that was the most wrong with today's action against us. He seemed to feel you'd know what that meant." William didn't sound convinced I was going to be on Oliver's wavelength. Couldn't blame him.

"Ah. Nothing else?"

"No, Ambassador, I'm sorry. Should I have not allowed him to leave? He was insistent."

"No, that's okay. He's a grown man and he's used to risk. I'm a little worried about him being off alone right now, though."

William cleared his throat. "Ah, he's not actually alone."

"Oh? Who's with him?"

"Len, Kyle, Jeremy, Jennifer, Adriana, and Walter."

"Wow. That's not an investigative team, that's a strike force. And really, Walter's with them?"

"All Security's been trained for Field actions now, baby," Jeff reminded me. "And Walter has nothing to do over here, since his job is currently evacuated."

"Good point. Okey dokey, please have all bases gently alerted that should one of those seven call in for help, they're priority one, got it?"

"Gentle alerts will be sent out." He sounded just a little too pleased.

"You already sent them, didn't you?"

"Ah . . ."

"I'm not mad. He's your little brother. And under the circumstances, we have a team waltzing around during a dangerous time. I call that good initiative, William, not insubordination."

"Thank you, Ambassador." He now sounded relieved, go me. "Anything else?"

"I'd love to tell you to come get Bellie and have her keep you company, but I realize, from the Death Glare Jeff's shooting me, that that won't be allowed. Could someone get a roomy cage with a very secure cover on it?" Sex booyah denied. Totally disappointing and really made me want to make Fried Parrot on a Stick.

"Actually, Ambassador, Pierre requested that he get to have Bellie stay with him tonight."

"Awesome. Send someone to collect the bird and make a note that Pierre needs a raise." Sex booyah reinstated! The night was looking up.

"Tell them to just walk at human speeds," Jeff said. "In fact, have them here in around fifteen minutes, if you would."

"Yes, Representative Martini." William signed off.

"You want more time with your avian mistress?"

"Yes, but I know where your mind's at, and I'm all for it. I never want you to lose your focus on the priorities."

"Good man."

"Good man! Good man! Captain is a good man!"

We both stared at Bellie. "Haven't heard that in a while," I said finally. "Jeff, try asking her some questions."

"Where is Mister?" Jeff asked in the lovey-dovey tone he always employed with Bellie.

Nothing.

"Is it Hammy time?" I asked.

"Hiding Hammy, hiding Hammy! Keep hiding Hammy!"

I was sufficiently shocked to realize that Bellie was responding to my questions more than to Jeff's. Sure, I'd worked with the bird during Operation Invasion, but Bellie was the winner of the Sluttiest Parrot of the Year, every year running, and she vastly preferred men to women, and almost anyone to me.

Meaning Oliver had told her to help me.

Say what I would about her, Bellie was one smart bird, especially for an Earth animal. But she was trigger focused, usually activated by a word or a phrase. "Bellie, what did Mister tell you to tell Kitty?"

"Bellie wants to go home."

"Don't we all. Anything else, Bellie?"

"Bellie wants treats!"

While Jeff went to the mini-fridge in the living room to request bird treats from the Elves, I pondered this. Bellie normally asked for treats after she thought she'd done her job. So, what word in her last sentence was "the" word? The only one I could come up with was home.

Jeff and Bellie returned, him feeding her treats while they both nuzzled each other. Controlled my gag reflex. "Jeff, you think Oliver and the others have gone back to the Embassy?"

"Why would they?"

"No idea. I just think we may need to focus on the word home."

"Bellie wants to go home! Bellie wants treats!"

"That's the word, see how she's reacting to it?"

"She just wants to get back to her normal routine, I'm sure."

"No. Pay attention to her. She's getting treats—but she's asking for them after she says she wants to go home."

"Maybe there's something going on at Oliver's place?"

"Does Bellie want to go home to Mister?"

"Mister wants to go home. Bellie wants to go home. Home, home, home! Bellie wants treats."

Thought about the clue Oliver had left with William while Jeff gave Bellie more food and loving. "What other home could she be talking about if it's not the Embassy or Oliver's place?"

"Home Base?" Jeff suggested offhandedly, still engrossed with his beloved birdie.

"Oh. Wow. That's it."

He stopped nuzzling Bellie and turned to me. "What do you mean?"

"Oliver said he's investigating the thing that's the most wrong with today. So, what's the most wrong?"

"Everything that's happened, starting with me being on the presidential ticket."

"No. I don't mean weird, or dangerous, or anything like that. Oliver is an investigative reporter, he works with words, and he chose them carefully. He chose 'home' and 'wrong.' And he said in today's action against us, not attack, action. Meaning something coordinated. And the only coordinated attack was what happened to us outside of Home Base."

"Okay, I follow that. And if I stand back and look at it, the thing that stands out as the most 'wrong,' versus unusual, to me is that Home Base didn't come to support us. But they were fooled by that fake presidential order."

"Yeah . . ."

"As Chuck likes to say, I know that look. What?"

"Colonel Franklin would have ignored an order like that. He'd have found a way around it, or pretended not to understand it, because he likes and supports us. The world's in one piece because he's willing to trust us over protocol. He's been a supporter of Centaurion Division since he's known about us, which was well before I did, and probably before you became the Head of Field."

"That's about right. That's why he was moved to Andrews."

"Right. So, who moved into Home Base?"

"We've met him. It's Colonel John Butler."

Tried to remember if I had any impressions of him. Not really. Honestly couldn't remember what this man looked like or that I'd met him. This was Alpha Team's bailiwick, and even though I was still technically the Head of Recruitment, being the Ambassador meant I didn't get out here much. If we were having a meeting with Alpha Team, most of the time these days it happened in D.C.

"What do you get from him, emotionally or otherwise?"

Jeff shrugged. "The usual. Nothing negative. Why? Are you thinking that he's one of our enemies?"

"I think Mister Joel Oliver is considering it as a possibility."

"Let him."

"Um . . ."

Jeff grinned as someone knocked on the door. "I'm not saying to ignore this, or that I don't think your suspicions have merit, baby. I just don't want to race off right now, and since things seem quiet and, per your mother, we have a world of political pain coming tomorrow, let's let the team that went out on this mission handle it."

"Who am I to argue with sound logic like this?"

"Wow, who are you and what have you done with my wife?"

"Hand off that bird and I'll show you."

Jeff grinned. "Ah, you *are* my wife."

CHAPTER 52

MY MAIN COMPETITION for Jeff's romantic affections left, squawking happily at the male A-Cs who'd come to take her, and Jeff and I got undressed.

"I still miss it here," I said as I dumped my clothes into the hamper. "Not all the time, but sometimes."

"Me too, baby," Jeff said as he did the same, then kissed the back of my neck. "So let's celebrate being back."

"It's been a pretty active day. You want to take a shower first?"

Jeff chuckled. "Sure, since I know I disappointed you by not ravaging you in the elevator."

Spun around and kissed him. "That's right. You owe me."

"Then let me pay up right away." Jeff picked me up and I wrapped my legs around his waist. We made out the entire way to the shower. I'd have been impressed that he didn't knock us into walls or trip while doing this, but I was too busy grinding against him while his mouth ravaged mine to stop to applaud.

Showers with Jeff were always well worth any water waste and always in my Top Five List of Things To Do as Often as Possible. He had us inside and me up against the tile in short order.

Pre-Jamie we could take hours on foreplay. Post-Jamie we'd really learned to go for the gusto right away, and then get fancy later if there was time. Sure, she was being babysat by both sets of grandparents, but why tempt fate? While he moved his mouth to my neck, which was my main erogenous zone, and I started the moaning that was likely to become howling shortly, I pushed against Jeff's perfect butt with my legs. This was my way of telling him I was more than ready for his thrusters to get into action.

He chuckled against my skin as he slid me up a little and slid his mouth down to my breasts. "You know I have a routine, baby."

Indeed he did. From day one, Jeff had made me orgasm at second base, and by now he considered it a point of pride to ensure this record remained unbroken. As his tongue twirled around my nipples and he sucked and gently bit them, sure enough, I flipped right into wailing as a climax washed over me.

While my body was still bucking, Jeff slid me onto him and I started to hit the high notes. He was incredibly well proportioned, for a draft horse, and any time he did this, it felt like I was having a continuous orgasm.

We ground against each other as the water poured over us, my hands running through his hair and over his back, while my legs shoved against the best thrusters in the world and he ran his teeth all over my neck.

Jeff bucked and I flipped even more over the edge than I already was and Jeff joined me. The soundproofing in the Lair wasn't up to the standards at the Embassy, but it was a lot better than when we'd housed on the transient floors, so I didn't worry that anyone else was listening to me yowling like a cat in heat.

My body's frantic thrusts slowed and he let me slide to the floor. I nuzzled my face between his impressive pecs, enjoying how the water ran through the hair on his chest, while he stroked my back.

It had been short and sweet, but that was fine, because we really did need to clean off. Oh, sure, we helped each other soap up and, once cleaned off, did a repeat performance, this time smelling springtime fresh. But still, for us, a quieter night.

We got out and Jeff dried off at hyperspeed. Technically I could, but it was always a little risky for me, and I just didn't feel like concentrating.

He kissed me as I wrapped a towel around my hair. "I'll just go warm up the bed."

"Oh, I like where your head's at. Both of them."

Got my hair down to damp and combed through and decided that was good enough for the work I planned to do in just a few moments. Was going to leave when I happened to glance at the back of the bathroom door, which wasn't fully closed or opened. The door had a hook and there was something on it.

As with every A-C facility, the Elves had it stocked with our clothes and other necessities. Because I was prevented by Algar from talking about him, and he blocked my thoughts about him from others, I found it easier to just still think of the Operations Team as the Elves most of the time. It caused me a lot less mental pain.

But, showing that Algar was indeed the one on the case, there was a slinky negligee hanging up here that hadn't been there when we went into the shower. Jeff had never needed sexy clothes to work up interest, but who was I to argue with the King of the Elves? Perhaps Algar was into this look and was watching us on his 24/7 Porn Channel. Or maybe it was just a nostalgic nod to our wedding. Decided to put the lingerie on and not care.

Heard music starting, "Moves Like Jagger" by Maroon 5 and Christina Aguilera. Excellent choice, since Jeff had Jagger's moves and everyone else's too.

Came out to see Jeff indeed in bed, on his side, head leaning on one hand, the covers pulled back. He looked Centerfold Sexy and I did my best not to drool. He saw me, his eyelids drooped, and he got the Jungle Cat About to Eat Me look on his face. I loved that look. It was probably my favorite look in the world.

"Nice," he purred. "When did you get that?"

"Tonight. The Elves apparently want us to celebrate, too."

"They need a raise along with Pierre."

Slid into the bed with him. Jeff pulled me to him and kissed me, deeply, his tongue twining with mine while his hand slid over the small of my back.

Wrapped my arms around him as he pulled me closer and

we rubbed against each other. The silky fabric of the negligee made a nice contrast to skin and hair, and, shocking absolutely no one, I was instantly ready to go again. My pelvis thrust against Jeff's and, happy day, he was ready and rarin', too. I loved when we were in sync like this.

However, while he was ready, Jeff was also going for nostalgia. He rolled me onto my back and his hands and mouth proceeded to wander my body, paying particular attention to my neck and breasts, sliding the negligee out of the way and then sliding it right back, but in no way letting the rest of my upper body feel left out.

Within short order, my hips were thrusting like mad and I was back to moaning. Jeff moved down, presumably because he wanted me back to yowling. As his tongue ran over me, I obliged.

He obliged as well, and delved his tongue deep inside me and I went for High C, while the music changed to "Addicted to Love". While I was singing the song of Being Jeff's Woman in harmony with Robert Palmer, Jeff flipped me over onto my stomach, his mouth still doing its good work downstairs.

He shoved my thighs up so my butt was in the air. He ran his hands over my back and down my arms, moving them so he could hold my wrists next to my knees. I couldn't really move in this position, but I was too busy having an intense orgasm to complain. Jeff growled against my tender, quivering flesh and I screamed into the pillows.

"Like that, baby?" he asked, mouth still against me.

Tried to reply. Only managed a yowl. He seemed okay with this, at least if his mouth's ministrations against me were any indication. He built me right back up and tossed me over the edge again, while I moaned, and yowled, and begged for him to stop and keep going at the same time.

As this latest orgasm subsided and "Love" from Elefant came on, he ran his tongue up and nipped my butt. I bucked as he nipped the other side. Jeff let go of my wrists and let my legs slide down, then he ran his tongue up my spine, which made me quiver easily as much as everything else had. He reached my neck and gently bit the back of my neck.

"What do you want, baby?" he purred into my ear, as my hips thrust against the mattress.

"Oh . . . God . . . you . . . Jeff," I wailed. "I want you . . ."

"Mmmm, that's what I like to hear." He put his arm around my stomach and moved me up onto my hands and knees, and with that, the music slid into Heart's "All I Wanna Do Is Make Love To You", he slid my legs apart with his knees, then he slid into me.

He always felt perfect inside me, but in this position the feelings were even more intense and he felt bigger and as if he was going even deeper inside me. I moaned as his hand went around my hip and between my legs.

We thrust against each other and he stroked me in time, building me up again and again, only to hold off just as I was about to go over. Jeff always played me as if I were a saxophone and he was Clarence Clemens. Fittingly, Bruce Springsteen's "I'm On Fire" came over our airwaves.

I was definitely hitting all the high notes when Jeff finally decided to be kind and let me crash over the edge. This time, he went with me, roaring as he exploded into me and I went from High C to High Wail.

He pumped into me, hands on my hips, until our bodies slowed down to match the rhythm of the song. As the song finished and "On Top Of The World" by Imagine Dragons started, he pulled out, and flipped us both onto our backs. I turned onto my side and draped my body over his, snuggling my face into the hair on his chest while he stroked my arm and kissed my head.

"I love you, baby," Jeff murmured against my hair.

Kissed his chest. "I love you, too. I'm really glad we didn't die today."

He hugged me. "Me, too. Feel better now?"

"Mmmm, yeah. But you know what would make me feel perfect?"

He chuckled. "No, what?"

Leaned up and kissed him. "Doing it again. And then again after that."

Jeff grinned. "Sometimes it just sucks to be me."

CHAPTER 53

AFTER MORE FANTASTIC SEX, and as Lifehouse crooned "You and Me", we fell asleep wrapped around each other.

Wasn't sure how long I'd been asleep when my dream started. Happily, it wasn't my favorite congressional hearing dream, and I wasn't in the gray formless mass, either. This was a new one—I was in the woods. I wasn't a fan of the woods, and these woods didn't look familiar.

They were kind of creepy woods, as I looked around. There were definitely "things" behind trees, or running past, that I could just catch out of the corner of my eye. I spun around to see what was there, but I couldn't get a clear look.

"*Kitty*."

The voice sounded very far away, almost whispered.

"Who's there?"

"*Kitty*?" The voice sounded a little closer but still far.

"ACE? ACE, is that you?" Something small bounded out from behind one of the trees. It was fluffy and adorable, but also hazy and indistinct. "Fuzzball?"

The Poof mewed at me and jumped up and down. Then it took off. I followed.

Fuzzball dropped out of sight. I ran to where the Poof had been to see a big, gaping black hole. "*Alice in Wonderland* much, whoever's in charge of this dream?" But I followed the Poof down the black hole.

Tumbled over and over, and as I did I saw not blackness but stars, nebulas, galaxies, and more. It was like a fast-moving panorama of the universe. This was better than the woods, but I wasn't getting the point.

Landed, and it didn't hurt, confirming that I was indeed dreaming. Got to my feet and looked around. More woods. Different woods, at least as far as I could tell, yet still creepy. What a lack of an improvement.

Saw a small body lying on its side and ran to it. It was Jamie, sleeping and looking quite peaceful, Mous-Mous snuggled to her chest and clutched in her hands. I reached for them but they dissipated like smoke.

Took this to mean that Jamie was indeed asleep. Wondered if she'd really been asleep when we'd gotten back or if she was disappointed in her inattentive parents. "ACE? Are you here? Is Jamie okay?"

"Yes, Kitty, ACE is here. Kitty should not worry. Jamie was asleep and is asleep now. Jamie is safe. Jamie had a busy day and was very tired."

The voice was much closer. Registered that I was hearing it through my ears, versus in my mind. Remembered that this was how dreams worked because they were all in my mind. Looked around to see if I could spot ACE. Nothing.

"Um, how busy was she, ACE? How much of our survival was dependent upon her?"

"Not as much as Kitty fears. Jamie . . . met Sandy."

Controlled my reaction, which was fear. Fear would wake me up and I wanted to talk to ACE as long as I could. Plus, Sandy hadn't actually hurt anyone. So far, and as far as we knew. Focused on the woods around me and tried to relax. The woods didn't help much. "How did that go?"

No response. Looked around again. Still nothing. Worried I'd woken myself up by worrying. Looked up. There, in the tree, was Fuzzball. "Where did ACE go?"

The Poof mewed and jumped up into a higher branch. It so figured. Well, at least I was still asleep.

Climbed up. This was easier than it should have been, but that was one of the benefits of dreaming—you could do things in dreams you couldn't in waking life.

Reached the very top. There were clouds right at my head. Fuzzball jumped to the top of another tree, and I followed. We did this for a while, until we reached a little house perched on top of a tree surrounded by a haze I realized was smoke. The house didn't have a chimney, but it wasn't burning, either. Just smoky.

The house was more like a shack, and it was also familiar. It looked like the prisoner shacks on the outskirts of Guantanamo.

"Curiouser and curiouser. That's my line right about now, right?"

Fuzzball mewed and went inside. I followed.

To see a small, dark-haired, Dazzler-beautiful older woman who still managed to look completely intimidating sitting cross-legged on the floor. "Hey, kiddo, how's it going?"

I wanted to run to Gladys and grab her, but figured she'd dissipate like Jamie had if I tried. Felt as though we were moving, but we were still inside the shack. Risked a look around. I could see a giant elephant-like thing underneath us. "Hey, the Pachyderm is part of ACE's collective consciousness? Really?"

"It's your dream, kiddo. Many things are in here. Some of them are really bizarre, too, let me tell you. But that's not why we're here. Relax. Take a load off."

Did as I was bid and sat down in the same way as Gladys. Fuzzball went to her and sat in her lap. "Things have been better. They've also been worse. What's going on?"

She shrugged. "Cause and effect. Plans put in motion. Many things are going on, as they always are."

I'd been too vague. ACE preferred it when I was literal and exact in my questions because it made answering questions easier, and clearly that extended to anyone who was part of his collective consciousness as well. I wanted to rephrase the question, knew that if I could figure out what the endgame was I could stop whatever bad was coming toward us. But I couldn't manage to grasp the right words.

"What should I do?"

Gladys gave me a long stare. "You need to focus on what matters most. You haven't been. You've been focused on finding enemies, not protecting friends."

"I saved Vander and Serene. Well, me and the others. And a good offence is the best defense."

"And he who fights and runs away lives to fight another day."

"I wish you'd run away."

Gladys shook her head. "I have peace here. So does Michael, and this one," she patted Fuzzball. "We aren't alone."

"What about Naomi?"

"Trust me, she's not alone. But you need to focus on what you can affect, kiddo."

"Jamie misses her almost as much as Chuckie does. I'm worried about him, about both of them, and all the rest of your family. Is that what I'm supposed to focus on?"

Gladys shrugged. "Every A-C on Earth is part of my family. Even the bad ones."

"Does that mean you think we should be trying to flip your half-siblings, even though Siler says we can't do it?"

"I think that you need to focus on the thing that will do the most good for my people. And that when top assassins speak, you should listen."

The house shook, and Fuzzball jumped out of Gladys' lap. The house tipped, and Fuzzball and I both fell through the open door.

"Hang tough, kiddo," Gladys said, sounding far away. "That's the ticket. Hang tough."

The sensation of falling while asleep isn't beloved by most and I was firmly in the majority on this one. Going down the hole hadn't been bad—it hadn't felt like falling. This did, in a big way.

As I fell, I heard ACE again. "Kitty must think right."

Landed before I could ask what right was in this case. Only I didn't hit the ground. I landed in someone's arms.

"Thanks," I said as someone put me down. Realized that someone was Michael Gower.

Even as a spirit, Michael was big, black, bald, and gorgeous. He flashed me his standard You So Hot, Babe smile that he'd given every woman over the age of eighteen when he'd been alive. "Any time. You look lost." Fuzzball jumped onto Michael's shoulder, purring like mad.

"I am lost. Fuzzball's my White Rabbit, Gladys was the

Caterpillar, so you must be the Cheshire Cat. Does that mean you're here to lead me out? Or do I get to visit the King of the Elves and whoever the heck Algar's queen would be?"

Michael cocked his head at me. "You're the queen, Kitty. You're always the queen. Remember that—the queen guards the king."

"I'm supposed to guard Algar?"

Michael kissed my forehead. "By guarding your king, you guard everyone, including him."

"Who is my king, then? Is it Richard, or Paul?"

"The king has always been your king." Michael grinned. "But don't worry—you're the best there is at guarding this king. Just remember . . . you're the queen, Kitty."

With that, Michael and Fuzzball faded away, and, in typical Cheshire Cat style, the last thing I saw was Michael's grin. But even that faded.

I was in the dark, literally and figuratively. Gave it one last shot. "ACE, I was able to think about Algar with you." Fantastic. That wasn't what I'd wanted to say.

But it garnered a response. "Yes. Algar cannot control ACE and ACE cannot control Algar. Algar and ACE have . . . an understanding."

"God and the Devil usually do."

"The Devil is in the details."

That didn't sound like ACE. Didn't sound like Algar, either. Looked around and, sure enough, Mephistopheles was waving at me, from quite far away, but I could see him and everything around him clearly. He was surrounded by video screens, and each one showed a scene from all that had gone on the day before. It was a confused, muddled view, just like my mind right now.

"Huh?" The darkness was fading. I could hear Maroon Five singing "Love Somebody". That meant my alarm was going off and I was going to wake up really soon. "Mephs, I sincerely would like to know who the Mastermind is."

"Guard all the power pieces," Mephistopheles said. "It's not time for the endgame. But it'll be the end if you don't think right."

CHAPTER 54

MEPHISTOPHELES and his detailed video screens dis-appeared, too, and all I heard was Adam Levine croon-ing about dancing the night away and taking him all the way. Wouldn't be a hardship to take Adam all the way, but I was happily married.

The song changed to "Wildest Dreams" by Iron Maiden. Had that right. Shoved my still-foggy mind back to the dream. Needed to remember everything.

Thought about what Mephistopheles had said, since his clues, if you could call them that, seemed the clearest. Why I was now getting regular visitations from the Fugly of My Nightmares was a special question I had no good answer for at this time.

"Up in Arms" by the Foo Fighters came on. Woke up fully and sat up. "Chess."

"What?" Jeff asked sleepily. I could get that Maroon Five hadn't woken him right up, but Iron Maiden should have, and if not them, then the Foos certainly should have done the trick.

"You okay?" I put my hand on his forehead. Felt normal.

"Yeah, just tired." He looked at the clock. "You got up with the actual alarm? I should be asking you if you're okay."

"Go back to sleep, Mister Funny."

"No, I'm wide awake now. What were you shouting about?"

"It's a chess game and we're not thinking about it right."

At least, I hoped that's what the various clues ACE and His Kitty's Dream Players had been trying to pass along. Either that or I should use less sour cream and butter on my baked potatoes. Chose to figure on the former, because I didn't plan to use less butter and sour cream anyway.

"Okay, you and Chuck always say it's chess," Jeff said as he sat up in bed and pulled me back to snuggle next to him.

"But we haven't been thinking of it like that this time. And I think we need to."

"Okay. You're always our queen. Chuck always says he's a bishop. Christopher and I are knights. Richard's usually the king, but it could be Paul. Paul was the other bishop, so maybe that's what Richard is now."

Thought about this. "The king is different this time." If the king was different, were the other pieces different, too? Our board had shifted a lot since the "chess game" Jeff was talking about. Michael had stressed I was the queen. Maybe because I was the only piece that hadn't changed positions?

"Why?"

"Things are different? I think."

Before we could continue this, the com sprang to life. "I'm sorry Ambassador, but Raj has asked me to encourage you to hurry up. You have an important press conference coming and you need to be briefed."

"Sure thing, William. I've totally been looking forward to today, promise."

"Briefing in the commissary."

"Tell Raj and Pierre I love and appreciate them."

Jeff and I zipped into the shower and, in deference to the rush, only did the deed a couple of times, and we used hyperspeed, too. That was us, always sacrificing for the cause.

Decided I'd better go out in the Armani Standard Issue because Raj and Pierre would tell me immediately if I needed to change clothes. There was a fedora sitting on the hamper. Looked at it fondly. Jeff looked amazing in a fedora. "Maybe you should wear a hat today."

"It's the middle of summer." Jeff looked at the hat and chuckled. "Later, baby. We're busy now."

Jeff finished up and left the closet. As I was putting my

shoes on the hat fell off the hamper and landed upside down. Which was odd because there'd been no movement near it. Picked it up and looked at it. There were some dark pieces of something dusting the inside. Spilled them out into my hand—tea leaves.

Apparently this was the same fedora Jeff had worn during Operation Sherlock and he'd been wandering around with tea leaves getting into his hair whenever he'd worn it. Put the hat back on the hamper and realized that made no sense. The Elves were nothing if not tidy, and leaving tea leaves in a hat for a year and a half was the opposite of tidy.

So it was a clue. And everything in my dream had been clues. Great. I needed some coffee and food so maybe what the Powers That Be felt were obvious hints would become clear to me.

Brushed the tea into a wastebasket, grabbed my purse and ensured it was full up with all the necessities, and joined Jeff. We headed upstairs, and again in deference to the urgency that was today, we took the stairs instead of the elevators. So no make-out session. Chose to show I was a big girl and not be bitter about it. Much.

Since the A-Cs tended to function like a military unit— albeit a giant, extremely well-dressed and good-looking one—mealtimes were at standard times. Therefore, the entire Science Center was in the commissary.

We were graciously allowed to give our daughter hugs and kisses, then dragged away from her to sit with the Briefing Team, which took up an entire, huge, long table. Jamie seemed quite content with Dad and Lucinda, but now Jeff and I were both bitter.

As we sat down I realized I'd been wrong in thinking everyone was here. Oliver's team was nowhere in evidence and when I asked about them, it turned out they hadn't checked in. No one seemed worried, other than possibly Ravi. I couldn't be sure because while they were a part of the briefing, we had so many people that Hacker International weren't sitting all that close to me.

I wasn't sitting next to Jeff, either. I had Raj on one side and Pierre on the other, with Reader across from me, and Tim and Serene flanking him. Got the feeling everyone was wishing I had an android counterpart somewhere they could just program with what needed to be said and how. Couldn't blame them.

The five of them filled me in on what had transpired while we were playing Quicksand in the Desert. More bombings, accusations of our involvement in said bombings, and then political unrest based on the bombings and fueled by every anti-alien group out there were the main highlights. Many of the streets of D.C. and elsewhere were plastered with anti-alien and anti-Armstrong-Martini posters, and all this before Jeff was even officially announced as the VP candidate. Apparently it had been a busy day for everyone, everywhere.

"We've set up a press conference," Raj said as he wrapped up and I shoveled food in and coffee down and hoped like hell I could remember anything about my dream and clues, let alone this information, by the time breakfast was over. "You're going to get hit with a variety of questions, but they'll all boil down to these points."

"Right, I think I have them. What are our thoughts about Jeff running for vice president? We think that if one of us is called to service, then we go, and since Senator Armstrong is our good friend, we will, of course, be happy to have Representative Martini represent us in higher office, if the voting public agrees."

Jaws dropped. "Well done, Kitty," Serene said without an ounce of sarcasm or shock showing. "That was perfect."

Raj nodded. "Yes. What else?"

"I'm sure I'll be asked if we did the bombings to garner attention or because we're closet terrorists. In which case my answer is a shocked, horrified, and offended absolutely not."

"What if someone insists they have proof, Kitty darling?" Pierre asked.

"Then I will insist that their facts are wrong and that we trust the good officers of the law, both state and federal, to get to the bottom of these terrorist acts. We fight the terrorists, we don't join them."

"Good." Reader nodded. "What else?"

"They're going to ask the follow-up, which is if we didn't do the bombings who did? In which case I'll point them back to the fact that we know the police and federal agencies are doing all they can to find the perpetrators."

"And?" Raj asked leadingly.

"And, if Bruce Jenkins is there, he's going to ask if I'm having a variety of affairs with anyone and everyone I know. To which I'm going to ask him if he's seen my husband and let the audience laugh at him. So, did I miss any?"

"What's happened to poor Missus Maurer," Pierre said. "I'd expect someone to toss that one at you, darling."

"She can't be officially listed as missing for another twenty-four hours," Reader said. "But Melville's confirmed that the Cleary-Maurer campaign called to alert D.C.P.D. that she hadn't come home from her afternoon stroll."

Mrs. Maurer was actually in the briefing session. She got up and came over. "Didn't want to have to scream. I think I need to go with the Ambassador, so it's clear I'm alive and not under duress."

"You mean you're ready to change sides politically?" Raj asked. "Because that's what you being seen with Kitty, in public, particularly in this way, will say."

She sniffed. "My own son sent people to kill me. I think that warrants a change of teams, don't you, young man?"

"We assume," White, who was on Serene's other side, said. "Though we have yet to confirm."

"Sadly, I have no issue believing it," she said.

White nodded. "I agree with you. You going along also tosses in a monkey wrench the other side won't necessarily see coming. However, that means monkey wrenches will be coming toward Missus Martini as well."

An idea dawned. "Can I have Raj and Richard with me?"

"Why?" Reader asked. "And why them?"

"Because I'm a troubadour and can calm the situation if needed and because Mister White is actually the best with human diplomacy," Raj said. "We'll bring along a few other troubadours, too, just to have a show of force that won't take any Field agents away from their other duties."

"Raj is my favorite." Heard Jeff groan from a few seats away. Which brought up another point. "What is Jeff going to be doing while I'm being interrogated by the press?"

"He and the rest of Senator Armstrong's team are going to be practicing their formal 'Jeff's our guy' speech," Reader said. "The National Convention is next week, remember."

I hadn't, but chose to not mention this. "Okay. So where are we doing this press conference?"

"You've scored the East Room of the White House," Mom, who was sitting between Jeff and Christopher, shared. "Try not to make the President regret it."

"Won't that be like the President is endorsing the Armstrong-Martini ticket?"

"He's the same party and he's already endorsed my candidacy," Armstrong, who was across from Mom, said. "And, as you know, he's pro-alien." He flashed me his Campaign Smile. "It'll be fine, Kitty. You're a natural speaker."

Senator McMillan, who was next to him, nodded. Caroline, who was next to McMillan, gave me the thumbs up. Tried to let their positivity fill me. I was filled with the positive feeling that we were all feeling far too confident, myself included, and that meant something was going to go wrong. Shoved it aside.

"True enough," Christopher said. "Never found Kitty to be speechless for long."

"Careful or I'll demand you come there with me."

"I'm part of the Presidential Ticket Announcement Team, sorry," he said with a grin, not a Patented Glare. Chose not to ask if he was feeling okay. He and Amy were sitting close together and I figured they'd had a good night and the effects hadn't worn off of Christopher yet.

Wondered for a moment if the President was the new king. Maybe. But he was on the last months of his second term—he seemed an unlikely target for what was going on. And Michael had said I always protected this king.

"I'd like to go with you, Kitty," Culver said. She was a little farther down the table but still near to the Senators. "And I think you should have Guy along as well. And not for the reasons I'm sure you think. We both have more experience dealing with the people you're about to be faced with, and I think you'll want the help."

"Thanks, Lillian, I'll take you and Guy on Team Press Conference gladly." Tried not to think about the message them coming with me was going to send, good intentions or not, and decided I'd deal with those ramifications later. "Nathalie, what about you?"

"Just like Don," she nodded at McMillan, "I'm going with Jeff and Vincent, to show my support." Knew without asking that Caroline would be with McMillan.

"Makes sense. I assume Chuckie can't come with me, right?"

"Right." He was on White's other side, so on the other side from most of the Presidential Ticket Announcement Team. "I'll also be with Jeff and Senator Armstrong. As will a large contingent of Field Agents, C.I.A. agents, and some Secret Service agents, along with most of the D.C.P.D."

"Why?"

Chuckie gave me the "what the hell?" look. "I think it's kind of obvious, Kitty. We'll be there to protect them. This is an outside event, and we've had a lot of terrorist and anti-alien activity going on. Hence, a large show of force and a lot of eyes and ears on the ground."

And there it was. I knew what Michael had been trying to tell me and, probably by extension, what the rest of those in my dream had been trying to tell me. Felt kind of stupid for it to have taken this long, especially with that gigantic clue Algar had tossed me, but hey, I had a lot going on and was distracted.

We all were. Everything yesterday had done the typical Bad Guy Double Duty, and distraction was always on the Bad Guy Plans Du Jour. But our enemies weren't distracted. At all. And they wanted to take the king. Or, as I thought of him, the guy I'd been protecting since, in that sense, we'd met.

Jeff.

CHAPTER 55

DURING OPERATION SHERLOCK, Jeff had been a target. However, based on all the clues, he was "the" target now, not just one of many. Though our enemies would undoubtedly like to take out as many of us as possible.

I wanted, desperately, to tell everyone that we had to bag all these plans and get Jeff under the strictest guard possible. Only, we didn't have that option.

If I didn't do my dog and pony show, I knew without asking that American Centaurion was going down in flames, at least in terms of approval ratings and such. And we needed approval, because we had a lot of people who hated us and they were getting good at getting together. Club 51 and the Church of Intolerance had made their love connection, and other groups like them were following suit.

The same held for the Presidential Ticket announcement. If Jeff didn't show, Armstrong could pretty much kiss his campaign goodbye. And it would mean we'd lose all our support in Congress, because if we bailed on one of the guys who was one of our staunchest supporters, then who could believe they could count on us at all?

Plus, even if I told the others what I was worried about, they'd all say the same thing: Jeff, like the rest of us in positions of power and influence within Centaurion, was always a target. So how did that make today different from any other day? My sharing that I was worried because of a dream and a hat with some tea leaves in it wouldn't convince or reassure anyone, either.

But Chuckie would be there with a ton of A-Cs and all those people focused on protection and maybe outside hadn't meant someplace dangerous. "So, where are you all going to be for the announcement you'll be making while surrounded by alert, watchful, and distrusting security personnel?"

"Steps of Congress," McMillan said. Swiveled to look at him. Hoped I wasn't going to get a crick in my neck from all of this. "Photo opportunity and all that. Hopefully the announcement will draw the press away from you on time. Vincent and Jeff go on shortly after your conference is supposed to end—just enough time for the reporters to leave you and come to us."

"Or to send two sets of reporters out." And just enough time for our enemies to blow us all up in succession. But I didn't say this aloud, score one for my learned diplomacy.

Armstrong shrugged. "Most reporters want both stories, not one."

"Love your optimism. But won't that mean the same people toss the exact same questions to you guys?"

"It will. But we're all prepped." Got another shot of the Campaign Smile. "Don't worry, Kitty. I've done this before and Jeff's a natural. It'll be fine."

Before I could list the ways that this could all be far less than fine, a Field agent I'd seen around but couldn't name if the fate of the world depended upon it arrived. "Excuse me, Commander," he said to Reader, "but the Embassies and the Pontifex's Residence are all cleared for rehabitation."

"Good." Reader stood up. "Then we can all go home after these events are over. Let's get moving—Kitty has to go on in less than an hour."

As we all got up and started moving toward the elevators, the Field agent touched my arm and we stepped aside. "This was waiting at the Embassy, outside the front door. Ambassador. I think it's for you."

He handed me a small package, wrapped in plain brown paper. There was no return address. There wasn't really a mailing address, either. Instead there was a small card, a cut and folded piece of the wrapping paper, taped to the top. This was addressed to Miss Katt.

Lifted the top of the card up. *Open immediately, before you leave for your meetings.*

Well. Either our enemies were aware that only a handful of people called me Miss Katt, or I'd gotten a package from the Dingo. Slipped the package into my purse. "Thanks. Could you let the others know that I'm going to visit the bathroom before we all hustle off?"

"Absolutely, Ambassador."

He turned to share my potty news and I zipped off to the bathrooms. Got into a stall, just in case I'd end up needing to flush whatever was in this. Put the package up to my ear. No ticking. Not that this meant anything.

The smart money said to take this to wherever the bomb unit was within the Science Center. It existed, I just didn't spend time there. However, speaking of time, I didn't have a lot before I had to gate it over to the White House.

Someone else came into the bathroom. "Kitty, are you in here?" It was Serene. Well, conveniently, the Bomb Squad had come to me.

Opened the stall door. "Yes." Handed her the package. "Think this is a bomb? I don't, by the way."

She examined it. "Why not?"

"I recognize the handwriting. And there's no way in the world anyone's going to make the Dingo or Surly Vic write a note they don't want to."

"It seems okay, but we won't know for sure unless we search it or you open it. I knew you were up to something."

"Blah, blah, blah, I wasn't trying to be stealthy."

She giggled. "Liar. Why were you in the stall?"

"So I could drop it into the toilet and flush whatever if it was a bomb."

"That rarely works."

"Rarely doesn't mean never. You ready to live on the edge?"

"True. And yes."

We went into the stall together.

Opened the package carefully, holding it over the toilet, to find a burner phone and a note. "Well, that was anticlimactic." Opened the note. *Please call the number programmed into this phone approximately 5 minutes before your press conference. No sooner, and definitely no later.*

"Huh. Well, this is certainly from my 'uncles' because they live for the cryptic cloak-and-dagger stuff." Had a feeling they found this to be the fun side of their jobs, protecting and messing with me. I was just lucky that way.

"I'm going to the press conference with you, then," Serene said. "Just in case."

"Works for me." Dropped the burner phone, card, and note into my purse. Serene checked the rest of the packaging and declared it interest-free. Tossed the paper and box into the trash and we headed out to rejoin the others.

Things were rather chaotic, in part because those who weren't going to the press conference were going to go home first, and then join Jeff and Armstrong at Capitol Hill, and we had a lot of people to relocate back to their places of residence.

Found Lucinda and Dad so I was able to give Jamie a hug and kiss. "Be a good girl for Grandma Luci and Papa Sol, Jamie-Kat."

She hugged me back. "I will, Mommy. You and Daddy be good, too."

"We'll do our best." Gave her, Lucinda, and Dad one last hug and kiss, then Raj came to drag me off.

We all went to first floor, which housed the main launch area, motor pool, and related moving-things-around functions and equipment. There were easily as many people here as we'd had when we were heading to Vegas to stop Kyrellis from blowing up half of Sin City. That entire thing seemed so much easier than what I was faced with today.

Speaking of Amazon fighters, Rahmi and Rhee had shapeshifted to look like a couple of female Field agents. Female agents were rare, but we had them, so this worked. They both assured me that they would not attack anyone without provocation and Chuckie's direct order, and that protecting Jeff, the senators, Chuckie, and anyone else we cared about would be their top priority. Was happy they were going with Jeff and tried not to worry that they'd forget the "Chuckie's direct order" thing the moment someone jostled them.

As I left the princesses, Jeff found me and hugged me. "You'll do great, baby."

"Picking up my stress?"

"Blocks or no, yeah." He kissed me, rather chastely for us. "Just remember, no matter what happens, you're always my girl."

"True enough. Jeff? Promise me you'll be extra careful and highly vigilant." Wondered if I should tell him he was the new king of this chess game. Decided he'd probably be more relaxed and less aggressive if I didn't.

He hugged me again. "Always, baby, you know that."

"Never that I've ever seen."

Jeff grinned. "That's why we fit so well together, Kitty. We both think the other one's the reckless one."

"And here I was thinking it was the great sex."

He laughed. "That too."

Reader joined us. "Jeff, Kitty, make out later. It's time to get this party started."

CHAPTER 56

CHOSE NOT TO WHINE at Reader and instead behave like an adult. Gave Jeff one last kiss, while sending a mental request to ACE and Algar to watch over him and the rest of Team Announcement. Then I went and joined Team Press Conference.

Guy Gadoire was there, of course, but this was the first time he and I had been near each other since all the fun had started the day before. "Ah, my dove," he said in his totally faked Pepé Le Pew accent, as he grabbed my hand and proceeded to do his "thing," which was to slobber all over it. "You look radiant as always."

"Thanks, Guy." Managed to extract my hand without jerking it back. "Really appreciate your coming to support us."

"For you, my dove? Anything and everything you ask." He winked. "Anything and everything." Really hoped he wasn't going to suggest I share a "bed of love" with him and Vance right now; I needed Diplomatic Decorum in charge, not the Inner Hyena.

White joined us as I controlled my gag reflex. "Ah, Monsieur Gadoire. Lovely to see you. Excuse me, I'm escorting the Ambassador." He moved us away, pulled a small pack of wipes out of his jacket pocket, and gave me one.

"You rock above all others." Wiped Gadoire's "kiss" off and dropped the wipe in a convenient trashcan. Made sure no one saw, to keep my façade of being diplomatic going.

White took my hand as we approached the gate. "I'd offer to carry you, but Jeffrey would object."

"True, but you're the best, Mister White."

"We're still assuming it's catsuit time?"

"We are. We definitely are."

With that he and I stepped through the gate, me with a death grip on White's hand. I was revved up just enough that I only had mild nausea, so I didn't toss the cookies in the White House, for which I was fairly sure everyone would be grateful.

Mom was already over there, along with the four troubadours Raj had selected, none of whom I knew well, and a bunch of White House staffers whose names I didn't even try to remember. They were all a blur. Not only was I nervous, but I had to call the top assassins soon and had no guess as to what wrinkle that was going to create. Wanted desperately to listen to tunes, but knew the reaction I'd get, so left my iPod and earbuds in my purse.

My Glock was in my purse, too, but we hadn't been screened for weapons, possibly because we'd come over via gate and into the vestibule for this area. Decided not to point this error out as we walked down a wide corridor with a large, red, gold-bordered carpet. The walls had white columns interspersed with portraits, and the whole corridor was lined with chairs I doubted anyone ever sat on and doorways to other rooms we weren't going into.

Gold and red was the definite color theme in this area. Culver fit in really well here—she looked far less out of place and even a little less angular. It also explained why so many First Ladies favored red as their color—why not blend in with the fancy décor where you'd be doing a lot of entertaining?

Vance had come along with us as well and he grabbed me away from White as we neared our destination. "Kitty, I heard from Mister Joel Oliver this morning."

"Is he okay?"

"Yes. He said to tell you that there are things he's about to bring to light about everything that went on yesterday. Should coincide with your press conference, depending on when he gets the go-ahead."

"Did he say anything about Home Base?"

Vance shook his head. "No, that's all he said. Other than that I should have my phone on and be ready to share a live web feed."

"Fantastic. Okay, thanks for the heads-up. Hey, did you work with Raj and Pierre on my stock replies?"

"Yeah. I'm also here to help them spot the reporters who are going to be the biggest problems, and to let you know who Bruce Jenkins is."

"How are you going to do that?"

"I have my ways."

"We're here," Mom said, before I could question just what ways Vance thought he had.

The East Room was really a giant ballroom—it reminded me of ours at the Embassy. There were incredibly ornate gold and glass chandeliers, tall windows with gold drapes all over the room, the ubiquitous old oil portraits hung tastefully on the walls, and a parquet floor mostly covered with a gold-and-red carpet. Yep, red and gold were this area's colors. Go ASU and USC. Thinking of those universities made me wonder how Caroline and Chuckie were doing and if they were in as much danger as Jeff, and if Len and Kyle were okay and if they were still with Oliver.

The room was set up with a dais at one end, topped with a lectern and a lot of chairs behind it, but with even more chairs on the main floor. As near as I could tell, other than those on the dais, all the seats were filled.

"I want to freshen up, just for a minute," I said before we walked fully inside.

Mouths opened to protest. "I'll go with her," Serene said quickly. "I know where it is." She linked her arm through mine and we hustled down the hallway and into the lovely Presidential Ladies' Room.

Didn't take time to look around. Serene made sure we were alone as I turned on the burner phone from the Dingo. Sure enough, there was only one number programmed into it.

"It's about the time they told you to contact them, but should I be here for this call?" Serene asked after she gave me the thumbs up that we were alone.

"Sure, why not?"

"They're your uncles and they sent it to you."

"If they mind, they'll tell me, I'm sure." Hit the number. It rang four times before it was picked up. No one said anything. "Um, Uncle Peter?"

"Ah, Miss Katt, it is you."

"In the flesh, so to speak. How are you and Uncle Victor? And what's the good word? I'm rushing because I go on, as you know, in five minutes. Thanks for ensuring we didn't all die yesterday, by the way. That was truly appreciated by all of us."

"We were happy to assist. Victor and I are both fine, thank you for inquiring. And the good word, so to speak, is that evidence has been planted that will show that, true to the accusations, Centaurion Division was responsible for all the bombings around the world yesterday. I would expect someone to have that information by the time your press conference begins."

"Fantastic. I knew we all felt too confident. So, is this evidence something we can get rid of, something we can explain, something we can prove to have been planted by the real mad bombers, or should I just tell everyone we're leaving the planet on the first spaceship out of Dodge?"

"Actually, I would strongly recommend you take responsibility for the bombings."

CHAPTER 57

LET THAT SIT ON THE AIR for a bit. "Excuse me?"

"Take responsibility for the bombings," the Dingo repeated, presumably because he thought I hadn't heard him. "At your press conference. Not before. Do not discuss this with anyone. Well, other than the young lady with you. I'm sure she will be able to offer some expert comments."

"I heard you. I really meant what the hell? Only stronger." So he knew Serene was with me. Wasn't even remotely surprised. For all I knew Surly Vic was in the audience and the Dingo was pretending to be White House staff. Nothing these two did surprised me anymore.

"There is a reason."

"God, I hope so. Care to share what that reason is?"

"Certainly." He sounded disappointed.

Tried to think fast. "Um, was there something far worse that we 'blew up' that will also be discovered in a timely fashion that will show us to be saving the day?"

"Well done." Now he sounded happy. Good, I was keeping my most dangerous "relatives" in the Proud Zone. Go me. "Yes. You can explain that the reason the bombs injured no one and only did minor damage is that they were set that way, in order to protect those the terrorists wanted to harm. And because there was no time to remove what the terrorists had placed."

"What were we destroying?"

"Ricin bombs."

"Um, for real?"

"Yes. Your enemies are terrible people."

"They used to employ you."

"No longer. They make most of our clients look like choirboys. Besides, technically, we were hired by the Pentagon for the job we were on when we met."

"True enough. Madeleine Cartwright probably figured out a way to pay you with taxpayer dollars. How'd you find out what was going on, though?"

"We were alerted to this by the contract on your embassy."

"Oh, so that's the poison they were supposed to release to kill us all?" Terrible people didn't begin to cover this group. And this wasn't the first time they'd used poisons. The Mastermind clearly liked them. Filed the fact away to discuss with the others later.

"Yes. I believe you have met our mutual friend?"

"Siler? Yeah. We have him 'captive' at the moment."

"Good. Be sure to let him 'escape' when he requests it. He is taking the contracts from your enemies, and then Victor and I are countering them. Our bombs burned hotter and went off sooner than the ricin bombs. High heat destroys the toxin."

"They planted these all over the world."

"They did."

"How did two of you manage to find and counter them all?"

"We did not work alone."

"Wow. The entire Assassination League is working on this?"

"Yes. Mass murder is very bad for business."

"Good point. Kill off a billion people, lose at least a million potentially high-paying jobs."

"Exactly."

Thought about it. "Did you guys happen to have help? As in, A-C help?"

"We might have."

"Can I trust those A-Cs?"

"You certainly have in the past."

Camilla was the only likely A-C who could somehow be working with the Assassination League and not let on about it. But one A-C, no matter how good, would have trouble blocking every bomb that had gone off yesterday. Even Christopher would have been hard-pressed to do it.

"More than one A-C?"

"Yes. They are all loyal to you, Miss Katt. Their leader in particular."

Leader. There was one other group of A-Cs who we'd certainly used for a kind of covert op in plain sight action. And they definitely had a leader. And he definitely needed a raise, too. After he and I had a long heart-to-heart chat about sharing with me and why it was good. However, I had a feeling my leader had his own leader as well.

"Gotcha. Um, for the announcement, should I go for offensive or defensive on this one?"

"The best defense is a good offense."

"You know, why is it so much easier to work with you than half the people I deal with?"

He chuckled. "Because you think right. We will be in touch. Keep the phone. I will send you a new number shortly. Good luck, Miss Katt." With that he hung up.

Dropped the phone back into my purse. "Serene, can you keep a secret for," checked my watch, "about another two minutes?"

"Sure, Kitty."

"Great. You're coming up with me when I make my speech. Because my speech has changed dramatically, and the Q and A is going to need your expert touch much more than mine."

"Why?"

"Lots of reasons. But, I need Scientist Serene onstage, not Airhead Serene."

Her lips quirked. "What do you mean?" Still sounded completely innocent and naïve.

"I mean I'm on to you. You're not a Liar, with a capital L, so much as you have some troubadour talent in there that no one's spotted. When you want us to think of you as Miss Innocence of the Year, we do. When you want to exert your authority, on the other hand, you do that, too. And no one notices that most of the time we think of you as a sweetheart who just manages to be the best bombs expert the world has."

"Not sure what you're insinuating, Kitty." I could feel it, now that I was aware of the talent, feel her using her voice and expression to make me think she had no clue. But this was the downside to the troubadour talent—if you knew it was being used, you could counter it.

"Not insinuating. Flat out saying—you have troubadour talent. So I'm wondering . . . why didn't you use it when you were young? Think carefully before replying. I *will* know if you're lying."

Serene looked at me closely for a long moment. Then shrugged. "It came on normally when I was a teenager. I already knew they didn't love me—why try to make them? I just wanted people to like me for who I was, not who I could make them believe I was. Besides, I'm not nearly as strong in that talent as Raj and some of the others are."

"Sure you're not. I'm wondering . . . how did Raj get assigned to our Embassy Mission?"

"I might have suggested him, in passing."

"I'll bet. Great choice, by the way. You know, around here, women are actually allowed to show that they know what the hell is going on." So were men. Unless they were troubadours.

It was easy to understand why Serene and Raj had kept most of what they were doing quiet—Christopher's disdain for the talent was indicative of most of the A-C population. In fact, the most action and respect the troubadours had seen was during Operation Infiltration. Wondered now how much of that disdain the troubadours actually encouraged and how much they simply allowed. Figured it was a bit of both.

She grinned. "I know. But this way is . . . more fun."

"I'll take your word on that. Why didn't you talk to me about this? I'm troubadour friendly."

"You are. Jeff isn't, Christopher is anti, and it's hard to do covert work if everyone knows and is telling you not to do it."

"Good point. So, are you running the Troubadour Underground Network?"

"Sort of. When I became the Head of Imageering I did a little searching and found Raj and the others who'd been trying for Centaurion Division or Embassy posts. I did some evaluation—they were all trustworthy and, as you said yourself, desperate to actually get to do jobs they felt were meaningful. When I realized that Imageering was compromised and we saw no way to fix it, I knew we had to do something. Raj was already in place, and then you had him pull in the rest of those I would have anyway."

"So you set up, what? The Centaurion C.I.A.?"

"Essentially, yes. Jeff and Christopher have affected James and Tim far too much—they're both focused on doing as good a job as those they replaced, and they are. But they're not looking to innovate, in part because they're human and afraid of being reprimanded or removed from their positions because they changed things."

"Never worried me."

Serene laughed. "No, you like to mix it up and keep everyone guessing. And we need to mix it up, to innovate, too, especially since our enemies have no lack of willingness to do so. I've seen what Chuck does—I set up our own people accordingly. And I may have asked Olga a couple of questions, off and on."

"I'll bet you're totally her favorite." Serene even sounded different right now; no one hearing her like this would think she was anything but hugely competent and totally in charge. Thanked God, ACE and Algar that Yates had never looked Serene up—she would make the best Mastermind in history. "Anyway, who's in charge of Mission: Fool 'Em to Protect 'Em, you or Raj?"

"I like to give people autonomy, Kitty. Just like you do."

"Super. So, is Raj prepared for what I'm going to announce?"

"Possibly. But I don't know what you're going to announce, Kitty. You haven't shared that yet."

"Oh, as to that, I have a funny story to tell you that I'm just betting you already know all about."

CHAPTER 58

WE LEFT THE BATHROOM just as a stressed-out White House staffer came to collect us. She took us through the Green Room, which was actually green and nowhere near as pretty as the East Room. Didn't have long to look at it—by now, we were officially late. Oh well, make an entrance, right?

Everyone on Team Press Conference was seated in one long row at the back of the dais, other than Vance. Got a lot of looks indicating everyone was aware Serene and I were late and none of them were happy about it. The President wasn't here, and neither was Mom. Presumably she was with him somewhere. Good. I wouldn't have to see my mother's expression when I dropped my bombshell.

I was graciously hustled onto the dais as a different White House staffer was doing a rambling introduction he immediately sped up and concluded when I arrived. Polite applause as I went to the lectern, Serene trailing me by a step or two. Was incredibly glad we hadn't had to walk through the scads of reporters in this room.

Since Oliver wasn't with us, no one had prepped me for the camera flashes. At least, I chose to believe it hadn't occurred to anyone else to mention them as I was blinded by flashing lights when I foolishly looked out at the audience in an attempt to see where Vance might be sitting. Spent some time blinking and was glad I wasn't going to have to read from my prepared speech any longer.

Despite being an ambassador and supposed lobbyist, I didn't have a lot of experience with this kind of situation. Most of my knowledge of how these things ran was based off of movies, or, since we're being honest, coaches and athletes doing their postgame interviews on ESPN or Fox Sports. Hoped I wouldn't end up channeling poor Coach Denny Green after the Arizona Cardinals had let him down one time too often way back when.

Cleared my throat. Couldn't spot Vance. Couldn't spot anyone familiar. I was about to have stage fright, mostly because I was actually frightened by what I was going to say. But, I could stand here like an idiot or I could talk.

Went with my go-to move—running my yap. "Thank you all for coming today." Camera flashes went off like crazy. Decided politicians and celebrities had it harder than I'd thought. How they smiled and managed to talk to the press when they were more than half-blinded was beyond me. Should have dug my sunglasses out of my purse before going on and just pretended I was trying to channel Jackie O.

Realized I was still holding my purse. So taking out the sunglasses was a possibility. The reality that I was going to look like the biggest dork in the world in every paper and news channel on the planet by taking my purse to the podium was a far more likely possibility.

Discarded the sunglasses idea and forged on. This was easier than Michael's funeral, right? Of course right. "I had a statement prepared for you, but certain information has just come to light, making that original statement inaccurate." More flashes. Was suddenly happy everyone I was here with was behind me. Not that I could have seen their expressions even if they were right in front of me right now.

"I'm sorry, but could you all just cool your jets on the camera flashes? I need my vision for later and all that." This earned some chuckles, but the flashes slowed down. They didn't all stop, however. "Yo, all of you in the back. The light's still bright even though you're far away. Please stop."

This earned more chuckles, but the cameras cooled it. Decided the party the reporters would have over this was worth being able to see something other than spots swimming in front of me.

Took a deep breath, let it out slowly. Nothing to fear but fear itself. And every single reaction of every single person here and elsewhere. Well, excitement kept life interesting. "There have been rumors that the many bombings yesterday were done by Centaurion Division, the military arm of American Centaurion." Heard a lot of cameras flashing, but the flashbulbs were off, so all was good there.

"I'm here to tell you that this is absolutely . . . true." Gasps from everyone in the room, especially from those behind me, and lots of low talking. I put my hand up and the room quieted.

Went on quickly. "However, we weren't attacking anyone or anything. Centaurion Division identified a terrorist plot to release ricin gas at strategic locations throughout the world, particularly here in Washington. Due to the timing of when we were able to confirm this intelligence, we had no time to safely remove or deactivate the bombs. Instead, we used quickly available, precise explosions to burn the ricin and destroy it."

"How is that possible?" someone shouted from the audience. "If you blew it up, you released the gas."

"Actually, as I believe evidence will show, we did not. For the scientific explanation, however, Serene Dwyer, our Chief Explosives Expert, will reply." Stepped aside and Serene stepped up.

"Ricin is made inactive by heat above eighty degrees centigrade, one-hundred-and-seventy-six degrees Fahrenheit. Because of our work with the American and other world governments, we have access to a variety of self-contained explosives that burn at double that heat or more." She sounded both in charge and soothing.

"Ambassador, why did you feel you had the authority to make that decision?" someone else asked.

A staffer ran in a cordless mic and handed it to me. Score one for White House efficiency. "As I said, we didn't have time to alert the proper authorities. We could have allowed a terrorist attack or we could have stopped it using the means at our disposal. We chose to stop it."

"Is that why you all disappeared yesterday?" another reporter shouted. "Because you were setting the bombs? Or trying to hide the evidence?"

"No. As I said, we used the bombs to stop the ricin gas from being released. Our embassy was one of the attack points. We weren't able to stop the gas from being released in our embassy and had to evacuate all personnel. We went to a safe location to be sure no one was contaminated and also to protect ourselves."

Normally, press conferences were well run. Despite my hopes, this one had devolved into chaos, with reporters shouting questions and accusations freely. Well, at least no one was asking if I was sleeping with someone other than my husband. Under the circumstances, had a hard time putting that in the win column, but did it anyway.

"I'd like to ask you to all calm down," Serene said sweetly. "The Ambassador can only answer one question at a time." The room started to quiet. Just as someone shouted.

"Listen!" That was Vance. He stood up, cell phone in the air. I couldn't hear anything, but the people around him started to get their phones out.

Decided this wasn't going to help if no one could hear what Vance's phone was sharing. Got off the dais and trotted over to him. Happily, no one tried to stop me. Handed him the mic, which he put near his phone.

". . . authorities have confirmed that evidence of ricin gas was found at the scenes of the majority of yesterday's bomb attacks, as well as evidence of multiple bombs at each site. Experts speculate that the explosions destroyed the ricin gas, preventing its release. Ricin is a deadly toxin . . ."

Took the mic away as a man in a full Air Force uniform entered the room and took Serene's place at the lectern. "No more questions," Colonel Franklin said. "We need to have the Ambassador and her staff back to continue briefing the President and his advisors of what transpired yesterday."

"So you're saying that you knew about this before this conference?" someone shouted at Franklin.

"Yes," he replied, not even sounding a little like he was lying. "We're the authorities who determined there were two bombs at each site—one containing the ricin toxin and one of clearly different manufacture that destroyed the toxin. That's all." He nodded to me as another guy in uniform I knew came and took my arm.

"Captain Morgan, it's great to see you." I grabbed Vance and dragged him along as Morgan led me out the back and to the corridor.

"Next time, give us a heads-up, will you?" Morgan asked. "We weren't planning to make a statement until after your press conference."

We were hustled into the Blue Room, which was, shocker, blue. It was a lot prettier than the Green Room, but again I didn't have time to examine the décor. I was too busy wondering if my mother was going to kill me or not.

Mom was in there, and she looked quietly angry. I went to her. "Sorry. I only found out about it a couple of minutes before I had to go on and it seemed important . . ."

Mom rolled her eyes. "You can't lie to me. Why you even try I'll never know. Which assassin gave you the tip?"

"The Dingo."

"Unbelievable. Raj, Serene, come here, please. Arthur, if you and Gil would join us?"

Uh oh. We were all busted.

CHAPTER 59

THE BLUE ROOM WAS AN OVAL, but Mom managed to get us all into what really felt like a corner. "Who'd like to explain themselves first?" Raj opened his mouth. "Not you," Mom said. "Or you, Serene. Kitty, what the hell were you thinking?"

"Honestly? I was thinking that the only people who ever seem to tell me the truth without my freaking begging for it or leaping through hoops to get it are assassins. What that says about everyone around me I don't know, but it's probably not nice. If you *knew* what was going on, Mom, why the *hell* didn't *you* tell *me*?"

Mom blinked. I rarely spoke to my mother like this, mostly because Mom was pretty much always right and, since I wasn't a teenager anymore, rarely upset me. But I was stressed out, worried about Jeff, and my feelings were more than a little hurt. I'd done my best. Sure, not the best everyone was expecting, but in my dream Gladys had said that when top assassins spoke I should listen. Had to figure that had meant more than that I should trust Siler.

Mom sighed. "I'm sorry, kitten. I didn't know until about five minutes before you went on."

"Interesting timing. Who contacted you and how?"

"Colonel Franklin found me and briefed me and the President. It's why we weren't in the room with you."

"I received a letter yesterday afternoon, via unconventional means," Franklin said.

"Unconventional?"

"Carrier pigeon. I wish I was joking but I'm not. This was the message." He handed me a piece of paper.

From the former to the current, look for signs of ricin gas, this is what A-C bombs destroyed. Home Base infiltrated. Watch your back and everyone else's.

"Wow, nice to see the kids these days holding onto the old ways and all that."

Bellie had said Hammy was hiding and should stay hiding. Now, how would she know that, and how would Hamlin get access to carrier pigeons without outside assistance? Clearly, Mister Joel Oliver had some serious sources.

"Obviously Colonel Hamlin is still alive," Franklin said. "I haven't tested this for veracity, but I had samples of his handwriting to compare it to and this looks legit. I contacted the F.B.I. and had the investigative team look for ricin, and we kept teams at it around the clock."

"Who did you call, Evander Horn?" I asked.

"Yes, and he can confirm it, I'm sure."

So, that's why Serene and Horn had been targeted to die. Because Horn could back up the tip and it was his team who was doing the main research. Serene had put the team in place that had foiled the toxin attack and she was also in charge of the A-C team that was doing the bomb site work. And Stephanie would have known most or all of this. So our enemies had rolled their plan fast, all things considered, meaning whoever was in charge was a nimble thinker. Meaning the person in charge was probably the Mastermind himself.

"While the toxin was rendered inert," Franklin went on, "there were traces at almost every bomb site from yesterday. We received conclusive results about an hour ago now. I knew where your mother was going to be, so alerted the President and grabbed her when I had the opportunity."

"I wish you hadn't used Centaurion personnel to do the tests," Mom said.

Gave Serene the hairy eyeball. "Thanks for mentioning that."

"Need to know," she said with her Innocent Face going strong. Chose not to argue. Or ask who else on Alpha Team, other than Serene and Team Troubadour, had known about this, mostly because I was fairly sure the answer would be "no one." I'd save the airing of dirty laundry for when we weren't in the White House surrounded by reporters and such.

"We did because we had to," Franklin said. "In cases like this it's standard procedure, because they can do the testing so much faster than humans can. However, we took steps to ensure that no one could tamper with the evidence. It'll hold in a court of law, if it comes to that."

"It's the court of public opinion that matters right now," Morgan said.

"I think the people who saved everyone are going to come off as the good guys," Franklin replied. Hoped he was right.

"So why is everyone mad at me? We saved the day, go us."

"We're upset, not mad," Mom said. "And we're upset because none of us were prepared for your statement. Politically, you just hung us out to dry."

"Actually," Raj said, "I believe the Ambassador ensured that the U.S. government could choose to either support Centaurion Division's actions or condemn then. We're hung out to dry, not anyone else." Managed not to say that Raj was my favorite, but it took effort.

"Go us again. Look, Mom, berate me later. I'm worried about Jeff and Senator Armstrong and everyone else with them. They're going to be the recipients of any and all backlash and they're out in the open and . . . I think Jeff's the main target for all of the whatever that's going on."

Mom shook her head. "I'm not berating you. I'm concerned about the fact that you made this announcement in the White House and you didn't let the President know you were going to do it. Protocol exists for a reason." Her expression softened. "Sadly, you and Jeff are targets far too frequently."

"So you think he's the target, too?"

"I have no idea. I've just accepted that you're probably right when you're worried." She looked around. "Where the hell is Malcolm?"

"You know, I didn't see him, or Siler, this morning."

"Mister Buchanan requested that he and Mister Siler eat separately from everyone else," Raj said. "For security. He also said that there was enough security here that he didn't need to come along."

Meaning either Siler had somehow knocked Buchanan out and taken off or . . . Siler had convinced Buchanan that the best option was to join forces and fight each other later. Based on yesterday's events, bet on the latter.

That meant we had three teams out—Team Announcement, who were probably the sitting ducks, Team Oliver who were doing who knew what, but releasing investigative tips to the media and bringing Colonel Hamlin snacks and pigeons seemed likely, and Team Bitchin' who were likely quietly kicking butt and eliminating names. Oh, and Team Assassin, too, out there being good and bad at the same time. This wasn't giving me a confident feeling of a coordinated effort. Could kind of feel Mom's pain.

"Malcolm was right, I'm safe here. However, I don't feel so confident about Jeff's situation, so can we go protect him now?"

"Too late," Morgan said, looking at his phone. "It's started."

CHAPTER 60

"DO WE NEED to send the police or the National Guard or something? Field agents?"

Morgan shook his head. "Sorry, I didn't mean to frighten you. I meant that the announcement has started. It's on the news."

"Let's go," Mom said. "There's a TV near enough."

"I want to go to Jeff."

"No. Trust me, he's got protection, and there's no way you could get from here to there via any conventional means. The last thing you need right now is to show up and give your enemies even more to question."

Mom had a point. So I didn't argue as she led us out of the Blue Room. Vance saw us and followed along. Decided Mom could yell at him, but if he wanted to watch the show with us, fine by me. We went across the corridor, to the left, and into the President's private dining room. Where the President happened to be. Hoped he wasn't going to bawl me out, too.

The President had the television on, turned to the channel we wanted. He nodded to us, then turned his attention back to the events going on outside Capitol Hill. Mom noted Vance, rolled her eyes, but didn't say anything as she sat in the chair I figured she'd vacated just a little while earlier. Franklin and Morgan didn't sit, so Raj, Serene, Vance, and I didn't either. We clustered near Mom and watched the show.

Our politicians were on the steps as promised, with press

clustered around them. So far, pretty standard for these kinds of things.

However, there was what looked like a giant mob curved around the press corps, held back by the police. Half of those in the mob appeared to be holding signs showing Armstrong-Martini circled in red with a line through it. Nice. Of course, there were also those holding Armstrong for President signs and even a few Armstrong-Martini ones without the red circle and stuff on them. The pro-Armstrong-Martini signs were clearly handmade, but the anti ones looked like they'd been printed up. Figured Club 51 had been busy.

Despite the mob, everyone on the steps of the Capitol Building looked fine and unfazed. Senator McMillan was at a microphone, talking, introducing and endorsing both Senator Armstrong and Jeff.

Armstrong definitely had his Senior Senator and the Guy You Want to Lead Your Country look going strong. Jeff wasn't imitating this look so much as it was how he looked naturally—like the leader you wanted but so rarely got. He had my vote.

McMillan finished, then Armstrong took the mic, listed all the ways American Centaurion and Jeff in particular were awesome, and officially stated that Jeffrey Martini would be his running mate should they get the nomination next week.

Then it was Jeff's turn at the mic. Hoped he handled his moment in the sun better than I had. Also hoped no one was going to shoot him while he was speaking.

"Hi, thank you, Vince, Don," Jeff said. He wasn't using his Commander Voice, but the Cheerful Politician Voice he'd learned over the past year and a half. "I'm honored to be considered worthy to support a man I'm proud to call my friend in a bid to lead this great country. And, as I've done all my life, I promise I'll do the best I can to represent you with honesty and integrity. Thank you."

Jeff waved and stepped away from the microphone. The press pressed forward. As they did so, the camera feed swung around to give us a good shot of the crowd while McMillan tried to get the press into a semblance of control. Spotted Chuckie, Reader, Tim, the flyboys, the K-9 squad, and a variety of others there, doing crowd and press control and clearly ready to protect and defend.

As the camera swung back toward the politicians it caught an average-looking guy, dressed in an average suit, straight brown hair, probably in his late thirties or early forties. There wasn't anything remarkable about him, other than that he was press and he looked smug.

"That's Bruce Jenkins," Vance said urgently.

"What's he doing with a microphone?" Mom growled.

"What's he doing with Jeff? I thought he was after me."

Naturally for my luck, Jenkins managed to shove forward and get a question in.

"Representative Martini, Bruce Jenkins, Washington Post, here with CNN. Do you have any comment on the fact that your wife just admitted that Centaurion Division was responsible for all the bombings yesterday?"

"Crap." Remembered where we were and who we were with. "Sorry, Mister President."

"I've heard the word before, Ambassador. Let's see how you husband handles this."

Shockingly to me, Jeff didn't look shocked. He looked cool, calm, and totally in charge. "I believe, Mister Jenkins, that my wife *also* shared that the reason Centaurion Division detonated those self-contained bombs was to thwart a large-scale coordinated bioterrorism attack. I'm proud that Centaurion Division saved countless lives, Mister Jenkins, with minimum damage, no casualties, and literally no injuries. Isn't that what leaders are supposed to do—protect the country and its people?"

This clearly wasn't the answer Jenkins was expecting, because he came through for me and looked shocked in Jeff's place.

"My God, your husband really is like Superman, isn't he?" Vance murmured.

"Yes, but drool later."

More reporters were tossing questions at Jeff, Armstrong, and McMillan. Many of them were about the bombings, and all three men were able to give coherent, cohesive answers. Of course, many of the questions were about other things, like their stance on immigration, the economy, and so forth, but the bombings definitely had center stage. Jenkins got shoved aside by other reporters, so it didn't look like he was going to get another shot to ask anything else.

"Mom, do we know if any of the press corps have left?"

"No, they're all here. None were allowed to leave and they've all been kept in the East Room. We have an official statement being made on the President's behalf regarding your announcement."

So, Jenkins hadn't been here and just raced over to Capitol Hill, and that meant he hadn't heard my announcement firsthand. Sure it was probably all over social media by now, but if he was in place to go for Jeff, then he probably wasn't checking for too many updates. Which meant he had an associate at the White House who'd filled him in. "Not sure if we care, Mom, but Jenkins has an associate here who's feeding him information."

"Then he or she is in the room with the press secretary. The press are allowed to report, that's why we let them in."

Chose not to argue this, since it was true and, though I still distrusted Jenkins completely, really, the reporters weren't necessarily doing anything but their jobs. But the question was—how did Jeff know what I'd said and what was going on? Looked at Serene. "Did you give Jeff the heads-up?" She shook her head. Raj shook his as well.

Thought about it. Christopher had been unnaturally cheerful this morning. And not only was he the fastest man alive, A-Cs could talk and hear at hyperspeed. Dug my phone out and sent him a text. My phone rang and I stepped to the far side of the room. "Hi Flash. Enjoying your busy day?"

"You sound so bitter."

"I am. Seriously, you were over here spying on me?"

"No. I was over there to ensure that, when you went off-script, I'd be able to get the information to Jeff immediately, so he'd be prepared. Which I did. Nice bombshell, by the way. The expressions onstage were priceless."

"I, and probably the others here, hate you."

"You'll get over it. By the way, you avoided this for the moment, but I heard the press talking amongst themselves while waiting for you, and once Missus Maurer showed up on the dais they got really curious. Expect to get questions about her. What's your answer going to be, by the way, for why she's with us?"

"She'd learned of the ricin attack and came to us for help."

"Really? You'd better brief her on that before you use it. And everyone else over there, too. Your mom in particular."

"Already got bawled out. Somewhat. So, yes, I'll run that by Mom, and Nancy herself, before I use it. By the way, are you still here or are you there?"

"I'm here, which for you is there. You're distracting me from lurking in the shadows and watching for snipers, bomb throwers, or tanks, so that I can grab Jeff and the others and get them to safety, you know."

"Then I'll blame you if anything happens to any of them."

"You'd blame me anyway."

"Speaking of bitter. Hey, Christopher?"

"Yeah?"

"Thanks for covering us on this one. It mattered. A lot."

His voice softened. "You're welcome. Kitty, I realize everyone's going to jump on you for what you did and how you did it, but honestly, I thought it was great. I'm really proud of you, and Jeff, too, for how you're handling all of this."

"Thanks. And, careful or I'm going to get all mushy and emotional."

"Can't have that, that's James' territory with you."

"And Amy's territory with you."

"True enough. And before you ask, she's with Caroline, Doreen, and Abigail, inside the Capitol Building, just in case."

"Doesn't anyone stay home and watch these things on TV anymore?" Glanced at the TV. "Looks like things are breaking up."

"Yeah. Hang in there, Kitty. We're at the start of a really strange road."

"It'll be a bumpy ride, but I'm sure we'll get there."

"I think the question is—do we want to get there? Reynolds just gave me the signal to help with crowd control. I'll talk to you later."

"Be careful."

"You, too."

"Always."

"Never that any of us have ever seen."

"I know you are but what am I?"

Christopher laughed. "You're the wife of the likely vice presidential nominee."

"Oh good. Totally not routine."

CHAPTER 61

HUNG UP AND REJOINED the others by the TV. "That went remarkably well."

Mom nodded slowly. "I'm amazed, frankly. Maybe the obvious show of force helped. However, there will be ample opportunities for mayhem beyond this morning, and just because Bruce Jenkins was shut up once doesn't mean he won't ask a question you don't have a good answer for next time."

"Speaking of which, Christopher mentioned that we dodged the Nancy Maurer bullet this morning, but he doesn't expect that to last long."

"Do you want me to fetch her?" Raj asked politely.

The President nodded. "She's been through an ordeal, I'd like to see her."

"Yes, sir." Raj zipped off.

"I heard your plan for what to say," Mom said. "I'm not sure if it's a good idea, involving her in the bombing plot."

"Mom, she was attacked by thugs her own son sent to 'protect' her, but we didn't catch the guys so it's her and our word against theirs. She has to have a reason to be with us that doesn't cause even more suspicion. The ricin story is out, it seems the easiest answer to me."

"I agree," Mrs. Maurer said as Raj ushered her in. "So nice to see you, Mister President, albeit under unfortunate circumstances."

The President stood up, hugged Mrs. Maurer, and gave

her his seat. "Angela tells me you're breaking ties with your son. I'm sorry you've been put into a situation where you feel the need to do so to protect yourself."

Mrs. Maurer nodded. "As I've been saying, he's not my son anymore. I don't recognize the man he's become."

The President looked at me. I mouthed the word "android." Then I did a little of The Robot dance move to be sure he got it.

His lips quirked, but he just nodded and looked back to Mrs. Maurer. "I feel confident that our friends at American Centaurion will protect you. However, are you sure you're willing to become what will surely be a focal point of the presidential campaign? I feel confident Senator Armstrong and Representative Martini will get the party's nomination, and you switching sides to join them will make the media's day, even more than the Ambassador's announcement did."

"I'm sure. I worry about the safety of my grandchildren, but I can't protect them if I'm dead or a hostage."

A staffer came in. "I'm sorry, Mister President, but you're due for a meeting in the Oval Office."

"I'll be right there. Fair enough, Nancy. Angela, I'll leave this to you and the Ambassador and her team." He nodded to us. "Ladies, gentlemen, please continue the good work you do and let's hope that the good guys win." With that he strode off with the staffer chattering to him about his meeting.

"I like him."

"I do, too," Mom said. "I've enjoyed this job."

"He's not the only president you've supported."

"No, he's not. But he'll be the last if Vincent and Jeff don't win the election."

This hit me like a bolt out of the blue. Why I hadn't considered that my mother's job would be in jeopardy if an anti-alien team was in the White House was beyond me, but I hadn't. The ramifications of Cleary-Maurer were larger than I'd paid attention to. The likelihood that we'd lose every ranking individual who supported American Centaurion was high. Chuckie, Horn, and Cliff would likely be out of their jobs before they could blink. Same with Kevin, Buchanan, and the rest of the P.T.C.U. Len and Kyle would be out of the

C.I.A. along with Chuckie, and Colonel Franklin and Captain Morgan would probably be sent to an outpost in Alaska.

Maybe we'd still have people at NASA Base, but Alfred would undoubtedly be removed from his position, and that Base had been infiltrated easily before. That it would flip to completely anti-alien seemed possible.

There were more people who supported us, all of whom would be removed from their positions or marginalized. Our enemies would be moved up into positions of power. And control. Control over Centaurion Division. Which was, still and all, what everyone wanted—the War Division, wrapped up in a nice, tight bow.

The good of the country didn't figure into this, I knew that without asking. The Cleary-Maurer ticket was pretty much anti everything we stood for and I cared about. It was time to stop complaining about Jeff being on the ticket and start campaigning.

Looked at Raj. "What do we need to do to ensure the nomination and the win?"

He smiled at me. "Glad to have you fully in, Ambassador."

"Yeah, yeah, some of us catch on a little slower than others."

"I've given it some thought already," Raj said. "But I believe this isn't the best place to discuss our strategy."

Mom nodded. "We need to vacate so the room can be straightened. And around here, someone's always listening."

"Is the Embassy safe and cleaned up for us to return?"

Raj nodded. "I believe we'll need to be seen leaving. This will give the press more chances to talk to you and Missus Maurer. We'll need the team to provide coverage."

"Make it so, PR Attaché Number One."

Raj grinned. "I'm glad I spent so many years watching TV. It's really paid off for this job."

We left the dining room and stood in the vestibule while Raj gathered the rest of Team Press Conference. The press corps was still in the East Room, and White House security was blocking them from leaving, for which I was extremely grateful.

"There will be press outside, waiting for us," Raj said as he herded the last of our flock over. "I want the Ambassador and Missus Maurer next to each other. Ambassador, you'll be holding Missus Maurer's hand."

"It would look better if I had my arm through hers," Mrs. Maurer said. "That way, it's clear I'm holding onto her, not the other way around."

"Squeaky, you amaze and impress me."

"The rest of us need to flank them," Raj went on. "We don't have the usual bodyguards here, so we're going to have to make do with those we do have. Lillian and Guy, if you two wouldn't mind going before the Ambassador, I believe you'll both be the best at warding off the press."

Culver grinned the Joker's Passing Out Killer Candy to the Kiddies smile. "Oh, trust me, we're both pros at that."

Gadoire nodded. "I suggest Vance be on the Ambassador's side. He also has experience with this."

In my experience with Vance, he was most experienced at running away screaming, but Raj was right—the guys who'd normally handle this were all MIA, so we had to roll with the punches.

"Raj should take Nancy's free side," Vance said. "Same reasons and he's stronger than me, if shoving is necessary. And, trust me, it'll be necessary."

"Actually," White said, "I think it would be better if I was with Missus Maurer, Raj was with the Ambassador, and you were with our Head of Imageering, Vance. She'll be asked questions as well and will need the protection, so to speak."

Vance nodded eagerly. He and Gadoire were married but both bi, and Vance's fondest fantasies now involved adding an A-C woman, or man, into their mix. Couldn't blame him, really. "That makes sense."

"Mom, what about you?"

She shook her head. "I need to stay here. I'm due in that meeting the President's having in about ten minutes."

Mom took me aside and hugged me, the usual breath-stopping bear hug. "You'll do fine, kitten. Just remember, silence is your friend in these instances. If you look like the press is attacking you, that can, many times, sway popular opinion toward you."

Hugged her back. "Gotcha. Air . . . air . . ."

She let go and kissed my cheek. "Remember that you're doing this for more than just yourself and your immediate family. The course of our country is going to be determined by this election."

"But no pressure! I'll do my best, Mom."

She gave me a rather proud smile. "That's all anyone can ask of you, kitten. And your best has been proven to be what we need. So, go get 'em, my little tiger."

CHAPTER 62

WE WERE IN OUR FORMATION, three lines of four people, the extra troubadours with Culver and Gadoire in front and Vance and Serene in the rear.

The troubadours weren't going to be doing a lot of talking. Raj felt that they didn't want to try to influence this particular crowd for a variety of reasons, most of them having to do with our wanting to look as beleaguered by the press as possible. Wasn't sure this was our wisest strategy, but since my idea would be to take a gate and avoid all of this, I kept my thoughts to myself.

We were about to go out the door when a thought occurred that I felt obligated to share. "Um, guys? Where, exactly, are we going? We didn't drive here."

"You wound me," Raj said. "And Pierre . . . when I tell him about your lack of faith . . ." he shook his head. "You'll probably have to console him for hours."

"Wow, your sarcasm knob goes from zero to eleven really fast."

"It does. Let's move, everybody. Stay with your line, and be sure it's one line to each car."

The East Room wasn't in the East Wing. Shockingly for D.C., it wasn't in the West Wing, either. No, we were in the official White House Residence section. This meant that we just needed to go out the North doors, down a few steps, and get into the gray limos that, now that I looked, were idling outside.

In theory, anyway.

In reality, there were a ton of reporters with microphones and cameras camped on the steps. Wanted to ask why they were allowed to be right at the President's front door, but figured it was standard procedure. Or else they'd been snuck in by people who didn't like us. Possibly both. Had no time to question or argue, so just rolled with it.

Pulled my phone out of my purse, which I had over my neck now, because this was just like going into battle. In case Jeff or someone tried to reach me, I'd never have a chance of hearing the ring, but I could feel the vibration.

"Just a moment," a man's voice called. Turned to see a variety of big, serious-looking men in suits descending upon us.

"Yes?" Raj asked.

"Secret Service, sir. The President's asked us to escort the Ambassador and her retinue out. Looks like there may be some trouble getting you folks safely into your cars."

"Thank you, we totally appreciate the help." Ensured I sounded droolingly grateful because I was.

"Even with us helping you, it's going to be a mob scene, folks," the Secret Service man in charge said. "So be prepared."

Everyone shared their preparedness and two Secret Service agents opened the doors.

We were out the doors and instantly it was like every movie or TV show where the attorneys are escorting the star witness or the famous mobster who's on trial—total bedlam. Crowds at a One Direction concert were probably better behaved than the press corps that was out here.

Having A-Cs on the perimeters along with the Secret Service was nice because, regardless of their body types, they could block like the biggest linebackers out there, due to their being naturally stronger than humans. The Secret Service guys were all, to a man, big. However, unless we were willing to toss the press aside en masse—which I was, but knew without asking no one else would go for it—we had to shove through semi-politely.

Our names were being screamed, mine and Mrs. Maurer's

the most, along with questions I couldn't even hear. "Hang on, dear," she said to me as we all got jostled, Secret Service assistance or no Secret Service assistance.

"Thought I was supposed to be guarding you."

"It's a mutual thing."

Most of the questions were being handled by Culver and Gadoire, who were in the lead, along with their A-C protectors, following behind three Secret Service men who were carefully shoving the crowd back. Couldn't hear a word either one of them were saying, nor make out the questions being shouted at them. For all I knew they were saying we were from Pluto and bent on world domination or the greatest hope for mankind. The smart money, however, was on a lot of "no comments."

"Are you sleeping with the man who has his arm around you?" This was shrieked by a woman nearish to me and Raj, who indeed had his arm around my waist so that I wouldn't fall and end up trampled.

I was able to identify the shrieker because she was close to us. Of course, a woman had yelled comments intended to incite a riot right after Jeff was sworn in and Cliff's car had exploded, thankfully without him, us, and Chuckie inside it. That woman had been Annette Dier.

Might be coincidence, she might just be a reporter. Or she might be something else.

Stopped walking and turned on the camera function on my phone. Got a good snap of the reporter accusing me of adultery.

"What the hell are you doing?" she yelled at me.

Took another couple of shots. "I like to remember all the rude people I've met."

Raj moved me on as a Secret Service man near us shoved her and those around her back. We'd made it down all of three steps so far. Fantastic. At this rate, we might get home by dinnertime. Then again, it was around noon, so maybe we'd be later.

Another woman's voice reached me. "You're all murderers!" Sounded vaguely foreign. Wasn't sure if this indicated foreign press or not.

Looked around and managed to snap a couple of shots of the woman I was fairly sure was accusing us of murder. She named no names, so there was that.

"Why are you taking tourist snaps?" Mrs. Maurer asked.

"For later." Took more random shots of the crowd, as many as I could get, while we were tossed around like rag dolls.

Seemed like forever, but the Secret Service in the lead managed to get to a limo and get the door open. They helped Culver, Gadoire, and their two A-Cs in, protecting their heads just like cops do when someone's being arrested or "helped" into a squad car. Four of us already in relative safety was good. Eight of us still out wasn't.

The press surged and got between my line and the next limo. "Missus Maurer, are you changing political parties?" a female reporter asked. Sounded legit. Took her picture anyway.

"I can't hear you, dear," Mrs. Maurer lied. "I'm sorry."

The Secret Service in the back chose to go sideways and take our last line with them, so they actually reached the third limo before we could get to the second. I could tell because we were still up on the steps, so could see Vance, Serene, and their two troubadours being helped in.

A microphone got shoved into my face. "Ambassador, why were you trying to kill innocent people yesterday?" a male reporter asked.

"We weren't." Snapped his picture. "We were focused on saving innocent people from a bioterrorism attack. As the F.B.I. will confirm or already has confirmed." I sincerely hoped.

Raj shoved the man away without seeming to, and now that all the Secret Service men only had the last four of us to deal with, they were able to form a human chain and move everyone back.

We were at the limo, and the door was open. "Get Nancy in first," I shouted to White. "And you, too." He nodded and the Secret Service got them in, doing the head protection move again.

I was almost there, just a step away from getting into the

car, when a woman shoved through a little gap between Secret Service men. "How does it feel to get away with murder?" she asked, as she shoved a mic in my face.

"I haven't murdered anyone."

"Yes you have." Her eyes flashed. "You killed Ronald Yates, Leventhal Reid, and Herbert Gaultier."

Once again, my recurring nightmare of standing before a congressional hearing paid off. Ensured I looked amused and affronted and did the only thing I could think of. Put my phone up and took her picture. With the flash on.

"She's trying to kill me!" she shouted as she staggered back. But I grabbed the mic.

"You're high, and highly misinformed," I said clearly into the microphone. "I have absolutely not killed the people you named, and I think you need to consider your career choice if this is what you think passes for journalism."

With that, I tossed the microphone back to her. It hit her in the face. Which might possibly have been an accident. But I sincerely hoped no one would ask me that question in a court of law.

Then the Secret Service helped me and Raj into the car, the door slammed, and we headed for the relative safety of the streets of D.C.

CHAPTER 63

AFTER THE SECRET SERVICE ran off the mob so that we could drive away, slowly, things were relatively calm. At least inside the limo. Outside it was still bedlam. Hoped we hadn't started some kind of riot on the White House lawn.

"Why were you taking pictures like a tourist?" Mrs. Maurer asked. For the second time, really. Chose not to point this out. There I went, flexing my diplomatic muscles. They needed the workout.

"Good question," White said. "I was wondering the same thing."

Was about to answer when my phone rang. "Hi Vance, you guys okay?"

"Yeah. Wanted to let you know that Serene and I figured out what you were doing. We both took video of the crowd."

"You amaze me. Good job."

"I'll try not to be insulted by that."

"Good. Wasn't an insult."

"Says you."

We hung up and I took the time to look at our driver. "Hey, I know you. Burton Falk, right?" He one of the human agents Buchanan used whenever he needed someone to handle driving and other sundry tasks. As far as I knew, Falk was part of Centaurion Division, but I figured it was better not to ask.

"Right you are, Ambassador."

"Who's driving the other limos, the rest of your team?"

"Yes. Everyone's in good hands."

"Good to know. Where's Malcolm?"

"He's busy, but asked me to make sure that you were taken care of. But I'm as curious as everyone else about your photo-taking obsession."

"Geez, everyone's a critic. Vance and Serene figured it out, but maybe that's because he's more paparazzi conscious than the rest of you and she's an imageer. I took pictures so that we could see if anyone in that mob was actually one of the Yates progeny we're trying to find."

"Oh!" Chorused by everyone else in the limo in unison.

"Makes sense," Raj said. "Sorry for not catching on right away."

"It's okay, you were busy being mauled. And I suggest the rest of you use that excuse, too."

Once off the White House grounds we made it back to the Embassy in short order. Our extra troubadours went to the basement to gate back over to the Science Center. Falk and the other drivers didn't stick around, either. They took one of the limos and drove off. Clearly they took their cues from Buchanan and were learning his Dr. Strange ways.

I had my own ways, however, and they said it was time to go to the kitchen.

Hugs all around from Pierre, along with the news that Team Announcement weren't back yet. However, Pierre confirmed that they'd checked in and everyone was accounted for and unharmed.

Grabbed a quick snack—Lucinda was in the Embassy and a gigantic plate of her brownies were sitting out on the counter, begging to be eaten. The others followed my lead, even Culver. Glasses of milk were also made available, which meant we could all have a couple more brownies without issue. Thusly fortified, I considered our options.

"I think we need to see what Serene, along with Stryker and his team, can get from the pictures."

"Let's go to them," Serene said. "They should be back in the computer lab by now, wouldn't you think?"

"Oh, they are, darling," Pierre said. "Believe me, they are."

"Lillian, Guy, do you want to go to the Zoo with us?" I wasn't suggesting we take a breather. We'd bought the building "next door" and had remodeled it to give us more space. We showed off the Poofs and Peregrines to the public at random times on the first floor, but the rest of the building was used for personnel, including Hacker International.

Culver shook her head. "I really do need to go to my office, and I should also check on Abner."

Realized I hadn't seen her husband, Abner Schnekedy, at any time over the past day. Culver had wisely kept her maiden name for business. "He wasn't brought to the Science Center?"

"No. He went to his mother's. He's fine, but I should be a good wife and check in."

Far be it for me to question anyone else's marriage parameters. "Okay. Before you go, what were the questions you and Guy got from the mob?"

"The usual. Were you mad bombers, why was Nancy Maurer with us, why were we with you, things along those lines."

"We replied with no comment, my dove," Gadoire said. "But cheerfully."

"Oh good."

"However, like Lillian, I feel I must not assist with your next tasks. Just as dear Lillian does, I expect calls to my office, and I'll need to handle them."

Culver nodded. "What's the party line? 'Ask the F.B.I.'? Or do you want us saying something more? Or less?"

I'd gotten so used to the fact that they were working with us on this one that the question only registered at about a three on my Shock-O-Meter. "Raj, I think that's your area more than mine. You, Pierre and Vance all came up with something, right?"

"Right. Before you leave, why don't the five of us have a short meeting to get our stories straight?"

Nods all around. "I'd like to join you," Mrs. Maurer said. "I think it's going to be important that I'm able to say the same things as the rest of you with confidence."

"Kitty, I'm going to stay at the Embassy when the meeting's done, to help out however you guys need," Vance said, as he held out his phone. "Just have the computer guys get this back to me as soon as they can."

"We will," Serene said, as she took the phone from him. Decided not to ask why she'd taken his phone instead of letting me do it. Right now.

"I'll leave you here in good care," White said to Mrs. Maurer, "while I accompany our young ladies."

Pierre ushered those staying in the kitchen to the larger table and Serene, White, and I headed up to the second floor and the raised, enclosed walkway that connected the Embassy to the Zoo.

The walkway was made of steel, concrete, and bulletproof glass, for which I'd been grateful more than once. Looked down at our street as we walked across. "No protesters are out."

"Give them time," White said. "They're probably regrouping just as we are."

"Speaking of which, I'm glad it's just the three of us going up to see the guys, Kitty," Serene said.

"Why? You don't want the others looking at the pictures and video we took? They all know you're an imageer."

"Yes, I know, and I'd be fine with them helping on the pictures. Besides, I'm sure we'll all end up looking at the pictures and video more than we want to."

"Speaking of which, did you take Vance's phone to try to get an early read?"

"Yes. I'm testing a theory."

"Which is?"

She sighed. "I'll tell you about it shortly, because it relates to what I was saying just now. I'm glad it's just us because I think you've forgotten something important that Benjamin wanted you to do. But I haven't."

"Probably. What?"

"It's time for you to make contact with Chernobog."

"That's great, but I have no idea how, and unless Hacker International, you, and Olga have figured that out, I might as well just click my heels together and make a wish."

"Well, we'll find out what progress has been made when we get upstairs," White said.

"What if said progress is none?"

"Then we figure out another way," Serene said.

"Open to suggestions here."

Right on cue, a phone rang. Only it wasn't my phone, Serene's phone, White's phone, or Vance's phone that was doing the ringing.

CHAPTER 64

DUG THE BURNER PHONE out of my purse as the three of us stopped in front of the elevators on the Zoo's second floor. "Uncle Peter?"

"Miss Katt, you did a lovely job today."

"Thank you. Thanks for not letting anyone shoot or blow up my husband."

"You're welcome. There was limited activity of our kind related to his excursion today."

"Nice to know. They saving it up for something better?"

"Indeed they are. I'm glad you've realized."

I actually hadn't, but decided now was the time to give it a shot. "They're going to hit us at the National Convention?"

"That seems to be the case, yes."

"Oh goody. Something to look forward to. Um, did you or Uncle Victor accept a contract on anyone there?"

"No."

"Did Siler?"

"You would have to ask him."

"Fantastic. Thanks for the heads up. So, anything else I should know about?"

"Only that we are leaving tonight."

"You are?" This wasn't good news. Of course, my feeling upset that the top assassins in the world were leaving town was indicative of just how bad things were and how far out of my depth I felt.

"We will be back next week. However, we have business elsewhere."

"I'm so glad you'll be back, I hope. And I don't want to know about your other business. Do I?"

"No, you do not. Keep your head down while we are gone. I fear our business might have been ordered to remove us from your proximity."

"Or it could be legit and that means you need to take the job." I was counseling an assassin about killing someone. Go me. Would have asked how my life got this complicated but I already knew. Just hoped they were going to kill someone evil versus someone good. Decided not to guess the odds on that being the outcome.

"Correct."

"Can I ask you an out of the blue question before you go?"

"Certainly. I do not guarantee an answer, of course."

"Of course not, but you're still more forthcoming than anyone else I work with."

He chuckled. "Perhaps because I see you differently than most."

"Probably so. Is there any way you can get me in touch with Chernobog the Ultimate?"

He was quiet for a few seconds. "Why?" Was glad he hadn't asked "who" because I was both sure that he knew who Chernobog was, and was also just not up to playing verbal and mental mind games at the moment.

"We have her son in severe custody, just like we have Annette Dier. But we need answers, and probably assistance, from her, and she's hella hard to find. She was in Cuba, but either she's gone underground or moved, because we've had teams searching there for a year and they've only found traces."

More quiet. "We need to meet with you before we leave."

"Not that I mind, because it would be nice to see you two, but why?" Chose not to ask why I'd said that, nor worry about the fact that it was sincere—I'd gotten as attached to them as they had to me, apparently.

"Because of who our next target is."

"Do I have to go to the cemetery?" I sincerely hoped not.

Any lie I could come up with for why I wanted to go there wasn't going to fool anyone.

"No. We will come to you."

"To our Embassy complex?"

"Somewhere nearby, yes. I'll contact you shortly. Hold onto the phone." With that he hung up.

Dropped my Special Burner Phone back into my purse and looked at Serene and White. "Well, that was weird. And yeah, I'll tell you about it later. But first, what's the plan on Chernobog?"

"You mean aside from asking your uncles to set up a meeting? I don't know, I've been with you." Serene hit the elevator call button. "Your uncles want to meet with you face-to-face?"

"Yeah. I've done it before. Usually means I'm the safest girl in the world."

"Jeff, Chuck, Malcolm, your mother, and pretty much everyone else wouldn't agree."

"Oh, I would support Missus Martini on this one," White said as the elevator arrived. He held it open, but didn't go into the car. "I'd like to ask if you've considered why, once you asked the Dingo to set up a meeting with Chernobog, he instantly wanted to meet with you."

"In the ten seconds since the call? Not really. If we'd like to ponder that right now, though, and I can see by your expression that you would, then my guess is that their current contract relates to Chernobog in some way."

White nodded. "That's my guess as well. Serene?"

"It makes sense to me, Richard. But what does that mean we do from here?"

He shrugged. "It means that, for right now, we need to keep this between the three of us, and we also need to hope that our computer experts and Madame Olga have come up with something."

"No argument, but why?"

"Am I right in thinking that the Dingo is going away?" Apparently White had learned my Dad's trick of answering a question with another question. Decided to support someone else using one of my favorite go-to moves.

"Yeah, he said he was leaving the area, and he didn't give any hint as to how far away he was going or where, but did say that he would be back in time for the National Convention. Where, by the way, he expects Jeff to be the target of murderous attacks. And Siler probably has contracted hits he hasn't told us about. So, you're both now all caught up on my call."

White looked worried. "All of that is troubling. But I can think of only two contracts that would affect Chernobog, and if the Dingo is leaving this area to complete his assignment, that removes one of them—Russell Koslov—as the likely target."

The reason White looked worried dawned on me. "Oh. Wow. You think the Dingo and Surly Vic have been contracted to kill Chernobog."

"I do."

"Wouldn't that ultimately be good for us?" Serene asked.

"Maybe," White replied. "However, the death of the person who hacked us means we will never have any hope of retrieving what she stole. I guarantee that while our data was erased on our systems, it still exists somewhere."

"And if I were Chernobog, I'd be holding onto that as leverage. Yeah. You know, I think the Mastermind is running this action personally." Explained my theory relating to the attack on Serene and Horn.

"Let's table the rest of this for later." White entered the car, still holding the door for us. "And hope that our team here has solved what's sure to be a thorny dilemma for us already."

"I love your optimism, Mister White, but I know how our luck runs," I said as the elevator doors closed.

"Well, perhaps the young men will surprise us with good news."

We rode the rest of the way in worried silence. In short order the doors opened on the fifth floor, where Hacker International ruled supreme.

Hacker International had moved into the Embassy during Operation Destruction and pretty much somehow never moved out. Buying The Zoo had made things a lot easier for all of us, since it meant they got their own space, blessedly far away from Jeff, who only rarely found them just this side of tolerable. And what a space it was.

As with all of our buildings, the Zoo was large, and the computer lab, which was state of the art, took up about half of the floor. Hacker International used the remaining space for their personal accommodations. It was nice work if you could get it, and, despite Jeff's protests and attempts to remove them, they had.

However, they'd felt the hit quite personally when Chernobog had hacked us, and hacked us easily, last year. This meant that after a short period of major sulking, they'd thrown themselves into the work of finding out what the hell had happened and ensuring it never happened again.

We entered the computer lab to see all five hackers there, along with Olga. It was kind of weird to see her without Adriana, and I had a moment of worry for Team Oliver. However, they were all more than competent and if something was going wrong, we'd probably find out soon enough.

I'd known Stryker Dane since Chuckie had found him while the two of us were in high school, meaning a long time now. It was why I knew his real name—Edward Simms—as well as other, less positive things about him. Stryker, like us, was from Pueblo Caliente, Arizona. Unlike us, Stryker's dedication to personal hygiene was limited.

He was an average-sized guy, with a reasonably impressive set of man boobs and a gut to match, topped off by a full, unkempt beard and long, curly, unkempt hair that, if he actually took care of it, would be quite lovely.

He was also a published author of the *Taken Away* series, wherein he made up alien encounters he claimed as being totally true that were nothing like the real alien encounters I had every day. Needless to say, Stryker's books did well, even after real aliens were shown to be living on the planet.

Big George Lecroix was tall, black, and skinny. He was to Europe what Dr. Henry Wu, who was small, scrawny, bald, and always just a little more nervous than anyone else, was to China—their best hackers.

Ravi Gaekwad and Yuri Stanislav were, particularly by

comparison to the other three, very normal looking. Ravi was India's best hacker, possessed a normal body build, and also was the leading ladies' man of Hacker International, having landed Jennifer Barone as his fiancée. They were still only engaged, even though both of them would have been happy to tie the knot by now, because his family was quite traditional and they hadn't finished whatever waiting period was required prior to marriage.

Yuri was from Russia, meaning he could now only claim to be Russia's second best hacker. But he was the only one you could find easily, so that counted for a lot in my book. Yuri was also blind, not that this stopped him from doing anything, and the only one who clearly worked out. Yuri was, all things considered, kind of hunky, especially compared to his hacker compatriots.

He was also cursing in Russian as we walked into the computer lab. At someone, if the headset he was wearing meant he was on a call of some kind.

"What's wrong with Yuri?" I asked Stryker by way of hello. Now wasn't the time to stand on formality. Or mention that I liked their array of *Firefly* T-shirts that were today's uniform of choice. They really had created a science fiction and fantasy T-shirt rotation with pride, after I made a joke about how they always wore certain shirts on certain days. Why encourage their special obsessive madness?

Yuri ripped the headset off, tossed it across the room, narrowly missing hitting Big George in the head, and answered for himself. "How many more dead ends can we hit before we admit the truth—we can't fight or find Chernobog?"

CHAPTER 65

"WELL, I guess that answers one of the questions we were here to ask."

"Sorry, Kitty," Stryker said. "But we're getting nothing. Less than nothing. Time-wasting, frustrating nothing."

"It's clear Chernobog has covered her tracks, and that anyone who knows something about her is afraid," Henry added nervously.

"We had a lead that she was in France," Big George added. "But it petered out."

"France is always suspect."

"There was a lead for Paraguay, too," Ravi said. "I think they were fakes, honestly."

"Why so?" White asked quickly, to forestall the arguments or offers of support clearly about to come out of the other hackers' open mouths.

Ravi shrugged. "Like Kitty said, we always suspect activity in those countries because of our past history. So, toss us some bad intel that sounds real, it sends us racing off to research a lot of nothing. Wastes our time and keeps us from finding the truth."

"The truth is out there."

"It is," Stryker snapped. "But unless we can call it a day and do an *X-Files* marathon, we're still not anywhere close to finding it."

Yuri finished cursing. "First, no one believes Chernobog

is real. Then she *is* real and everyone's terrified of her. Make up your minds!"

"Deep breaths, Yuri, think calming thoughts. You guys have only been at this for a few hours."

"No, we've been at it for a year," Stryker said, patience clearly forced. "You don't think we've spent time on this? Sure, we've been working to recreate the lost data and shore up our security, but the fastest way to do that is find Chernobog and figure out how she hacked us and where she hid her copies."

"We've done the other work you guys wanted," Big George said quickly. "But that's slow going, as you know. Plus, after what happened yesterday, we were hoping to get a solid lead that could help the team."

"Wow, Jennifer's been working with you guys on the right way to talk to people who control your paychecks and living situation, hasn't she?"

"Speaking of whom, have you seen her?" Ravi sounded worried.

"Not since yesterday. She's on a mission."

"She hasn't checked in with me. At all. We always check in."

"Maybe she can't. Not that she's hurt or something," I said hurriedly. "But I think they're doing something very covert. She just might not be able to check in without blowing cover or something." From his expression, this didn't comfort Ravi all that much.

"I'm sure she and the others are fine," Olga said reassuringly, as she rolled her wheelchair over to Yuri's station. She shot me a look that said she was lying, however. Great.

"What I don't understand," Serene said, in her Innocent Voice, "is how anyone, even Chernobog, could hide her tracks so well. Our enemies found her before. And Kitty figured out where she was a year ago."

"She's got access to the highest-grade stuff," Stryker said. "We've got the best, but she's got better."

"We have the best money can buy, at least per my husband. So who could have better?"

"Major world powers," Henry replied.

"Jennifer should have been home by now," Ravi fretted under his breath.

My brain nudged. "Home. Wait a second . . . no one say anything for a moment." I could tell Reader, Tim, and the flyboys weren't here—the room went dutifully still.

There was information Serene and I had that White and the others in this room didn't. Information sent to Colonel Franklin via Colonel Hamlin, who I was now sure was being assisted in some way by Mr. Joel Oliver. I'd focused on the part about the ricin bombs. But Hamlin had said more.

"He said, point blank, that Home Base was infiltrated. But Franklin got the note after Oliver's team had gone out, meaning they probably confirmed this for him. And he told Franklin to watch his back, and to watch everyone's backs. Now, why would he say that?"

"Who is this he?" White asked politely.

"Colonel Hamlin," Serene replied for me. "I saw the note, too. Kitty, you think Mister Joel Oliver went to investigate Home Base?"

"Yeah, I do. I also think something else. You've met Colonel John Butler over at Home Base, right, Serene?"

"Yes. He's a nice enough man. Pro-alien as far as we've seen. I'm not used to the resistance his office gave us yesterday."

"His office? Wait, was the colonel at Home Base yesterday?"

"No, per his secretary, he was overseeing something at Luke."

"Have you met his secretary?"

She nodded. "A couple of times. She's an older woman, seems pleasant enough."

Looked at Olga, who looked surprised, but in a really pissed off way. Started to laugh.

"Kitty, what is it?" Stryker asked. "You okay?"

"I am. I'm all kinds of thrilled because I just figured out something before Olga did. Mark this as a total red-letter day. Also, Siler's right—I'm going to get along really well with Chernobog. I like the way that sneaky Russian beeyotch thinks."

CHAPTER 66

"YOU CAN'T GO TO HER ALONE," Olga said. "And all who I would suggest go with you are elsewhere."

"I know. But I have Mister White here. And I think I'm going to have some serious support, too."

"Want to catch the rest of us up?" Stryker asked, sounding more than annoyed.

"Sure, because someone should know where we're going, just in case. Chernobog was hiding in Cuba these past years, right?" Heads nodded. "But she was hiding *on* the Naval base and its surrounding areas, on the American side. I'm sure she went over to the Cuban side a lot, especially since we couldn't find her, but she was spending most of her time on that tiny patch of American soil around Guantanamo."

"You think she's still in Cuba somewhere?" Ravi asked.

"No. I flat out know she's not there anymore. Frankly, I know exactly where she is. She's somewhere the only person who could pick her out of a lineup never goes, but where she still has access to the best damn equipment in the world."

White jerked. "Oh. Oh dear."

"Put so much more diplomatically than I would say it. Yeah, Chernobog is at Home Base. In fact, she's got a great job there—she's Colonel Butler's secretary. Bet he thinks she's the greatest and trusts her completely, too, doesn't he?" I asked Serene.

"Yes, he does. She came over after his former secretary

took ill." Serene looked a little ill herself. "She made that poor woman sick, didn't she?"

"At least she didn't kill her. I hope. But yeah."

"But how?" Serene asked. "There are security checks, a large number of them."

"If Madeleine Cartwright could infiltrate the freaking Pentagon, why would we think that the best hacker *in the world* couldn't make herself a shiny, perfect persona that would pass muster anywhere and everywhere?"

"She always had a plethora of identities when we worked together," Olga said. "What trouble would creating one more be? I'm sorry, this should have occurred to me, and it did not."

"Well, it only occurred to me because of what all's gone on and Hamlin's note. Telling Franklin to watch his own back makes sense. But telling him to watch everyone's backs? Really? That seems like overkill, and I've met Hammy, and he's not an overkill kind of guy. But what he *is* is former military intelligence. He knows how to leave a coded message without writing in actual code."

"When are you going there?" Big George asked. "I mean, we all know you're going."

"As soon as possible." But not before I talked to the Dingo and Surly Vic. However, I had no way of knowing when they were going to call. On the other hand, I should be ready when they did call, because I was sure we were heading to Home Base again the moment I told them what I knew was going on.

"Before you run off, why does Serene have two phones?" Henry asked.

"Oh! Right. Let's get the pictures downloaded. We can start facial recognition or whatever and see what we come up with. Do mine first. I need to go change but I'm expecting a call."

Stryker snatched my phone from me, plugged it into a computer, tapped some keys, and pulled up my photo file. "Just take the ones from today."

"We don't want to see your naked pictures of Jeff, don't worry," Stryker muttered.

"Careful, Eddy. I'm not against hurting you."

The pictures were downloaded quickly and my phone was back in my hand. "Mister White, I need to change clothes. You coming or staying?"

This caused Yuri and Big George to almost choke to death on their respective Big Gulps. White chuckled. "If you promise to call me when you're ready to go, I'll stay here and peruse the pictures of the crowd for a bit."

"Works for me. Serene, you coming along or staying here to run point?"

"It'll depend on what we get before you're ready to leave. Check with me, because I can get us into Colonel Butler's office without an issue."

"Sounds good." Gave Olga a hug, and took off. I was revved, so I took the stairs at hyperspeed, and did so well I kept it up across the walkway and up to our apartment.

My father and Lucinda were there along with Jamie. And our dogs. Had to greet the canines first. Then gave Lucinda and Dad big hugs. Then I finally got to actually hold my daughter for the first time in a day, which was nice.

Cuddled her and took her with me while I changed out of the Armani Fatigues and into jeans, my Converse, a short-sleeved Iron Maiden T-shirt, in order to look intimidating, and a light Aerosmith hoodie, because I was going into action and that required my boys to be on my person.

Made sure I had plenty of clips for my Glock in my purse, verified that anything and everything else I could need was in there, gave my hair a fast brush and pulled it into a ponytail, and I was ready.

Through all this, Jamie had been happily cuddling her Poof and prattling about her day and all the fun things she'd done with her grandparents. "We watched you and Daddy on TV!" she said in summation, as I slung my purse back on and checked—Harlie and Poofikins were in it, snoozing. Poofs on board was never an issue. "You looked really pretty, Mommy."

"Thanks, Jamie-Kat." Kissed her head.

"You look pretty now, too," she said judiciously.

"I appreciate that. Daddy looked handsome as always, didn't he?"

"Yes! Gran'ma Luci said Daddy looked proud and happy."

"I hope so. I'm very proud of Daddy."

"Me, too. Papa Sol said that Daddy is going to be a heart-beat away from the presidency. What does that mean?"

"It means that, if Daddy and Senator Armstrong win the jobs they're trying out for, that Senator Armstrong will become the President and Daddy will have a very important job, helping him."

"Oh." She was quiet as I picked her up. "Mommy?"

"Yes, sweetie?"

"You need to take Mous-Mous with you."

"But Mous-Mous is your Poof. Harlie and Poofikins are in Mommy's purse."

Jamie shook her head. "You need to take Mous-Mous with you." She kissed the Poof, which purred and rubbed against her. Then Mous-Mous purred at me and jumped into my purse.

"Are you sure, Jamie-Kat?"

She nodded. "Lola will cuddle with me." As she said the Peregrine's name, Lola dechameleoned. She was right next to me and looked up as I looked down. Lola winked.

"Lola, where's Bruno?"

Lola cooed, flapped her wings, bobbed her head, and cooed again. Bruno was on the job with Jeff and the rest of Team Announcement, along with half of the other Embassy Peregrines. Lola recommended extra Poofs if I was going into danger, since the remaining Peregrines were on guard in the Embassy.

"Gotcha. Okay, I'll take good care of Mous-Mous, Jamie, I promise."

"I know you will, Mommy. And Mous-Mous will take care of you, too."

"Good to know. Any Poofies who want an adventure get into Kitty's purse. Any Poofies who want snuggle time with Jamie stay here." Several Poofs joined the ones already in my purse.

The rest of the unattached Poofs, all of whom lived with us because I was the Ambassador and I could make that rule stick, stayed on their luxury Poof Condos, snuggled around our cats. All but two. Those two jumped down and into Jamie's arms, purring like mad. Had a feeling they'd have names by the time I got back. Oh well, Poofs for everyone and more Poofs for me and my little girl was my motto.

Left the bedroom, gave Jamie back to Dad, gave everyone more hugs, with extra hugs and kisses for Jamie, then got out of the apartment before I didn't want to do anything but stay and be a mom doing mom things with my little girl.

My timing was good. The burner phone rang as I reached the elevators.

"Uncle Peter?"

"Yes, Miss Katt. We are nearby."

"Where?"

"Conveniently close."

Thought about it. "You're on the Embassy's roof, aren't you?"

"Yes, we are." And they could be up there because Walter was off with the rest of Team Oliver. Had no idea if we even had someone running Security now, but based on the fact that Lola had told me to take Poofs with me because the Peregrines were staying put, my bet was that we didn't. William was probably monitoring from Dulce, but that wasn't the same thing as having someone here. "Are you able to join us?"

"Yes, but I'm bringing two people with me. Both unarmed and friendly to the cause."

"As you wish."

We hung up and I sent a text to White and Serene, then headed for the stairs to wait for them to join me. They were both A-Cs so they showed up within a couple of seconds. "What's the word on the pictures?"

"Olga spotted some similarities throughout the crowd, so we're running full facial recognition on everyone the three of us captured," Serene replied. "And I gave Vance his phone back, so we should be good. The meeting's still going on in the kitchen."

"Great, then let's head upstairs."

We trotted up and onto the roof. Sure enough, as we stepped through the roof access door, no one was there. "Why would they be hiding?" I asked White.

"To ensure you did not bring people we wouldn't want to see," the Dingo said, as he closed the door behind us and Surly Vic stepped out from behind the roof entrance room. They were both dressed in black T-shirts, black painter's pants, lightweight boots, black baseball caps, and leather gloves, and were carrying backpacks, also black. They were also carrying guns. Not pointed at any of us, however, so we had that going for us.

Managed not to scream and only jumped a little, go me. "You know Richard White from the last time you visited, and this is Serene Dwyer. Serene, these are my uncles Peter and Victor Kasperoff."

The Dingo nodded to White and Serene, but Surly Vic gave her a wide smile. "Pleased to meet you." He rarely smiled, so, clearly, Serene was his type.

"She's married," I pointed out.

He laughed. "All the beautiful women are, aren't they?"

Serene blushed and I didn't think it was faked. "Pleased to meet you both."

"Your embassy is safe again, I see," the Dingo said.

"Yes, thanks to you. Oh, you know, I have a question about all that's gone on, unrelated to what we're here to talk about. What was the bio-weapon you destroyed for me when it was delivered to our embassy a year and a half ago?"

He gave me a small smile. "Exactly what you think it was."

"It was a ricin bomb, wasn't it?"

CHAPTER 67

THE DINGO NODDED. "A particularly nasty one, yes."

"That's why you knew what to look for this time, it's a signature poison for our enemies."

"Yes," Surly Vic said. "Ricin is easy to make but hard to survive."

"Fabulous. Thank you again, even more, for all you've done for us."

"We are happy to help you," the Dingo said. "You help us as well."

"Yes, speaking of that . . . I'm sure it's against protocol, but can you tell me who hired you to kill Chernobog?"

They both looked pleased. "You figured it out?" the Dingo asked.

"Yeah. I know where she is, too. But, I need to talk to her, and get things back from her that she took. And, if possible . . . get her to help me. And she can't do that if she's dead."

"We cannot disclose our client, in part because we don't know who it is, specifically, ordering the job. However I can tell you that the contract came to us through the U.S. government. Your government is one of our best clients these days, since Raul was eliminated."

"Aha, well, that confirms our expectations—that the Mastermind is up there politically in some way. Was the hiring organization the C.I.A.?"

"No. And that's all I can tell you." The Dingo looked at me seriously. "We do have to complete the assignment."

"Yeah, I know. But does it have to be this week?"

"Yes, it was requested to happen before the National Convention next week."

"That's a big coinkydink and I've been trained not to believe in them. Therefore, logic says it's totally related to what's going on. My bet is that the Mastermind is who hired you, him more than the government, I mean, and he wants to get rid of Chernobog before she can have a change of heart in any way, or leverage what she has to the highest bidder."

"That could be, in which case the assignment would work against what we want, personally. However, unless you can prove this contract is not actually condoned by your government . . ." The Dingo spread his hands out. "We have a job to do."

"I know. But I'm wondering—could the three of us come with you? Or, rather, do you want to come with us? We're heading over there, and we can get there faster than you can. I want to talk to Chernobog, and she might be a lot more chatty if the two of you are with me than not."

"We were not planning on an up close and personal elimination," Surly Vic said.

"Yeah, but I know you're more than capable of it. I have no idea how formidable Chernobog is physically, especially at her age, but nothing makes you play nicely with others like the two best assassins in the world asking you to."

"She'll want to bargain, and we have no leeway," the Dingo pointed out.

"Well, as to that, I have an idea. Can you return your fee and refuse the job? If she's willing to cooperate, I mean. If she's not, by all means, kill her."

"You would allow that?" the Dingo asked.

"She's the reason we lost all our data, and she made it easy for our enemies to kidnap and murder our people. People we loved. A lot. Yeah, I'd allow it."

"I want to ask her some questions before we kill her," Serene said quickly. "Not that I'm condoning killing her."

"We enjoy being paid," Surly Vic said.

"My idea includes you getting paid. Just potentially not for killing Chernobog."

"The fee is quite high," the Dingo said.

"And I'll bet Chernobog has access to all that and more."

"It's against the rules to allow your target to bribe you," Surly Vic shared.

"But it's not unheard of, I'm sure. Besides, as your protégé Siler likes to say, the enemy of our enemy is our friend. And I think we can show Chernobog that we're her friends. And if that's the case, then I can say with some confidence that we can set it up so everyone's happy, alive, and paid what they expected to be if not more."

The Dingo said something to Surly Vic in Russian, who replied in kind. At least I assumed it was Russian. Sounded like Yuri only no curse words, so Russian or a similar language. They stepped a few feet away and carried on their conversation.

"Care to share your plan?" White asked quietly. "Both of you?"

"Once we know if they're buying in or not on mine. But I'd like to know what Serene wants to ask Chernobog."

"I want to know what she did to Imageering. I don't believe what the others do, that it's something they were able to put into the digital airwaves. That explanation made sense at the time, but if that's what it was, we should have been able to counter it by now, and we haven't."

"That could just mean we haven't found the right digital bits or whatever, you know. Hacker International's been mostly focused on data reclamation and the Hunt for Red Chernobog."

"Yes, but they have been working on it about a quarter of the time and can't find anything. Plus, if the virus was in the digital airwaves somehow, we should still be able to read film, and most of Imageering can't even do that anymore. It's impossible for something digital to move to film, and even more impossible for it to move to old prints. Most imageers can't read photos from when they were children anymore. We're getting weaker in the talent, not stronger, and I think, especially because we're dealing with people who use bio-weapons, that they poisoned us somehow."

White and I let that one sit on the air while the assassins argued quietly. "How would they do it?" I asked finally. "If that's what happened?"

"My guess is that they isolated a gas or poison that would affect imageering talent and only imageering talent. I have no idea how, though. But the empaths aren't affected—they can still feel as long as there are no blockers or enhancers around. Same with troubadours. No dream readers have identified restrictions or loss of powers. It's just the imageers."

"Why target them?" White asked.

"I can think of why. Realistically, it's your most potent talent. A good con artist could imitate an empath's abilities, maybe not to Jeff's level, but good enough for the average mark. It's the same with a good actor imitating the trouba-dour talent. You don't have a lot of dream and memory read-ers anyway. But imageering talent is like magic—touch a picture, know all about the person shown, manipulate the images as you see fit. You've used the talent for good, but it's terrifying if you think about it clinically."

"But they didn't do whatever they did because they were afraid of the talent," White said.

"Actually, I'd say that fear is exactly why they did what-ever. We took pictures today—a little over a year ago, Serene would have been able to tell us which of those people in the mob were our enemies and which weren't. Today? We're re-liant on facial recognition software, not imageers. And, spe-cifically, a little over a year ago, if Serene or Christopher had touched the right picture, they'd have known who the Mas-termind was, and where he was."

"Christopher used a camera to reassure Amy she was fully human," White said slowly. "Meaning he could tell if, say, Cameron Maurer was a human or an android."

"Past tense. Because he can't any more. Other than using Tito's OVS or ripping Maurer's head off."

"That means the Mastermind isn't just politically con-nected, but is someone who is either a public figure or close enough to us that one of our imageers touching a picture would be a likely risk," White pointed out. "I'd assume Christopher is who they're trying to avoid."

"Probably. As for how they did it, speaking of Christopher, they had him as a drugged out, unwilling guinea pig for far too long. Plus, LaRue went to Alpha Four before she took off for space parts unknown. And I'll wager the Z'porrah were more than happy to help with whatever experiments would mean they could screw us over. Bottom line, I think Serene's on the right track. So we need to know what they released, and if it's still out there somewhere."

"It's worldwide," Serene said. "But it would only have to have been released in the Science Center. Every imageer will come to Dulce at least once a year for mandatory routine checkups."

"Yeah, this I actually know. It's required for all talented A-Cs, whether they're in active roles or not, right?"

Serene nodded. "And we had all personnel come in after we were infiltrated, too, as a security measure, to ensure all were okay worldwide." She looked ill. "That's our standard practice. Richard's right—the Mastermind knows us well."

"We will go along with your plan for now," the Dingo said as he and Surly Vic rejoined us. "Though we would like to know how you plan to get close to Chernobog without us all being detected."

"Oh, that's easy," Serene said brightly. "You two just need to change clothes."

CHAPTER 68

"I CAN'T BELIEVE WE'RE DOING THIS," the Dingo muttered to me.

"Oh, come on. I know for a fact you two have done undercover work before. Besides, you look good."

They did. Serene's plan was brilliant in its simplicity. Dress the assassins in the Armani Fatigues, so they looked like any other human Field agents. And the Head of Imageering showing up with a couple of Field agents for protection wouldn't cause anyone at Home Base to even blink.

The Elves had come through with our clothing requests, and it had been easy enough to sneak two extremely sneaky people into the Embassy, especially since we were on the roof anyway. We hadn't even used hyperspeed.

Getting past everyone in the kitchen hadn't been hard, either. Serene stopped in to say we were leaving while White and I got the Dingo and Surly Vic downstairs into the basement.

What to do with all the equipment our assassins had was the bigger issue. They refused to travel without it, and I didn't want to leave it at the Embassy anyway. White solved this by requesting two of our nifty cloaked missile launcher cases, minus missiles. The assassins put their guns and other equipment, backpacks included, into the cases, and hit the cloaking button.

"Amazing," Surly Vic said, as he turned his case back to

visible and then cloaked it again. The Dingo nodded with enthusiasm as he tested his case as well. Had a feeling they were going to ask for these cases as parting gifts. Had a worse feeling that I was going to let them have them.

Focused on flowers, lest Jeff be choosing this moment to monitor me. I'd found out it didn't do much more than tell him I wanted privacy, but so far, that had meant he'd ignored me, so hope again sprang eternal.

White spun the wheel and calibrated the gate. "You're sure we want to use the internal gates at the base, not the exterior one?"

"Yes. We won't have a lot of time and we don't want to get held up."

"I agree with Kitty," Serene said. "When Tim, James, and I go over, we usually use the internal gates." Most gates were in bathrooms. Every airport in the world, even the tiniest, had a bathroom with a gate in it. Home Base, however, also had a regular bank of gates in their Administration building, so that important people didn't have to go in and out of the most active human-alien base in the world via the toilet.

"We have to go one at a time," White warned me. "And normal procedure would be for one of the Field agents to go first and one last."

"Uncles Peter and Victor, who wants to go first?"

"I will," the Dingo said. "Victor will bring up the rear."

"Peter, Serene, myself, Missus Martini, and Victor, then," White said. "Agreed."

"Yes," Serene said. "Let's do this." I saw her shift her expression, just slightly. She looked like Innocence on the Hoof again. She was good. Complimented myself on my hiring skills.

We went through, one at a time. I had the "pleasure" of watching three people do the icky, slow fade in front of me. At the last second, changed my mind. "You go before me. It won't throw anyone."

Surly Vic chuckled. "Everyone has their fears. What happens if I go through, but hold your hand and you follow after?"

"I honestly have no freaking idea. For all I know, nothing

happens, we lose our hands, or we're conjoined forever. It's sort of a mystery to me how these things really work. Though Jeff carries me through all the time. But the gates have to be calibrated for that."

"What is life without risk?" With that, he grabbed my hand and stepped through the gate, pulling me after him.

It was nauseating, but a little less so, mostly because I was too busy wondering if we were about to channel *The Fly* or worse. I stumbled out, though, and it was good Surly Vic still had hold of my hand or I'd have fallen.

Administration was one of the more bustling areas of Home Base, in part because it housed a typical military headquarters setup. As with Dulce's Bat Cave level, there were lots of terminals and screens of all sizes, many desks with papers, many busy and intent Air Force personnel, but fewer busy and intent A-Cs than I'd seen here in the past. Under the circumstances, didn't figure this was a good sign.

"See?" Surly Vic said quietly as he let go of me. "We still have our hands."

Nodded but didn't speak, in part because I wanted to be sure my stomach was settling and in other part because Serene was talking to some airmen.

"Oh, I'm sure I have an appointment. It's on all our calendars." She sounded like the sweetest ditz in the world.

Serene was a Dazzler, and as Surly Vic had made clear earlier, she, like every other Dazzler, was a hottie. The human airmen she was talking to weren't immune, especially because I could tell she was sending out flirt signals.

"I'm sorry, ma'am, but . . ." one of the airmen said regretfully. "But the colonel is in closed doors all day."

"Maybe we could help you," the other airman suggested eagerly.

White cleared his throat and stepped up. "We were told it was urgent. We left a very important meeting for this. I'd like to see, for myself, why your colonel has asked for half of Alpha Team to come to a meeting he now won't let us join."

The airmen still looked unsure. Time for me to take a crack at it. "As far as I recall, Commander Dwyer outranks every single person on this base, potentially even the colonel.

I have no problem calling in the rest of Alpha Team and having Commanders Reader and Crawford ask you in far less pleasant ways why the hell we're still standing here. Nor do I have a problem reminding you of my diplomatic status. My husband is both a Representative in Congress and also running for vice president. How much of an incident do you two want to create? Or, let me put this another way—take us to your leader or I get really prickly about American Centaurion being insulted and call many people to complain, all of them far above your pay grades."

That seemed to do it. Clearly these two were more stick than carrot focused. Pity for them. The airmen nodded. "Follow us, please," the first one said.

The building was huge, and one side of it was given over to a giant gate, similar to the two at the Dome, that was used to send and receive heavy equipment or transfer large numbers of personnel. There was also a huge sliding door by which vehicles entered or left the building, and the related transfer staging area. The gate wasn't active, the doors were closed, and there weren't any vehicles or personnel in the staging area.

We weren't headed there, but rather to the back, toward the private conference rooms and offices of high-ranking personnel.

Home Base's set up wasn't as fancy as Andrews, but the commanding officer still had a bathroom and conference room attached to his office, and his secretary's office was basically the antechamber to all of this.

However, there was a Do Not Disturb sign on the outer door, the one leading into the secretary's office. All the blinds were down and closed as well.

One of the airmen knocked politely. There was no answer. Exchanged a glance with the Dingo and Surly Vic. They both looked suspicious. Good, so was I.

"We'll take it from here," I said quietly.

"But—" the one who'd been doing most of the talking started.

"That's an order," Serene said, in a voice that had absolutely no ditz attached to it. "We will let ourselves in. Dismissed."

The airmen nodded, and scuttled off.

"What do we expect to find?" White asked.

"Oh, could be anything, but my money's on Chernobog holding someone hostage. Maybe many someones."

"You think the team that hasn't checked in is here?" White certainly sounded like he thought so.

"I think there's a real possibility of it, yeah. One way or the other, there's something going on that Chernobog doesn't want anyone to know about."

"The name she's using here is Zoya Darnell," Serene said.

"She went with a Russian first name? She's not worried about being found out, is she?"

"I would imagine that if you're the best at what you do and no one can find you, there must be a certain thrill to hiding in plain sight," White suggested.

"She's been found," the Dingo said darkly.

"We hope. How are we doing this?"

"I'll go in first," Serene said. "Be ready in case someone shoots at us." And with that cheery warning, she opened the door.

CHAPTER 69

I WAS READY TO DODGE, run, or attack, but nothing happened. Serene stepped into the room, held the door for us, and the rest of us came inside.

That the room was empty was immediately clear—no one was at the secretary's desk and there was no one else in this room. The blinds to the colonel's office were drawn and closed, however.

"It's too early here for a lunch break," White said softly.

"I wonder where Zoya is," Serene said, at a normal tone, in her Innocent Voice. She pointed to the computer on the desk and White and I came over to look. It was off. It was also a laptop. I unplugged it and handed it to the Dingo.

Our assassins were busy. They had their cloaked cases off and were getting guns and other weapons out and about their persons. More than they'd had on them already. All done silently. The Dingo took the laptop and put it inside his case, also without making noise.

Serene went to the door to the colonel's office, opened it, and stuck her head in. I waited for it to be blown off and readied myself to leap for her.

But nothing happened. "Huh, the colonel's not here, either," she said into the room. "I guess they left for an early lunch or something. We'll have to come back." She shut the door in a normal way but ensured it made noise. Then she went to the outer door, waited a few seconds, opened it, waited another few seconds, and closed it.

While she did this, I tiptoed to the door that led into the colonel's office, leaned carefully against it, being sure to make no sound myself or against the wood, and listened as hard as I could. Didn't hear anything. At all. But what Jeff called my feminine intuition, my Mom called my gut, and I called a funny feeling told me there was at least one person in there, being incredibly still.

Backed away and went to the Dingo. The others joined us in a little huddle.

"I didn't hear anything," I said in a low voice. "But it feels like someone's in there now."

The Dingo nodded. "Good instinct. Continue to speak softly, but assume that, despite Serene's good efforts, they know someone is in here. We will go in first."

"I think I should," Serene said. "It could surprise them."

He shook his head. "If they truly believed we had left, they would have come into this room. They have not, meaning whoever is in there, be it Chernobog or some other enemy, they know we are still here. No, Victor and I go first. We will try to disarm and not kill, but if it's between us and them . . ." He shrugged.

"Yeah. Just . . . I think some of our people may be in there as prisoners or hostages."

"We're professionals," Surly Vic said. "We aren't paid to kill random strangers." he gave me a small smile. "At least, not on this job."

"Ah, Operation Assassination. Good times . . . good times . . ."

"I agree, they were," the Dingo said with a chuckle. He patted my shoulder. "It will be fine. Be prepared to hold off the military, however, because we may not be able to be silent."

"You realize that the three of us could do this fast enough that no human could see us," White said. "And, as such, I believe that if you gentlemen will cover me, I'll be the one to go in first. I should be able to disarm anyone before you have to fire."

The Dingo looked skeptical.

"Mister White is good. I think he's the best agent we have."

"I'm flattered," White said.

"It's risky," Surly Vic countered.

"Less for me than for the two of you," White replied calmly. "Frankly, less for Serene and Missus Martini as well. However, I would prefer our young ladies hang back, hold the extra weapons, and cover the rear, while simultaneously being ready to save us menfolk if necessary."

"As you wish," the Dingo said. He went to one side of the door, and Surly Vic went to the other. They both had impressive-looking handguns with silencers on them out and ready.

White motioned for me and Serene to get out of the potential line of fire, and once we did, he nodded to the assassins, and took off.

He had the door opened and was in the room in the blink of an eye. The assassins followed him in, but they didn't have much to do.

Proving where Christopher got his butt kicking abilities from, White had the three people who were in the room knocked down and their weapons taken away in about two seconds flat.

Serene and I trotted in as the assassins pulled zip ties out of their suit jackets and had the three people bound, hand and foot, in less than a minute. They also had duct tape, and put it over the prisoners' mouths.

Which was awkward, because when I actually looked at the prisoners, I recognized them. "Um, guys?"

"What?" Serene asked. Then she took a good look, too. "Oh. Oh! Gosh, we are so sorry!"

She and I raced over to untie Len, Kyle, and Adriana, all of whom were looking betrayed and more than a little pissed.

"Wait," the Dingo said. "Be sure they are really who you think they are."

"We don't have an OVS on us. Other than asking them questions, how would we know?" Pondered this and pulled off Kyle's gag. "How did we meet?"

"You were hanging off a ledge at the Hooters Hotel and

Casino in Vegas and Len crawled out a window to save you. Why the hell are you guys in here like you're all S.H.I.E.L.D. agents or something?"

"It's Kyle. The others who we think they are?"

"Yeah. Geez, Kitty, we're on the job."

"Apologies," White said. "I didn't stop to look at faces."

"If you'd checked in we'd have known it was you. Besides, Mister White disarmed you for your own protection." This didn't earn me any looks of love.

Once we'd unbound and de-gagged our "captured" members of Team Oliver, I checked the bathroom—no one was in it.

"What are you doing?" Adriana asked.

"Checking for enemies."

Len sighed. "Kitty, I think you guys have the wrong idea about what's going on."

"Wouldn't be the first time. What is going on?"

White opened the conference room door, to show the rest of Team Oliver, a man I didn't know who looked to be in his fifties wearing an Air Force uniform, and an older woman who looked like she was Everyone's Grandma all sitting around the conference table.

Mr. Joel Oliver looked amused, Jeremy, Jennifer, and Walter looked slightly guilty, and the Air Force guy whose stripes and such indicated he was a colonel, and so likely to be Butler, looked shocked. Everybody's Grandma, however, looked both concerned and as if she was calculating a wide variety of odds.

"Wow, would have been nice of you guys to let us know you were powwowing with Chernobog the Ultimate all this time. Some people have been worried about you. Not me, mind you, but others."

"Ah, Ambassador," Oliver said cheerfully. "Allow me to introduce you to Colonel John Butler, who shared that he hasn't yet had the honor of meeting you. And to Zoya Darnell, at least as she's called at this moment." He looked at the assassins. "Oh, gentlemen, please put your guns away. I'm sure you don't need to protect anyone in your assignment from those of us here."

I nodded to the Dingo and Surly Vic, who did indeed put their guns away. Right now, no one other than Oliver seemed to realize who they were, score one for Serene's Armani Fatigues idea. Went with the undoubtedly safe assumption that Oliver knew exactly who they were, based on him being pretty much as hard to fool as Olga. Or Chuckie. Who I figured I was going to need to call, and soon. But not just yet, apparently.

Instead, I took the weapons case off and handed it to the Dingo. Serene did the same with the one she was holding for Surly Vic. "Doesn't look like we'll need these right now, but hold onto them, just in case."

The Dingo nodded, took the case, and stepped back, so that he was leaning against the wall near the door. Surly Vic did the same. They both looked like they were Secret Service, but that was kind of what half the human Field agents resembled anyway, so hoped they'd stay incognito.

"So, MJO, want to explain why you guys are holed up here and, more importantly, why none of you checked in?"

Butler answered before Oliver could. "We're in the middle of delicate negotiations, Ambassador. I'm going to have to ask you to leave."

CHAPTER 70

OPENED MY MOUTH TO REPLY, but Serene beat me to it.

"No." One syllable, but she packed a lot of authority into it. "The woman you've had as your secretary for the past year is considered one of American Centaurion's most wanted war criminals. Either we're now a part of this meeting, or the Ambassador will call in the C.I.A. while I call in the rest of Alpha Team."

"I will not work with them," Chernobog said imperiously. Caught Adriana's eye—she rolled hers, shrugged, and made the "duck" with her hand, fingers flapping against thumb, or what I thought of as the Universal Blah, Blah, Blah Sign. So, Chernobog had been stalling things out, and Butler had been allowing it. Good to know.

"Oh, you will." I sat down and Serene and White followed my lead. "And let me explain just why you will. There's a contract out on your life. We can stop the assassins. But we won't—in fact, we'll tell them exactly where you are—unless you cooperate with us. I'm sure everyone else has been really nice. But this has taken too long, and Team Hardball just showed up."

"You have no authority here," Butler said, albeit rather more nicely than I'd been expecting. He looked like he'd be about Christopher's height standing, but was much stockier. Normal features, black hair, blue eyes. Average nice-looking man.

Had to figure he was worried about being brought up on charges of treason for having been fooled by her for a year, with good reason. If I was Chernobog—and she was in the Megalomaniac League and, therefore, experience said I could think just like her—I'd make damn sure I had all the incriminating evidence there was on Butler, real and faked, in a safe yet easily accessible place so that I always had a bargaining chip.

Also, it wasn't likely that Butler had a ton of experience with negotiating spies in from the cold. Chuckie should have been here at least half a day ago, but I knew without asking that Chernobog had said she wouldn't talk if the C.I.A. or other government agencies showed up. So, needed to make sure that both Butler and Chernobog realized I was now in charge.

"Sure we do. Lots and lots of authority. I also have a direct line to your bosses' boss, Colonel." Well, I had a direct line to Mom, and that was, essentially, a direct line to the President. "He's kind of pissed about everything that's happened these past couple of days. I'm sure he'll be happy to have someone to blame. Tag, you're it."

Butler blanched. "I'm not your fall guy."

"So," White said pleasantly, "someone might perhaps want to catch us up, and quickly, before the Ambassador uses her itchy phone trigger finger."

"You complete me, Mister White."

"Madame Darnell—" Oliver started.

"Call her Chernobog. That's who she is. I don't care what name she's used for the past year. It's no more real than any other she's had over the decades. But Chernobog is who she *is*."

Chernobog gave me a long, appraising look. "Why do you insist?"

"Two reasons. One, you don't deserve to be called something pretty like Zoya or Madame Darnell. You're a terrorist, a murderer, and someone who released a bioagent into Centaurion's main research facility which has ended up crippling a good number of our people. That the three of us aren't trying to strangle you right now is a testament to our restraint, not our lack of desire."

"What's two?"

"You're the best of the best of the best when it comes to hacking. That deserves its own level of respect. Zoya Darnell isn't the Ultimate. Chernobog is."

She smiled slowly at me. "You, I am willing to talk to."

"Fabulous. So, MJO, where are we at? I'm looking for bottom line information. Stop worrying about offending Madame Prickly here. I can guarantee that what I'll have to offer her will be the best deal she could ever hope to be offered."

"This capture belongs to the Air Force," Butler said.

"Bull. It belongs to my team. If they're here with you, hanging out, there's only one reason—they're the ones who brought to your attention the fact that your secretary is the biggest security risk in, possibly, the history of the United States. And you had her working under you for a year . . . and you didn't figure it out."

Butler flushed. "I can't deny that," he said stiffly.

"Good. I like to know if I'm dealing with an idiot blowhard or just a guy who's been caught totally by surprise and is trying to do the best he can with absolutely no prep."

Butler gave me a long look. Not as appraising as the one Chernobog had given me, but close. "Colonel Franklin speaks highly of you."

"Arthur's my kind of guy." There were times to use Franklin's first name, and this seemed to be one. "He rolls with the punches better than any high-ranking military I've ever met. Other than Major-General Mortimer Katt." I smiled nicely. "My Uncle Mort is, of course, the best at rolling with whatever's tossed at him and handling it."

Not for the first time was I happy that I had a family member I knew and loved in a position of rank within the military. Butler straightened up. "Oh! You're Mort's niece? I'm sorry . . . I didn't make the connection."

Controlled myself from calling him on this one. There was no way that someone in charge of Area 51 wouldn't know that Mortimer Katt's niece was the American Centaurion Ambassador. However, I could spot someone trying to save face, and Butler didn't seem to be an idiot blowhard.

"No problem, Colonel Butler. It's been a trying time for all of us."

"Please, call me John, Ambassador."

Butler was definitely covering his butt. Good. It showed intelligence versus belligerence. It was also making Chernobog nervous. I could tell because she was fidgeting, just a little, but she sure didn't seem nearly as relaxed as she had earlier. Also good.

"Thank you, John. And it's Kitty. So, let's get to it, shall we? What has Chernobog offered and what has she asked for? MJO, you were saying?"

"She would like full immunity for her promise not to be a bad girl computer-wise ever again."

"And?"

"That's it," Oliver said.

"Wow, such a deal. Here's the counteroffer. You give us back all the data you stole and wiped from Centaurion Division and any other U.S. department over the past, oh, let's call it twenty years. You will give us all the information you have on the people who put you into motion to steal Centaurion's data and so forth a year ago. You will tell us, in detail, what was released in the Dulce Science Center and potentially elsewhere that has caused our imageers to lose their powers. And you will also tell us who created it and how to fix it."

"And if I refuse?" Chernobog asked.

"Then," the Dingo said from behind me, "you die."

CHAPTER 71

"WHAT OUR AGENT MEANS," Serene said smoothly, "is that we'll alert the assassins who are after you. We'll give them your exact location, and we'll tell them we won't stop them from killing you."

"You cannot protect me from assassination," Chernobog said.

"You know, a couple of years ago, I'd have agreed with you. Now? Now, as long as you do two more things, I can guarantee you'll be left alone. But we aren't going to discuss those things until I have the answers and data I want."

"Oh, and spare us the protestations that you've destroyed all you took," White said conversationally. "Because we know you're just not that stupid."

"It will take some time for me to do all you ask," Chernobog said.

"She's stalling," Surly Vic shared.

"I agree. Jeremy, what are you getting?"

"Not much. She's a little agitated, but that's all."

"Adriana, has she been strip-searched?"

"No, the colonel wouldn't allow it."

"Well, I'm here now, and I demand it. You and Jennifer strip her down and see where she has the emotional overlay hidden about her person. The bathroom's free. Len, Kyle, you go with Jeremy and make sure Chernobog doesn't manage to overpower anyone and escape."

"Are you sure this is necessary?" Butler asked me.

"Dude, right now, if you know what's at all good for you and your career, you'll shut up and smile and nod. A lot. I can't believe you refused to strip-search a known terrorist." Looked him right in the eyes. "As far as the C.I.A. will see it, you're in it with her. Now, are they right or are you just too damn chivalrous for your own good?"

He swallowed. "No. Go ahead."

Adriana and Jennifer each took an arm and escorted Chernobog out. "Leave the door open," I called to Len as the guys went after them. He nodded and did so. Surly Vic shifted so that he was able to see the office and, therefore, the bathroom.

"She had all the proper qualifications," Butler said, a little desperately.

"I'm sure she did." While we were talking, had an unsettling thought. There was one other reason Butler might have been stalling. Sent a text. "She's hella old, dude. Did you not consider that?"

"She showed as having worked for the State Department and Department of Defense for her entire career, then retired. She asked for part-time work when her husband died, and was given a secretarial job at entry-level wages. She was so good that she was kept on, and then moved up to my office last year."

"Impressive. All a lie, but still, impressive."

"Who are you talking to?" White asked.

"Tell you shortly. John, where were you stationed before you took over here?"

"In Germany. I ran the Spangdahlem Air Base."

"Impressive post." My phone beeped. "Excuse me a minute." Got up and went to the outer door. "Tito, good to see you and your special wand."

He shook his head. "Hilarious. Who am I wanding?"

Led him through. "He's with me," I said to my assassins, who nodded. "Run it over our good colonel here, please. John, stand up, would you?"

Serene and White stood up and moved to flank Butler. Walter followed their lead and stood behind him. "What's going on?" Butler asked as he stood slowly.

"I'm just a super-suspicious girl. This is noninvasive and won't take a moment."

Tito ran the wand all around Butler. "Thanks," he said calmly. Then he moved near to me. "Ninety percent inorganic."

"What?" Butler asked. "What the hell are you talking about?"

"Show us your artificial limbs, or we're going to shut you down."

Butler looked confused. "I don't have artificial limbs."

Walter karate chopped the back of his neck, hard. Nothing happened.

Butler spun around, but he didn't attack. "Why did you do that?" He sounded hurt and confused.

Backed up near the Dingo, who wisely had his big gun out. "He's an android," I said softly. "But he doesn't seem to know, meaning he hasn't been activated yet. We could use him, if he can be contained."

Butler heard me. "What the hell? I'm not an android!"

"Sensors say you are," Tito said.

Oliver looked shocked. "Are you sure? He's acted perfectly normal."

"No, he hasn't. Colonel Franklin wouldn't have let Chernobog sit here for a day without calling in reinforcements, of which the seven of you were not. But someone who's been programmed to ignore and protect Chernobog would."

Butler shook his head. "I don't know what you're talking about. I'm not an android." He blinked, rapidly, several times in succession. Had the proverbial bad feeling.

"Everyone? I think it's going to be time to go."

Oliver got up and trotted to me and Tito. "Are you sure?"

"Is that man acting normal?" Pointed to Butler, who was jerking. "He's either the best actor out there or he's about to self-destruct."

"We need what he has," Serene said, somewhat desperately. "We can reverse engineer him."

"N-n-n-ot annnn an-d-d-droid," he said. Then looked at me with horror. "Help. What . . . what have they . . . d-d-d-done to me?"

The Dingo was ready to shoot, and I was ready to run. But it was clear Serene didn't want to give up. And Butler was terrified, I could see it in his eyes. There was ten percent of him that was still human, and that ten percent didn't want to die.

Gave it one last shot. "John, you're trying to self-destruct right now, there's some mechanism or chip in your head that's telling you to blow yourself up. If you can stop it, can keep yourself from exploding or self-destructing, then we can help you. And we're the only people on Earth who will be willing to."

He was still jerking. The women came out of the bathroom. "What's going on?" Chernobog asked.

"He's an android, and I'm betting you knew."

"What? No!" She sounded freaked out. "He's going to self-destruct!"

Turned to her. "Unless you stop it. I'm betting that you can."

"Why save him?"

For whatever reason, this question made me flip from worried, scared, and angry to enraged. "Because he doesn't want to die. He might be mostly machine, but they took whoever John Butler was and turned him into that machine, and I guarantee it was against his will." He was fighting too hard for me to believe he'd chosen this willingly. "And you probably helped them do it. If not this, then you've helped them do so many other horrible things you owe this, much more than this. But it's a start. Save him. Or die with him."

"I need codes to deactivate, and I don't know them, and we don't have time for me to find them." Chernobog sounded terrified. Unfortunately this might mean she was telling the truth.

I grabbed her and shoved her toward Butler. Racked my brain. During Operation Invasion Bellie had known the trigger codes to stop and then control the androids. Butler could be a newer model, but if he'd been in Europe when the invasion happened, then he might be one of the older models. This wasn't my area of expertise, though.

Had my phone in my hand and I used it. Thankfully he picked up right away. "Kitty, we don't have anything yet—"

"Shut up, Ravi, and listen to me or we're all dead and by

we I include Jennifer. What were the codes that Bellie gave you during Operation Invasion?"

"We lost them along with all the rest of our data."

"Great. Will call you back if we're alive." Hung up and hit the speed dial of the one person who might be able to save the day. He also answered on the first ring.

"Kitty, what's—"

"What's up, Chuckie, is the usual deadly crap. I need the numbers that Bellie gave us during Operation Invasion that gave Ravi control of the androids. Do you remember them?"

"Hang on." He was quiet for a few long seconds while I pulled a pen out. "Got it. Protocol two-two-six-three-seven-one-two. Protocol eight-seven-one-four-five. Protocol six-six-six-one-four-nine-two." Wrote those down on my hand.

"I love you." Shoved my hand at Chernobog's face. "See what you can do with that. Meanwhile, Walter, Jeremy, take Len and Kyle and evacuate the hangar, get everyone out. Now. And be sure Len and Kyle are with you and safe." Walter grabbed Len, Jeremy took Kyle, and they raced off. Alarms started immediately. "Jennifer, get MJO, Tito, and Adriana out of here, too." She nodded, grabbed Oliver and Adriana, who grabbed Tito. They took off, too.

"Kitty, what the hell is going on?" Chuckie asked. Well, shouted, because the alarms were loud and I assumed he could hear them, too.

"Home Base is double infiltrated, we have Chernobog and the android version of Colonel Butler, who's going to explode if she can't use those codes to deactivate his self-destruct. He's fighting it, so we have a shot."

"Get the hell out of there!" He was bellowing. Not quite up to Jeff's standards, but pretty close.

He was right, of course. Even though hyperspeed meant that we could probably get out before Butler exploded, it was stupid to stay here to try to save the android version of a guy I didn't know.

But I hadn't been able to save Michael or Fuzzball, Gladys or Naomi. Or so many people before them. This one life wouldn't make up for theirs. But still, Butler, the human part of Butler, didn't want to die.

"No. We'll be fine."

"Kitty, get out, now!"

"Mister White, get the others out of here. I'm staying until we have to run." I nodded toward Chernobog.

White shook his head. "I'm not leaving."

"Me either," Serene said.

"I need an entry point," Chernobog said. "Short of ripping his head off, I have no idea where to start. I don't work on these and if I were hacking I'd go in differently. And with more time."

Serene made a call. "Ravi, you need to talk us through defusing an active android. You're on speaker now, try to ignore the alarms."

"Serene, I lost all that a year ago," Ravi sounded freaked out and far away, because the alarms were drowning him out. "I can remember some but—"

Butler looked at me. He wasn't shaking or blinking any more. "I can't stop it. I can feel it trying to tell me to explode something in my brain."

In times of trouble, I'd found one thing that always worked for me. I went for the crazy. "John, look at the numbers on my hand." He did. "Internalize them. Tell them to the whatever that's trying to blow you up."

"What?" This was shouted in unison by Ravi and Chuckie. Still wasn't a huge fan of the unison thing, but this was kind of cool, since they were both on different phones and, presumably, not together.

Serene had a hold of Chernobog. The Dingo and Surly Vic were still with us, too. White was between them, presumably ready to grab them and run. They had their guns trained on Butler, presumably to kill him before he blew up.

"Try, John," I said gently, as I pulled up the trigger phrase that had worked on Bellie. "This is for the survival of the fittest."

Butler blinked, and jerked, big time. "You need to run."

CHAPTER 72

SERENE AND WHITE both took off, Chernobog and assassins in tow. I pretended to. It's easy enough to fool someone going at hyperspeed—by the time they figure out you're not with them, they're far away. Hung up my phone and put it in my purse, all while keeping my hand in front of Butler. "Try harder."

"I can't."

"John, the mere fact that you're still here, fighting, means that you can. You're the only android I've come across that could realize what was going on and stop it, even for a little while. That's the John part of you doing it. You're a strong person. Be stronger. Look at these numbers."

"Why are you staying with me?"

"Because she doesn't want to let you die alone," Christopher said.

He entered the room, dragging Jeff & Chuckie with him. Jeff and Chuckie were gagging a little, but I could say from experience that being revved up made the effects of Christopher's Flash Level less intense.

"But we've lost enough people to this fight. Baby, we need to go." Jeff took my hand, the one without the numbers on it.

"Wait," Chuckie said. He was on his phone. "Yeah, Ravi, got it." He tossed his phone to Christopher. "Act as relay, speakerphone won't cut it while the alarms are going off."

He went behind Butler and pulled a pen out of his pocket. "This may hurt," he said to Butler. Then he slammed the pen into Butler's right ear.

Results were immediate. They also didn't involve any of us going boom.

Butler dropped to the ground. "Now what?" Chuckie asked, which Christopher relayed.

"No," Christopher said to Ravi. "He's not moving. Looks dead, honestly. Really? You're positive? Okay." He looked at Chuckie. "We don't do anything now. He's in stasis, Ravi says you've hit the suspension mechanism. He's still active, but nothing can happen as long as your pen remains connected to whatever the hell it is you hit."

Jeff got on his phone. "We need an emergency containment team here now. Yeah, an active android that's just managed not to self-destruct. Yes. Sooner than that. I'm here because my wife is here, why shouldn't I be here?" Heard someone yelling. Said someone sounded like Reader. "You weren't nearby when she called Chuck, Christopher and I were. Yes. No, we didn't take a gate." He sighed. "Yes, he can, he really can. Could we discuss this later? Great, thanks." He hung up.

A dozen Field agents showed up, in what looked like riot gear. They were accompanied by six Dazzlers, also in riot gear, and a gurney.

"Don't let that pen move out of his ear or everyone goes boom."

"Yes, Ambassador," one of the Dazzlers said. "We know."

"Him going boom is not what we want. Especially not if all of you are around him, but even if you're not."

"We'll do our best."

"You need to leave, please," one of the Field agents said. "Commander Reader's orders."

"Happy to," Jeff replied as he took my hand. I grabbed Chuckie, Christopher took Jeff's other hand, and we zipped outside.

Found White and Serene with Chernobog, Tito, and the rest of Team Oliver in the middle of Groom Lake. It was time for a flashback. Really hoped quicksand, javelinas, and combine tractors wouldn't be in our near future.

The Dingo and Surly Vic were nowhere to be seen. Decided I'd ask White where they went later. Like when Jeff, Christopher, and Chuckie weren't around later.

"Are you crazy?" Jeff asked all of us, me in particular. "Is that your problem?"

"Grouchy much? We're all alive and well." And I was still enraged, meaning I could have gotten away because when I was this angry, all the skills flowed like I was Jet Li, Jackie Chan, Jean-Claude Van Damme, and Chuck Norris combined.

"Miraculously," Christopher said.

"How did you know?" Chuckie asked. "About Butler, I mean. Stryker told us how you figured out where Chernobog was."

"He wasn't acting right, for a military man in that position. He was stalling. At first I thought he was working with Chernobog, but he seemed sincere, which was when the thought that he could be an android hit me and I asked Tito to come over. Then I asked where he'd been stationed last. The moment he told me he was in Europe, the likelihood of him being an android seemed much more, um, likely."

"I feel chagrined that I didn't realize that," Oliver said.

"You were busy negotiating to bring in our Public Enemy Number Five. I get why you all missed it, really."

Chernobog sniffed. "I should be higher than that."

"It took hours for her to admit to being Chernobog," Adriana said, ignoring her. "Half the team shadowed her while the other half searched Home Base for proof. We had nothing to report for quite a while, but we didn't want to be called off, either."

"Hence why you broke protocol and didn't check in," Jeff said in a resigned tone.

"When did you make real contact?" Chuckie asked.

"Early this morning," Oliver replied. "The Home Base team was waiting in her office, and the Shadow team came in with her." He chuckled. "And then the verbal gymnastics began. She's quite good."

"She's been hiding in plain sight for decades."

"Thank you, and I'm right here."

"And once he was there, Colonel Butler wouldn't allow us to call anyone in," Walter said, also ignoring Chernobog. "Ostensibly because it could cause her to shut down and not give us anything."

"See? And you're at the correct slot at five," I said to Chernobog. "So stop whining."

"Public Enemy Number Five?" Jeff asked. "Who are the first four?"

"The Mastermind, his Apprentice, the new and not improved Leventhal Reid and LaRue Demorte Gaultier. Unless you have other people who should be up before Chernobog."

"No, no, that's the right list. I just hadn't thought of them like that." Jeff ran his hand through his hair. "I may never sleep again, now that we've listed them out and given them numbers."

"Oh, poor baby. I think a non-exploded android is one for the win column, though."

"I don't know how he fought the programming," Chuckie said. "Or if we'll be able to save him or not."

"I know. But I hope we can. He just seemed so . . . scared and horrified. He didn't ask for this, I can guarantee that."

"Whether Cameron Maurer did will be the question." Chuckie looked at Chernobog. "Nice to meet you. I'm the head of the C.I.A.'s Extra-Terrestrial Division. As such, that gives me unlimited approval to do whatever the hell I want to get back what you took from Centaurion and other government divisions."

"I'll talk to her," Chernobog pointed to me. "Not you."

Chuckie smiled the nasty, wolfish smile I knew he'd learned at the C.I.A. "Oh, that's nice. I'll be with her when you're talking to her. And, in case you weren't sure, I'm not the nice one."

"Neither am I, honestly. Look, Chernobog, we have requests. You'll either meet every request, or I'll let the C.I.A. do whatever to you and then tell the assassins where you are, so they get to finish the job."

She shrugged. "As you said, I'm an old woman. I've seen more than all of you put together. Your threats don't scare me."

"Yeah? Let me give you a threat I'm fairly sure will. If you ever want to see your son alive again, you'll cooperate."

Her eyes narrowed. "I have no son."

"Oh my God, we know you do, okay? And we have him. And you know it. Maybe you think that a changing of the political guard will mean he's freed. But I'll just tell the assassins where he is, and then let them in."

She looked a little less sure of herself. "You will not."

"Babe, we lost people we loved because of what you did. *Loved*. Close family members. Take a look, a good look, at the expressions on the faces of the people with me, and then ask yourself if you really think that at least one of us, let alone all of us, won't say it's more than okay to let your loser son die?"

Chernobog sniffed. "It's easy to threaten. Your government has laws."

"And I have Poofs."

On cue, Harlie, Poofikins, and Mous-Mous came out of my purse, and Fluffy and Naomi's Poof, Cutie-Pie, jumped out of Chuckie's pocket. All five went large and instantly in charge. They all roared at her. Chernobog gasped and stepped back.

"Oh, did I forget to mention? You helped kill a Poof. One of their brethren. You helped kill two of the people they belonged to, too. They're as pissed about everyone we lost as we are. Guess what? Poofs are carnivores. See those teeth? They will chew you up and not even spit you out. And they can get in where your loser son is and eat him up, too. Alive, I might add."

Had no doubt the Poofs would do this. They were still grieving Fuzzball's loss, Cutie-Pie was grieving Naomi's loss as well, they were all upset about Michael and Gladys as much as they were about Naomi and Fuzzball, and I didn't like Chernobog, meaning they didn't like Chernobog.

Chernobog gaped, her eyes bugging out. Then she collapsed on the ground.

CHAPTER 73

FORTUNATELY, Tito was there, and down next to her in an instant.

"Did you just kill her with terror?" Christopher asked.

"She's fainted, that's all." Tito looked up at me. "Apparently you've found her weakness, Kitty."

"Go me. No snack right now, Poofies. Back into Kitty's purse and Chuckie's pocket, please and thank you."

Got five booming purrs, then the Poofs went small. Harlie and Poofikins hopped back into my purse. Checked. They were curled up with a bunch of other Poofs. Well and good. Fluffy and Cutie-Pie jumped onto Chuckie's shoulders, rubbed against him, and then went into his pocket.

Mous-Mous, however, was still out. While Tito brought Chernobog around using smelling salts and much more gentle slaps to her face than I would have managed, I tried to see what the Poof was doing. Looking around, as near as I could tell.

There were some shimmers, off in the near distance. Could be floater gates, could be dust devils forming, could be Sandy being a dust devil. Wasn't sure. But the Poof was definitely looking where these shimmerings were.

But, right when I was about to ask the Poof what was going on, it gave a satisfied snort, jumped up onto my shoulder, gave me a nuzzle and a purr, and joined the others in my purse.

I still might have inquired about this—because there was more than one shimmering I'd seen, and if Sandy manifested using the stuff around him, then the likelihood of others like him doing the same was high. But Tito's ministrations were working and Chernobog's eyes opened. I'd table my shimmering questions for later, especially since there was nothing to see now and I didn't relish being told I was crazy.

Tito helped Chernobog sit up. "What . . . what were those things?"

"Alien animals who don't like you or the people you're working with. Answers. Now." While the Poofs and Peregrines were "outed" as aliens, we'd kept the fact that the Poofs had their Extra Large With A Side of Giant Teeth side hidden. So I knew Chernobog wasn't faking her reactions, because the only people who weren't on our side who'd seen the Poofs large were all dead.

"Yes," she said shakily. "I can retrieve the data taken, and no, your enemies don't know where it is. I didn't give it to them. I kept it in a safe place."

"Why?" Chuckie asked.

She shrugged. "Leverage." This checked out with my assumption, so that was good. "As for what was released into your main research facility, that was alien in nature."

"From Alpha Centauri?" Jeff asked.

She shook her head as Tito helped her stand up. "No. I don't know where it came from or how it was created, but my impression was that it's from far away. My guess is it was created by the invaders."

"How did you release it?" Serene asked. She and Christopher both looked angry and upset, not that I could blame them.

"Cloaked, time-released aerial bombs."

Serene went pale. "They used my designs."

Christopher put his arm around her. "This wasn't your fault. At all."

"Can it be reversed?" Jeff asked, Commander Voice on Full.

"Not that I know of. I didn't create these. I didn't set them, either. Your own people did that."

"No way—" Christopher started.

"They were mind controlled," I interrupted. "And I know which person set them, too. Gladys. She was the only one who would know exactly where to put them so that no one would detect them." No wonder she'd killed herself once she knew Ronaldo Al Dejahl was dead. Living with the knowledge of what she'd done, unwillingly or not, would have killed her, only much more slowly and with so much more emotional pain.

"Why didn't she tell us?" White asked. "If she was the one who set them."

"Maybe she didn't remember right away, or even at all. She said things were fuzzy when she was mind controlled." Not that this made anything better.

"I've told you what you want to know," Chernobog said. "Now let me go."

"Oh, it is to laugh. Look at us, do we look to be in laughing moods? No, you owe us all the information on the people who hired you to hit us, and you need to actually give back what you stole. And then there are those two other things I mentioned. You do those, and then we may have an accord."

"What are the other things?" she asked suspiciously.

"They're dependent upon returning the data and giving us the intel on who hired you. They're irrelevant if we don't get that, because you'll be dead and then these other parameters won't matter."

She cocked her head at me. "You are of Russian descent?"

"Maybe, back there somewhere."

She chuckled. "You have a Russian viewpoint. You would have done well in the KGB." She looked at Adriana. "And you, you are KGB, aren't you? Raised in the old ways."

Adriana shrugged. "My training isn't the same as yours. I'm not on the side of people like you. But I do know what to *do* with people like you."

"And I know you already know what my people do with people like you when you're not considered worth enough to trade," Chuckie said. "I'm sure you think you're going to get traded. But I mentioned that leeway I have? You aren't going to be registered as our prisoner until we have everything we want. That means if you die, no one will actually know."

"And if they do trade you, let me mention those assassins after you again."

Chernobog sighed. "Fine. I am your prisoner. It would be helpful to have my laptop."

"We took it." Of course, it was with the Dingo, but still, sort of in our possession.

Tito opened his medical bag. "Yeah, we have it." Managed not to ask him how he'd gotten it. Obviously the Dingo had given it to him. Why, was the question.

"I asked that we hold the laptop while the agents helping us went to investigate the base," White said. "So, yes, we do have the laptop." Managed not to tell White he was the greatest, but it took effort.

"Good. Then, you will take me somewhere and we will start in with your demands."

"I want her in the Embassy."

"What?" Jeff shouted. "Why?"

"Because the hackers she's going to be verifying every single keystroke with are there. Why else?"

Jeff shook his head. "I know where this leads."

Rolled my eyes. "I'm not moving her in permanently or something."

Christopher sighed and made a call. "Hey, yeah. Situation under some form of control. Kitty wants the prisoner at the Embassy. Because it's Kitty, why ask why? Yes, of course under heavy guard. Yes, because she wants our hackers watching closely. Yes. Yes." He eyed Chernobog. "She looks harmless. Figure that means we need triple the number you just suggested. Yes, around the clock. Yeah, we'll transport her there. Thanks." He hung up.

"How many agents are you going to be having watching Everyone's Grandma here?"

Chernobog snorted and Christopher shook his head. "At least a dozen, at all times. We'll have some of our more computer-minded science staff there, too. That should pretty much fill up the fourth floor of the Zoo, by the way."

"The more the merrier. Who's taking her back?"

"I will," Christopher said. "Home Base is safe and we can use the gates there."

"I'm going, too," Serene said.

Adriana stepped next to Chernobog. "I as well."

"Jeremy and Jennifer, you go, too," Jeff said. "Walter as well. We need you back at your post." He gave me the hairy eyeball. "Too many people have been sneaking in and out without someone paying attention."

"I'll go too, in case she faints again." Tito looked at Chernobog. "But in case you're not sure, if they want to rough you up, I'm going to let them. So don't give them any incentive. My friends died, too."

"When will you be coming?" Chernobog asked me.

"In a while. Why? You're not exactly safer if I'm there."

"You have honor. You tried to save the colonel when everyone else ran, and not for his information, but for him. I'd have run sooner than you had the others go, if I'd been able. But you tried to save him. I would like to think that, if things work out right, you would also try to save me."

Stepped closer to her. "Perhaps. There are a lot of marks against you in my book. If you do everything we want without trying to screw or double-cross us? Then yeah, I'll save you from the certain death hunting you."

"You said assassins. Many have tried." She shrugged. "None have succeeded."

"Got two words for you: the Dingo."

Thought she was going to faint again. "But . . . they promised . . ."

"That they'd never send the top assassin in the world after you? Well, guess what? They lied. He's coming for you and I'm the only one who can stop him. And you have a lot to do in order for me to have a prayer of stopping him. So, my recommendation is for you to get busy, because time's a'wastin'."

She nodded. "If what you say is true, if . . . he . . . is after me, then I'll need your help. And I'll do as you ask."

Chuckie handcuffed her, gave Christopher the key, and then the team escorting Chernobog back left.

"Now," Chuckie said nicely to Oliver, Len, and Kyle, "why don't you three tell us just what's really going on with Colonel Hamlin?"

CHAPTER 74

"HOW DID YOU FIND OUT about that?" I asked Chuckie before the others could respond.

"Your mother tends to share important information with me. A lot sooner than you do."

"So bitter. So, MJO, can I guess and you tell me where I'm wrong?"

"If it makes you happy."

"Oh, I'm sure it will. You've been hunting for Colonel Hamlin and you found him. You've helped him set up his carrier pigeon network, and you're his eyes and ears, and he's also yours. He trusts you because he's had to. But on days like today that trust is quite valuable. He told you what was going on with the bombs, you got the note to Colonel Franklin, leaked the information to the media, and then he sent you after Chernobog, or maybe even to check out Butler."

"I didn't leak anything. I filed a report that was instantly picked up by all the other news outlets."

"Go you Mister Joel In The Know. Nice to have some respect?"

"It's pleasant but sometimes complicated things. However, Hammy sent us to investigate issues at Home Base. That Colonel Butler was an android and his secretary was Chernobog weren't told to us. His information was more along the lines of something has to be wrong at the top there, and you need to figure out what."

"Adriana was the one who suspected that Missus Darnell was Chernobog," Len said.

"I'd like to know how you found Hamlin," Chuckie said.

Oliver shook his head. "He has my trust and I have his. I won't tell you and, since I'm not a war criminal and am a journalist, I'm going to hold with protecting my sources."

Chuckie sighed. "I don't want to hurt him. We want to protect him."

"He's doing better on his own," Oliver said. "That's not an insult. However, he's aware that Mister Buchanan was attacked shortly after they parted, and Hammy's not willing to risk it, or put someone else in danger." Oliver shot me a quick look. Had a feeling there was more to why Hamlin didn't want us knowing where he was, but I'd have to get it from Oliver later, when we were alone.

"Well, we still don't know for sure that Malcolm was attacked because of being with Colonel Hamlin. But anyway, when you talk to him next, say hi for me, and thank him for letting us know there's a Mastermind."

"Now what?" White asked.

Jeff's phone rang before any of us could reply. "Yeah, James? Oh. Good. Really? Yeah, she'll be glad. Keep him under guard. Yeah, I agree. Glad we can sleep at home then. Yes, I'm sure we'll be back in D.C. soon. Oh, really? Maybe we'll have lunch out here, then." He laughed. "Yeah, actually, you were all this big a pain when I was Head of Field. It's your turn now, enjoy it." He hung up.

"What's up with James?"

"Colonel Butler is stable. Still in stasis, but the team feels confident they can safely keep him from self-destructing until we get our data back and can then figure out how to keep him from exploding, permanently. But because he's explosive, he's being kept in one of the prisoner cells on the fifteenth floor of the Science Center."

"Well then, I'm happy we'll be in the Embassy tonight, too. You want to get lunch somewhere? We could gate it over to Pueblo Caliente and hit one of our old faves."

"Jeffrey really can't be seen to have been making a presidential announcement in Washington at eleven eastern and then appear in Arizona at eleven pacific," White pointed out. "I think that would create issues we'd all rather avoid."

"Wise man takes all the excitement out of life."

"It's my gift, Missus Martini."

"Seriously, it's not even noon here yet?" Jeff asked. "I feel like we've already been up for twenty-four hours today."

"Yeah, I know what you mean." Chuckie rubbed the back of his neck. "What else can possibly happen today?"

Right on cue, we found out. My phone rang.

Sighed and pulled it out of my purse. Recognized the number. Clearly I should put him into my address book. "Bruce Jenkins, how goes it?"

All the men with me groaned. Yeah, that was my reaction, too, but I showed off my diplomatic skills by not groaning out loud. But I was groaning in my head, big time.

"Ambassador, impressive announcements from you and your husband this morning."

"Glad you enjoyed them. Why are you calling?"

"I'd like to do that interview now, more than ever."

"Dude, what part of 'call my people and set it up' did you just not comprehend? I don't take meetings with gossip columnists whenever. I take them when they're scheduled on my calendar. Protocol, it exists for a reason." Per Mom and Jeff, anyway.

Was about to hang up on him, but the next thing he said caused me to pause. "Do you know Cameron Maurer?"

"Not personally, so I'm not in a position to set up an interview for you with him, either." Waited for him to ask to talk to Mrs. Maurer.

"There's something wrong with him." Well, that was unexpected.

"Why are you telling me this?"

"Ah, because I think I need help."

"Excuse me?"

"Help. I think I need it." He sounded frustrated and a little freaked out. "I don't know who else to go to who will believe me."

"Why do you think coming to me is the right answer for all your help needs?"

"Because you have a reputation."

"Yeah, as to that, I'm not having an affair with anyone, other than my husband. Our affair it quite torrid, but since we're married, I hear that's okay these days."

"I don't mean that! Look, I know we got off on the wrong foot."

"You think?"

"But I need help. I've discovered something terrifying, and I think it's the same thing Nancy Maurer discovered and that's why she's hiding with your diplomatic mission. Please . . . if I'm crazy or ask you inappropriate questions, kick me out. But I need to talk to someone."

Great. I had the reputation for being the go-to girl for anyone with a scary issue. Go me. However, if what Jenkins had discovered was that Maurer was an android, then that was indeed why Mrs. Maurer was hiding with us. If Jenkins was acting as a spy we'd find out fast. And if he was using this as an excuse to ask me interview questions, then we'd kick his butt onto the street.

"Fine. Understand and accept that you'll be strip-searched because I just don't trust you."

"That's fine. I have nothing to hide. Well, I do, but it's what I'm coming to you about. So I don't have to hide that."

I'd talked to this man before. He wasn't this scattered normally. Meaning he was either acting or really stressed out.

"Okay, come to my Embassy. We'll be waiting for you."

"I'll be there in less than ten minutes. If I'm longer than that, do me a favor and call me back."

"Why should I do that?"

"Because if I'm later than ten minutes, it probably means I'm kidnapped. Or dead."

"Gotcha. Will do."

"Thank you. I really appreciate this."

We hung up. "Time to go," I shared with the menfolk. "Either Bruce Jenkins is playing me, or he's discovered that Cameron Maurer isn't human any more. He's meeting us at the Embassy in ten minutes. If he's longer he thinks he might be dead."

"Wonderful. You had to ask?" Jeff said to Chuckie.

Who shrugged. "This could be good for us. Or we have an enemy trying to infiltrate. Kitty already told him he'd be strip-searched, I think we're okay."

Sent a text to Raj, who replied quickly. "Okay, Embassy staff is prepared to receive Jenkins, strip-search him, and scan and search anything he's bringing with him. We need to get back. And I'm starving, so I hope this guy doesn't mind if I eat while he shares his tale of woe." Those brownies had been far too long ago.

"I'd like to be there, when you sit down with Bruce," Oliver said.

"Oh, MJO, as if I'd let you miss this? Yeah, we want you there. Frankly, Bruce is going to have quite an audience." Sent Pierre a text telling him we'd probably have to have the meeting in the dining room and to get the Elves busy making some food. "You know, should Nancy be a part of the meeting, too?"

Oliver nodded. "I think so, unless you've learned all the reasons why she called you in the first place."

"Uh, I haven't. Guys?" The rest of the men shook their heads.

"Too much else going on," Chuckie said ruefully.

"Then, yeah, we'll have her participate, too." Sent Raj another text.

As Jeff reached for my hand my phone rang again. We all sighed this time. Embassy number this time. "Eddy, what's up?" Heard a lot of background noise.

"Chernobog is here," Stryker said, as if this explained everything.

"Yes? I know. I sent her there."

"Yeah, well did you remember that Olga was with us?"

"I did indeed." Realized the sounds were people shouting in a foreign language.

"Did you also realize they hate, and I do mean *hate*, each other's guts?"

"I knew they were no longer close, yeah."

"Well, they're close right now. And I'm not sure the computer lab is going to survive the meeting."

CHAPTER 75

"ON OUR WAY." Hung up and grabbed Jeff's hand. "We need to get home pronto. Apparently there's a KGB catfight going on."

"Where is Christopher?" White asked.

"Stryker didn't say. Not sure if he's elsewhere or what, but Stryker called me, so I have to figure whoever's around isn't cutting it in terms of stopping the fight." Grabbed Chuckie's hand.

White took Len and Kyle, and Jeff grabbed Oliver, and we took off for Home Base. About two seconds later we were at the external gate. "Why this one?" I asked Jeff.

"Because I don't trust anyone at Home Base right now. We had an android running things, the ultimate hacker was his secretary, and the remote radio tower was turned into a floater gate mechanism for our enemies. I mean, God alone knows what else has been negatively affected."

"I agree with our future vice president's concerns," Oliver said.

"Hilarious," Jeff said as he calibrated the gate.

"I'm quite serious. I fear for our country if the Cleary-Maurer ticket wins."

After my realization this morning that Cleary-Maurer winning would be bad for pretty much everyone I cared about, I was one with Oliver's concerns. I squeezed Jeff's hand. "Like with everything, you'll make a great VP, Jeff," I said quietly.

He gave me a very loving smile. "As long as I have you next to me, baby, I can do anything. Okay," he said in a louder voice, "everyone else through first, then I'll bring Kitty through last."

Happily, no one argued with this. White went first, then the boys and Oliver. Chuckie looked around. "Don't dawdle. I say that because you two always dawdle and right now, I don't like the idea of you being here alone."

"We'll hurry, Chuck. I promise. You okay?"

Chuckie shrugged. "You know, the same."

Jeff looked worried, meaning he was picking up emotions from Chuckie that weren't showing on Chuckie's face.

"Let's dawdle and discuss the elephant in the desert. You keep on trying to tell everyone that you're okay, but you're not. Your wife was taken from you in a really awful way before you two had made it past six months of marriage. And you're nowhere near to over the loss."

"It's been a year." But the way he said it I knew it felt like yesterday to him. Most days it felt like yesterday to me, too. "But Jeff's right—my emotional state hasn't been . . . very good."

"Dude, no duh. I'm aware of the huge amount of time the Peregrines as a group are spending with you, not to mention all the unattached Poofs, along with our cats and dogs. We haven't let you move out of the Embassy for a *reason*."

"You know, we're here for you. Uncle Richard would be more than willing to talk to you about what you're going through. And I know you haven't talked to him because he mentioned it to me the other day. He's as worried about you as the rest of us are."

"I appreciate the concern, I really do. I just . . ." Chuckie looked around and stiffened. He pulled us into the shed that housed the external gate and closed the door, but not all the way; it was open a crack. He looked through said crack. "Jeff," he said in a low, urgent voice, "tell me if you recognize the people who are coming out of Administration."

They sort of switched places and Jeff also looked through

the crack. "Now, what the hell are Gideon Cleary and Cameron Maurer doing here?"

"Nothing good. Can I look?"

"No," Jeff said quietly. "You need to get back for your meeting with Jenkins."

"Convenient timing, isn't it?" Chuckie asked. "That Jenkins calls Kitty and wants to meet her on a matter of life and death, and then, when we should be gone, the opposition is doing some kind of tour of the Home Base. Right after we've taken the base commander and his secretary into custody."

"You think our enemies knew she was Chernobog?" Sent Raj and White a text, telling them what was going on and to be super-suspicious of Jenkins. Or to expect him to be dead.

"Fifty-fifty shot," Chuckie said. "What I want to know is how they got here so fast. I know for a fact they were in D.C. this morning."

"They used a gate." Algar's main concern came back to me. "Or they have access to the last Z'porrah cube. The one I'm pretty sure the Mastermind has in his possession."

"So they know the Mastermind, then. They went back into Administration. You two go back to the Embassy, I'm going to investigate."

Jeff grabbed the back of Chuckie's jacket before he could leave the shed. "The hell you are. You're not going anywhere alone any more than Kitty is. I'd tell you to go to the Embassy, baby, but I know better than to waste the breath. But Chuck, we go together or we don't go at all."

Raj sent a text back. "Jenkins is there. He's been strip-searched, no emotional blockers or enhancers, no bombs. Jeremy says he's freaked out beyond belief."

"Have them tell him where we are and who we're seeing here," Chuckie said. "Just make sure his phone is taken away and there's no other way for him to send a message."

Relayed these instructions to Raj and we waited. Got a text from White in the meantime. He was refereeing the Old Ladies' War in Hacker Central and felt that I could remain on the job at Home Base.

Shared this with Jeff and Chuckie, then Raj replied. "Huh. Jenkins is telling Raj to tell us to get the hell home. Jeremy says his overwhelming emotion is terror and from what he can tell, Jenkins isn't lying, though he'd like you, Jeff, to read Jenkins."

Someone shoved against me, from behind. "None of you want to come home, right?" Christopher asked.

"Didn't you worry about landing on one of us coming out of the gate?"

"Figured one of you would cushion the blow. Thanks for that, Kitty. Jeff, James is really unhappy you're still here."

"Too bad." Jeff told him what was going on. "Think you can take a look at what's going on, safely, and report back?"

Chuckie nodded. "We don't want to create an incident if this is some planned tour, and it could be."

"Yeah, give me a second." With that, Christopher zipped out, closing the shed door behind him.

He was back quickly, and this time he left the shed door opened a crack again. "It's not a planned trip at all. I think they came to keep us from getting Colonel Butler—they're asking for him. No one on the base actually knows what happened because you evacuated them. So no one seems clear that Butler's gone. But what I also heard indicates that they were outside when Reynolds spotted them to make sure all of us who'd been here were gone, so they obviously knew we'd been here, meaning they probably realize that we have the Butler android and are either trying to continue faking it or create chaos. Or both."

"They could be trying to find Chernobog, too, if they know who she is. Which I give at fifty-fifty odds. What do you think, Chuckie?"

"I agree with you and White both."

"Are there any A-Cs there?" Jeff asked. "Because I want our people out."

"Hang on." Sent a text to Reader. Got a really snarky reply back. Reader was not enjoying our being the Team on the Scene. Or rather, he was fine with Chuckie being on the scene, but felt that Jeff, Christopher, and I should be home in the Embassy. "He's pulling all personnel into the Science Center. Excuse is an emergency drill and inspection."

"We need to know when they're all clear," Jeff said.

Someone else shoved against me. "They're all back," Reader said, as he moved me to the side so Tim could come through.

"That was fast. Even for A-Cs."

"Girlfriend, despite what all of you seem to think, I'm not an idiot. I brought the majority of our personnel in when you discovered the base commander was an android set to explode. And now that we're here, you can go back."

"Ha ha ha, you're not A-Cs. Nice try, but unless Lorraine and Claudia are right behind you, we're staying. Not that we can fit many more bodies in here."

"Not my fault you've been eating six meals a day, girlfriend. Though, honestly, you look the same as you always have."

"He means great, Kitty," Tim added.

"I still love my Megalomaniac Lad, the best suck-up on the planet."

Jeff grabbed me and Chuckie, Christopher took Reader and Tim. "No," Jeff said flatly. "We're not leaving. However, we're all going to find out what the hell is going on right now. Together. Think of it as a fun campaign team-building activity."

We zipped out, closing the shed door behind us, and headed back into the Administration building. There were a lot of human airmen but not any A-Cs I could spot, other than us, so assumed that no one had lied to Reader and stayed behind just in case.

Things seemed less busy and more chaotic than they had earlier, which was probably to be expected, especially since the head guy was gone and those next in line were undoubtedly searching for him. However, the large gate staging area was no longer empty—there were a number of missiles stacked there on a large flatbed truck. Right next to a missile launcher.

We could get in and remain unseen using hyperspeed, but that meant we had to run around constantly. Fortunately, Jeff found an empty office that had its blinds down and closed that provided a good view of the majority of the interior, and we hid in there.

"Could you launch a missile using a gate?" I asked Reader in a low voice, while the others stationed themselves at each side of the two windows this office had. "Because those missiles and that launcher weren't by the big gate even an hour ago."

"Yeah, you could. But why would Cleary want to be a part of that? He's ahead of Armstrong in the polls, or at least he was until today. Jeff's acceptance helped the Armstrong ticket a lot. But even so, blowing things up when you're not in a war isn't great political strategy."

"It is if you can blame your opposition for the explosions," Chuckie said. "Think about it—if bombs come out of Home Base, then Centaurion Division is immediately suspect. The ricin situation becomes instantly fishy—no longer will the public believe that Centaurion Division blew up the ricin bombs to protect the public; they'll think that the attempt just failed and you're all trying again. That means that Jeff will be so beleaguered by accusations, innuendo, and negative public opinion, that he'll have to withdraw."

"They tried blowing us up from Guantanamo and we stopped that. This does strike me as the next inevitable phase. And, by the way, I hate these people so much. Okay, look we have to find out just what's going on."

Jeff stiffened. "Stephanie's here."

"Well that freaking cannot be good. Who is she here with?"

"Appears to be with Cleary," Tim said. "You know, she could be telling him she's representing Vander. I don't think anyone's shared that she's a traitor."

"And even if they had, that would probably make her more appealing to them, not less." Pondered our options. They seemed slim. Went to the window near Chuckie and peeped out.

Gideon Cleary was in profile to me. Florida's governor was tall with an average build, though he was going a little soft around the middle and it showed, even in a suit. His hair was blonde and thinning, features were okay but he definitely possessed a weak chin and a look I found familiar—Oily Reptile. He wasn't as bad as Leventhal Reid—after all, who was—but he definitely wasn't going to win any looker prizes in my book. However, he could turn on the charm when voters were paying attention.

Maurer, meanwhile, had been a congressman for a while and he had the bearing of someone who'd spent years in positions of power. He was a normal-looking man, under six feet, trim, light brown hair, and pleasant features.

Stephanie was standing in between the two men, but a little closer to Cleary than Maurer. Might mean nothing, though. They were talking to several airmen, but I didn't read lips so I had no idea what they were discussing.

A thought occurred. "You know, Siler put a tracker on her. And he and Malcolm are off doing something. Just like Oliver and his team were."

"See if we can spot them," Reader said. "Because it would just figure."

"Look," Chuckie said. "On the far side, in the shadows."

We all stared. "That's Buchanan," Jeff said finally. "I think Siler's with him. Damn, they're gone now."

"No, they're invisible now. I guess Nightcrawler wasn't lying—he can't hold a blend for too long."

"We can't let them know we're here without blowing their cover," Tim said. "Buchanan may have his phone off or on mute, but it's not worth taking the chance."

Looked at Reader. "You know, I have an idea."

All the men with me groaned, albeit quietly. "I hate it when you say that," Reader said. "Can I just say no now and get it over with?"

"Only if we want to let them start World War Three."

CHAPTER 76

READER SIGHED. "I'll bite. What bizarre and foolhardy thing do you want to do?"

"Oh, not me. Jeff and Christopher, but not me."

"As if that's any better?"

Jeff gave me a long look. "This is going to be just like in Florida, isn't it? Where you have us doing something incredibly dangerous?"

"Yep. We need to get those missiles somewhere they can't be sent into targets. They're heavy, but you're both superstrong and superfast."

"You made wrangling alligators sound reasonable, too," Jeff said. "It wasn't."

"But it worked."

He sighed. "It did. You seem remarkably willing to let me risk blowing myself up."

"I'm not. I just know you two know how to handle a bomb. I figure if Malcolm sees bombs disappearing he'll realize we're here, or at least that some A-Cs are here. And we'll get the bombs out of here."

"I actually don't think Kitty's idea is that bad," Christopher said. "Because I agree we need to get those bombs away from the gate. But where are we going to put them?"

"Stephanie blew up one option and Kitty burned down the other," Jeff said.

"We could send them to the Science Center."

Reader shook his head. "Then we're stealing them, and I guarantee that will blow up in our faces, pun intended."

"If we could get them to Luke, or any other nearby Air Force Base, that wouldn't be stealing so much as rearranging," Chuckie said. It was nice to see everyone getting in on my plan.

"We'd need the gate for that," Christopher said. "I could do it, but I'll be wiped out, going back and forth, and I'm sure we'll need my speed. Plus, this gate calibrates slowly due to the mass of things normally going through it."

"And these missiles would be a great example of mass," Jeff said.

"What about using the Poofs?" Christopher asked.

"Oh, good idea. Let's ask if they can handle things of this size."

"Wait, baby." Jeff shook his head. "Even if they could do it, we'd still have to go, and I think it'll be harder to explain to the base commander at Luke what the hell we're doing with all these weapons if they're busy thinking they're being attacked by alien animals."

"I hate to say it, but Jeff's right," Reader said. "I don't think it's wise to use the Poofs for this, because they'd have to be seen in Attack Mode and they don't say 'coming to help' to someone who's never seen that before."

"The missiles are on a truck," Tim pointed out. "And that's a mobile missile launcher. Calibrate the gate for Luke, drive them through, leave them there, use a gate at Luke to get back."

"I like Tim's plan," Reader said. "The problem is that Jeff and Christopher can't drive, and that means you and I will have those honors."

"We have to go," Jeff said. "Because if something's wrong over at Luke, too, we have to be able to get the two of you out."

"No argument from me, Jeff," Reader said. "The more the merrier. But that means we're going to be seen. Which sort of blows the whole element of surprise thing."

"Not if there's a distraction."

They all looked at me. "And let me guess who you're going to suggest for the distraction," Jeff said, sarcasm knob heading toward eleven.

"Well, there are only three of us with hyperspeed and I can't calibrate this gate, nor do I trust myself to drive a missile launcher. I mean, I could drive the truck, since I'm still a great driver, nifty A-C skills or no. So, if you want me driving the bombs through the gate, just say the word."

"No," Jeff and Reader said in unison.

"I'll keep her safe, Jeff," Chuckie said.

"See? I have Chuckie's big gun and badge on my side. We'll be fine here."

"I hate your plans. I know I say this all the time, but they just get progressively more terrifying every time." Jeff ran his hand through his hair. "However, I don't see any other options. We can't get the proper authorities here in time to see what's going on, and who'd believe it anyway? This is a military base. So there are missiles and a launcher here, so what?"

"Then we're agreed. I'll be sure to make the distraction really spectacular." Trotted over, hugged Jeff and gave him a kiss. "I promise we'll be fine and this will work."

"And I promise you that I think it's going to be terrifying before it's over." He hugged me tightly. "Be careful, baby. And if you get in trouble and can't get back to Chuck safely, get to Buchanan."

"I will." Pulled out my iPod and portable speakers. Spun the dial. "Feed the Gods" by White Zombie would do the trick. And I was revved up, and due to all that had happened today, it was easy to tap into rage, because I really hadn't stopped being angry for a while now. All I had to do was think about the fact that these people probably planned to blow up the Science Center or the Embassy while they were hitting other targets and, bam, enraged.

Nodded to Christopher, who was manning the door. "Go as soon as they're paying attention to me." He nodded back, opened the door, and I zipped out.

He and I had spent a lot of time working on my control over the past year, and I was confident in my hyperspeeding abilities now. I set up my iPod and speakers near to where everyone was, but on the side opposite the gate, and hidden so they wouldn't be easily found. Turned the volume up to eleven, hit random play, and raced away, still on the side away from where Team Missiles would be.

The music started, and it was loud and jarring. Everyone jumped and, to a person, spun toward the sound, which was my cue. I appeared to be coming in from the far door. They saw me and I "froze."

"Get her!" Cleary yelled. But the person who responded wasn't one of the airmen, or Stephanie. It was Maurer.

He barreled toward me, and I recognized the way he was moving, and how fast. He was an android for sure. And that meant he was faster than a human.

This was going to be hard, because in order to maintain the distraction, I had to stay within the building and not get caught. However, I couldn't use hyperspeed, because then no one would see me.

Waited until Maurer was close, then I took off, toward Cleary. Once again, being a sprinter and hurdler all through high school and college was paying off in my current career as bait. Swerved away from Cleary before I was close enough to grab, Maurer hot on my heels.

Fortunately, this setup had a lot of open spaces between clumps of desks or equipment. Ran around as many airmen as I could. Some tried to catch me, and a couple would have succeeded if I hadn't had increased strength and if Christopher hadn't drilled me on how to use bursts of hyperspeed.

The positive on all of this was that it was working—pretty much everyone was paying attention to what was going on. It's not every day you see a vice presidential candidate chasing an ambassador around in a gigantic air base administration hangar. Even the airmen who weren't trying to catch me were paying attention.

The negative was, of course, that Maurer was right on my heels.

The music changed to "Alpha Dog" from Fall Out Boy. Fitting, since the lyrics were about megalomaniacs. As I hurdled over a lone desk in my way I risked a glance toward the gate. The truck was starting to go through. Good.

Distraction, even for an instant, is rarely a good thing, and even though I landed well and was able to keep on running, Maurer merely slammed the desk into me. I went down, thankful that I'd also gotten the faster A-C healing from Jamie. Sadly, faster healing didn't mean no pain, but it did mean the massive bruises I was sure a desk hitting me with great impact would cause would be gone quickly.

Maurer picked me up by the back of my neck, feet off the floor. Yep, this was an android move. What a pity that the two people who could actually fight an android physically were getting a truck loaded with missiles and the corresponding launcher through the gate. On the plus side, they were almost through.

Maurer carried me like this back over to Cleary. "What now?" he asked.

"Did they do it to you willingly?" I asked through gritted teeth. Being held like this wasn't comfortable.

"Do what to me?" Cleary asked.

"I'm talking to Cameron. Or what's left of Cameron in there. Did they make you into an android willingly, or did they force it onto you?"

"I don't know what you mean," Maurer said.

"Yeah? Think about it. How could you have done what you just did, and how could you be holding me the way you are, if you were still a human being? You're not The Rock." I'd have given a lot to have The Rock show up right about now. He was a hero, he'd save the day, right?

Heard a gun cock. "Put her down," Chuckie said. "Or I'll blow you away."

CHAPTER 77

OH, RIGHT. I had Chuckie backing me up. Booyah.

Looked around. Chuckie and his gun were up against at least a hundred airmen, Cleary, Stephanie, and the Maurer Android. Booyah denied—Chuckie and I were going to be toast.

Wondered where the heck Buchanan and Siler were, as well as if the Dingo and Surly Vic were around. And if they were around, why weren't they shooting at someone? Well, someone other than me or Chuckie.

"You have no authority here," Cleary said to Chuckie.

"I have a hell of a lot more than you do. Put her down." Chuckie had his gun aimed at Cleary. "Or I'll put you down."

"I'm not the one holding her, why are you pointing your gun at me? Unless this is an assassination attempt."

"No, assassins rarely stop to tell you to put someone down. They just shoot you." Though I had a much better track record with assassins than most. Didn't think now was the time to share that, though.

"Can he just kill her?" Stephanie asked. "Please?"

"I have authority right here," Reader said, Commander Voice on Full, as he and Tim appeared, escorting a guy in uniform who I was fairly sure was a lieutenant colonel, and therefore probably the second in command of the base, over to us. Booyah reinstated. "It's me and the man with me. And I'm telling all of you men to take the governor, the congressman, and the young lady with them into custody. Now."

The man with them nodded. "You heard Commander Reader. Stand down, all of you, and that includes you, sir," he said to Maurer. He was a little taller than Tito, but had the same build—slim but muscular—and I guessed him to be of Hispanic heritage too. Also like Tito, he was pretty cute. That he seemed to be on our side in no way colored my opinion of his looks, either.

"Who are you?" Cleary asked him.

"Lieutenant Colonel Sergio Gonzalez, second in command. In the absence of Colonel Butler, I'm *in* command. I just came on shift and was informed of the chaos that's been going on around here for the past couple of hours. I want that woman's feet on the floor immediately or I'll have you all under military arrest, is that clear?" Decided I liked him.

"Do it," Cleary said softly. Maurer let me go. Dropped to the floor but landed well, so I didn't fall or turn an ankle. Trotted over to Chuckie and his big gun. The music changed to Nine Inch Nails' "The Hand That Feeds". "Thanks," I said to Gonzalez.

"Yes, ma'am. Explain yourself, sir," he said to Cleary.

"What's going on here?" Cleary asked. Sadly, he knew my dad's trick of answering a question by asking another question. "We came for a tour and we're being attacked."

"I wouldn't call *you* chasing *me* to somehow equal your being attacked."

"Where is Colonel Butler?" Cleary asked. "I'd like him to take charge of this."

"I'll bet you would. He was taken ill. He's in a medical facility." Looked at Maurer. "You could use one, too."

Maurer expression showed no belligerence, only confusion. "I don't know what you're talking about."

"Maybe you don't. Seriously, think about what just happened and ask yourself what's wrong with that picture."

"What have you done with my mother?"

"She's being protected. At her request. From you."

"I'd never hurt her."

"She no longer believes that. Have to be honest, particularly after the past fifteen minutes, I don't believe that, either."

"We didn't realize the woman running around here was the Ambassador," Cleary said to Gonzalez. "Honestly, she was acting crazy, and we feared for our safety." U2's "Love and Peace or Else" came on. "And can someone shut that horrible music off?"

"Well, now that I'm on the ground and not being attacked, sure." Trotted over and got my stuff, turned my iPod off, and noted that Cleary not liking my music was just another mark against him.

"So, you're trying to tell us you were afraid of one woman?" Tim asked. "While you happened to be in a base full of soldiers? You're not really confident in your ability to handle a low-risk situation, are you?"

Cleary sniffed. "We know what . . . you people . . . are capable of." He gave Chuckie a dirty look as I sidled back next to him and his nice cocked and aimed gun. "Oh, put your gun away. You're just an alien's lapdog."

"Actually he's not," Jeff said, as he and Christopher stepped out of the regular gates, along with a goodly number of Security Forces Specialists, which were the Air Force's Military Police. "This base is under military review, based on certain events and information being passed along to the proper authorities." He smiled at Gonzalez. "Nice to see you, Sergio. Didn't realize they'd moved you over here."

Gonzalez smiled in return. "A couple months ago, Jeff. Haven't seen you in at least, what, five years? But you look like political life is agreeing with you."

"Six, I think, but who's counting? You haven't aged a day. And it's being married that agrees with me." Jeff turned to Cleary. "Speaking of which, I'm willing to pretend to believe that you didn't recognize my wife. But if either of you touch her again, I'll ensure we both press assault charges. If you're lucky."

"Is that a threat, Congressman?" Cleary asked.

"No, a promise."

Gonzalez pointed to four of the Security Forces guys. "Please escort the governor, the congressman, and their assistant back to their vehicle."

"We used a gate," Cleary said stiffly.

"Oh, so you used our technology to come here and attack us? Good to know you're the usual hypocrite."

"Supposedly you have that technology for all of us to use as appropriate," Cleary snarled. "Not just your friends."

"Stephanie, you should come with us," Jeff said, before Cleary and I could continue to snarl at each other.

She sneered. Literally. Figured she'd practiced it in the mirror, potentially for hours. "Never. You're not my family anymore." She put her arm through Cleary's.

Jeff looked upset. "This isn't you. You're going to break your mother's heart."

"As if you care about that? You murdered my father. You think that didn't break her heart?"

"Your father was a traitor," Christopher said. "And self defense isn't murder. In any state in the union."

"My father was a patriot. He understood where we fit here. And it wasn't under your rule." Her eyes narrowed. "And to think I used to love and look up to the two of you. You'll never fool me again, so stop trying. You're not my family anymore. I have people I *belong* with. And we support the man who's going to save our country." She looked up at Cleary with a total "my hero" expression.

He gave her a fond smile in return. "I understand that Stephanie had to leave the employ of the F.B.I. due to discrimination. I'm taking her on as my personal secretary."

Repressed the shudder this gave me. I didn't trust the majority of politicians with anyone under thirty, be they male or female. Precedent was too much in favor of the young person being used and many times discarded, usually as a dead body. "Does your wife know?"

Cleary gave me a long look. "Yes. She approves. I plan nothing untoward with our Miss Valentino. But she needs a job, and protection, and we're pleased to be able to provide both."

Managed not to say that I didn't believe him, but it took effort.

"And I'm pleased to finally be with decent, right-minded people," Stephanie declared. She shot a snide look at me and Chuckie. "And you're really one to talk. Everyone knows about the two of you."

"Oh, I'm sure they do." Ensured I sounded bored. "Just remember—it's really hard to cross over a bridge you've burned."

"Some bridges need to be burned," she hissed. "Besides, I never want to come back to any of you."

Jeff stared at her for a few long seconds, then he shrugged. "Okay. You win. You're not family anymore. And you're an adult. So, do what you think is right, not what you're told is right. That's what we all have to do—what we think, what we know, is right."

With that he turned and walked away.

Christopher shook his head. "One day, Stephanie, you're going to realize what you've done, and that day is going to be the worst of your life." He did the same as Jeff.

"I know you're happy," I said to her. "So, enjoy the bed you're happily lying in. Don't make the mistake of thinking we'll ever give you the benefit of the doubt now, and also don't expect special consideration due to relationships or age. You're made your choice, and you may end up very sorry we're going to abide by it."

"That's fine," she snapped. "I'm willing to take the so-called risk."

"Then that works out for everyone, doesn't it?"

"Let's escort the governor and his retinue back and ensure their gate is calibrated correctly," Gonzalez said.

An airman ran up to us. "Sir, the President just called and asked that we fly the governor and congressman back to Washington."

Cleary chuckled. "Fine. The delay will be helpful. It'll give us time to get press assembled."

"Ah, as to that, sir," the airman said, "I believe you're flying to Andrews. And will be in an immediate closed doors meeting. Just the two of you, sir. The young lady and any others are not to be on the aircraft or in the meeting. This is a presidential order, Governor, not really a request."

Cleary seemed nonplussed for a moment. Then he recovered. "As the President requests." He patted Stephanie's hand. "I assume you'll actually ensure the young lady is sent safely to our campaign headquarters?"

"We'll ensure she goes wherever she wants, within reason," Gonzalez replied.

"I'd like to walk the governor to his flight," Stephanie said haughtily.

Cleary nodded. "Most appreciated. I'll advise you when we're done with the President. But contact me immediately if they don't send you where you want to go." He smirked at me. "Round one to you, Ambassador."

"Really? You think this is round one? Dude, you've joined a game in progress."

Cleary laughed. "Think of it how you like." Then he turned to follow the airman who'd come with the news of their meeting, Stephanie trotting along with him like an eager puppy. The really pretty kind, like an Afghan hound. But still, a puppy who had no idea her new master was a bad person, and probably wouldn't care as long as the master was good to her.

Put my hand onto Maurer's arm as he started to follow them. He turned, but didn't attack. "What?"

"Seriously, think about this event. Think about it like Cameron Maurer, not like whatever they've turned you into. Your running mate used you like a trained animal. Since when are you an attack dog?"

"I . . . you were dangerous." He sounded unsure.

"I was standing there. He told you to get me, and you ran after me, with serious intent to harm. Why? I don't believe you'd have done that before they turned you into what you are now. I just want you to think, about this, about all the things that are wrong. And if you want help, you know where we are."

He blinked slowly. "Is my mother safe?"

"Yes. She'd like her son back. Her *real* son."

Maurer twitched. "I . . . don't know what you're talking . . . about."

"You do. Cameron Maurer knows. If you're strong enough, you can fight it. It would be good—for you, for your mother, for your children, and for your country—if you fight it. If you can become Cameron Maurer again, not Gideon Cleary's trained and very well-controlled attack dog."

Maurer stared at me. Then he turned and followed Cleary and Stephanie.

"Good try," Reader said quietly. "But I don't know if he can fight it. He's a newer model, you know."

"Yeah. But a girl can dream, right?"

"Yeah." Reader put his arm around my shoulders and hugged me. "You've done all you can, and more than you should have here. Go comfort your husband and cousin. They're trying to hide it, but I'm sure they're not handling it well."

Leaned my head against his shoulder, but not for long. We weren't in a place where this was a good idea. "I will. Lieutenant Colonel, I just want to thank you for your timely arrival."

Gonzalez grinned. "I was at Luke when a truck filled with missiles showed up, followed by a missile launcher. Considering who was in the truck and launcher, I didn't question that there was a problem here. Commander Reader called for a floater gate and he and Commander Crawford returned with me to help me get my base under control." He winked at Reader and Tim. "Oh, and please call me Sergio, Ambassador."

"And I'm Kitty."

"I've heard you were informal. It's a nice trait in any politician."

"I want a full rundown on why you weren't advised about anything that went on here today," Reader said, Commander Voice on Full.

"Assume this base is severely compromised," Chuckie said. "Nothing that's happened here the last couple of days has been following any form of proper military protocol."

"True enough," Gonzalez said. "No one advised me of anything. I'd have been at Luke all day if you hadn't had your men bring in such a big surprise, Ambassador."

"I love it when a plan comes together."

CHAPTER 78

READER AND TIM headed with Gonzalez to his office. Chuckie and I joined Jeff and Christopher. "You guys okay?"

"Yeah." Jeff sighed. "I want so much to believe that she's trying to save the day and is actually acting as a double agent."

"But she isn't," Christopher said sadly. "You can see it in her eyes."

Chuckie shook his head. "I should have put more stringent bugs on her."

"It wouldn't have mattered," Jeff said quietly. "But . . . I think you need to investigate the rest of my family. Just in case any of them have been turned, too."

"I will. And . . . I'm sorry."

Jeff shook his head. "Not your fault, Chuck. It has to be done, and I accept that. Now."

We needed to get out of here, before everyone was completely depressed. "Let's go home. We have a frightened reporter and the top computer hacker in the world to chat with."

"Where did Buchanan and Siler go?" Christopher asked as we headed for the internal gates.

"You know, I have no idea." Had no idea where the Dingo and Surly Vic had gone, either. Hoped Buchanan was okay—three assassins to one Buchanan could mean bad things.

Thought about it. The Dingo and Surly Vic could have

stolen a vehicle and escaped. Same with Siler and Buchanan. But Siler was following Stephanie, I had to figure, meaning they were probably still here.

My "uncles" were likely willing to wait for me to get what I wanted from Chernobog and then either kill her or let me negotiate a mutually beneficial deal. White or Serene might know where they were, but it was going to be hard to ask them where someone else wasn't going to see the answer in some way.

Siler and Buchanan could get home because Siler could calibrate a gate. For all I knew, Buchanan could, too. But the Dingo and Surly Vic couldn't. And I didn't want to strand them here if I could help it.

"You know, before we go, let me make a call." All three men gave me suspicious looks, but no one argued. Stepped away and pulled out the burner phone. Dialed the last number that had called me. It rang but no one picked up. Tried the other number. Same thing. So much for that idea.

Didn't want to send Buchanan a text in case he was in a situation where that would blow his cover. While I was contemplating my lack of options, the cosmos did me a solid and my phone played "Secret Agent Holiday" by Alien Fashion Show, which was my ringtone for Buchanan.

"Malcolm, where are you?"

"With some good friends of yours. They assume you're dithering around at Home Base because you're worried about how they're going to get back to D.C. Figured they were right and that I should let you know that we'd all appreciate it if you'd all get back to the Embassy."

"Wow. They're good. And so are you. Are you okay? I mean really okay, not being held against your will by the top three assassins in the world?"

"Yes, I'm fine. As I mention frequently and you and the others like to ignore, I have a lot more in common with them than you realize."

"No, actually, I realize it a lot. I just happen to appreciate the similarities. And the differences. Cameron Maurer is definitely an android. Gideon Cleary is an oily, evil man. Stephanie's fully on the Dark Side and I think will very shortly be sleeping with Cleary. There's a slim chance Maurer can over-come the android within and come to us for help."

"There's an even bigger chance that he'll pretend to and self-destruct inside the Embassy when you're all there."

"No argument. Just wanted to catch you up on the excite-ment that is our lives. I'm sure your new friends caught you up on the happenings with Chernobog and Colonel Butler."

"Yes."

"Good. Chernobog's in the Embassy now. Tell them she will make it worth all our whiles or I will bring her to the roof. They'll know what that means."

"Missus Chief, I know what that means, too, you know."

"Good! Um, somewhere in all of this, I was warned by someone—and I swear to you that I can't even remember who now—that the National Convention was going to be giv-ing the term 'chaotic goat rodeo' a new meaning. Oh! And Colonel Hamlin is alive and well and requesting that we not try to protect him since we did such a bang-up job letting you get attacked and almost killed."

Buchanan chuckled. "Good to know. And, we'll be pre-pared for the convention, at least as much as we can be."

"They're after Jeff, much more than me."

"Maybe so. But if they hurt you, they hurt him. Don't forget that."

"I won't."

"You could have fooled me with that distraction technique you used just now."

"We thought we'd spotted you and Siler! So, um, why didn't you do anything?"

"We were prepared to blow every single person around you, other than Reynolds, away. Fortunately, we didn't have to assassinate the opposition candidates. That's not really good for your husband's campaign, by the way. Public opin-ion tends to flow toward the party whose nominated candi-dates are killed by agents working for the opposition."

"Good point."

"So glad you think so. Go home. Get what you can out of Chernobog. We have some things to clean up here, and then we'll be back with you."

"Did you find the cell that Stephanie was a part of?"

He was quiet for a few seconds. "Do you really want to know?"

Considered why he was asking. Considered what Siler and, more significantly, Buchanan were likely to do to a group of people they knew were actively out to get me and mine. Considered if I could sleep with the confirmation of what I suspected the answer would be. "No."

"I knew you were smart."

We hung up and I rejoined Jeff and the others. "They're fine. Let's go home."

"Do we want to know?" Jeff asked.

"I guarantee we don't," Chuckie replied.

"What Chuckie said."

Jeff calibrated a gate. "I know, I know," he said to Christopher and Chuckie. "Don't dawdle."

"Hey, dawdling worked out this time," I pointed out.

Christopher shook his head. "You two have been dawdling at the gate since the first day Kitty was with us. So don't dawdle too long." He stepped through.

Chuckie looked around. "I see nothing else untoward. I promise I'm not going to kill myself. And yes, I'll talk to Richard when we have some breathing space. Oh, and humor us all and don't take too long, in case something else bad wants to happen." He stepped through.

"So, are we dawdling?" I asked as Jeff recalibrated.

"Nope." He swung me up into his arms. "I want to get home where it's a different brand of chaos. But it's the brand I prefer."

I'd have chimed in, but Jeff kissed me, and I focused on that instead of my witty reply, the gate transfer, or anything else. Like Buchanan said, I was smart.

CHAPTER 79

AFTER ONE OF THE BETTER gate transfers of my life, we joined the meeting, and luncheon, in progress in the main Embassy dining room.

Most of the Embassy staff were here, though we were pointedly missing Serene, Gower, Abigail, Amy, Doreen, Irving, White, and Hacker International. Jennifer and Adriana were in here, as was Vance, though, so I figured those not here were assisting White in calming down the KGB War over at the Zoo. But also figured I should verify.

"Pierre, is everyone who isn't here helping Richard?"

"Or doing their jobs, such as running or assisting with daycare and being adorable little ones, yes." Took this to mean Dad and Lucinda were helping Denise with the kids, or as I was sure they thought of it, having a wonderful time. This meant the Embassy pets were with them as per Jamie's daily demands.

Jenkins looked relieved to see us. "Thank you for believing me, Ambassador."

"Not sure what you think I believe, because right now what I believe is that I'll have a double helping of everything on the table."

"I'll get that for you, Kitty, darling," Pierre said as he helped me to a seat next to Jenkins. "You and Jeff just get things handled."

"Okay. So, Bruce, what's got you so spooked?"

"Cameron Maurer. He's not . . . normal anymore."

"Ah, as to that . . ." Looked at Mrs. Maurer, who was on Jenkins' other side, with Raj next to her. Raj patted her hand.

"It won't . . . affect me," she said. "I mean, I've already rum the gamut of emotions in this past day, and I've heard what Bruce had to say. What's one more horrible thing?"

"Then, I can say without a doubt that your son is an android now. Has Jenkins here said anything different?" Probably asked that a little more snidely than I'd intended, but I was really focused on getting the food Pierre had placed in front of me into my mouth.

"No. Look, Ambassador, I know I came off badly before—"

"You came off as being in the employ of our enemies. We have a lot of enemies, so it was hard to accurately guess which set had hired you. But hired reputation hit man was definitely how you came across. It's what, as far as I'm concerned, you probably still are. The timing of your call to me was incredibly suspect, and for all we know, you're here to perpetrate some evil and are just a really good actor."

"Ambassador, I can see why you'd think that. Though I believe I've given your staff plenty of proof of my intentions."

"Which are?"

"I need protection and want to help you. And I want the Armstrong-Martini ticket to win."

Stopped with a bite halfway into my mouth. "Seriously? That's a hell of a party switch in the course of an hour or so."

"Well, discovering that the vice presidential candidate you're trying to support is actually some evil robot being controlled by the presidential candidate is more than unsettling. And I got a look at the bomb debrief information—you were telling the truth. And I was at the political protest yesterday, meaning I'd have been killed by the ricin gas, too. With friends like these, who needs enemies?"

"Who are your former friends, Bruce? We'd love some names."

"Harvey Gutermuth is one."

"Oh, the head of Club Fifty-One. Great company. Who are the others? Names, Bruce, I want names."

"Well, what Harvey says, Farley Pecker supports. They're

the ones responsible for the ricin bombs. Club Fifty-One has the largest worldwide reach of all those who oppose the A-Cs being on Earth, and Pecker's people make enthusiastic guerillas."

"Church of Hate and Intolerance covered, check."

"You're certain Club Fifty-One set all the bombs?" Chuckie asked.

"Yes, but I'm sure they took direction from someone. Harvey likes to act like he's in charge, and he does run the Club itself, but it's clear that he has someone who tells him what to do and when."

"Not a surprise." It was certainly how Club 51 had worked in the past, so why change a successful setup? "However, I find it almost impossible to believe you're taking all your cues from these combined groups of total wackos, Bruce."

"Sorry, I thought it was obvious. The Cleary-Maurer campaign asked me to support their efforts. For my support, I got unlimited access to their campaign, exclusive interviews with the candidates, hot tips, and so forth. And the support of Gutermuth and Pecker, which isn't an insubstantial thing, given their numbers."

"Political insider trading. I can see why it was appealing. So, what changed you from the Side of the Sith to Return to the Jedi?"

"I was early to join the campaign on a tour of Area Fifty-One. It was supposed to be my first time using your gate technology, so I was rather excited. No one was in campaign headquarters, which was odd. I'm an investigative reporter, I investigated." He looked chagrined. "Honestly, I was thinking that perhaps your people had done something to Gideon or . . . Cameron or one of their people." He swallowed and looked ill.

"Go on," Jeff said gently. He leaned next to me. "He's telling the truth, so you may want to lighten up on him," he whispered in my ear.

"Mmmm-hmmm." Whenever Jeff did this, all I actually wanted to do was rub up against him. Controlled the impulse, though it took great effort. Score one for my massively impressive diplomatic skills.

"The door to a back room was slightly ajar. I heard voices,

and my reporting instincts kicked in. So I snuck over and remained outside the room, but was in a position where I could see in. And . . . I saw Gideon and several women, one of whom was very young and also quite beautiful."

"Stephanie," Jeff said.

"I didn't catch her name, any of their names. They were . . . working on Cameron. They had the back of his head opened like small double doors, his shirt was off and his chest was opened the same way. There were no organs I could see, just machinery. They were talking about calibrating his programming, saying that the doctor hadn't done it quite right. Someone else joined them, a man, but I didn't see him. However, whoever he was, Gideon and the women instantly acted like he was in charge."

"Could have been the Mastermind," Christopher said. "Would you recognize his voice?"

Jenkins shook his head. "It was too muffled. I could tell it was a man, and that's all. If I'd been able to stay longer, I might have. I certainly wanted to see who this was. But someone else came in through the front door, and I realized I was going to be discovered. I had to pretend I was looking for everyone, so I called out. Gideon came to greet me, shutting the door behind him. I don't know if I looked guilty, but I told him I'd just started to feel ill and feared food poisoning, and asked if I could beg off this visit."

"What did he say? I mean, I know you didn't go."

"He expressed concern for my health, then Cameron came out of the same room. But he was acting strangely, so I think they just slammed his doors shut."

"Probably," Chuckie said. "By the time we see him again, though, they'll have recalibrated him. Cleary was there when Kitty was trying to get through to Maurer. They won't wait to get him locked down."

"Then what?" Jeff asked Jenkins.

"Then I hightailed it out of there and called the Ambassador and came here. Where, honestly, I don't want to leave." He shot Mrs. Maurer a commiserating smile. "I'm very happy to follow Nancy's lead and hide with the people who aren't actually trying to put a robot into the White House."

"Oh, I'm sure they're trying to do worse than that. Who was it who came in after you, did you see him or her?"

Jenkins nodded. "Senator Zachary Kramer."

"And yet Kramer didn't make the trip to Home Base." I exchanged a very meaningful look with Vance. "Thoughts?"

He grimaced. "Zachary and Marcia are fully against you, and have been for ages, I told you that before. He must be jockeying for some kind of position within Gideon's cabinet."

Had a very bad thought. "You know, Cameron Maurer is now a detriment, not an asset. They know we know he's an android, and they know that we know how to destroy but also deal with androids."

"Every android has a self-destruct mechanism," Chuckie said. "And I'm sure they can be remotely destructed, too."

"Does that mean we need to change Colonel Butler's location?"

"Wish you'd mentioned that before we moved him into the Science Center," Christopher snapped.

"It'll be fine," Jeff said, in a warning tone. Christopher rolled his eyes, but stopped snarking.

"Didn't think of it at the time, sorry," Chuckie replied. "I was too busy keeping him from blowing up at Home Base."

Jenkins went pale. "He's an android, too? My God, how many are there?"

"Do you read Mister Joel Oliver's columns?"

Jenkins cast an ashamed look in Oliver's direction. "Not as often as I should."

"Damn straight, dude. You need to get caught up. But to be clear, unlike you, MJO here doesn't actually write fiction. You can learn a lot from him, and you might want to." Looked around the table. "I go back to my original concern—are we at risk of someone blowing Butler up before we can help him?"

"Probably." Jeff sighed and pulled his phone out. "Hey James. Yeah, it's been so long. Chuck just pointed out that Butler might have a destruct sequence that can be triggered automatically. Oh? Oh. Great. No need to take that tone. Yes, fine, I'll relay that to the others. You're really tense, I think you need a vacation." He hung up.

"That sounded fun."

"Yeah. James said to tell all of you that he's already thought of that, and a fail-safe room has been constructed within one of the cells. They're also close to having him completely offline, and are already checking for external triggering mechanisms. In other words, we need to stop trying to do Alpha Team's jobs and do our own."

"You're right, he does sound tense. So, Bruce, we're going to want to get a full debrief on everything you have regarding the opposition's campaign to see where they've planned to perpetrate more evil, and we'll need that pronto."

"Already started, Ambassador," Raj said. "Most of us have heard this story for the second time now."

"Blah, blah, blah, but good job. Does anyone know why the President called Cleary and Maurer in for a private 'not a request' meeting?"

Jeff cleared his throat. "Ah, I do, baby. I called your mother and told her what was going on."

"Okay. I'm now worried that they're going to set Maurer off to explode while they're with the President and Mom."

"They won't," Jenkins said. "If they did that, the vice president would take over, and the party would run him for President and Armstrong for vice president. And that ticket would not lose."

"Why isn't the current VP running?" Despite living in D.C. and having a career where knowing all this stuff was considered vital, I just couldn't bring myself to care most of the time.

"He's spent eight years watching what the President's gone through and decided that playing golf is a lot more rewarding," Jenkins said.

Oliver nodded. "He's older and just wants to retire. If he had to step in for the end of the term, however, he would be the good soldier and run for president to support the party and the country."

"Well, that's good, then, because that means Maurer won't be killing my mother and the President, along with whoever else. But unless we can get him right after this meeting, he's lost to us forever, I think. I'm sorry, Squeaky."

Mrs. Maurer looked at me. "Can you help him, if we save him somehow? Or will he always be a robotic copy of my son?"

"We don't know," Chuckie said. "Butler's the first android that could fight programming, and appears to have retained a sense of self as a human. We think it's because he was turned unwillingly."

"There is no way the man I raised would willingly become what he has. I know you're all worried that I'm horrified by his being turning into this . . . thing, and I am. But this is honestly a better explanation than him just turning against everything his family has ever stood for on a whim. I'm asking, though, because I'm willing to try something, but there's no point if there's no hope."

"There's always hope. Always. It might be a tiny sliver of hope, but it's always there. What's your plan, Squeaky?"

She pulled her phone out of her purse and dialed. It took a few seconds, but clearly someone picked up. "Cameron? Yes, it's me. No, I'm fine. It's you, dear, who are not fine." She sighed. Could hear someone talking and assumed Maurer was telling her whatever party line he'd been programmed with.

Looked at my hand. The numbers I'd written there were smudged. Pulled a pen out of my purse, got up, handed the pen to Chuckie, who was next to Jeff, and shoved my hand at him.

The benefits of knowing someone since ninth grade were without number. He got it without my saying anything and wrote the numbers down clearly. Trotted over to Mrs. Maurer. "Squeaky," I said softly, "read these to him."

"Cameron, dear, I'd like to share something with you." She read the numbers slowly and carefully. "Cameron, did you hear me?" She repeated the numbers. "Dear, if you're still in there, please come to the American Centaurion Embassy. We want to help you, dear. I miss my son and I want my son back. *My* son, not what they've turned you into. Yes." She said the numbers one more time. "I hope to see you soon, Cameron dear." Then she hung up.

"How did it go?"

She shook her head. "I honestly have no guess."

My phone rang. Jeff tried to dig it out of my purse, without success. Christopher put his hand in and pulled it out. "First try. Hello? Oh, hey, Angela. Yeah, it's Christopher, Kitty's just not near her phone. No, she's fine, hang on." He tossed the phone to me.

"Hey Mom, what's up?"

"Cameron Maurer took a call from his mother and then took off running so fast that no one could stop him. We're fortunate that he didn't break down White House walls. What's going on?"

"Mom, I'll call you back. If anyone says we killed Maurer, it's a lie. It'll be that he self-destructed on us." Hung up. "Com on!"

"Yes, Chief?"

"Walter, we need a containment unit here pronto and all the kids and non-military trained personnel moved to the Pontifex's Residence immediately. We have an android trying to come in from the cold depths of Hell."

CHAPTER 80

"WE'LL WATCH THE DOOR," Len said, as he and Kyle jumped up and ran to the foyer.

"I'll go with them, just in case," Raj said, as he zipped off.

"I'm going to get Grandmother and ensure she goes," Adriana said, as she ran off.

"Ah, Ambassador?" Pierre asked nervously.

"You and Vance and whoever else get the heck out of here. Make sure the kids are all over safely."

"I'm staying here," Mrs. Maurer said firmly. "You need me. Cameron needs me."

"I agree. Bruce, MJO, staying or leaving?"

"I want them leaving," Jeff said, Commander Voice on Full. "Jennifer, Jeremy, get everyone out of here and do like-wise." The Barones grabbed people and they took off at hyperspeed. This left me, Jeff, Christopher, Chuckie, and Mrs. Maurer in the dining room. Flung my purse over my neck.

"Chief," Walter shared over the intercom, "your father suggests going to the Israeli Embassy instead of the Pontifex's residence. Agents stationed with the Israelis report that embassy to be secured."

"Dad wants to party some more, doesn't he? What does the Paul think?"

"Pontifex Gower agrees that under the circumstances, our personnel being with others who can both protect and vouch for them is probably wise."

"Make it so, Walter. Immediately if not sooner, for all personnel. Tell the Pontifex we include him in the people we expect to go over. Tell Rahmi and Rhee I want them guarding the Pontifex, Jamie, the other kids, and their caretakers—they need to be on full alert. And please advise Alpha Team of what's going on." Why stress Reader out any more than we already had? "I want all visitors and residents of the Zoo transferred with extreme care, our prisoner in particular."

"Ah, the Pontifex says that the prisoner doesn't wish to leave the premises. She insists it's not because she's afraid of the Israelis but because she thinks she's figured out how to, ah, hot-wire an android."

"Gotcha. We'll bring our android to the Zoo, then. Keep all fifth-floor personnel there, Walter, but get anyone else like Amy or Abigail out of there. And tell them to have the floater gate in the computer center calibrated for the Pontifex's Residence in case we all have to fling ourselves through it really, really fast."

"Speaking of fast," Christopher said, "we need to decide who's grabbing the android when he shows up."

"Has to be you and me," Jeff said. "I'll grab him, you shove a pen or whatever in his ear."

"It has to be exact," Chuckie said. "I know it looked like I just shoved that in randomly, but Ravi gave me specific instructions."

"Conveniently, you still have my pen in your hand. I'm willing to sacrifice it to the cause." Hey, it wasn't my Mont Blanc.

"He's here," Kyle called.

"Walter, are all the kids out?"

"Yes, Chief, just now."

"Okay, keep the com open and be prepared to run really fast." We all raced to the foyer to see Cameron Maurer come through the front door.

"Mother?" he sounded funny. Fuzzy and almost metallic. This wasn't a good sound.

"Hurry, guys."

"Let them help you, Cameron," Mrs. Maurer said. "Don't fight them."

Jeff grabbed Maurer from behind. It was a good thing that Chuckie was the assigned Ear Stabber, though, because despite his mother's admonition, Maurer almost tossed Jeff off. It took both him and Christopher to hold Maurer still.

"Mother . . . I'm-m-m-m sorry."

"Hurry, Chuckie."

"Hope this works and we're lucky a second time. Otherwise, been great knowing all of you." With that, Chuckie slammed my pen into Maurer's ear.

Thankfully, the same thing that happened with Butler happened now. Maurer went still as if dead or inactivated. "To the computer lab," Jeff said, then he and Christopher disappeared.

Grabbed Chuckie and Mrs. Maurer, Raj grabbed Len and Kyle, and we took off after them, using the stairs because hyperspeed was faster than any elevator could ever hope to be.

Met up with those who'd remained in the Zoo in a couple of seconds. Maurer was already flat on his back and Chernobog was giving instructions to Hacker International.

A team of Field agents were setting up a 10x10x10 metal box at hyperspeed while another team impressively moved all the equipment to a safe distance while also not unplugging it or actually disturbing Hacker International and Chernobog. In addition to thick metal walls and a thick door, the containment room also had windows made out of the thickest glass I'd ever seen.

Serene pulled me aside while White held Mrs. Maurer as she gagged. All four of us, just like everyone else in the room, were still poised to run. "Once Richard calmed things down, Chernobog cooperated. We have all our data back. We're not done verifying, but it looks to be all here. Chernobog was motivated to find our work on defusing androids."

"Thank God."

"Yes, she's terrified of the Dingo, though she's trying to pretend she isn't."

"She's incredibly smart, and her being afraid proves it."

"Serene, we need you," Stryker called as they rolled Maurer onto his stomach and opened the back of his head just as Jenkins had described. Was glad White was holding

Mrs. Maurer, because it was horrible to see as a relative stranger, so it had to be infinitely worse for her to see her child this way. Her freaking out and sobbing was also a clue that this was, indeed, horrific for her to experience.

"Commander, the containment room is ready," one of the agents said.

"No time," Ravi said urgently. He had a Bluetooth in his ear and was clearly talking to someone, probably at Dulce. "You have to start right now."

Jeff and Christopher were asked to move out of the way, and Serene went to work. I'd have watched but my phone chose this moment to ring again.

I was glad for the distraction—medical stuff wasn't my "thing" and while this was the least bloody medical stuff I'd seen, ever, it was still horrible. The tension in the room was high, too, because we were all waiting to go boom. Could tell the Field agents were wondering why they'd bothered to build a containment unit if we weren't going to use it. Kind of agreed with them, but oh well.

So, I happily answered the call as Jeff moved me near to the stationary floater gate we had in the lab—that always sounded like an oxymoron, but wasn't.

"Hi Mom. Kind of in a situation here."

"So your father's told me. Thought you'd like to hear the latest, however. Per a statement Gideon Cleary just released, Cameron Maurer has taken ill and resigned from the campaign. They're announcing that Zachary Kramer is stepping in as Cleary's running mate."

"That's hella fast. Wasn't he just there with you and the President?"

"Yes, and the moment Maurer left Cleary shared that this was something they were both about to tell us."

"Unreal. No one believes him, do they?"

"Well, the Secretary of Transportation claims to."

"Langston Whitmore will side with anyone who hates us, so no surprise there. What about the rest?"

"Varying degrees of suspicion. Frankly, I think most feel that Cleary made the decision because Maurer just acted like a crazy person in front of them."

"Makes sense. But can he do that? Isn't their convention over?"

"Yes, but precedent exists for this. Since you're certain Maurer has been turned into an android, and we think Kramer's still human, this is a positive."

"I'm not sure that Maurer's going to come out of this as anything but an inoperable piece of machinery in a Cameron Suit." Glanced over. Serene was deep inside his head.

The positive, if you could call it that, was that I could see gray matter in there, surrounded by wires and such, but there. Meaning they'd presumably left his brain intact in some way. Maybe that's why he and Butler had been able to fight the programming. Maybe we'd live to find out. However, I didn't like Serene's chances if he exploded, though, nor Ravi and Henry's, since they were assisting her.

"Just ensure that none of you die trying to save him."

"Doing our best and thanks for reminding me to be stressed out of my mind. I'd forgotten for all of one second. On the plus side, Serene says Chernobog gave us back all our data."

"Don't trust it."

"Well, it seems to be helping. She's motivated to not be assassinated."

Gasps in the room caused me to jump. Apparently they were gasps of appreciation, as Serene dropped some circuit thingy into Henry's open palm. Went back to focusing on Mom's latest warnings.

"This is a woman who redefines the term 'sly fox.' Keep her where you can see her, keep her under the severest form of lock and key, and ensure that your computer experts aren't so awed to be in her presence that they allow her to pull one over on them. Because she will if she can. Captivity isn't something she enjoys."

"Gotcha. We'll have Chuckie devise a clever plan once we see if, you know, we all survive this sorta rescue attempt. Oh, and tell me there are going to be amazingly stringent protections going on at our National Convention."

"There are."

"Great. Where's it going to be, by the way."

"Why am I even remotely surprised that you don't know? At the Baltimore Convention Center. Wisely keeping close to D.C. this year."

"Good to know."

"I'm sure it is, kitten. Try not to die, I'd miss you."

"Good to know. And, same here, Mom."

CHAPTER 81

WE HUNG UP and I unwillingly turned my attention back to the drama happening on the computer lab floor.

Serene was still digging around in the back of Maurer's head like a brain surgeon. Or a computer technician. Kind of both.

Henry was holding a lamp directly over Maurer's head with one hand and all of the spare exploding parts with his other, which impressed me with Henry's manliness more than anything he'd ever done before. Ravi was functioning as the Head Nurse and handing Serene instruments or taking them away, depending, while also passing along tips from whoever he was talking to at the Science Center.

Omega Red was assisting Chernobog and passing along information as well. Stryker and Big George, however, seemed to be continuing the download of our old data.

Sidled over to Stryker because my staring at Serene wasn't going to help anybody, me especially. Distraction, that was the key. Otherwise I'd probably cause Jeff to overload empathically. Hey, it was my excuse and I was sticking with it.

"Eddy," I said in a low voice, "my mother doesn't trust that Chernobog's giving us the real goods, so to speak."

He nodded. "I think what we have so far is the real deal. But we had to download it quickly to get to the information on androids. We kept it in a separate server we have here. It's isolated, not connected to the rest of the system, or any other system."

"Good security."

"Only if the data coming is bad in some way. If it's good, that means that much more of a delay in getting the information back out to Dulce and elsewhere." He looked over his shoulder. "And if that explodes right now, then we've lost everything."

"Yeah, thanks for the reminder. But Mom's right. This woman's spent decades hiding, in plain sight most of the time, and all of that time covering her butt. If she's helping us, there's going to be more to it than her hoping we can call off the assassins after her."

"Yeah, and if it were me, I'd build in a fail-safe so that if I didn't check in with whatever my special codes are at a specified time or similar, the data would corrupt, or worse."

We looked at each other. "Enjoy searching for that."

"I won't be able to find it quickly, none of us will." He grimaced. "It's kind of tough on the ego, to discover that there's some old lady who's so much better at your life's work than you are."

"She's had a lot more years at it." Patted his shoulder. "You're still number one in my book, Eddy."

He gave me a rather nice smile. "Thanks, Kitty. Always nice to be appreciated versus threatened."

Stared at him for a moment. "Yeah," I said slowly, "you're right. Flies to honey and all that." Turned around and went over to Chernobog, who seemed to be done with her part of the medical stuff, at least for right now. "Thank you."

She eyed me suspiciously. "For what?"

"For giving us the data so swiftly so that we'd have a hope of saving what's left of this man and Colonel Butler."

"It was in my best interests."

"Maybe. But you could have stalled it out. I just wanted you to know that we appreciate this."

"Enough to let me go?"

"No. I wasn't kidding. You need to give us what you've taken from the U.S. government, and we need to verify that this data, and what you've given back to us today, is secure and not rigged with something."

"Why would I do that?"

"Because it would be smart, and if there's one thing I know you are it's smart."

She gave me a long look. "True. I realize you're holding back the other things you say I need to do so you get all the information you want. I'd like to know what those are."

"And I'd like to know who hired you to hit us last year. You go first."

"I didn't meet them face-to-face."

"Oh, come on. Why would they trust you without meeting you?"

She rolled her eyes. "Why would *I* be willing to meet with *them*? Until today, I've managed to be known to only a handful of people. Why in the world would I allow people who obviously have no morals or scruples to see who I am?"

She had a point. And it was interesting that she seemed to feel that she, unlike her employers, had morals or scruples. Hoped that was true, versus the Sly Fox playing me. "They were able to find your son."

"Because I told them where he was. That was my price of participation—that they free Russell."

That was confirmation of our strong suspicions already, which tracked. Then again, she could have figured we'd have already guessed this. My brain was already tired of trying to extrapolate all the potential if-then statements regarding Chernobog's motivations. "We know that's not his real name."

She shrugged. "Who cares? It's the name that works for right now."

"Ronald Yates was his father, wasn't he?"

"Yes." Her lips quirked. "You seem to know quite a lot of things about me I'd thought were well hidden."

"We kind of have an edge on all things Yates. Not as much of an edge as our enemies do, but enough to make some educated guesses. So, what's Russell's talent?"

"He has none."

"Bunk."

"No, it's true. He has no talents. Believe me, I paid attention."

"What did Yates think of that?"

"I have no idea. I never let him know we had a child."

"Oh, come on. I'm supposed to believe that?"

"Believe what you want. I know what he did to his other children. I didn't want my child to become some sick scientist's laboratory rat."

"How old is Russell?"

"I'm sure he's told you, and you can guess from looking at him. He's forty-five."

This didn't track. Chernobog turned away from me and started giving Serene some instructions. Decided now was as good a time as any to risk it and sent Buchanan a text to call me if he could. My phone rang almost immediately. Trotted back to my spot right by the floater gate. "What's up, Missus Chief?"

"I have a question for your new bestest bud. Was the name Russell Koslow on the his list?"

"Hang on." Heard voices murmuring. "No. But we're assuming that's not Koslow's real name."

"Yeah, but he's about the same age and wasn't listed."

More background murmuring. "Siler knows of no other sibling in his age range."

"Interesting." So, Chernobog was probably telling the truth. "Thanks." Caught him up quickly on what was going on here—trying to downplay the danger, mostly so I wouldn't freak out anyone in the room, or stress myself out even more—which he relayed to Team Assassin. "So, Chernobog says she hid the fact that they had a kid together from Yates," I said by way of wrapping up.

"Per your uncles, she's extremely cautious. They feel that this tracks much more with what they know of her than her being a Yates groupie."

"Gotcha, and thanks. See you soon if we don't blow up."

"I'd tell you to be careful but no one in that room other than Chernobog seems to comprehend what that phrase means."

We hung up just as Serene gave a shout and I jumped. "Got them!" she said triumphantly as I landed. Thankfully, no one but Jeff was looking at me. He put his arm around me and hugged me, without even chuckling. Too much.

"The bombs?" I asked.

"Essentially, at least some. The self-destruct mechanism is fully removed." Serene carefully closed the back of Maurer's head. "Now, let's turn him over."

"Why?"

"Because the remote destruct wasn't in his head, Kitty. So I have to assume it's in his sternum somewhere." Goody. We still had another bomb defusing scenario to go through. Couldn't wait.

"It might not be an explosive," Chuckie said. "If they can simulate a heart attack, that would work just as well."

"Not if paramedics showed up," Kyle pointed out.

"Oh, I imagine they'd have an ambulance standing by in that case. They're not blowing someone up on a whim."

Serene nodded. "Good point, Kitty. I'll look for both, Chuck."

"There are different intricacies," Chernobog said. Then she started listing a lot of very detailed scientific things that my brain decided Chuckie should listen to. He'd advise me when I needed to pay attention.

"Commander, I'm going to have to insist that the containment room be used," the Field agent said when Chernobog paused for breath. "We can move the body for you, and do the work if you want."

"I'll let you move him, but you're not doing the work," Serene said, in her Commander Voice, which was a lot like Jeff's and Reader's in timbre.

The agents nodded and moved Maurer into the room, putting him flat on his back. This room was set up inside like an impromptu medical lab, too. Serene and Henry were able to go in, but Ravi couldn't get the Bluetooth signal through the thick metal, so he stood outside the door and relayed instructions. Fortunately, there was plenty of light, so Henry was able to show his range and hand her implements while also holding bombs.

This was great in that, if Maurer exploded, most of the room would be protected. However, in order for Serene to hear anyone, the door was opened toward the rest of Hacker International, Chernobog, and a ton of equipment.

Tried not to wonder if this was worth it or not. Forced myself to believe that Serene would be able to get herself and Henry out, and the door closed, before everything blew up. Figured this was how Reader had felt about all of us for this entire day. Made a mental note to ask Pierre to send him a gift basket with chocolates and spa certificates should we all survive.

This train of thought wasn't helping my mental state at all. So, while Serene, Chernobog, and the rest went back to work or kibitzing, depending, I went back to thinking and pretending I wasn't watching a game of High-Stakes Operation.

We'd countered every move thrown against us so far. But the other side had also bounced back from our counterattacks. Whatever happened with Maurer, Cleary had already given us an out by saying that Maurer was quitting because he was ill, which seemed oddly wrong.

"What is it?" Jeff asked me in a low voice. "You're worried, but not just about what Serene's doing."

"Well, if we, hopefully, don't blow up, I'm indeed worried about other things."

"About what?"

"About everything. Because it's been too easy."

CHAPTER 82

"EASY?" Jeff's voice was still low, but he managed to get a lot of outraged surprise in there anyway. "You call all of what we've been through for the past, what, a little over a day easy?"

"Yeah, in a way." Tried to figure out what felt so wrong to me. "It's like they're . . . testing. Nothing's been coordinated, in that sense. Sure, they've hit us with one thing after another, but, last time, they'd guessed almost every move we'd make."

"Last time they had Ronaldo mind-reading Gladys."

"Yeah. But there's more than that. I mean, they've announced that Maurer's out of the race because of illness. If he blows up on us right now, or deactivates in some way, well, then we can call the President, tell him, and he'll have his people make up a very believable lie. Heck, we could do it ourselves." That was me, focused on the positive idea that if Maurer blew up we'd all be around to make casual calls to the President and such.

"We could also share that Maurer is an android with the entire world," Jeff said dryly.

"Only if he's not blown up. But say he survives essentially intact. Our sharing this news would panic the world, and they know we won't do that unless we have to. And you know that if we show off one android, we have to be able to say 'and these people made the android' and we can't do that right now, because we don't know who's carrying on Antony Marling's heinous work. And the next question is 'how many androids are there' and we have no idea. So they give us this Get Out Of Jail Free Card to share, and if we take it, awesome for both sides."

"That just seems like convenience for them they'll generously share with us because, in the grand scheme, it doesn't matter. So far, you're not showing me that anything happening against us was actually easy. All I see is a lot of bad coming at us, from all sides."

"But they seem so . . . scattered."

"So? Sounds like the usual three or four plans acting against us at one time."

"Yeah, but in the past, all actions against us were related. And I know they're all related now. Somehow." Considered past Operations. "You know, Operation Sherlock was all about Apprentice Tryouts. What if this is similar, but with different goals? Or a different form of competition?"

"I honestly have no guess, baby. Do you really think the Mastermind showed up personally at the Cleary campaign headquarters?" He ran his hand through his hair. "Because that means that Stephanie knows the Mastermind."

"Well, her father knew the Mastermind, I guarantee it, so why not her? But no, I doubt the Mastermind was dropping by, though his Apprentice might have. Or, rather, one of the several people who think they're the Apprentice. Despite my numbering system from earlier, Leventhal Reid pretty much confirmed that more than one person thought they were the New Apprentice. But Reid is the real Apprentice . . ."

"What? I can tell you just made some connection. Do you think Reid was who Jenkins heard?"

"Maybe, but that's not what I'm thinking about. I'm thinking about what Reid said last year . . . and Stephanie. What if this isn't about us so much as it's about us cleaning house for the Mastermind?"

"What? How the hell do you get that from anything?"

Chuckie came over. "I heard you, and no, you weren't talking that loudly, I'm just trained to listen very carefully. Kitty, go on with that idea."

"Okay. Survival of the fittest."

"What?" Jeff said. "Are you testing to see if one of us is an android?"

"No," Chuckie said. "She means that the Mastermind is culling his herd."

"Exactly. See who survives against us, they're worthy to keep around. Whoever isn't skilled or sneaky enough we kill or remove as a threat. If they destroy us, great, they move up in the hierarchy. But if they don't, then us getting rid of them means we've culled a weak one and the side benefit is those who are left hate us that much more."

"I can see that," Chuckie said. "And that's a long-game strategy, and that's his style."

"Where does Stephanie fit in?" Jeff asked.

"She's someone primed to hate us who we're all going to be loath to kill. She knows it, the Mastermind knows it." And guaranteed she'd be Reid's type. Heck, she was a Dazzler. She'd be anyone and everyone's type, maybe even the Mastermind's. "So Stephanie is valuable not only for what she can do but also as much as what she can get away with doing without recrimination."

"You threatened to kill her," Chuckie pointed out.

"But we all know she'll have to be ready to kill one of you, or Jamie, Mom, Dad, someone I love, or be about to, you know, drop poison into the city's water supply, before I actually do it."

"I don't think I can," Jeff said quietly.

"If it were her or Jamie you could," Chuckie said calmly. "But I know what you mean. Reid or LaRue I'd like to kill on sight. But Stephanie is different. And believe me, they all know it."

"Sentimentality is the ultimate weakness." Chernobog came over to us. "Serene is quite talented. We believe we have removed all the destruct sequences within the android. But you might want to be ready to run if we're wrong when we turn him back on."

While one Field agent recalibrated the floater gate, two more zipped off with a pan filled with circuits and the like. Hoped they were taking them to the middle of nowhere, but they were probably taking them back to Serene's Bomb Shop so she could play with them at her leisure.

"Thanks." Chose not to mention that I'd been ready to run this entire time. If I was coming across as calm, cool, and collected to Chernobog, so much the better. "May I ask you something? Well, probably more than one something."

She shrugged. "Why not?"

"Do you know or have a guess as to who the Mastermind is, or who his Apprentice is or are, in case you know of more than one?"

"Someone in your government. Because I was hired via a government contract."

Let that sit on the air for a moment. "Which division?" Chuckie asked finally.

She shrugged. "Didn't say and I didn't care. There are many slush funds used by the Alphabet Agencies to get dirty work done. This request bounced through many different channels, but, ultimately, the buyer was from the U.S. government."

"That's why you were in Guantanamo, isn't it? Whoever it is suggested you stay there."

She shook her head. "No, I was already there. Whoever it was *knew* I was there. It was part of why I agreed to take the job—they had a line on where I was. But they met my price, so . . ." She shrugged again.

Ran through my list of potential suspects, which were people we'd met once we'd come to D.C. Anyone dead and not regenerated via clone or android was, of course, no longer suspect.

Cliff had been a target during Operation Sherlock, and Horn had been one now. Considering how close both had come to being blown to bits, that removed them from my list. Langston Whitmore remained at the top of this list, as did Gideon Cleary. Same with those running Gaultier Enterprises, Titan Security, and YatesCorp. And yet, none of them were our intimates, so how would they know our strategies and game plans?

Mom and Dad were out. Chuckie was the Mastermind's ultimate target. Senator Armstrong had so much more to gain from being our friend that he seemed unlikely. The President already had power and the Vice President just wanted to play golf, so again, not really high on the list of possibilities.

Lillian Culver and Guy Gadoire both seemed more and more unlikely every day. The other lobbyists we worked with weren't nearly as intimate with us. Vance could be the Mastermind. He was smart enough and hid it extremely well. But why the hate for Chuckie if that was the case?

Senator McMillan? Maybe. We all loved and respected him. He was a possibility, but one I couldn't bring myself to believe. Maybe that meant the Mastermind *was* McMillan. Or Colonel Franklin, someone else we trusted and I couldn't believe would be a bad guy or against us. Same with Captain Morgan. Hell, maybe it was my Uncle Mort.

This speculation was getting me nowhere. Gave up and went back to the relevant conundrum. "Did you know Butler was an android?"

"No. Absolutely not. I would never have stayed. Honestly, I thought he was a nice man. Good to work for, always polite, never demanded more from anyone than he demanded from himself."

"So, you liked him?" Jeff asked.

"Yes, I did."

"Did he change how he behaved at all in the time you were working for him?" Chuckie asked.

"No. He was always the same. I assume this means he was always an android, as long as I knew him?"

"Probably." My turn to ask a question. "Did he have a meeting with the Cleary-Maurer ticket on his calendar for today? And don't say you don't know or don't remember. You were working as his secretary, and you were actually doing the job."

"It was interesting and put me where I wanted to be. But you're right, I have his schedule memorized. And no, there was no meeting with anyone on today's books, because he was supposed to be at Luke Air Force Base still. He came back because I sent him a text, telling him I felt I was in danger."

"So, why were Cleary and Maurer there, then, let alone Stephanie?" Jeff asked. "They had to have come for a reason."

Had to give it to stress, things were falling into place in my mind. "Cleary's an Apprentice. Or maybe an Apprentice to an Apprentice. Just because he was respectful toward someone else doesn't mean he doesn't think he's the Mastermind's right hand man. And even if he's Apprentice the Lower, that doesn't mean he doesn't want to get rid of his competition."

"Makes sense," Chuckie said. "But why visit Home Base for no reason?"

"They had a reason, it's just not the one we'd originally thought. They weren't there to kill Butler, they were there to get rid of a loose end. And Stephanie was there to make sure it happened."

Chernobog stared at me. "You think they came to kill me?"

"Abso-damn-lutely. They rolled really well with the punches, but they wouldn't have known we were there. Because we evacuated the building, no one knew what had happened to you or Butler, and I guarantee only a handful of people knew we'd come over at all. But Butler wasn't where Cleary and his team thought he'd be, which was in another state, and he was only at Home Base because Team Oliver was following you and you caught on."

"And you're a huge loose end," Chuckie said. "Especially because we have the one thing you care about under custody they can't affect."

"Not without giving themselves away, at any rate," Jeff added.

"How would they have done that?" Chernobog asked. "There would have been witnesses."

"Cameron the Android would have held you and one of them would have injected you with the heart attack poison or whatever. Then they're there to be all upset over your death. You're an old lady, who would question it, especially because a presidential candidate was a witness. Done, confirmed, and moving on up in the ranks."

Jeff nodded. "I can see it. Kill her, we never get our data back, we can't offer to release Kozlow as incentive, it's all just gone."

"And you can't tell us they're in the government. Which is more of a confirmation, but still, it's a confirmation we didn't have until three minutes ago and would never have if you were dead."

"But they hired the Dingo to kill me."

"They did that in part to get him the hell out of D.C. for a while and possibly as cover for Cleary and his team if your death looked suspicious to someone. And if Cleary, Maurer, and Stephanie failed, well, there's a better team coming along in the next day or so. But the Dingo would have had to take a flight to get to you and Cleary used a gate." Or the Z'porrah cube, but I managed not to share that with the best hacker in the world.

She gave me another long look. "So, the rumors about you are indeed true."

"And they are?"

"That you're the Dingo's quite beloved niece. 'Maybe I'm Russian back there somewhere' my ass. That's why you feel you can stop him from killing me, if I do what you want. Because you'll ask him for that favor."

Quite beloved? Wow. I was really and truly moving up in the world of Assassins International. Felt all flattered. At least someone cared. Oh, sure, they were cold-blooded hired killers, but not when it came to me, apparently. Put this one in the win column. It would undoubtedly come back to bite me in the butt, but I could enjoy it for right now.

"Essentially, yeah. It'll have to be worth his while, in a big way, but I'm pretty damn sure that the world's best hacker, by far and bar none, can probably make a big way happen without too much trouble."

"So the enemy of my enemy is my friend." There was a lot of that line going around this Operation. And for once it was working in our favor. Another one for the win column. Truly a red-letter hour, as long as Maurer didn't explode. Chernobog looked around the computer lab. "This is not such a bad place to spend time."

Jeff groaned. "I knew it. You're planning to move in and stay, aren't you?"

"What, you'd leave an old woman on the streets? I thought you were a nice boy."

Couldn't help it, I laughed. "I hate to admit this, but I like her, I really do."

CHAPTER 83

CHERNOBOG SMILED AT ME, and it looked genuine. "I may like you, too. You're all far too trusting for your own good, however."

Tensed for an attack. There was none. She rolled her eyes at me. "I don't do physical violence. As has been pointed out, I'm an old woman, and, unlike Olga, that was never my strong suit. I meant you're too trusting with me and with everything, in general. Trusting people are much easier to fool."

Jeff shrugged. "We just like to believe the best about people. It's a failing, I know, but it's one I'm glad we have."

She stared at him. "You mean that."

"I do. I'd rather trust that most people will do the right thing, and the brave thing, most of the time, than to think that everyone's an evil, cowardly creep just waiting to stick it to me and mine."

"I cover that side," Chuckie said.

She chuckled. "Well, it's good that one of you does." She looked up at Jeff. "But it's no wonder the opposition doesn't want you on the ticket. You're an impressive man, and that's a rare thing these days."

"I think you're impressive, too," I said to Chuckie.

Jeff sighed. "Always there's someone impressing my wife more than me."

Chernobog snorted. "I doubt it."

"I have another question. Why do you think what's going on now is going on?"

She blinked. "Excuse me? English isn't my first language, though it's rarely an issue. However, I have no idea what you mean."

"So few ever do, Boggy, so few ever do."

"Boggy? What?"

"It's a nickname."

"My God. Please, call me Bogdana."

"Um, you realize that I'm still going to get Boggy from that, right?"

"You could just give us your real name," Jeff suggested.

Chuckie looked at her closely. "She did. That *is* your real name, isn't it?"

"No. But I'm willing to use that name."

Chuckie laughed quietly. "You're lying. Why toss out a name that sounds so close to your pseudonym, especially after Kitty gave you a nickname you don't like? That's actually your real name."

"Yeah, it is." Jeff nodded to me. Good, he'd read her emotions. Always nice to have that working for us.

"Go me and my awesome interrogation skills. But back to what I was asking Bogdana, sometimes known as Boggy, here. We've had a variety of attacks over the past twenty-four to forty-eight hours." Gave her a high-level recap. "So, I'm asking if you have insights or thoughts about why our enemies rolled all that they've been rolling yesterday and today, versus, say, last week or next month?"

"The election? It seems obvious."

"Yeah, and I can buy the stuff with Bruce Jenkins in regard to that. But not a bunch of bombs, that bizarre quicksand attack, the attempted assassinations of Vander, Serene, yourself, and so on. Just wondering if you might see something, some pattern, that we're missing because we're too close to it."

"Or, short of us dying or my stepping down as a candidate, what you think we might be able to do to stop it," Jeff added.

Chernobog seemed to be giving this some thought, but we

were all distracted by the containment room door slamming shut.

Once I landed from my jump for the ceiling, turned around to see Serene, Henry, and Ravi all outside and hopefully out of harm's way.

"Okay," Serene said. "I reactivated him. He'll be online momentarily." She reached out and took Mrs. Maurer's hand. "I hope I did it all right."

Mrs. Maurer nodded. "You did your best, dear. That's all I can hope for." She looked over at Chernobog. "What do you hope for? If they could do this to my son, they can do it to yours, too."

Chernobog gave her a long look. "I would like your son returned to you as I would like mine returned to me."

"But even if this works," Mrs. Maurer's voice trembled but she held it together, "I'll only get a part of my son back. He'll never be all him again."

"No, he won't be." Chernobog cocked her head. "Why are you asking me these questions?"

"Because I don't trust you," Mrs. Maurer snapped. "And these are decent people trying to do good, and they're also trying to trust you. If you love your son, truly love him as I love mine, then you'll help them, and not betray them."

"I—"

Mrs. Maurer sniffed and interrupted Chernobog. "You can say anything you want. It's your actions that will matter. Prove that you're worth what they'll do to protect and help you. Prove that your son deserves a full, normal life, instead of being turned into a robotic version of himself."

With that she turned away and stared through the window at the robot with her son's skin and brain.

"Are we sure those windows are safe?" I asked Jeff, somewhat to change the subject and somewhat because I was still kind of freaked out.

"Yes, Mrs. Martini," White answered for him. "They are. Remember, we're good with fail-safes."

True enough. White, Chuckie, and I had experienced a major one at the end of Operation Confusion. "Great. Just want to be sure and all that."

We all clustered around the containment room. Really questioned our wisdom, but decided hyperspeed would just save the day as it tended to.

Maurer was lying there, looking like a dead person or a robot whose plug had been pulled; I couldn't decide which. But all of a sudden his eyes blinked slowly, once. Then rapidly, several times. Color came back into his cheeks and his chest rose and fell. He sat up and looked around, and once again he looked just like a real man.

"God, Antony Marling did good work. I mean, it's horrible work, but the man really was an artist. What a damned pity he was totally evil and completely batshit crazy."

Maurer got off the table and came to the window where his mother and Serene were, which was where Jeff, Chuckie, White, and I were, too. He banged on the glass. "Mother, what's going on? Why am I in here? Where are we?" He sounded far away, like he was in a giant fishbowl, which he kind of was. But still, he was in a containment room. Was shocked we could hear him at all.

"We can hear because it's set up for that," Jeff said quietly to me. "And yes, I read you, and yes, even though we can hear him, we won't be hurt if he explodes."

"Don't let him out," Chernobog said. "Trust me, he's not safe yet."

"As in not safe because he's going to explode, or not safe because we don't know what program he's currently running?"

"Both."

Serene nodded. "We need to wait until Ravi hears from the Science Center. We need to know if what I removed explodes or not."

"What do we know if it does or doesn't?"

"I think it's still active, so if it explodes, it means we got everything and the destruct sequence was triggered by someone. If it doesn't explode, it may mean nothing or it may mean that I didn't get everything."

"What about his self-destruct things? You got all of those."

"Again, we'll know soon."

"Just wait, Cameron, dear," Mrs. Maurer said. "This is for your own protection."

So we all waited, and while we did, I thought again. I was getting better at thinking to myself, versus aloud, but there was still nothing better for my mental processes than running my yap.

Gave up the silent treatment. "So, who set the bombs in the Israeli and Bahraini embassies? Not the ones Night-crawler set, but the ones that were set to go off sooner."

"Stephanie," Christopher said. "She has hyperspeed, and she was in D.C. working for Vander. Take your coffee break, plant bombs to kill your family, grab a Starbucks on the way back as cover."

"Makes sense. We figure Ronnie's Kids helped Club Fifty-One and the Church of Hate and Intolerance set the ricin bombs, right?"

"Yes," Serene replied. "Per everything we've learned."

"Boggy, can we fix what was done to the imageers?"

"I hate that nickname. And I don't know. I don't know where the toxin is or what it is, specifically. But that's what it is, I believe—a toxin that affects whatever part of the brains that control the talent. But it's definitely in your main research facility, the one I accessed to take your data."

"Nicknames are given out of love, babe."

"So you claim. Even nicknames someone hates?"

"Yes. It'll grow on you."

"What do you call Olga?"

"The Oracle. Or Olga. Or She Who Knows All."

"And I get Boggy. I see who you like better."

"She's never worked against us. So, we need to have a more thorough search of the Science Center done pronto."

"Just sent James a text," Jeff said. "Walter apparently gave him the heads up and he's started literally an inch-by-inch search. He said to tell you that, yes, they're starting in the air vents and circulation system."

"Wow, he definitely needs a vacation. And good initiative Walter."

"Thanks, Chief," Walter said. Didn't shock me—I'd told him to keep the com open.

"Walter, did we miss anything that you and the rest of Team Oliver might have heard, seen, or experienced that's key?"

"No, Chief, I don't think so. But, ah, would you like my opinion?"

"I'd love it, Walt. What do you have for me?"

"I think we need to consider why Colonel Hamlin thinks he's safer if he doesn't let us protect him than if he does."

There were a lot of comments I could give to this. Buchanan had been attacked right after dropping Hamlin off somewhere. We were really public figures now. We were public figures constantly under attack. And more. But I chose to, instead, ask a question. "Walt, why do *you* think he feels that way?"

"I think he's figured out who the Mastermind is—and it's someone very close to us. So close we won't believe it without solid proof, which I don't think he has yet."

CHAPTER 84

BEFORE ANYONE COULD COMMENT, or I could share my musings on this from a little earlier, Serene's phone rang. "Yes? Yes? Great! No, good job. Yes, good work. Thank you." She hung up.

"What happened?" Jeff asked.

"The remote destruct just went off. It was in a contained room, no one was injured. Huge blast radius, though. If it had gone off here it would have leveled the Embassy. Same with Colonel Butler's destruct. But," she said quickly as all our mouths opened, "they were able to deactivate his bombs, too. Dulce has been online with us and doing the same procedure we have. Both were a success."

"Walter, I want a portable OVS given to every Field agent, and I want a set for the Embassy, the Pontifex's Residence, my parents, Kitty's parents, the Israeli and Bahraini embassies, and all bases worldwide. If James has a problem with this, tell him it's a congressional decree."

"Yes, sir, Congressman Martini."

"And tell him Imageering agrees with the congressman," Serene added.

"Yes ma'am, Commander."

"I also want Field teams assigned to the Armstrongs and the McMillans, and if we already have teams on them, add on more personnel. That goes for every non-Centaurion location getting an OVS as well, and yes that includes Kitty's parents, regardless of what Angela may want to say about it."

"Got it, and have relayed. Commander Reader agrees and has also assigned three teams to protect Lieutenant Colonel Gonzalez. He's been verified as ninety-five percent organic, by the way. Commander Reader said you'd want to know."

"We did, thank you. Move Caroline into the Embassy, please," I added. "She may protest, but she's been an attack point before." Unless she was the Mastermind. Heck we totally trusted her. But if she hated Chuckie, I'd never seen any indication of such. And we knew the Mastermind was a man. So, great, unless Caroline was doing Mastermind work in drag, she was out as a suspect.

"Yes, Chief. Do you want family and friends brought into lockdown?"

"No, not yet," Jeff said.

Had a thought and made a call. "You're still alive, kitten?"

"Yeah, for now. Mom, I think you need to increase security on Russell Kozlow." Chernobog's head swiveled toward me.

"Why so?"

Brought her up to speed on the android and android destruct situation. "We need to create metal detectors that somehow include OVS detection in them." And why this hadn't occurred to me or anyone else before now was beyond me.

"We were, but all the data was taken and it was a lower-level restoration requirement," Mom said. Ah, it had occurred. Go team. "However, if the data is truly back now, we can probably do so fairly quickly. Possibly before the National Convention, but I wouldn't count on it."

"Why not? I'd bet Dulce could get those suckers out fast."

"Yes, they could. And for the half of Congress that feels that they'd be signing up their constituents and themselves to be probed by aliens, that's a frightening idea. It's not the creation alone that's the issue, Kitty. It's the legal use of this kind of scan that will be the bigger holdup."

Managed not to say that we used the OVS all the time. We

did because we could—the law for us was the Pontifex, the Diplomatic Corps, and Alpha Team. All of whom were all for using the OVS. But Mom had a good point. Heaved a sigh. "They're risking being blown up by an android that looks like the congressman next door."

"We're all at risk every day, kitten. But unless you also think we should be tapping everyone's phones twenty-four-seven, you have to go through the proper channels and procedures. Otherwise you have a fascist dictatorship. Or anarchy."

Refrained from making a snippy comment about the NSA. Because, you know, they might be listening. "Think the Mastermind is in the NSA?"

"That would be too easy and too obvious."

"Yeah. Bummer. So, anyway, I think they're going to make a move to get or kill Kozlow. We have Chernobog and I'm sure the Mastermind knows that by now. Whether that means they'll make a move on the other prisoners or not I have no bet."

"They're hard to get to."

"Whoever hired Chernobog is in the U.S. government."

Mom was quiet for a few seconds. "She could be saying that to create havoc. Or to get you to ask for us to release him into your custody."

"Or it could be the truth. Frankly, we know the Mastermind's got connections. It's not a surprise that he'd be in a position of some kind of power."

"I'll advise that guard should be increased. Anything else?"

"Yeah. Any suggestions for how to handle the Cameron Maurer situation, since he hasn't blown up so far?"

"Not really. I'm sure his mother will have some ideas."

"Really? You have nothing for me on this one?"

"Nope. You're the diplomat, not me. Keep me posted, kitten."

We hung up as Serene opened the containment room door. Couldn't speak for anyone else, but I was prepared for Maurer to blow up anyway, or to attack us.

He did neither. He walked out of the room and went to his mother. "Mother, I had the weirdest, most horrible dream."

He looked around. "I really have no idea where we are. What's going on?"

"We'll explain it to you," Raj said, Troubadour Tones set on Soothe. "In a few minutes. Right now, why don't you and your mother have a reunion?"

"Why did you leave?" Maurer asked her.

"You weren't yourself." She took his hand. "Let's go have that little reunion, dear."

"If it's alright, I'd like to escort you both," White said.

Raj nodded. "I as well. We'll figure out what to tell the press, and run it past you first, Ambassador, don't worry about that."

"Yes," Mrs. Maurer said. "I believe it will help having you both with us and helping craft our statement." She took my hand for a moment. "Thank you for giving me back at least part of my son."

"Glad to."

Maurer looked confused, but he didn't ask any more questions. The four of them left, presumably to go to one of the salons in the Embassy, or to the rooms Mrs. Maurer was staying in.

The agents with us broke down the containment room and took it away, in about two minutes. Which, at hyperspeed, was kind of a long time. Then again, if they needed to take some time constructing and deconstructing the thing that could stop the giant explosions, that was okay with me. They all left with the equipment.

"Now what?" Jeff asked.

"Ah, Chief? We have protestors outside. All bases in populated areas are reporting protestors, as is the Pontifex's Residence, as well as the embassies that are friendly to us, such as Israel's, Bahrain's, and Romania's. All buildings with shields have them activated, ours included. The Bahraini and Israeli embassies say this is no big deal to them and we shouldn't worry. We have overflow personnel with the Bahrainis again."

"Oh joy, oh rapture, the Loon Squad has arrived. Tell our friends sorry and thank you, please. We're on our way to take a look-see."

We left Hacker International, Chernobog, a dozen Field agents who arrived sharing that Reader had sent them over, and Serene in the computer lab and headed downstairs.

Went onto the bridge. Sure enough, we had a ton of people clogging the streets around us, holding more of those Armstrong-Martini signs that had the red circle with a line through it on them.

There were also a nice complement of "Aliens Go Home", "The Only Good Aliens Are Dead Aliens", "Probe Elsewhere", and similar. There were also a lot of anti-gay signs joined by a lot of Biblical verses and such that undoubtedly didn't actually mean that God wanted us all dead, but which the Church of Intolerance was also undoubtedly using as proof that God despised us and wanted us burning in hell.

They saw us and started shouting, waving their signs, and throwing things. We couldn't hear them, the waving made the signs illegible, and the shielding bounced all the rotten veggies and the like right back onto them. So we had that going for us.

"What do we do?" I asked everyone and no one.

Len cleared his throat. "Ah, I have an idea."

"Go for it."

"I say we do nothing."

CHAPTER 85

WE ALL STARED AT HIM. "Say what?" Christopher asked before I could.

Len looked uncomfortable, but he went on. "We do nothing." He looked to Kyle. "It's just like the UCLA game when we were juniors, remember?"

"Oh, yeah." Kyle nodded enthusiastically. "We were being accused of cheating, which we absolutely were not doing. So UCLA had a bunch of supporters come down to our campus and protest our team."

"Coach told us to ignore them," Len said. "And pretend they weren't even there. Because giving them attention was what they wanted and the media would do plenty of that anyway."

"Yeah, he said that the best way to deal with them was to practice hard, play harder, and win the game fair and square. Which we did." Kyle beamed proudly. "It was my best game that season. Len's too. It was like he couldn't throw an interception or miss a receiver."

"Protest is part of being in a political campaign," Chuckie said slowly. "I think they have a really good point."

"We have enough going on that we need to prep for anyway," Jeff said. "But how do we get in and out? I mean so that the public sees? And how do we keep random people on the streets, or who live and work around these protest areas, safe?"

"Well, that's not actually our job, is it? So, we do what every other politician in these circumstances does. We ask for governmental assistance and police protection. And, I know just the police I want protecting us." Pulled out my phone and sent Officer Melville a text.

He replied quickly. D.C.P.D. had been advised of the various protests and were already scrambling teams to cover. They'd also requested the National Guard, but hadn't heard if that request was going to be fulfilled or not.

"The K-9 squad are on their way. One quarter with us, one quarter with the Israelis, one quarter with the Bahrainis, and the last at the Pontifex's Residence. They're sending regular police to cover the rest of our street and Romania's embassy, as well as other areas."

"I want to keep Paul with us, and James, too, if he's able to come out," Jeff said.

"No argument. But they expect attacks on the building, so they want people there."

"That's fine," Chuckie said. "I've got Angela alerted—we'll also have P.T.C.U., F.B.I., C.I.A., and Homeland Security support, in addition to those of us already here."

"So, now what?" Christopher said. "We just wait around and pretend this isn't happening?"

"Sort of," Len replied. "But Jeff's going to be going up onstage at the National Convention. He needs a speech, which I'm sure Raj already has written, but he also needs to practice it. Kitty, same thing—they may expect you to speak, and you need to be prepared."

Chuckie nodded. "This isn't the time to wing it, I'll say that. There will be other things we need to prepare for as well."

"So, we just hunker down and wait?" Christopher asked. Considered this. "Yeah."

Everyone looked at me. "That was easy," Chuckie said.

I shrugged. "It's a chess game. We're black. We've just made our move in reaction to white's. Time to wait for them to make their next move. Because I don't think the protests are that move. I think they're just filler and distraction, and we've been distracted enough. Besides, I'd love to actually see my daughter for more than a second, and we could all use whatever downtime we can grab."

"Are you sure we're not going to be attacked in the next fifteen minutes?" Christopher asked.

Thought about what Mom had said. "We all face danger all the time. Driving is a risk. Taking a walk is a risk. I'm willing to be on full alert, but also not trying to guess the next move. In part because I don't think we can. We have two recovered androids and Chernobog. Let's get what we can from them and see what we can rebuild or regain from her. We have the pictures from the crowd at the press conference to go through. We probably have a lot of other things that we've forgotten or put off. Let's spend the time doing them versus trying to guess what our enemies are going to throw at us next."

"Speaking of androids, what are we going to do with the Maurers, Jenkins, and Oliver?" Jeff asked.

"They all stay here. We'll ask James to send teams to get their stuff."

"Once they move in, are they ever moving out, is my question," Jeff grumbled.

"Oh, the more the merrier. Let's get everyone back here who should be and then you can practice your nomination speech."

Jeff sighed. "Can't wait."

The doorbell to the Embassy rang and we trotted to get it. Officer Melville, along with the officers I called Larry and Curly, was there. Melville didn't like me calling him Moe, but the other two guys were either flattered by the Three Stooges comparisons or were really named Larry and Curly.

There were other police on the street, moving the protestors back and off our property, as well as getting them off the street.

Prince greeted us with great joy, while sharing that our separation had seemed almost eternal and he was thrilled to see us.

While we got our three officers and their respective dogs into rooms, the rest of the Embassy staff and related personnel returned via floater gates. Within a short time, things were humming along as if the last day and a half hadn't really happened.

It was great to get Jamie back and be a family. Jeff or I carried her around, and she and Mous-Mous had a nice little reunion. There hadn't seemed to be a real reason she'd had her Poof go with me, and I mentioned that to her.

"Mous-Mous made the things go away," Jamie said.

"What things?"

"The ones that want to take Fairy Godfather ACE away."

"But they didn't come to visit us today."

She hugged Mous-Mous. "Because Mous-Mous is a good Poof!" The Poof purred loudly and they nuzzled each other.

Decided now wasn't the time to argue this or ask more questions, especially because I'd seen those shimmers when we were in the desert. Meaning that Jamie could be 100% right. And she'd said things, plural, meaning that there was a good chance Sandy had friends or co-workers of some kind following up on his work. How fantastic for all of us.

"Okay, Jamie-Kat, whatever you say." Wondered if I was right in thinking we should take some breathing room, especially under these potentially new circumstances.

She stopped nuzzling the Poof and looked at me. "You're right, Mommy. We can wait for the next move." Then she turned back to the Poof.

Thanks, ACE, I said in my head. I didn't expect a response, which was good, because I didn't get one. But Jamie hugged me, and I figured that was from her and ACE both. And these days, that was good enough for me.

CHAPTER 86

THE WEEK FLEW BY. I spent most of my free time with Jamie and the pets, which Prince felt included himself. Officer Melville was okay with this, mostly because I didn't have all that much free time.

In addition to the steady stream of protestors outside our doors, we had a steady stream of politicians coming through those doors. Armstrong and McMillan, of course, and Nathalie, but also others big in the party in some way.

Culver and Gadoire were over all the time, as were other lobbyists, but, interestingly enough, none of the other Dealers of Death Vance had told me about. Presumably they'd thrown in with the now Cleary-Kramer ticket and were avoiding us. Which was okay with me.

Culver took it upon herself to work with Nathalie and Pierre to determine my "color." She felt it was vital that I have one, and Pierre agreed, meaning that deal was sealed. And, naturally, my color couldn't be black or white.

Sure, when forced to wear only the Armani Fatigues, I longed for other colors. But being told I was going to be choosing one color and sticking with it pretty much for the foreseeable future seemed like a cruel irony.

Though I begged for green, that was turned down flat. Apparently green was only okay for other people or holidays. Pierre called in our designer, Akiko, and she, traitor that she was, also turned down green.

We finally all agreed on blue. Or rather, the four of them chose blue and I said okay. But not just any blue. An iced sky blue was considered to be the right color for me. This vital decision made, it was time for Akiko to whip up something for me to wear.

On this I put a foot down. I refused to wear a fancy dress, because precedent said that when I was really dressed up, I was going to end up attacked and bedraggled. Nathalie backed me on this one, and I was allowed to wear a suit.

Crazed with success, I put the other foot down and insisted the suit jacket and skirt had to be black, leaving only the blouse to be blue. This was met with approval as a "test run" of the color. Decided this was one for the win column and quietly rejoiced.

The rest of my work time was spent in a variety of "fun" ways. Raj, Oliver, and Jenkins had me practicing several prepared speeches and peppered me with both prepared and surprise questions so that I'd be prepared for anything. Prepared—that was the PR and press watchword for Mission: Convention.

Jeff and I, along with the rest of our delegation, got to review the pictures Serene, Vance, and I had taken of the mob of reporters to ensure that we could identify our suspected Yates progeny should they show up at the convention.

Spent time hanging out with Hacker International Plus One to ensure that we got what we wanted from Chernobog and so I could set up what the Dingo would need to cancel her contract. Siler had been right—she and I definitely had an understanding. She and Olga had made a sort of peace brokered by White, so Olga and Adriana were over a lot, too, and this helped me get the agreements from Chernobog I needed.

Speaking of Siler and agreements made with assassins, I spent a good deal of time wondering where in the heck Buchanan, Siler, the Dingo Dog, and Surly Vic actually were. While they'd checked in via phone—and the Dingo had agreed to the terms I'd brokered with Chernobog—they hadn't shown up physically. Buchanan insisted they were all fine, himself in particular, but it was still a little unsettling to have him gone.

So I had a lot to occupy me during this short time before our big show, but even so, the time flew by and before I knew it, the convention was starting.

The National Convention was scheduled to run for four days. Though Jeff had to be there pretty much the entire time, mercifully, I wasn't required until the last day. This was supposedly because I was being saved as a "big deal" for the last night. I figured it was so that I would have fewer opportunities to say the wrong things to the wrong people. Not that I wanted to be over there anyway. Plus it gave me extra time to prep and stress and worry about Jeff.

Christopher wasn't part of our daily delegation, though White, as the former Pontifex, was. As was Amy, since she had sway in the legal and business world, the Gaultier name, and a great deal of public speaking experience.

Doreen and Abigail were also going to represent our principality, Mrs. Maurer was going along as well, to represent the "we've changed sides" standpoint, Brian Dwyer was going to represent NASA's support of our ticket, and of course Caroline was there with McMillan.

Naturally, Gower was part of the delegation, and Reader, Tim, Claudia, Lorraine, and the flyboys were there as well, to represent but mostly to protect everyone else. Similarly, Kevin Lewis was going as part of the P.T.C.U. and he promised me that everyone would be focused on protecting Jeff. And Chuckie, Len, and Kyle were also part of the protection section of our delegation, as were the Barones.

Raj, as our Embassy Public Relations Minister, had a huge role, and he had several other troubadours helping him as well. We had my troubadour "double," Francine, in reserve, in case of emergencies, meaning she was with the delegation, but mostly in the green room, hanging out.

I had Rahmi and Rhee shape-shift to look like Dazzlers, so they could fit in with the delegation as well. Them I gave specific instructions to protect Jeff at all costs and to figure that somewhere along the way he was going to get attacked. Prayed I wasn't sending them in to be a two-woman demolition team, but they assured me they were clear on what they should and shouldn't do.

Christopher was more than a little bitter about all this, especially when Raj shared that he was considered the next likely to blow it right after me, which was why we both were staying in the Embassy until the last possible moment. Considering the K-9 squad was with our delegation, too, dogs and all, it was kind of a big slap to the old ego.

This left only a few of us actually in the Embassy most of the day. Walter, of course, Pierre, Irving, Tito, Nurse Carter, Mahin, Denise and the daycare kids, Christopher, and me. Mahin, like Christopher, was bitter about not getting to go, but Irving was all for having Doreen handle this and had thanked everyone for letting him stay home. Denise, like Irving, was thrilled to be "forced" to stay home to care for kidlets, and Tito and Nurse Carter both said they appreciated having a few days of down time.

Serene requested to stay in the Embassy, partly to keep an eye on Christopher and me, and partly to see what we could spot on TV. Hacker International had brought in extra screens, meaning we almost had a Mini Command Center in the computer lab, so we all hung out with them, Chernobog, and the dozen random A-Cs assigned to guard duty at whatever time.

We watched the first three days' worth of coverage like we were C-SPAN junkies. We spotted nothing untoward—none of Ronnie's Kids, none of our assassins, none of our other enemies. And while Club 51, the Church of Hate and Intolerance, and a host of other anti-alien groups were protesting the convention, the National Guard was out in force and they were kept away from the convention and the delegates.

Our delegation was getting a lot of airtime, in part because Jeff was the vice presidential candidate and in part because they were so damned photogenic. If I had been running the cameras, I'd have focused on all the beautiful people, too. The good side of this was that we could keep an eye on pretty much everyone we cared about. The bad side was that we weren't getting all the coverage we could hope for, meaning that while we hadn't spotted anyone evil, that didn't mean they weren't there.

Somehow the entire place seemed covered with posters of Armstrong and Jeff. Had no idea when they'd taken the picture of Jeff they were using, but he looked amazing—serious, authoritative, but accessible, with his arms crossed over his chest, gazing straight at you. Bottom line, he looked gorgeous. Figured we probably had the straight female and gay male votes locked up.

Our massive team went over early each morning, stayed until late at night, and came back safe and sound. This should have made me happy and calm. Instead, it stressed me out.

"Why are you so tense?" Jeff asked through yawns, as he staggered into our bedroom after another eighteen hours at the convention.

"Just wondering why nothing's happened yet."

"Maybe they're actually going to leave us alone."

"Maybe."

"You'll be great tomorrow, baby."

"Yeah? I hope so." I snuggled next to him. He pulled me close, kissed my forehead, and went right to sleep. Another reason to hate politics—it was making my husband so tired he wasn't up to having sex. For the third night in a row. And I, of course, was wide awake and nervous.

Jeff needed the sleep, and so did everyone else I'd want to talk to in order to calm my nerves. Tried to sleep, but I was too jittery. Got up and went into the closet. Sat on the floor near the hamper. "I can't sleep."

Algar appeared, sitting cross-legged on the hamper. "I noticed. Would you like a cup of cocoa?"

"Not really. You told me Jeff was the target, and yet, he's been reasonably safe."

"Is that all that's bothering you?"

"No. Jamie told me that her Poof kept the 'things' away. I think she meant Sandy the superconsciousness and maybe some of his friends or relations. But for all I know she didn't."

"Anything else?"

"Yeah. I'm worried I'm going to blow it tomorrow in some way."

"What matters more—you coming off as politically perfect, or protecting your husband and other innocent people?"

"Gosh, let me think. The latter. Protecting Jeff and others."

Algar hopped down from the hamper and patted my cheek. "Then you're all ready for tomorrow. And everything else you've been waiting for."

And with that, he snapped his fingers, and I was back in bed with Jeff, as if I'd never left it.

"Very funny," I grumbled quietly.

"Hmmm?" Jeff said. He pulled me closer. "You awake?"

"Sorta. Worried about tomorrow and having trouble falling asleep."

He pulled me on top of him. "Then let me help you out with that, baby." He pulled my head down and kissed me, and all my stress floated away, along with our nightclothes.

Short and sweet for Jeff was still fantastic for me. He stayed on his back and I straddled him, enjoying the slow, sensuous way his hips bucked while his hands fondled my breasts, slid over my stomach, stroked me everywhere.

He flipped me over the edge and kept on, still bucking slowly while his fingertips traced my neck, nipples, and back. As I got closer to the edge again, he sped up and pulled me down, so that my breasts rubbed against his chest and his lips were on mine.

Still kissing me, Jeff slid his hands to my butt, and squeezed gently while shoving me down against him just enough that my lower body went wild. He moved his mouth to my neck, bit me gently, and I climaxed hard, while he exploded inside me.

As our bodies slowed, I stayed draped over him as he pulled the covers back up and over us. I snuggled my face into his neck. "I love you."

"I love you, too, baby. Get some sleep now. Tomorrow's going to be a busy day."

"Busy's fine. It's dangerous I'm worried about."

Jeff chuckled. "No worries. It'll be routine." He nuzzled my head. "But if you need me to help you relax some more, just say the word."

"The word."

He laughed. "I see."

"Hey, you just took two nights off. I have needs. But I know you're exhausted and need the sleep."

Jeff rolled us over so he was on top of me. "I'm never too exhausted to make you happy, baby."

"Well then, rest assured—you have my vote."

CHAPTER 87

AFTER MORE GREAT SEX, we fell asleep wrapped around each other. The sounds of Oingo Boingo's "The Winning Side" woke us up far too early. Sun-just-coming-up too early. However, duty called—it was time to test-drive iced sky blue as "my color." Could not, literally, wait.

Had a fast shower wherein we didn't even have time for sex, bitterly got dressed, and had a quick but nice breakfast with Jamie as Dad, Lucinda, and Alfred came over to watch her.

Normally, we'd have brought her, and our parents, and any other family members we could, to the convention, so we could all shake as many paws as possible and smile like crazed hyenas. Under the circumstances, Jeff had put his foot down as hard as possible and Jamie and everyone else who wasn't me, Jeff, or Mom was staying home.

"You're going to be great today, Kitty," Alfred said with a twinkle. Jeff was a slightly taller, slightly buffer version of his father, complete with the charm and sense of humor.

"I hope so."

"You will be," Lucinda said with utter confidence as she kissed my cheek and took her eager granddaughter out of my arms. "You look so poised, beautiful, and professional. The other women will be jealous."

"Love you for saying that. And look at how well you managed to lie, too."

She chuckled. "Trust me, you look perfect for today."

Dad hugged me. "They're right, kitten. Just do your best and remember—when it comes down to it, you're your mother's daughter." He kissed my forehead. "And you're mine, too. We're both so proud of you. Take a deep breath, and just let things happen as they will."

Hugged him and the others. "Thanks. I'm just hoping we survive the event."

Jamie handed her Poof to me again. "You need to take Mous-Mous, Mommy."

Considered arguing, but what could it possibly hurt? And Jamie had felt so certain her Poof had helped the other day, why not humor her again? "Sure, Jamie-Kat. Thank you. Mous-Mous can tell you all about the convention."

She nodded. "Yes. Be yourself, Mommy."

Kissed her head. "I will. You and Fairy Godfather ACE can be sure of that."

Jeff hugged everyone, while they told him how awesome he was and how he shouldn't be nervous at all, and other parental rah-rah things. Then he kissed Jamie, took my hand, and we left.

As we walked to the elevators, I looked around. "Bruno my bird, what's the avian word?"

Bruno appeared beside us. He squawked, bobbed his head, flapped his wings, and scratched the carpet.

"What's he saying?" Jeff asked, in the tone of voice of a man who hopes no voters learn of his real home life.

"The Peregrines are sticking around the Embassy. They're worried that the kids are too exposed with the rest of us going over today. They also want to keep an eye on Chernobog, just in case. Bruno's worried about us going over without him, but says he's briefed the K-9 dogs and feels that they'll make reasonable stand-ins and a good Poof Support Team."

"So how many Poofs are going?"

Bruno squawked and clawed the ground several times. "Huh. Most of them. There are about three Poofs to a person in the Embassy and Zoo, all the attached Poofs are with their people, and the rest of the unattached Poofs will be with us."

"Oh. Good." He didn't sound like he thought it was all that good, but I chose to ignore it.

Gave Bruno a scritchy-scratch between his wings, and then we headed downstairs to the ballroom so Jeff and I could have our hair done and I could sit through makeup.

Pierre was in charge of doing all the hair and makeup for our delegation, and while he'd assigned some of Team Troubadour to assist with this, he insisted on doing me and Jeff himself, which was great with me.

Other than my wedding, I'd never really bothered with this elaborate process, but Raj had insisted and everyone had backed him up. So even the men were being carefully coiffed and groomed. The less said about the number of Patented Glares Christopher was shooting around while he was getting styled the better, but as Serene gently pointed out, everyone had looked great on TV, so it was time to man up and accept that hairspray was going to be used.

Finally, Pierre and his team had us all looking nothing short of fabulous. I'd been sprayed with the Dove Extra Hold hairspray so near and dear to my and Pierre's hearts. He'd also sprayed me and some of the others with some sort of makeup hairspray thing that he insisted Hollywood types used all the time. And those riding with the K-9 dogs were all issued lint brushes and rollers. Thusly prepped, we all headed to the underground garage.

We literally had a fleet of limos taking our delegation over and back. Saw Burton Falk and the other guys on his team, so felt like Buchanan was watching us somehow, which made me feel a little better. I'd gotten used to knowing that he was out there, and it was unsettling now that he wasn't.

Serene was going along today, and Christopher had taken pity on Mahin and insisted that if we got to go over finally, she got to go with us. Tito was also coming along, mostly because he said he was getting cabin fever, and Nurse Carter was in the Embassy to handle any medical emergencies.

Found out why I was denied green as "my color"—Amy was in an all-green ensemble and I realized she'd been in green every day of the convention. Chose not to be bitter. If one of your besties claims a color you wanted, you move on to other colors, that was my motto.

Jeff and I were in a limo with Gower, Reader, Raj, Officer Melville, and Prince, with Len and Kyle driving. D.C.P.D. had the protestors cleared back so we could get out of our garage and onto the highway without a lot of issues.

Kyle, proving why I loved him, immediately put on music. As the soothing sounds of Green Day's "Wake Me Up When September Ends" hit my personal airwaves, the others ran through what I should be expecting. Well, other than Melville, who was literally looking everywhere as we drove, and Prince, who felt my only worries should be if I was petting him enough.

Fittingly, "Good Days Bad Days" by the Kaiser Chiefs came on. Because, basically, today was a lot like the other days. Minor dudes and dudettes getting to have their say, finalization of the party platform, which happily covered a lot of alien rights, marriage equality, immigration, a strong economic plan, and an even stronger defense plan that didn't involve turning Centaurion into the War Division. Those of us kibitzing in front of the TV for the past three days had approved the party platform.

"Jeff doesn't really get voted on," Raj said by way of summation, as "You Can Do It" by No Doubt started. "These days it's just assumed that whoever the presidential nominee wants is who he or she gets. But the VP decision affects the nomination process."

"Yeah, after three intensive days in front of the TV, I actually think I know this stuff. The state's roll call was supposed to be yesterday evening, but they've moved it to today because media coverage has been so good."

"Yes. It's the first thing going on. Expect to glad-hand a lot when we first get there, but Vincent has the bigger role here," Raj said.

"Don's doing the keynote," Jeff reminded me. "Then it's acceptance speeches. The order is going to be me, you, Elaine, then Vince."

"I get why Elaine's speaking, she'll be the First Lady. But why do they want to hear from me?"

"It's not unusual for the wife of the VP candidate to speak," Raj said.

"They want to hear what you're going to say," Reader added. "We've held you back for a reason, Kitty."

"To keep me from blowing it, I know."

He shook his head. "No. You're considered our loose cannon, yeah, but everyone's heard the eulogy you did for Michael, and everyone knows that was done on the fly." Fittingly, "Crazy Days" by Adam Gregory came on.

"Well, sane people know that," Gower said dryly. "The crazy ones insist I planned to break down and have to be led away so you could amaze everyone with your oration skills."

"Let's focus on the sane people. Why do they want to hear me?"

"Because you gave an incredible speech, girlfriend. And there's a lot of anticipation about what you'll say today."

"Is the nomination in the bag?"

"Pretty much, yeah," Jeff said. "Vince is the clear party frontrunner."

"And they're thrilled Jeff's on the ticket," Reader added. "Not that he'll tell you himself. But he's helped the ticket a lot." He shot me the cover boy grin. "And you getting Jenkins under control has helped even more. The Tastemaker's column yesterday was very good for us."

"Haven't read a thing, we've been too busy watching you guys on TV. What did it say?"

"Aliens good, those who oppose them bad." Gower grinned. "Nice work, Ambassador."

"It's a gift." Tried not to be nervous. I'd been a lot more relaxed when I'd thought everyone was worried about me blowing it. Now that I knew they had positive expectations, the pressure got that much higher. Wondered how fast I'd forget all the speeches that had been drilled into me.

Raj sighed. "I wish you'd done what I told you and not mentioned that to her. She's nervous now, and she wasn't before."

"Sorry." Reader took my hand in his. "Kitty, you're going to be great, whether you remember all the speeches Raj wrote for you or not. You're the best we have at winging it. It'll all work out."

"I'm more worried about being attacked." Whoops.

Hadn't meant to blurt that out. Maybe it was because Agent Orange's "Too Young To Die" had just hit our airwaves.

"Security is the best I've ever seen," Melville said.

Prince barked. At me. "Yeah? Thanks."

"What did he say?" Jeff asked for everyone.

"Prince would like to stay with me. As in, with me, the entire time. He feels he'll keep me calmer and safer if he's right there by my side. And I don't think he's wrong."

"Say he's her emotional assistance dog," Reader said. "And it'll fly without issue."

"And give our enemies some fantastic ammunition," Raj said, sarcasm knob heading toward eleven.

Melville shrugged. "I'm assigned to the Ambassador and congressman anyway. That won't be an issue." Prince whined. Melville petted his head. "Yes, you can stay with *her*, you traitor." Prince flung himself against Melville to share that he still loved Melville best. Just barely, but still, best.

"Just for the record and officially, Prince is my favorite."

Jeff sighed. "Beaten out by a dog. Such is my life."

CHAPTER 88

AS "TAKE ON ME" from A-Ha came on, we arrived. To see a massive number of protestors encircling the convention center, held back by the National Guard. Well, nice to make an entrance.

There wasn't parking at the convention center itself, but it was near the Inner Harbor, meaning there were plenty of parking lots nearby. So the limos were letting our delegation out, then parking as a group. Field agents under Falk's command would guard our fleet. Our drivers who were an active part of our delegation, like Len, Kyle, and the flyboys, would then come back to the convention center as a group, ensuring that none of them walked anywhere alone, important due to everything going on, but more important because of the protestors.

Chose to ignore the many shrieks, catcalls, and insults coming as soon as our limo doors opened. Why grace the Loon Patrol with a response?

Proving that the security inside wasn't all I'd hoped it would be, though, we were ushered in via the Candidates' Entrance, and we weren't searched at all. This was good, because I'd insisted on taking my regular purse with me, and I had my Glock and several clips in it. Sure, I'd forgotten they were there until we walked in, and also sure, it was nice not to have my weapon taken away, but if I could bring in a Glock, what could someone else bring in?

Then again, maybe Mom knew we'd all be packing and wanted to ensure that we could. Chose to not worry about this any more. Succeeded only a little.

However, there were so many people here it was like being at the largest, most crowded Aerosmith concert ever, times ten. Decided that the biggest risk we all faced was being trampled to death, and also felt it was a real possibility. However, you could tell who had a K-9 dog with them—one step onto a paw resulted in a lot of loud barking and a little circle of space. I was graced with just such a circle and was even more grateful to have Prince along than I already had been.

Baltimore had a very nice convention center, and it was decorated like a patriot's wet dream, some of which hadn't been shown on TV. There were American flags everywhere, along with a lot of state flags up on the walls and being waved wildly by delegates. Yet more posters of Armstrong and Jeff, all telling everyone to vote for them. There were Armstrong ones, Martini ones, and Armstrong-Martini ones, where they'd put their separate campaign photos back to back. There was a riot of red, white and blue streamers, garlands, flag banners, and more all over the place. My blue blouse didn't clash with the décor, which was nice.

The stage had a huge screen behind it, and there were giant screens throughout the area, ensuring that no one could miss the happenings onstage. There were cameras on the mezzanine level above us, and a stationary media console in front of the stage, about a hundred yards back. There were also cameramen roving on the floor, and several on the stage as well. Pretty much anything that was happening, someone was going to film it and toss it up onto those jumbo screens and to the television networks.

American Centaurion, while also being its own principality, was also a US territory. I'd stopped trying to figure out the intricacies ages ago. However, what it meant was that we had a vote. And I was the one who was designated to cast it.

This meant that one of my speeches was about how awesome American Centaurion was, and how much we loved the nominees, as well as sharing our delegation's vote count.

This process went in alphabetical order, so Alabama was first and Wyoming was last. And American Centaurion was, therefore, going third, after Alaska and before American Samoa. So absolutely when everyone was still paying attention to the speeches.

But no pressure.

It was so packed, even in the staging area, and Jeff and I had to shake so many eager hands along the way, that by the time we reached the spot where we needed to be in order for me to get in place to go on, Alabama's head delegate had already finished and Alaska's was on the stage. Tried not to let the butterflies in my stomach get to me.

Jeff had his arm around my waist. "You'll do great, baby," he said in my ear. I was too stressed to find this arousing. That did it—I was officially far too worried.

"Don't argue," I said, as I pulled my iPod and earbuds out of my purse. Took off my jacket, clipped the iPod to the top of my skirt, and ran the earbuds up my back and under my blouse's collar with Jeff's help. Ignored the looks of horror Raj, Reader, and Gower were all shooting at me. Put my jacket back on, shoved the earbuds into my ears, and hit play. The soothing sounds of "Breathe" by The Prodigy hit my ears, and I relaxed.

Happily, Alaska's dude wanted to talk a lot, so I had plenty of time to run my speech over and over in my mind. In fact, I got to hear "All That Money Wants" by the Psychedelic Furs, "Keep It Together" by Puddle of Mudd, and "God Is On The Radio" from Queens Of The Stone Age before Alaska finally shut it down, said they, like Alabama, were giving all their votes to Armstrong-Martini, and got off the stage.

Jeff gave me one last squeeze. "Knock 'em dead, baby." I pulled my earbuds out, tucking them under my jacket, though I left my iPod on. Figured I'd need to listen to music again the second I was off the stage. Then it was time for me to trot out for the first part of my dog and pony show.

The main floor of the convention center was, as all main convention center halls are, gigantic. We were in the space normally reserved for the exhibit hall, but they'd set this up really well, with a ton of bleachers and a giant stage, as well as open floor space between the bleachers and the stage, with only the stationary media area blocking anything.

The entire area was packed to the gills with people. As I looked around, it appeared to be filled to the standing room only, no space between anyone level. People were trying to climb onto the media station, though they were immediately pulled down by security. It really was like a concert—some people from various areas were shoving forward to get closer to the stage, some politely, some rather rudely.

Cleared my throat, took that deep breath I'd been advised to take, and stepped up to the microphone. The room quieted down. Not that this meant it was silent—there were too many people for it to be still. But the sound dropped from a loud roar to a quiet hum.

"Fellow delegates and patriots, those of us from American Centaurion are pleased to be joining you at this historic time." So far, so good. I had the first sentence out, and out correctly. "In our time as part of this great country, we've faced trials and tribulations, just as all of you have. But, like the rest of you, we've come through them better and stronger."

This earned me a smattering of applause, which was pleasant. The people shoving forward were near to the stage now. As I opened my mouth to deliver my next line, one of them shouted. "Murderers!"

Closed my mouth and took a look at who'd spoken. Because I'd heard that clearly, and there was no way that someone who wasn't using a microphone—or had troubadour talent of some kind—could have been heard.

Sure enough, I recognized her. She was the woman who'd accused me of murdering Reid and others when we'd left the White House. And she didn't have a microphone in her hand.

Saw some of our security team moving toward her, so I forged on. "Over the decades we've worked closely to ensure a better life for all citizens."

"Other than the ones you've murdered in cold blood," the same woman shouted. I could tell her voice was carrying because people too far away to have heard her normally were shifting uneasily, murmuring to themselves, and so forth.

"So we're incredibly proud that one of our own has been deemed worthy to lead more than just the Second Congressional District of New Mexico and our own people, but also to stand with Senator Vincent Armstrong as part of the team that will lead all of us into the future."

"If we have a future!" This chick was really getting on my nerves and hashing my speech-giving buzz. And I could tell most of the room was hearing her.

Looked right at her. "You know, if you're a delegate, you get to talk. If you're not, save it for later."

"You won't have a later," she snarled. And then, true to my expectations, all hell broke loose.

CHAPTER 89

PROVING THAT RONNIE'S KIDS—in addition to Ma-hin and the dead earthbender, and our airbender in custody—had another bender in their ranks, this chick waved her hands and water came out of nowhere. And splashed all over me.

The water tasted salty, meaning she'd probably pulled it in from the harbor. Considering that was a couple blocks away, she had impressive range, power, and control. Lucky us.

I'd jumped back so I was at less risk of being electrocuted, but the microphone for sure shorted out. Not that it mattered. My speech was, essentially, over. The less said about the state of my clothing the better, but then again, looking like a bedraggled cat was one of my Action Go-To Moves, so I had that going for me.

Because action was definitely needed.

Apparently her drenching me was a go sign for whoever was working with her. Team Yates went into action.

In addition to our waterbender, we had a group who were shoving delegates away while also attacking them, others who were moving kind of at hyperspeed, and a group who must have been manning the main doors, because a variety of Club 51 and Church of Intolerance protestors were inside now. These weren't the real problems.

The people with the guns were the real problems.

Those people weren't ours, because our team didn't shoot over people's heads and yell that they had to get down or die. But I was suddenly really glad that we'd been able to bring in our guns.

Heard Jeff bellow for our team to get Armstrong and others to safety, meaning that most of the A-Cs were now racing off to do just that. Security forces moved toward the various trouble points as well, but there were a lot of those points, and most of security were humans.

All this happened as if it was in slow motion, possibly because I was seeing it via hyperspeed vision, since this chick drenching me ensured that I flipped from nervous to enraged in less than a second. But this was good. I was able to spot trouble areas and, because of where I was, point them out to the good guys and have them actually see me do it.

Raj had found a microphone and was relaying information as well. But even though security was involved, there were a hell of a lot of people, and anyone not fighting was panicking.

Some rushed the stage—there were clearly some of Ronnie's Kids in this group, but also regular delegates who were trying to get to the stage to get away.

Jeff came onstage to get me off. And then the people with the guns changed where they were shooting, and started shooting at us. At him, really.

As Prince and I tackled Jeff to the ground and Len and Kyle tackled Raj so that the bullets flew over all of us, and I then rolled us out of easy range, what Algar had said the night before clicked. It was all going to happen here. This was the place where I had to defend our king. With all the cameras rolling. Well, no problem. As Dad had reminded me, I was my mother's daughter.

"Stay down, they're after you." I scrambled to my feet, shoved my earbuds back in, and hit play. My jacket was a hindrance. Took it off and tossed it to the side. As the sounds of Garbage's "I Think I'm Paranoid" started, I opened my purse to get my Glock. There were a lot of Poofs in there. Got out my gun and gave the signal. "Poofs assemble!"

They poured out of my purse. "Poofies, Kitty needs you

to help out. Get people to safety, help the good guys, stop the bad guys. Sadly, no eating anyone right now. Only go big if you have to. Got it?"

Poofs purred at me, then disappeared, other than Harlie, who jumped over to Jeff, and Poofikins and Mous-Mous, who stayed with me. "Ready, boy?" I asked Prince.

He barked that he was born ready.

"Then let's show these mutated, vengeful assholes how we do things downtown."

This would have probably been a lot more impressive if, right after I said it, I hadn't been hit with another wave of salt water.

Happily, my iPod was still running. Hoped that meant Algar had it under some kind of protection. Probably. He liked to communicate with me this way. The song changed to "Right Between The Eyes", also by Garbage. Wasn't sure if this meant I was on my Garbage playlist or Algar was trying to tell me something. Decided I'd freaking find out.

We got back to our feet and Prince and I charged the waterbender. She was our main nemesis and it's always good to take out the front line.

She appeared to need time to recharge, or to grab more water from the harbor, so we were able to get to her. I hit her high with an arm to her throat and Prince hit her low, knocking her to the ground. I spun and grabbed her head, intending to slam it into the ground.

But I was knocked away by someone who, as I bounced off some innocent bystanders and got to my feet, looked familiar. Stephanie helped the waterbender to her feet and then smirked at me. "Hope you enjoy watching Uncle Jeff die."

That did it. I headed straight for her. She in turn grabbed the waterbender and took off as well, at hyperspeed.

No worries, I had hyperspeed, too. However, there were a lot of people willing to block me and not as many blocking Stephanie. Always the way.

Prince cleared the area by shaking himself off. Amazingly enough, even people in a panic don't want a soaking wet dog to shake himself on them. "Good boy!" I slammed my fist into the face of a guy pointing a gun toward Reader, who was nearby. Took the time to ensure the creep was knocked out, took his gun away, and moved on.

Raj was still onstage and was using his talent to try to calm people down as well as point out trouble areas. And it might have worked if we hadn't heard a very loud, unpleasant sound—like an airplane engine starting up, only louder and less friendly. As it did so, "Gear Jammer" by George Thorogood came on. Yeah, this was a tip from Algar. Good. I needed the help.

Hoisted Prince up under one arm and flipped the hyperspeed up to eleven. At this rate it was fairly easy to get around people, as well as hit bad guys in the face, stomach, or back of the head as we zoomed by.

Despite being told to stay down, my husband was up, tossing bad guys off of delegates and into protestors who were really filling the place up even more than it had been, which seemed impossible.

The others were all fighting as well, some doing better than others. But I couldn't spot Stephanie and the waterbender anywhere. The sound was still going, and I had to figure that I needed to find it and stop it.

Worked my way to the outer part of the room, where I could see out. It was chaos on the streets, with the rest of the protestors basically attacking the National Guard, meaning said Guard couldn't come in to help, and other help was going to have a hard time getting through as well.

"Time Bomb" by Godsmack came on, and I figured it was time to really find that sound and make it stop.

Looked up and around. The sound seemed to be everywhere, so that either indicated it was coming through the sound system or it was above us. Most of the press corps was higher up, on the mezzanine level, which allowed them to look down on the exhibit area and therefore keep cameras stationary. So the whatever it was might be up there.

Raced off, found a set of stairs, and went up them. To see a tank, a literal tank, sitting there. Only this was a special tank, loaded with bells and whistles and what appeared to be a lot of maneuverability. It reminded me of a shorter, wider, less random-limbed supersoldier, while at the same time clearly being a tank. I'd worry about how it had gotten in here later, though someone using the Z'porrah cube was my most likely answer. I'd also worry about who'd created it later, since this kind of tech pretty much screamed Titan Security.

No, I needed to pay attention to the tank itself. The tank that had its very maneuverable gun aimed down, toward the stage below. Where, naturally, my husband was. And of course, he wasn't alone. Reader, Chuckie, Tim, and Serene had him surrounded, trying to protect him. And Raj was still onstage, trying to calm things down and direct the good guys to the bad guys.

So, naturally, this very loud, very nasty looking tank was primed to wipe out all of these people I loved, and probably take a good number of the random people I didn't know but still didn't want to die, too.

And who was protecting the tank but dear little Stephanie and her pal the waterbender.

Always the way.

CHAPTER 90

PUT PRINCE DOWN as more water hit us. I really hated this chick. Happily, my iPod was still working. The music changed to "Hi-Fi Killer" by American Hi-Fi.

Had no idea if my Glock was still going to work, but gave it a shot anyway and aimed right between her eyes. Naturally, the gun was waterlogged and nothing happened. However, I had another gun in my other hand. Tried that one. Nope.

Dropped my Glock into my purse and advanced. Just because the hunk of iron in my hand wasn't going to shoot didn't mean it wasn't still useful.

Stephanie jumped out in front of the waterbender. "You should run away now."

"Nah. You may not be sure, but it wasn't Jeff, or Christopher, who actually finally killed Clarence for real. It was me. And I'm not remotely sorry."

That did it. She charged, as I'd known she would.

There are a lot of rules of fighting, most of which I'd ignored at one time or another. Don't fight angry was a biggie I tended to not pay attention to. However, there was a reason it was an important rule. Angry people normally didn't think clearly. Because I was enhanced and rage was my friend, I was the exception to this particular rule.

But Stephanie wasn't really a trained fighter, though I was sure she'd had some training by now. And she was mad.

She flailed at me and I sidestepped her, spun around, planted my foot against her back, and kicked, hard. She went flying. I spun back and headed for the waterbender. Who'd had time to get more water.

However, I'd shoved my way through a water entity not too many days ago, and I just told myself the wave of water was Sandy when he was Sloshy and shoved on through.

The waterbender hadn't been expecting this. Either that or she was auditioning for a role that required her to look shocked out of her mind. Slammed the extra gun I had into her face. I enjoyed the hit probably a little more than I should have, but oh well.

Jumped up onto the tank as the music changed to "All Kinds of Time" by Fountains of Wayne. Based on the song's lyrics, this meant I only had a few seconds. Ripped the hatch off to see a very surprised guy in there. Reached down, pulled him out, and tossed him over the side and onto the main floor below. If he lived, someone else could enjoy killing him.

Realized I had no idea how to stop this tank and if I went inside I was far too easily trapped. "Poofies, can you get this tank to Home Base or somewhere else safe for Kitty? And if possible, ensure it can't go off?"

Poofikins jumped out of my purse and onto the tank, then mewed at me. Moving it, yes. Stopping it, no.

Heaved a sigh. "Gear Jammer" had certainly been a clue. There was a space in the gun turret where I could shove something in. Took the useless gun that wasn't mine and so shoved. The horrible noise I'd been hearing increased.

Jumped down. "Time to go, Poofikins." The Poof mewled again and several other Poofs appeared. Then they and the tank disappeared. Awesome. Poof powers rocked. Hopefully they were taking it somewhere where, if it exploded, things wouldn't be hurt. Assumed Groom Lake was going to enjoy another gift from our team.

Looked around to see Stephanie up and holding the waterbender up. Said bender spoke. "You killed my father, and my brothers."

"Maybe. Not sure who your brothers are."

"You murdered them! In their sleep!"

"Um, no, no I didn't. I haven't killed anyone in their sleep, ever."

"Yes you did. All this week. We've lost so many."

"Um, how many?" Good to get confirmation of what Team Assassin was up to. Not a surprise Buchanan hadn't wanted to share what was going on. But it made sense—Siler had written these people off, he knew they were dangerous, and presumably Stephanie had led him to a lot of them. Truly hoped Buchanan and the others had been sure that who they'd killed were bad guys. "And were these brothers people you grew up with or dudes you've met in the last year or so?"

"It doesn't matter how long you've known someone. If they're your blood, they're your blood."

Okay, that felt like proof that these brothers of hers were more Yates Kids found in the last year. "I didn't kill any of them. Neither did anyone here."

"Yes, you did." Her eyes were wide—crazy eyes for sure. "You, all of you, are murdering bastards and we're going to wipe you off the face of the Earth."

"Technically, you and your siblings would be the murdering bastards. But whatever makes you happy. I'm not going to allow you to kill anyone, especially not all those innocent people down there you seem hell-bent on hurting. They've done less than nothing to you. There's no reason to attack them, other than the fact that you know we'll do everything we can to protect them."

Stephanie was backing the two of them away from me. Wasn't sure why. Neither one of them could be hurt that badly, because I hadn't actually done any kind of real beat down on them. So she was either trying to get away from me, or trying to get me to move somewhere.

Risked a look around. In addition to some press who were still here, there was a guy trying to sneak up on me. Pity for him that Prince was here. The dog tackled this guy silently, took him down, and stood on his chest, growling, fangs right against the guy's throat.

"Good dog!" Turned back. Stephanie and the waterbender

had disappeared. Cursed, ran over and did a side blade kick against the guy's head so he was fully out, and then took off running at human speeds, just to be sure I didn't miss anything, Prince bounding along at my side.

Reached the stairs again. "You stay here," I said to Prince. "I'll be right back." Raced upstairs. There were two more levels, one loaded with meeting rooms, one with the ballroom. As I reached the third floor, someone grabbed me.

"It's me," Christopher said quickly, as I spun to hit him. "I already checked everything. It's clear."

"You saw the tank and didn't do anything?"

He shrugged. "You were handling it."

"Gee, thanks. Stephanie and the waterbender have escaped, no idea where they are."

"Not upstairs."

"Well, that's good. There's a bomb somewhere, though, I'm sure of it."

"Bombs work best when they're low, to bring a building down. And there were none on these top floors, or the roof, which I also checked." He took my hand and we raced back downstairs, Christopher grabbing Prince on the way.

A fast check of the outer lower level showed no bombs. My music went to "Mobscene" by Marilyn Manson. This combined with what we hadn't found meant the bombs were in with all the people, for maximum damage. And, based on what had gone on before, they were ricin bombs.

Rejoined the mob of panicked, fighting people. "You search," I shouted to Christopher. "You're the fastest." He nodded, put Prince down, and took off.

Prince heaved all over someone waving an anti-alien sign. I grabbed the sign and hit them with it. Hit a few others holding nasty signs, too. The benefits of hyperspeed and superstrength meant that I knocked these people out on the first try.

I needed to get the room cleared and get to Jeff, not necessarily in that order. "The Angry Mob" by the Kaiser Chiefs came on. Decided this meant I needed to bang some more heads.

Did so—they were really easy to spot what with all their

signs and such. As I broke one 2x4 over someone's skull, I just took their sign and kept on going. I was so enraged that I was fairly sure no one knew what hit them, because I was pretty sure I was going far too fast to be seen by anyone except maybe Christopher.

As I finished taking out about a hundred people there was a shout and collective gasp. Looked to the stage. Everyone else was down, and Stephanie had Jeff on his knees, with a gun to his head. The waterbender was with them, and she had a tube of water spinning around them. It was deflecting bullets, at least as near as I could tell.

Two women came to me as "Come Hell or High Water" by Poison hit my personal airwaves. Had that right. "What would you have us do?" one asked, and I realized they were Rahmi and Rhee.

"We need to take those two women down before they can kill Jeff."

As I said this, I spotted someone I wasn't expecting—Cameron Maurer. He trotted right by us and through people, knocking them out of his way. Tried to get a bead on where he was headed. "Lift me up please," I said to Rahmi, who obliged. I followed his trajectory—which, despite the chaos, was simple due to people being knocked aside—and realized he was going to end up near to the stage. Where Christopher was, with Chuckie, working feverishly on something.

Rahmi put me down. "Follow our android," I told them. His route would put us close enough to the stage and we'd get there quickly because he was clearing a path. Picked Prince up again, and we all took off.

Got onto the stage in a matter of seconds. Stephanie was enjoying her moment in the spotlight, and hadn't shot Jeff in the head yet. But it was only a matter of time.

The people who'd been around Jeff were alive, I could see all of them breathing. As I grabbed Tim's gun, which was, happily, a Glock, something I'd really been hoping wouldn't happen did.

The air around us swirled, as if there were a variety of dust devils forming without dust. Looked around. Spotted

Mahin—she was fighting with a couple of people I was pretty sure were half-siblings—so it wasn't her doing this.

The air devils formed into shapes. Eight shapes. Eight humanoid shapes. One of which was far more defined than the others. "I am sorry," Sandy said. "But the time for judgment is here."

CHAPTER 91

"THIS IS REALLY BAD TIMING. Give me a couple of minutes to save my husband's life and ensure the nasty bomb that's going to kill and/or poison everyone here doesn't go off. Then I'll be glad to let you all toss your weight around, okay?"

"This is the leader?" one of the others asked Sandy.

"No, I'm not the leader. Well, I'm ACE's leader, yes. And I lead our people. Somewhat. But I'm not 'the' leader."

As I said this I noted a couple things. One of which was that Cameron Maurer had reached Christopher and Chuckie. He wrested something from them, and took off running, again bowling people over left and right.

The other was that if Maurer was doing this, then the Superconsciousness Council hadn't moved us out of time. Meaning that the entire world was seeing this particular showdown. Oh good. I was drenched and bedraggled, so totally ready for my close-up.

"We look around and see how unworthy all of you are," one of the other shapes said.

"Well, as I look around, I can easily find us unruly, even though we're all definitely quieting down due to confusion, fear, and the sheer awesomeness of being in your august presences, but unworthy? No. We're not unworthy. Younger than you, yeah, by millennia or more, I'm sure. Different, absolutely. But unworthy? A few of us, sure. But the vast majority? Worthy. At least as worthy as you. Maybe more so."

"We find you unworthy," the one said again.

Contemplated my options. I could beg and such, but I wasn't in the mood. I could ignore them and try to get to Stephanie, but they'd probably stop me. However, Sandy had told me what their ultimate weakness was, and now I realized exactly why Sandy had done so. It was good to have friends all over.

"And I find you rude. Okey dokey. Guys, or gals, or whatever you are, I hate dealing with formless, nameless beings. Particularly nameless. So, there are seven of you. Line up, names are coming."

"What are you saying?" a third asked, sounding horrified.

"Well, Doc, I don't know. Grumpy seems to think we're unworthy. Happy wants to know if I'm the leader. Sneezy, Sleepy, Bashful, and Dopey haven't spoken yet, but I'm sure they'll add in."

"Who are you naming Dopey?" another one asked, sounding outraged. Despite the situation, heard some giggles from the crowd.

"You, congrats on stepping up. Everyone, meet the Super-consciousness Seven. Sneezy, Sleepy, wave to the audience. Bashful, don't bother, we'll figure out who you are. Eventually." There were a few more titters from the audience. Keeping it light, that was me all over.

"Stop it," the one I'd named Doc hissed. "You have no right."

"My world, my rules, my rights. You have no right to come here and try to order us around, Doc. You haven't come to help us, you've come to interfere with us. So you and Grumpy, Happy, Dopey, Sleepy, Sneezy, and Bashful go back to wherever you came from and leave us the hell alone."

"Stop using those names. I am not named Sleepy!"

"Yeah, you are. You chose it, actually, not me. Isn't that right, Sneezy?"

"No," the sixth one said. "I am not Sneezy either."

"Bashful, what's the good word? Okay with your name?"

"Not really," the last replied. "I don't . . . understand it."

"Oh, you will. Soon enough. By the way, I heard a lot of I's in there. Good. Enjoy learning what being an individual feels like. You'll feel very alone, and then you'll realize that other individuals can join with you and make you feel less alone, make you stronger, safer. So, in that sense we're just like you are, only we have to choose to be joined with others. Some of those other individuals are bad. Most are good. That's pretty much our world in a nutshell. Like it or leave it, but seriously, we have a lot going on, so back off, I'm working here."

With that, I turned away from them and toward the nasty tableau on the stage next to me. The waterbender had managed to keep her water tunnel going all this time, but it looked weaker. And I was, by now, the very definition of seriously pissed.

I could see the water, see the individual drops that formed it, and therefore see the spaces in between them. I aimed my gun. "Stop with the water, or I shoot. And I won't miss."

"Why are you aiming for her, not me?" Stephanie taunted. "I'm the one with a gun to your husband's head. Or don't you care about him at all?"

"Oh, I care. I just know when to let someone else handle the big save."

As I said this, Rahmi and Rhee broke through the water barrier. Rahmi slammed her battlestaff onto the arm Stephanie was using to hold the gun on Jeff, while Rhee pulled him away and out of the range of fire.

Stephanie screamed as her gun dropped to the ground. I was pretty sure her arm was broken. The waterbender stared at me.

"Try me," I said conversationally. "Maybe I'm wrong and I can't shoot your head off. But, before you decide, tell me, bitch . . . do you feel lucky?"

She waited another long second. Then the water sloshed onto the stage, and she put her hands up. Apparently she did not.

Claudia and Lorraine hypersped over and put her and Stephanie into restraints, despite Stephanie screaming and starting what sounded like a tantrum. Much nastier restraints than handcuffs.

Looked around. There were a lot of people in the same kind of restraints. Apparently all the good guys had been spending the breather Sandy and his folks had provided in getting the bad guys tied up. Wondered if Sandy had considered this might happen. Decided that he probably had.

Mous-Mous jumped out of my purse and started mewling, meowing, and jumping up and down. It was clear that the Poof was talking to Sandy and the Seven Superconsciousnesses, not anyone else. I let the conversation go on while I went to Jeff and hugged him tightly.

"Can I say, once again, how much I hate how all the bad guys want you on your knees so they can kill you dramatically?"

"It's because I'm tall. And as long as they don't actually kill me, I don't care." He kissed me. "You were awesome, baby, as always."

"Yeah." Surveyed the scene. There were bullet holes through almost every poster, half of the décor was down or halfway down. The video screens were shot up. Many people looked as bad as I did.

Raj came over and handed me his microphone. "Cast your delegation's votes."

"Seriously?"

He nodded. "We've had the stage long enough."

I laughed, and turned to the audience. "American Centaurion gives all its votes to the Armstrong-Martini ticket."

Wasn't sure what to expect. But someone started clapping, then a few more, and a few more. And all of a sudden the room was cheering again, as if this horrific battle hadn't just happened.

Sandy set down on the stage next to us. He'd pulled some downed flag streamers in to make himself look solid, just like he had with water and sand. It was no weirder than any of his other looks. No better, either.

"This is us," I said to him. "We get knocked down and we get back up again." "Tub Thumping" by Chumbawamba came onto my airwaves as I said this. I laughed again and pulled my earbuds out. "If you try to hurt us, we'll fight back, and we won't stop until you go away and leave us the hell alone."

Sandy shook his head. "No. You've proven your worth. You defended the helpless when all you had to do was run away and remain safe."

"We don't run away," Jeff said. "We came to this world and asked for refuge. And in return we promised to help and to protect it and the people on it. That's still what we're here for. And that means protecting people we don't like, who don't like us right back. Not all the time, but many times."

Sandy looked around. "Many of your enemies are dead or down."

"There are always more. Trust me." Realized that, because I still had the microphone, everyone in the room had heard us. Decided not to care. But I turned the mic off, because what we were going to discuss with Sandy now wasn't for general consumption. "But, what's the plan? The Seven Superconsciousnesses going to try to destroy us, take ACE, or similar?"

"No. They're going to leave." Sandy sounded amused. "I warned them not to come, but they had to see it for themselves."

Reached out and took his hand. While I could feel his hand as a real thing, it also felt insubstantial, as if, were I to squeeze it, it would dissolve into nothing. "Thanks for your help."

"You are welcome. I am not going to join with Paul. Right now, anyway."

"Why not? Too much excitement for you?"

"No. I wish to visit other worlds, see what their inhabitants are like, learn their good and bad. And unlike those who protect you now, I have less restraint in terms of helping you. I would do what the others are able to avoid—I would help you too much. I would make you dependent upon me, and I would become the despotic god I do not want to be."

He squeezed my hand, and didn't dissolve. Instead, he formed, from the inside out. Which was icky, but masked greatly by the décor he'd used as his form outline. Sadly, there were a lot of bullet holes in that décor, so I could still see his internal organs and bones and such. Managed not to gag, but only because I was still so revved up.

Once his skin and hair were on, he smiled at me. "Thank you."

"You're going to stay as a human? I don't think we travel well through space."

"No. But now that I know how to form as you are, I can do so when I want to or need to."

Mous-Mous came over, jumped onto his shoulder, and purred. "Mous-Mous, are you staying with Sandy?" Tried not to sound horrified. Failed. I'd promised Jamie I'd protect her Poof. How would I explain that I'd let it go off with some superconsciousness that might or might not ever be back?

"No," Sandy said gently. "Your daughter's pet will never desert her. It argued quite eloquently on your race's behalf, and for you in particular. But just now it was merely sharing its thanks with me as well, in its own way." Sandy took Mous-Mous off his shoulder, patted the Poof gently, then handed it back to me.

Clutched the Poof to me. "Back into Kitty's purse." Mous-Mous purred at me, then did as requested. Checked. I had a lot of Poofs back in there, including Harlie and Poofikins, so all was well in Poof Land. "So, Sandy, what now?"

"Now we leave you. But I will do you one small favor." He waved his hand and everything was put back in its place, everything was repaired, every single thing. The room, and presumably the rest of the convention center, looked as if nothing had happened.

"Thank you, but yeah," Jeff said, "we need you to leave. Miracles like that make humans and A-Cs very desperate to bow down and worship."

"We know. All of us will be leaving. And while we may visit from time to time, we will ensure that the majority never know of it."

"One thing, before you go?"

Sandy nodded. "I know what you want to know. And as much as I want to tell you, I can't. It will . . . disrupt the balance of things. This great secret you all must learn on your own."

"One little hint?" I asked. Okay, I wheedled. Hey, I really wanted to know who the hell the Mastermind was.

"No. I will give you some advice instead. Offer the truce. It will be in everyone's best interests." Sandy took my hand and squeezed it one last time. Then he dissolved into thin air, and the others with him did as well.

CHAPTER 92

"TRUCE?" Jeff asked.

"Later. Trust me."

There was a lot of chaos still, because you don't witness what truly looks like a miracle and not talk about it. A good chunk of time was spent with security forces removing the Club 51 and other protestors, loading them into police vans, and so forth. The higher-level terrorists, as in Stephanie and the ones we could tell were Ronnie's Kids, we held onto.

The American Samoan delegation's representative suggested the rest of the fifty-plus speakers pass on all the state and territory speeches and just share their delegate votes. Some states wanted to do a fast recount, which, under the circumstances, was allowed. So, while security was doing its thing, the delegations did theirs.

Our delegation was moved back to the Candidates' Staging Area, which was different from the regular staging area by being about fifteen feet farther away from the stage.

Went over to Reader and Tim. "Do we have any idea what happened to Cameron Maurer and the bomb he wrested away from Christopher and Chuckie?"

Tim nodded. "He deactivated it, then brought it back to the Embassy. It's over in the Science Center, in a containment room."

"What? How?"

Reader shook his head. "I have no idea. But I think Serene and Chernobog tinkered with his programming."

"Thank God for that."

"Yeah. Good job, girlfriend. And thanks for having your special friend fix up the convention center. I wasn't looking forward to the repair bills."

"What about all the people who were hurt?"

"All fixed, too," Tim said. "Other than any bad guys we killed. They're still dead."

"Interesting."

"I think that means they cast their votes with American Centaurion." Reader flashed the cover boy grin. "At least, that's my party line."

"We can hope that's how it was interpreted. By the way, where was all the security everyone told me was going to be so very effective? And where the hell is my mother?"

Tim grimaced. "Interesting thing. Every agency— P.T.C.U., C.I.A., F.B.I., Homeland Security, and any other Alphabet Agency that was supposed to be here—was called off this morning due to what was considered an extremely credible threat to the White House and the Pentagon. The only security left were D.C.P.D., Secret Service, and the National Guard. But we had a smaller Secret Service contingent because of all the other security that was supposed to be here, D.C.P.D. was spread thin because of all the street and crowd control they had to do, and the National Guard was kept busy and then overrun by the protestors."

"Reynolds was supposed to go, too, but he pretended he didn't get the message," Reader added. "The problem, of course, is that there was no actual threat, credible or otherwise, and the order, which was again supposedly presidential in nature, did not originate from the President or anyone on his staff."

"So, was Chernobog behind it, do we think?"

"No," Tim said. "Because Stryker and his team insist they've verified every keystroke she's made. She's also the one who determined that the order hadn't really come from the President."

"So, who hacked in if the top hacker in the world and the next five best didn't do it?"

"I think we have her in custody," Reader said. "Because right now our money's on Stephanie. Or else it was the Mastermind."

"My money's on Langston Whitmore."

"Could be," Reader allowed. "Bottom line? We don't know."

"Is my mom okay?"

"Pissed as hell, but yeah, she's fine," Tim said. "So are all our bases, the Embassy, and so on. The faked order was clearly to get security away from here."

"Oh well, it is what it is." As I said this, I felt like someone was watching me. Turned around to see the guy I'd knocked out on the mezzanine level. He was right behind Jeff who was somehow standing somewhat alone and sort of in the shadows, with no one nearby. And the guy I'd knocked out but hadn't killed had a gun pointed at the back of Jeff's head.

I opened my mouth to scream, but the guy never fired. Because Jeff wasn't actually alone.

Prince leaped out from the darkness and grabbed the guy's gun arm in his mouth as he pulled him to the ground. Ran over and kicked the gun away as Prince bore down with his jaws and the guy screamed. Tim got the gun, Prince moved to stand on the guy's chest and growl his regrets for not killing this guy before. Reader joined us and Prince let him get the guy into cuffs as Jeff spun around, looking shocked.

Slammed my foot into this guy's groin. "I've kicked you in the head, and now I've kicked you in the balls," I said as he whimpered. "If you ever try to hurt someone I care about again, I'll kick your balls up into your stomach and your head off of your neck."

Prince sniffed at the prisoner intensely, barked, growled, and barked again.

"What?" Jeff asked.

"This is the guy who attacked Missus Maurer." Made sense. He'd gone for me and Jeff from behind, just as he'd

done with her. "Good boy Prince. You always get the perp."
Had an incredible urge to kill this guy. But I resisted the urge,
because, despite what our enemies had been told and clearly
believed, I didn't kill people in cold blood. Plus, this particular prisoner would be extremely useful to have alive and in
our severest form of custody.

All the security that was supposed to have been here already finally arrived and we gave this guy, Stephanie, the
waterbender, and all the others identified as high risk and
somewhat in the know to the P.T.C.U. Reassured my mother
that all was well, after she stopped hugging me and Jeff and
allowed us both to breathe again.

With the rest of security here, the other politicians were
brought back in. Thankfully, none of them were hurt and no
one had taken the opportunity to try to kidnap Armstrong or
something.

Finally the rest of the delegations were ready again. The
Armstrongs and McMillans stayed with us as the delegation
representatives went up one by one. And, one by one, they
cast all their votes for Armstrong-Martini. As Wyoming cast
the last votes, it was official—we had a unanimous vote.

While everyone was happily congratulating everyone
else, I slipped out and went to the bathroom. In part because
I figured I needed to give fixing myself up a shot. But also
because I knew what Sandy had meant. Made sure I was
alone and locked the main door.

Sent Buchanan a text. He called me back. "Sorry I wasn't
there, Missus Chief." He sounded upset and worried.

"It's okay, Malcolm. I think you were off doing things that
are bad yet helpful. But that's not why I'm calling. I need to
talk to my Uncle Peter."

"Hang on."

The phone was handed off. "Miss Katt, you are well?"

"Yeah." Risked a glance in the mirror. "I look just like I
did when we went swimming in the Potomac. But otherwise,
I'm good. So is pretty much everyone else."

"We saw. Impressive use of otherworldly forces."

"Yeah, that was a lucky break."

"The news reporters are calling it a legitimate miracle."

"How lucky we all are. Your contract on Chernobog, it was contingent on your killing her before the National Convention, right?"

"Yes. However, we received thanks of the confirmation of our kill along with the monies owed to us. And a substantial bonus."

"Yeah, about that . . . Chernobog's really amazing with all the computer stuff. And old ladies die all the time, of natural causes and all that. Apparently hospital records are amazingly easy to hack and alter, too. Who knew?"

"So, she has faked her death and given us the credit?"

"Yes. She died of a 'heart attack' that you gave her. I'm not sure how long it'll be before the person who hired you realizes they've been duped. But I do figure they'll find out. However, Chernobog is tracking the money trail. I'm hoping she can figure out who paid you, and therefore, possibly who hired you, before they figure out she's still alive. Is this enough for you to not kill her?"

"She's already dead. Why would we kill some old woman living in your Embassy?"

"You're the best."

"You ensure we keep on getting paid and also receive credit for amazing kills. We consider you the best, too."

"I think you're compromised, though. Because of me. People know you care about me."

"They do. They also now know I care about someone who has friends who can wave their hand and perform a miracle on national and international television. I am less worried about this weakness than you are."

"How many of the Yates offspring are left alive?"

"More than we would like."

"Did you kill some of them in their sleep?"

"Yes. It is more humane." He sighed. "Your protector does not want me telling you this."

"He thinks I'm going to dwell on it and feel guilty."

"Are you?"

"Honestly? No. I didn't ask you or tell you to do this, and I understand why you did. But I do think you need to stop."

"Then we will stop."

"That was too easy. You've run out of cells to clear out, haven't you?"

"It's nice when goals align, isn't it?"

"It is. Thank you, again, for all your help. Could I talk to Malcolm again, please?"

"Yes. We will be in touch. And if you need us, just go to your roof."

"Gotcha."

Buchanan came back on. "Sorry, Missus Chief."

"It's okay, Malcolm. You've said it enough, and, as I told my Uncle Peter, I know why you did it. I need to know if you know how I can reach Gideon Cleary on a private, secured line, where no one else will be able to tap or hear our conversation."

"Yes, give me a moment." He gave me two sets of numbers. "Dial the first one, when you click through, then call the second number. You'll be on a secured clandestine ops line. Why are you calling him?"

"To try to prevent you and our friends in the Assassination Squad from having to kill a lot more people, on either side. By the way, come home. It's weird without you shadowing me everywhere."

He chuckled. "It's always nice to be appreciated, but don't let your husband know you miss me when I'm gone."

We hung up and I sent a text to Stryker. He also called me right away. "She found it. Interesting money trail. Led straight to where you thought it would. She has access to all his bank records now, as well as all those who are connected to him. And she took the bonus out of one of his slush funds. He won't know for a while."

"Awesome. The Dingo was happy to take the deal."

Stryker relayed this. "She's pleased. She says she's happy to play dead in the Zoo. She likes our setup."

"I'm sure she does. Thank her for whatever she, Serene, and you guys did to Cameron Maurer. And remind her that the Mastermind and his gang will figure it all out sooner as opposed to later and she shouldn't get sloppy. That goes triple for the rest of you. Especially since I'm sure you and the other guys are more than excited to get to learn at her knee."

"You know it. Oh, Olga says that it's time for you to play hardball. But nicely."

"Yeah, I will."

"By the way, you really need to fix your hair and makeup before your speech. But the wet T-shirt look is a good one, so I'd stick with it if I were you."

"It's a blouse, not a T-shirt."

"Trust me, Kitty, right now, it's about the same."

"Ha ha ha, I'll hurt you later, Eddy." Hung up and dialed the numbers Buchanan had given me. Worked just like he'd said it would. Cleary answered on the second ring. "Hello?"

"Gideon, hi. This is Kitty Katt-Martini. We're on a secured line, just FYI. We've met, when your pet android was holding me up in the air."

"Yes, I remember. What can I do for you?" He sounded like he'd just eaten a lemon.

"This call is about what we can do for each other. Which is why I called using a clandestine ops channel that can't be traced or recorded."

"Go on."

"I realize that you think you've won by killing off an old lady who had some serious skills, by getting the Secretary of Transportation to send out fake presidential orders, and by getting the easily led Club Fifty-One people and their ilk to attack us en masse. However, I think we've just shown that we have some powerful friends in really high places, as well as other friends in very low places, all of whom are very willing to help us in their own special ways."

"Yes, what's your point?" Interesting. He didn't deny the Secretary of Transportation or Club 51 things. Always nice to be right.

"I want us to call a truce."

"Why would I want to do that?"

"You can dig up skeletons we don't want revealed to the public. And then we can produce Cameron Maurer and open up his chest for the world to see. You can dig up more dirt. We have the guy who tried to kill me, Jeff, and Nancy Maurer in a severe form of custody, and we'll share what he tells us about your dirty dealings with the world. Maybe you toss out more dirt on us. We'll make you pay for that financially, trust me. You can kill some of ours and we'll kill some of yours. Or . . ."

"Or what?"

"Or we can agree that you want to be president and Vincent Armstrong wants to be president, as well, and just run normal campaigns. Less mudslinging, more issues. I realize this goes against the majority of political precedent, but let's agree to be the first in a long while to give it a go, shall we?"

"What if I refuse?"

"We empty your coffers. Easily, I might add. We call back our friends who think we're sort of worth helping and who also think you are not, and we let them wave their very powerful hands around. We do other things you aren't aware that we can do and make your life, or what will be left of it, a living hell. Or, you and I just agree to be polite, decent human beings and run non-smear campaigns, keeping each other's skeletons safely in each other's closets."

"I can see you've given this some thought."

"Yeah, despite my reputation, I do, occasionally, think."

"How long can I have to think about this?"

"About now is long enough. Pick your side, Gideon. Choose Team Escalation or Team Truce, but pick it now. I'm a busy woman and I have an acceptance speech I need to give."

He was quiet for a few long seconds. Used the time to look in the mirror again and try to decide what fixes to my so-called look I could possibly manage.

"If I pick Team Truce, how do I know you won't use that advantage against me?"

"Because I'm not like you."

He laughed. "Frankly, I think you're just like me."

"No. I have morals, scruples, and things I'm just not willing to do."

"But you have other people do those things. So we are alike. And despite your likely expectations, I'm going to take your offer of a truce and . . . accept it. You probably think what happened today will help your side, but I know people. You've just shown how frightening you all can actually be.

We won't need to resort to dirty tricks to beat you, so I accept your offer of truce."

"Super. Oh, and as for your whole beating us fair and square without using dirty tricks boasting, we have a little saying where I come from—prove it."

"I will. See you on the campaign trail, Ambassador. I look forward to hearing your husband's concession speech on the first Tuesday in November."

"And I look forward to hearing yours. I'll be in touch should it seem as though your side isn't holding to our agreement, and I'm sure you'll do the same."

"Yes. Good chat, Ambassador." He chuckled. "I'm quite looking forward to the next few months now. A new challenge is always invigorating, don't you find?" He hung up without saying goodbye. Decided I could find the will to go on.

I could either go home and have Pierre fix me up or give that idea up and just go for being me. Chose what had been working for the past four or so years. Washed the sad remains of my makeup off, brushed my hair, pulled it back into a ponytail, and headed out of the bathroom.

Jeff was waiting outside, leaning against the wall opposite the bathroom door, holding my suit jacket. He was a little rumpled, but that just made him look rakish and, if possible, even more handsome. "Want to tell me about it?"

"When we're home I'll fill you in on anything you somehow missed while you were out here reading me."

He grinned as I pulled my hairbrush back out and ran it through his hair. "I just missed being fussed over. You think they'll stick to the offer you made?"

"Yes, because I just gave them another Get Out Of Jail Free card. Cleary's many things, but stupid and foolhardy aren't two of them." Jeff helped me back into my damp jacket. "Can't wait to give a speech looking like this."

He laughed. "You looked good before, baby, but you look like you now, and that means perfect."

"Flatterer."

"Nope. I only tell the truth, remember? Ready to go accept the party's nomination?"

"About as ready as I was to become a superbeing exterminator way back when."

He kissed me. "Then that means you're not only ready, but you'll be the best. Just like always."

"Well, to paraphrase someone I love, adore, and respect, as long as you're with me, I can do anything."

Jeff put his arm around my waist and we headed back to smile, wave, and try, in whatever ways worked best, to continue to do what we truly did best—protect and serve.

THE FIRST TUESDAY IN NOVEMBER

TRADITION SAID that the candidates watched the election results in their home states. This meant that both campaigns were hanging out in Florida.

While the opposition had rented out the Miami Beach Convention Center for their election night viewing party, the Armstrong campaign was hanging out at Jeff's parents' estate, what I called Martini Manor.

Per the truce I'd brokered with Cleary, the campaign had actually been fairly civil. They'd left our many skeletons in our closets and we'd done the same for them.

Oh, sure, the usual anti-alien muckraking and mudslinging had reared its ugly head, coming mostly from Club 51, the Church of Hate and Intolerance, and the various news channels that loved them. But the hysteria or accusations or whatever were always quelled from the top before they got too in-depth or too close to real facts. In fact, we'd ended up sort of covering for each other when the press asked awkward questions.

The debates had been decent—if you ignored all the "why are you aliens really here" and "what are you hiding" questions, all of which were softballed and easy for Armstrong and Jeff to sidestep or answer safely—and kept to the issues. As well as any other debates over the past few decades had at any rate. Plus, no one had taken out contracts on the other side, and our various enemies had left us alone, so it was definitely the best option we could have hoped for.

This was good for us in a lot of ways, but not necessarily in the polls. Sure, Cleary-Kramer was still the Hate Ticket, but Cleary had been correct—they had a lot of support. A lot of people still feared us because, well, aliens. Plus, Sandy's "miracle" meant that many people expected us to perform daily miracles and when we didn't, they turned against us, too.

So much so that, despite what felt like nonstop campaigning for three straight months—or as most of us called it, Our Own Private Boot Camp In Hell—we had no idea which candidate was going to win. Pollsters, pundits, and every reporter we knew, including Jenkins and Oliver, felt that Cleary-Kramer were going to take the election, potentially in a landslide.

Martini Manor was packed, though. We had people in the giant Guest House and the giant for normal people Servant's Quarters. All of our people, all of Armstrong's staffers, press, Secret Service, and more.

A huge outdoor tent had been erected on the grounds, and this was where Armstrong and Jeff would either wave and thank everyone for electing them, or wave and thank those who voted for them but concede to the opposition.

We'd voted in D.C., since that was where Jeff and I officially lived, as soon as the polls had opened in the morning. Then we'd gated it down to Florida and spent the rest of the day pretending we weren't stressed out and worried.

Despite the National Convention, or because of it, I was in an iced sky blue dress. Jeff was, of course, in the Armani Fatigues. Jamie was allowed to be all in pink, which was still her favorite color in the world. We all looked great, Pierre having done his magic and no one having dumped water all over us. The Armstrongs looked great, too. As did every other political ally who was here with us. All dressed up and potentially nowhere to go.

The first few states came in. Cleary-Kramer had Maine, Vermont, and New Hampshire. Pundits immediately started suggesting Armstrong-Martini start preparing those concession speeches.

Then more results. Cleary-Kramer got West Virginia and South Carolina. And more. They had Tennessee. Armstrong-Martini concession speeches were being discussed, along with the Cleary-Kramer landslide.

Until, all of a sudden, we got New York and Pennsylvania. Then Virginia and Maryland. And D.C. and North Carolina. And on it went, rolling across the country.

I was sitting with Jenkins and Oliver when they both started laughing. "What is it? What's so funny?"

"We just got Texas," Jenkins replied.

"Yes?"

Oliver smiled at me. "Get ready."

"For the concession speeches?"

He shook his head. "No. To win. We have Ohio, thanks in no small part to the Maurers, Illinois, and Indiana, along with several others with double-digit electoral votes. We know we'll get both New Mexico and Arizona because they're your home states and were the only two polling Armstrong-Martini from the get-go. If we get California, it should seal the deal."

"Florida's results are coming," Jenkins said.

This was a biggie, not only for the votes, but because both presidential candidates were from this state. Cleary was expected to take it; the state had polled Cleary-Kramer from day one.

And yet, when the results were in, Armstrong-Martini had taken Florida. By a wide margin.

The realization that we were suddenly winning a race we'd been told we were about to lose sank in, as the pundits started changing their tunes. The word landslide was still being bandied about, but the word "unexpected" was added to it, as were the words Armstrong-Martini.

Time rolled on, and the party actually started. It was a cautious party, based on the fact that pretty much everyone had expected to not be partying at all, but it was a party nonetheless. Some of the younger staffers were dancing. Realized music had been playing but I'd been too nervous to hear it. Was still too nervous to focus on it.

I rejoined Jeff, who had Jamie cradled on his shoulder. She'd fallen asleep. "You're such a good daddy."

He smiled. "Doing my best." We sat down a little apart from the rest and he put his arm around me and I snuggled next to him, put my hand on Jamie's back, and closed my eyes.

Heard a snapping sound and something bright went off. Opened my eyes. What looked like the nation's entire press corps was standing there, taking pictures of us. "What the hell?"

Jeff chuckled. "Sorry. You fell asleep, baby, and I didn't want to wake you. But the press felt this was a good photo op, so I let them have it."

Yawned. "Good photo op for what?"

"To show how confident and relaxed the Martini family was about the election," Jenkins replied.

Managed not to say we were tired and stressed. I'd learned to shut up faster these past three months. "So, how much longer until we know?"

Someone screamed. Not out of fear, but excitement. Then more screams. Then cheers.

Raj took the stage and the mic. "Ladies and gentlemen, they said it couldn't be done, but hard work, perseverance, and fighting for what's right pays off. It's official—despite the polls, the voters have spoken and Vincent Armstrong and Jeffrey Martini have taken this election by a landslide. Please help me greet the next President and Vice President of the United States of America!"

Lots of applause, cheering, and far too much flash photography. Jamie woke up a little fussy, but Jeff kissed and cuddled her as we walked to the stage and she cheered up and stood next to me, holding my hand.

On stage with the Armstrongs. Hugs all around. While "Hail to the Chief" played, Armstrong took center stage, grabbed Jeff's hand, and threw their hands up in the victory clench. The crowd went wilder than it had been.

Elaine and their children and grandchildren joined Armstrong, and Jamie and I joined Jeff. Everyone waved, myself included. I kept on waiting to wake up.

As we stepped back and Armstrong gave his acceptance speech, the reality of the situation hit me. "You're really about to become the vice president. Wow. What does that make me, the Second-Best Lady?"

Jeff grinned, swung Jamie up into his arms again, and put his free arm around me. "Baby, you're second best to no one. And you can have whatever title you want." He looked around. "We won. We really won."

"Yeah. And let me be the first to say how proud of you I am." Saw all our friends and family clapping and cheering. "Nothing's ever going to be the same, is it?"

"No. But you know what we call that."

I laughed. "Yeah, I do. Routine."

Available December 2014,
the tenth novel in the *Alien* series
from Gini Koch:

UNIVERSAL ALIEN

Read on for a sneak preview

THE FORMER PRESIDENT OF INDIA, Abdul Kalam, shared a lovely sentiment—Look at the sky. We are not alone. The whole universe is friendly to us and conspires only to give the best to those who dream and work.

He's totally right that we're not alone, of course. But with all due respect, Former President Kalam is dead wrong about the entire universe being friendly to us. There's a lot of "others" out there, and while some are all for helping good ol' Earth, there are plenty who think we should be avoided, enslaved, or destroyed.

George Carlin said that if it's true that our species is alone in the universe, then I'd have to say the universe aimed rather low and settled for very little.

I know he's right. I just know there's more out there than we've seen. I look for it, sometimes, when I feel alone. I look for all the "others" out there. So far, unless they're in a comic or a book or a movie, I haven't found them.

I'm not sure what's actually more surreal—that the universe is teeming with life of all kinds, or that I've somehow gone from being a single marketing manager to the wife of the Vice President of the United States in just under five years.

Oh sure, there was a lot in between "there" to "here"—much of it filled with having to fight many very bad things, both extraterrestrial and very terrestrial. Humans are really the worst, though. We're devious and nasty on a scale that, thankfully so far, none of the aliens showing up to visit or move in seem able to manage. I'll take a fugly space monster over most of the human megalomaniacs I've dealt with over the years.

Being married to an alien, at least one from Alpha Four of the Alpha Centauri system, is the highlight. Well, our hybrid and scary-talented daughter is a highlight, too. Jeff and Jamie make all the change and general surreality that has become my daily life worthwhile.

Sometimes, I wonder what it's all about. I mean, we have a pretty great life, and I love my family. I'm a good wife, mother, and daughter, and I do things that matter. But there are days when I just can't do anything right, and I wonder what's wrong with me.

Oh, of course, I have bad days. Sadly, since becoming the Second Lady, or whatever I'm really supposed to be called now, there's a lot of pressure. Shockingly, with more public scrutiny comes more ways for me to screw up. And there are days when I wonder what's wrong with me.

Sometimes, I just want to see what it would be like, if things were just a little different. Maybe not a whole lot different, just enough so I could do something more, be something more . . . be something else.

Sometimes, I just want to know what it would be like if I was me, but maybe a little less unwillingly famous and a whole lot more competent on the regular people things I sometimes seem incapable of managing with anything resembling smoothness or skill.

Some days, I just want to be somewhere else. A place where I do everything right.

Some days, I'd really like to be somewhere else. Where everything I do is right.

Hey . . . is there an echo in here?

*   *   *

My brains oozed out of my ears.

Not from being shot or something. From boredom. Massive, stultifying boredom. Boredom on a scale so epic I didn't think anyone could really fathom it. I could barely fathom it and I was living it.

Cheers went up from those around me. Well, not most of those immediately around me. I was surrounded by Americans. Sure, more than half of them were actually aliens either originally or first generation out from Alpha Four in the Alpha Centauri system, but still, living and raised as Americans. And this was *not* an American pastime.

"You're sure this is cricket? I mean, the game. The game that millions of people around the world supposedly love?"

This earned me a dirty look from everyone near me, American or no. I'd tried to keep my voice low, but apparently cricket shared something in common with that most boring of Scottish games that had immigrated to the U.S., golf, in that the fans were hushed unless something "exciting" was happening on the field.

I wasn't actually sitting next to my husband. As the newly minted Vice President of these non-cricket-mad United States, Jeff was sitting a couple of rows below me, with now-President Armstrong, and the Australian Prime Minister. Technically, as his wife, I should have been sitting with them.

Wiser heads had prevailed, however. Despite a great deal of effort and patience on the part of the Head of the C.I.A.'s Extra-Terrestrial Division and the American Centaurion Public Relations Minister—otherwise known as Charles Reynolds and Rajnish Singh—after a week's worth of immersion, I still hadn't been able to grasp or enjoy cricket.

Since we'd been in our mid-twenties Chuckie had lived half the year in Australia, and Raj had been born and raised in New Delhi. Ergo, they both actually enjoyed cricket. In fact, Raj was quite a rabid fan, and Chuckie had an Aussie team he supported. Meaning if anyone was going to get this game through to me, it should have been them.

Only, it took the complexity of baseball, the slowness of golf, and the bizarreness of croquet, and managed to turn them into something that, sports lover that I was or no, I just couldn't manage to follow, let alone like.

The hope had been that I'd have picked up enough to have the light bulb go off while watching a live match and suddenly become an expert. Hope might have sprung eternal, but it was definitely being dashed against the wicket today, because I still wasn't sure where the wicket was, let alone what it was, or why it existed, other than to be the current bane of my existence.

It didn't help matters much that the entire point of this extravaganza was that the Australian government was visiting to show support for not only the new administration in particular but also aliens in general.

Because of Operation Destruction, the entire world knew aliens lived here. The entire world also knew that there were a lot of different alien races out there, and some of them really hated humanity. Of course, some of them liked us just fine, in part because we'd given the exiled A-Cs a home.

However, there were still a lot of people around the world who felt that aliens were the worst things to hit Earth, and they wanted us gone. Off planet, in work camps, or merely wiped off the face of the Earth, they weren't picky. What with Jeff and then-Senator, now-President Armstrong having had a surprise landslide win, having a known alien a heartbeat away from the presidency had all these anti-alien groups in a tizzy of epic proportions.

Australia had its share of alien haters. Club 51, our biggest, most coordinated anti-alien enemy, had made a lot of inroads into Australia, meaning one of America's biggest allies had a huge anti-alien population.

So it was vital for us to make the Australian Prime Minister and his retinue feel happy and comfortable. The PM was a huge cricket fan, hence this game. That I was supposed to feign excitement about.

Wished I'd studied acting instead of business in college, because, despite my desire to be a good wife and representative of my constituents, I was failing to convince anyone that I liked this sport.

The fact that we'd spent money to fix up the stadium where the Redskins played football to look like a cricket field didn't help. They weren't my team—we might live in D.C. now, but I remained true to my Arizona Cardinals and their tradition of usually losing—but I'd have committed many major felonies to have seen the Redskins trot onto the field and toss the pigskin around. I couldn't pick a Redskins player out of a lineup, but still, football was a sport I understood and enjoyed.

I loved baseball, too, but neither the Washington Nationals nor my beloved Diamondbacks were going to be showing up to save my day. There were lots of guys on the field who, from the program, were quite cute. Not that you could really see them. So I didn't have that distraction going for me. And when I could see them they were standing around in a giant circle or running back and forth along a small strip of dirt in the middle of the field, so far, far away. For whatever reason, this didn't make my Sports Gene go wild.

My phone beeped and I dug it out of my purse. At a normal sporting event I'd never have heard it. At this one, not a problem. Of course, I wasn't supposed to spend time on my phone when we were at public events such as this one, but our daughter wasn't with us and the text could be about her.

Sadly, it was from the head of Alpha Team. Reader was none-too-gently suggesting I plaster a look of enjoyment onto my face. He wasn't technically at this event—Alpha Team's job was to protect, not to be the face of American Centaurion. Had no idea where in the stadium Reader and the others actually were, other than nowhere I could see them. However, they could see me, and I looked, if I took his text to be accurate, "like you're about to die while passing gas."

Sent a reply text with one word—"charming"—in it. Wanted to say other words. But my Secret Service detail had clued me in—I had no such thing as privacy anymore.

Dropped my phone back into my purse as people nearby gasped. Something was happening on the field. It appeared to be exciting, based on the crowd's increased murmuring. Couldn't tell what the heck it was. Looked around. Right now would be a great time for a parasitic superbeing to form, or for an intergalactic invasion to happen, or something else that would alleviate the boredom. Waited hopefully. Nothing. Apparently the Powers That Be liked cricket. Or had been bored into inactivity.

"When is the halftime or intermission or whatever?" I asked Raj. Again, tried to keep my voice down, but apparently the acoustics in this stadium were great, because I got another host of dirty looks.

"There isn't really a break like that, as I've explained." He managed not to add "over and over again" but I could see the thought written on his face. "We're watching a T-twenty game, so there will be a short intermission in about an hour."

We'd already been watching this for an hour and had been here even longer. I wasn't sure I could stay conscious for another hour without moving around. And there were at least two more hours to get through after the short 10-20 minute intermission. And this was a "short" game. "Real" cricket could go on for days. Had to figure this game had been created to use as torture for political prisoners and wondered if I could invoke the Geneva Convention as a way out of the boredom. Probably not. My luck never went that way.

Plus I was uncomfortable. Under normal circumstances— you know, before my husband had somehow become the Vice President—I'd have been in jeans, my Converse, an Aerosmith thermal of some kind, and my nice, warm snow jacket. Or I'd have been in what the A-Cs, who were love slaves to black, white, and Armani, always wore—a black slim skirt, a white oxford, and black pumps, with a long black trench coat.

Because we were now among the most public of figures, I was required to pay a lot more attention to what I was wearing. I'd also been assigned my own color—iced blue. I was in iced blue as much as I'd been in black and white before. In fact, I missed black and white, I was in this blue so much nowadays. This meant, therefore, that for this event I was in an iced blue pantsuit, with an off-white Angora sweater, and high-heeled boots that were of a neutral color. And pearls. Supposedly I looked great. I felt remarkably stupid dressed like this at a sporting event.

Chuckie got a text and grunted. "You need to pretend to be having fun," he said.

Either his voice hadn't carried or everyone else agreed with him, because no one shot the Evil Eye toward us.

"I'm trying."

"It's not working."

Made up my mind. "Then I'm out of here."

"What the hell?" Chuckie sounded ready to lose it, though he managed to keep his voice down.

"You can't leave," Raj said, as he tried to watch the so-called action on the field and look at me at the same time, with limited success.

"No freaking duh. I'm going to the concession stand. Now."

Raj, sensing that the emergency was about a negative three on a scale of one to ten, turned his full attention back to the match.

"Couldn't we just send someone?" Chuckie asked, sounding relieved. "You're going to have to go with a contingent, and that's going to be noticed."

"I need to piddle." I didn't, but I needed to splash cold water on my face and drink about a gallon of coffee to make it through this ordeal. Of course, I was in makeup, so cold water on my face was probably out. It was also February and we were outdoors in the freezing cold. I was at risk of dying from hypothermia as well as boredom.

Hypothermia sounded better.

Chuckie heaved a sigh. "The Secret Service has to escort you."

Gini Koch lives in Hell's Orientation Area (aka Phoenix, Arizona), works her butt off (sadly, not literally) by day, and writes by night with the rest of the beautiful people. She lives with her awesome husband, three dogs (aka The Canine Death Squad), and two cats (aka The Killer Kitties). She has one very wonderful and spoiled daughter, who will still tell you she's not as spoiled as the pets (and she'd be right).

When she's not writing, Gini spends her time cracking wise, staring at pictures of good looking leading men for 'inspiration', teaching her pets to 'bring it', and driving her husband insane asking, "Have I told you about this story idea yet?" She listens to every kind of music 24/7 (from Lifehouse to Pitbull and everything in between, particularly Aerosmith) and is a proud comics geek-girl willing to discuss at any time why Wolverine is the best superhero ever (even if Deadpool does get all the best lines). Because she wasn't busy enough, she's added on featured guest columnist and reviewer for Slice of SciFi and It's Comic Book Day.

You can reach Gini via her website (www.ginikoch.com), email (gini@ginikoch.com), Twitter (@GiniKoch), Facebook (facebook.com/Gini.Koch), Facebook Fan Page (Hairspray and Rock 'n' Roll), or her Official Fan Site, the Alien Collective Virtual HQ (http://aliencollectivehq.com/).

Gini Koch
The Alien *Novels*

Diana Rowland

"Rowland's delightful novel jumps genre lines with a little something for everyone—mystery, horror, humor, and even a smattering of romance. Not to be missed—all that's required is a high tolerance for gray matter. For true zombiephiles, of course, that's a no brainer."

—*Library Journal*

"An intriguing mystery and a hilarious mix of the horrific and mundane...Humor and gore are balanced by surprisingly touching moments as Angel tries to turn her (un)life around." —*Publishers Weekly*

My Life as a White Trash Zombie
978-0-7564-0675-2

Even White Trash Zombies
Get the Blues
978-0-7564-0750-6

White Trash Zombie Apocalypse
978-0-7564-0803-9

To Order Call: 1-800-788-6262
www.dawbooks.com

DAW 201

Seanan McGuire

The InCryptid Novels

"McGuire kicks off a new series with a smart-mouthed, engaging heroine and a city full of fantastical creatures. This may seem like familiar ground to McGuire fans, but she makes New York her own, twisting the city and its residents into curious shapes that will leave you wanting more. Verity's voice is strong and sure as McGuire hints at a deeper history, one that future volumes will hopefully explore."

—*RT Book Reviews*

DISCOUNT ARMAGEDDON
978-0-7564-0713-1

MIDNIGHT BLUE-LIGHT SPECIAL
978-0-7564-0792-6

HALF-OFF RAGNAROK
978-0-7564-0811-4

"The only thing more fun than an October Daye book is an InCryptid book. Swift narrative, charm, great world-building . . . all the McGuire trademarks."

—Charlaine Harris

To Order Call: 1-800-788-6262
www.dawbooks.com

DAW 143

Tanya Huff

The *Confederation* Novels

"As a heroine, Kerr shines. She is cut from the same mold
as Ellen Ripley of the Aliens films. Like her heroine,
Huff delivers the goods." —*SF Weekly*

A CONFEDERATION OF VALOR
Omnibus Edition
(*Valor's Choice, The Better Part of Valor*)
978-0-7564-0399-7

THE HEART OF VALOR
978-0-7564-0481-9

VALOR'S TRIAL
978-0-7564-0557-1

THE TRUTH OF VALOR
978-0-7564-0684-4

To Order Call: 1-800-788-6262
www.dawbooks.com

Laura Resnick

The Esther Diamond Novels

"Esther Diamond is the Stephanie Plum of urban fantasy! Unplug the phone and settle down for a fast and funny read!"   —Mary Jo Putney

DISAPPEARING NIGHTLY
978-0-7564-0766-7

DOPPELGANGSTER
978-0-7564-0595-3

UNSYMPATHETIC MAGIC
978-0-7564-0635-6

VAMPARAZZI
978-0-7564-0687-5

POLTERHEIST
978-0-7564-0733-9

THE MISFORTUNE COOKIE
978-0-7564-0847-3

To Order Call: 1-800-788-6262
www.dawbooks.com

DAW 145

Jim Hines

The Jig the Goblin series

"Clever satire… Reminiscent of Terry Pratchett and
Robert Asprin at their best."
—*Romantic Times*

"If you've always kinda rooted for the little guy, even
maybe had a bit of a place in your heart for Gollum,
rather than the Boromirs and Gandalfs of the world,
pick up Goblin Quest."
—*The SF Site*

"This exciting adult fairy tale is filled with adventure
and action, but the keys to the fantasy are Jig and the
belief that the mythological creatures are real in the
realm of Jim C. Hines."
—*Midwest Book Review*

"A rollicking ride, enjoyable from beginning to end…
Jim Hines has just become one of my must-read
authors." —Julie E. Czerneda

GOBLIN QUEST   978-07564-0400-0
GOBLIN HERO   978-07564-0442-0
GOBLIN WAR   978-07564-0493-2

To Order Call: 1-800-788-6262
www.dawbooks.com

DAW 100